These Fes ᵍⁿᵗˢ

These Festive Nights

Marie-Claire Blais

Translated by Sheila Fischman

Published in 1997 by
House of Anansi Press Limited
1800 Steeles Avenue West, Concord, ON
Canada L4K 2P3

First published in French as *Soifs* in 1995 by
Les Éditions du Boréal

Distributed in Canada by
General Distribution Services Inc.
30 Lesmill Road
Toronto, Canada M3B 2T6
Tel. (416) 445-3333
Fax (416) 445-5967
e-mail: Customer.Service@ccmailgw.genpub.com

Canadian Cataloguing in Publication Data
Blais, Marie-Claire, 1939-
[Soifs. English]
These festive nights

Translation of: Soifs.
ISBN 0-88784-601-7

I. Fischman, Sheila.   II. Title.   III. Title: Soifs. English.

PS8503.L33S6313 1997   C843'.54   C97-931679-0
PQ3919.2.B53S6313 1997

Cover design: Bill Douglas @ The Bang
Text design: Tannice Goddard

Printed and bound in Canada

We gratefully acknowledge the Canada Council for the Arts and the Ontario Arts Council for their support of our publishing program.

This book was made possible in part through the Canada Council's Translation Grants Program.

To Pauline Michel, artist and writer,
incomparable friend and reader
from the very beginning of this book.

Let me now raise my song of glory. Heaven be praised for solitude. Let me be alone. Let me cast and throw away this veil of being, this cloud that changes with the least breath, night and day, and all night and all day. While I sat here I have been changing. I have watched the sky change. I have seen clouds cover the stars, then free the stars, then cover the stars again. Now I look at their changing no more. Now no one sees me and I change no more. Heaven be praised for solitude that has removed the pressure of the eye, the solicitation of the body, and all need of lies and phrases.

VIRGINIA WOOLF, *THE WAVES*

These Festive Nights

*T*hey had come here to rest, to relax, side by side and far from everything, the window of their hotel room opened onto the peaceful, blue Caribbean, where almost no sky could be seen in the powerful glare of the sun, the judge had had to uphold his guilty verdict before his departure, but it was not that sentence, a fair one, that was worrying his wife, he thought, rather it was the young man, who was unaccustomed to the courts, already the question of delinquents and pimps in prison had overwhelmed him, he might not practise much longer the awe-inspiring profession of magistrate, formerly his father's, he thought, Renata had suddenly stopped pleading and she didn't enjoy being inactive for months at a time, but it was more than just his sudden concern about her health, which all at once had been delicate and threatened, though there was that, it was always present at the centre of their embrace or their anger, but now an event that had seemingly occurred some distance from them, from their lives, in a room or a cell where the cold vapours of hell would prevail for a long time, namely the execution in a Texas prison of an unknown black man, death by lethal injection, a death that was veiled and discreet because it made no sound, it was an intravenous liquid-death of exemplary efficiency because the condemned man could inflict it on himself during the first rays of dawn, he knew that she had been thinking about that man, about his body, still warm or scarcely cold after being jolted by the imperceptible shocks, his body which a few hours later would still give off a sharp, foul smell, the smell of fear, of the sterile anguish he had had time to experience, for a second perhaps, before his appalling end, all night long they had both thought about the condemned man in Texas, had talked about him at length, then they had forgotten him when they threw themselves into each other's arms amid a joyous frenzy they now found it difficult to explain, for barely had they emerged from their tender embrace when both felt the same helplessness, that man should not have died, Renata said over and over, stubbornly, he may have been innocent, she said, her concern creasing her forehead, this thinker's forehead on a woman, the judge thought to himself as he looked his wife squarely in the eyes, the man in her who assumed the other sex, not only was she opposed to him, she was fierce, why did he not hold onto her hand, she was going to get away from him, to go out, already she was dressing to go to the casino, and although she was not a frivolous woman, suddenly a disarming frivolity seemed to come over her, and when he saw that she was already moving away from him, that stern crease in her brow and the look of worried vigilance in her gaze, which no longer enveloped him, for he had been banished from it to make way for loftier preoccupations, such as the death of a condemned prisoner in a Texas prison, he had thought Renata's stubborn expression was constantly urging him to feel the grimness of resistance, for what she wanted was to make him a better man, different or better, that was the hope she had always invested in the young men she loved — that they would be able to surpass themselves, as Franz had done in music, but Franz had told her that we cannot hope for honourable actions from someone with an irresolute, sensual nature, and as for the irresolute nature of men, thought the judge, Renata had observed that of all the judges, only one had spoken out against the death penalty in the United States, and no one had listened to him, the irresolute nature of man, it wasn't all that long since Claude's father — a father, a grandfather — not all that long since judges approved of women and men in their country being executed by hanging, thought Claude, no matter what we do we can never expiate the sins of the fathers, would there ever be a generation of fair-minded men, he thought, despondent, and her earrings, she mustn't forget to wear earrings when she goes to the casino, and as he reminded Renata to think about earrings he was concealing his own despondency, his sudden sense of discomfort with himself, in this hotel room, and it struck him that men always looked at Renata when they were out on the street together, or was it the perfume of life, of death, of convalescence that drifted around them, his wife struck him as vulnerable with her broad forehead, her naked ears, the lobes struck through with a pink light, like children's flesh when they're injured, those naked ears must be adorned, must be covered with earrings, it's prettier, he said, but why are you going to the casino, it's full of smoke, it's bad for you, and as he walked to the window he had felt Renata brush against him, felt her majestic head against his shoulder, she had disappeared in the direction of the elevator, the hotel lobby, she was already part of the crowd, lighting a cigarette so quickly and then

another, she had waited so long for this moment and no
tenderness, no solicitousness on his part could hold her
back, he thought, that trembling thirst was her own, Renata's
thirst, how obscure, how ungovernable it seemed, when she
knew that it could bring about her death, so many times he
had seen her in this same attitude of aloof distraction when,
without moving, without looking at him, she would suddenly
grow animated and go through some automatic sequence,
staring avidly at the cigarette and quickly expelling its
smoke, putting down the sparkling lighter on a night-stand
next to the bed, the malevolent object would pursue them
into the folds of their secret destiny, and now, he thought, he
must erase those sinister traces from the room, what was left
of the night's conversation, a newspaper they had read
together the night before, the condemned man's name, his
photograph, what good was it now, it was too late, the
irresolute nature of men, the human soul is laden with an
eternity of grief but even so it continues to live amid oblivion, pleasure, insouciance, he could hear the murmur of
frivolous laughter on the beach, in hotel rooms, Claude was
like those vacationers, he indulged in the water and suntan
lotion, each of them was alive, triumphant, satisfied with his
own precarious permanence on this earth, but if Renata was
running away from him to slake her thirst, he thought, it was
no doubt because he had been too harsh in imposing that
sentence on the delinquents and the pimps, he saw again the
expression of commiseration that was frozen on her face,
thinking about those disturbing things they had said during
the night, once again he had forbidden her to smoke in bed
and she had rebelled, then suddenly they had been talking
about Dostoevsky, a dreamy czar had granted Dostoevsky a
last-minute reprieve, otherwise he'd have been assassinated
like his father before him, and was it not surprising that this

corrupt sovereign should have saved a man, but the thought of that final second had never left Dostoevsky, for a long time he had heard the crack of the salvo, and Renata was walking alone to the casino, alone, for a woman the sense of her freedom, of her dignity, still counted for something, for she was always being observed, watched, the gaze of others was intimately linked with the way she walked, with the movement of her hips, her neck, with the sparkle of the jewels she wore to mask her frailty, just there, so close to her temples, where Renata smoothed her fine silver hair with her fingers, higher, towards the forehead, and it was from there that the illumination came, the flash of pale truth that sometimes pierced the soul with uncertainty, it seemed to her that she could hear those words very distinctly, the destiny of a woman, my destiny is incomprehensible and formless, God's plans did not anticipate me, what sensation of painful idleness had urged her to tell her doctor, remove that malignant tumour, what was most painful was the thought of the lighter she'd left behind in the hotel room, for her senses would always be too poor to savour this world that was hers, not the one belonging to Claude and Franz but this one, a magnificent garden, fragmented and broken but hers, thought Renata, to be thirty years old like her nephew and niece, Daniel and Mélanie, whom she would soon see again, her only relatives, to be thirty like them, to experience the carefree joy of raising one's family here, tomorrow she would visit a museum, she walked with a loose, enthusiastic stride, she had not thought about the audacity of what she was doing, but it was essential to shake off the yoke of a forbidden freedom, when she had summoned to her side a white-suited man and asked him to light her cigarette, he was a black American, slender, he leaned towards her, she too was tall, his hand created a shelter for the flame, the flame that rose between their gazes while she meekly thanked him, the man had raised his head, haughtily observing this woman who had approached him when he was himself with a woman, then he had seen her take flight, for in the act of requesting a light, overcoming her helplessness, Renata had acquired a little more space in this territory where she was now grappling with her thoughts, that was what was remarkable about her destiny, she thought, daring to perform these acts that made her certain of her own free existence, of being independent and rebellious, and the name printed in black letters on a gold-coloured plaque on her door — Renata Nymans, Attorney — served only to accommodate, to defend the status of women, which was constantly under assault, and it was also a name linked with her captivity, her bourgeois captivity to a husband, her professional captivity, with all the privileges of her social class, and now her convalescence was just beginning and already she was being reborn in another way, she thought, she had felt the man's breath on the small flame, above the cigarette, he was from Los Angeles, a flame had brought them together for a moment, on an unfamiliar island, Claude would never be one of those old judges stagnating with indifference and boredom over the fate of men, she recognized his moral quality, but he was too harsh with the delinquents, with the young drug dealers arrested in miserable apartments, lying surrounded by garbage, he should have rehabilitated them first by providing medical attention, Claude's concern was exacerbated by their constant arguments, nor would her husband approve of these insubstantial challenges with which she enhanced her life during these days of rest that felt so long to her, the gaze of the black American, which she had sought, had displeased her, it was a cold and mocking gaze, while she

walked she could still feel the attractive force of his dark
eyes, it was like when she was living with Franz, she always
provoked the phenomenon of inexplicable pity when she
passed, she would have done anything to please Franz, even
giving herself over to the care of a manicurist in Paris, she
had watched as the humble servant of the place bustled
around her in her heavy nurse's shoes, holding a box of
cotton-wool as she stood amid the hair clippings that
strewed the polished black floor, she saw again her
polished nails shining in the feeble light of a winter
afternoon, she had been leafing through a magazine and
suddenly she had felt ashamed, why should she attend a
benefit function with Franz when he no longer loved her, the
manicurist wadded damp cotton between her fingers, Renata
could see herself in the mirror, the austere face, the hair the
hairdresser had dampened, he had brushed it back, and
she'd thought, I'll wear my hair like this from now on, it was
that head, that skull which emerged victorious from the abyss
of her humiliation, of Franz's unfaithfulness, but why should
she suddenly provoke this obscure effusion from the
manicurist, did Renata suggest to her one of those stigma-
tized faces that one often sees in a crowd, our faces do not
altogether belong to us, they go back to the ravages of times
before us, to the cruelties of history, a face that is closed and
silent becomes that of a mother, an aunt, a cousin who died
under mysterious circumstances, and the face that Renata
now saw in the mirror had suddenly been stripped of those
ornaments that gave her a cheerful, a scatterbrained look, for
without earrings her ears seemed tiny, close against the rigid
skull, you could see the pink spot where a needle had
pierced the delicate earlobes, and in the hot and noisy streets
of a foreign city Renata wondered if it was that face, the one
the manicurist had seen in the mirror, which the black

American had spied, had come close to and then brushed
aside with his haughty smile, and now the judge was pacing
the hotel lobby, feeling the cold contact of Renata's lighter,
of her gold cigarette case, he had refreshed himself after
their argument by playing tennis, then swimming in the
pool, they had needed that painful incident in their lives, he
thought, Renata's operation in New York, to make him take
some time off with his wife, he had walked around their
hotel room nude for a long time, all those hours in an office,
taken up with files, both of them sometimes working late
into the night, and as he slipped on his shirt he had thought,
what a disguise a judge's robe is, to feel oneself invested
with the power of the law and then to rule by force, by
terror, as my father did, Renata had reproached him for
keeping his father's servants, a cook, a chauffeur, ex-convicts
Claude couldn't part with, housing them in a cottage near
their home, how sad to no longer feel the sun's caress on
your back, your hips, while he was standing at the window,
delighting in his unfailing vitality, this always happened
when you finally agreed to relax, the unfailing vitality of
youth was being restored, he would go out now and not
wait for Renata, wouldn't he be irritated to be suddenly
walking at her side without her turning her head towards
him, for when she ran away like that, striding briskly, she
stopped seeing him, finding irresistible the click of the gold
cigarette case which she would open proudly, afraid of
meeting her husband on the street, Renata gave in to her rit-
uals privately, in solitude, thoroughly savouring one cigarette
after another, leaning against a wall as she exhaled the
smoke, for most likely she had already been walking for a
long time, though she didn't know exactly where she was
going, in fact had no sense of direction, she had walked
around many European cities that way, and in notebooks

which she fiercely kept from his eyes she would write on how to reconcile love and wandering, and the art of the magistrature struck Renata as inhumanly hostile, men, thought the judge, no doubt exceeded their own powers when they brought down sentences, for men became fiendishly weak when they were given a power, a task of monstrous proportions, yes, they exceeded their powers, he was walking in the warm, humid air of the street, he would say nothing when he saw Renata bring another cigarette to her lips, he would knead the gold cigarette case, the lighter, between his fingers for a long time, all the while hesitating to catch up with her. And all along the ocean, along the military buildings that lined the periphery of the beach, Pastor Jeremy's children were playing, chasing the roosters that crowed themselves hoarse all day long on the rough lawn in front of the house that had been painted the same rather dreary dark green as the military buildings, this is a real house, thought Pastor Jeremy, even if it still looked too much like a box flattened by the white sun striking it, you could hear the rumbling of the waves there from the nearby Atlantic, it was time to round up the children for prayers, Pastor Jeremy called out in his strong, resonant voice, come and get ready for church, and what were you doing at the neighbours' place, you were stealing fruit again, the professor would be here any moment now, his friends were already waiting at the airport, what will the professor say when he sees these thieves in his garden, eh, what will he say, they're climbing all over my lemon trees, my orange trees, now it's true that for a long time there was no one to harvest the fruit, the professor was a strange man, but you never know how these white folks live, and those garrulous roosters that never stop singing, Pastor Jeremy would tell all the children to reread the Gospel according to St. Matthew,

the Lord is my shepherd, has He abandoned you even once,
and you're just good-for-nothings who steal from the trees,
and they would reply in chorus, the Lord is my shepherd,
amen, amen, the girls in front, in their starched white dresses,
with ribbons holding back their heavy hair, braided or curly,
the celebration of the Divine Office would scarcely have
ended when the pastor saw them tumbling around in the
dust, but in the meantime let them be still, soon enough
the pastor would have before his eyes a row of curly
heads shaking with nervous twitches, with mischievous
movements, yes, the rippling of all those heads during his
sermons, if the big red rooster didn't come into the temple
as well, let them all come, squawking and laughing amid a
cloud of feathers, welcome to all, the pastor would say,
come, this is the church of the prophets and the chosen, and
as we do every Sunday at noon, we will have a feast of barbecued meat, on the sidewalks and in the backyards of
Esmeralda Street, what will your mothers say if you get your
dresses dirty in the mud, and they didn't listen but fluttered
about among the hens and roosters, a slap on the cheek,
that's how your mothers will punish you, they'll shake you
and we'll be able to hear you all the way to the church, and
little by little Pastor Jeremy's flock would be rounded up,
wearing their Sunday best, and he thought, no, don't let the
airplane touch down right away, it would be so good to drop
to the bottom of that crystal-clear water now, to get it over
with, to be transformed into the morning dew on the cool
grass, near the beaches, to ripple in this air, this water, to be
dissolved already in the clouds, no more of this battle against
matter that can only conquer you from below, through the
degeneration of your cells, and it was moving to observe
all those blue craters that appeared beneath the waves, islets
of underwater vegetation he'd never noticed before today,

surrounded by the ocean, too soon the professor's plane would touch down, causing all the houses on Bahama Street to tremble, up in the blue sky Pastor Jeremy could see the professor's plane as it descended slowly towards the runway, soon the professor would be in his house, so long had his garden been abandoned, had his cat been alone, scaring the chickens and roosters that ran around free, recite with me, the Lord is my shepherd, said the pastor with his powerful voice as he guided his family to the temple, in the sunlight that blanched the skin of Uncle Cornelius and his musicians as they marched in procession, lanky in their stiff Sunday clothes, dancing and skipping all the way along the graveyard to the church, sometimes rolling their eyes to the sky, and this bubble of champagne or blessed air in which Jacques had been confined during the flight suddenly burst, evaporated, the plane touched down, still bounding into the air in fitful shudders, now Jacques would no longer be alone with the convulsions of his nervous, impatient, bruised flesh, he thought, Luc and Paul and a woman who was already at the wheel of their car when he arrived had taken charge of him, what a sad mission had been entrusted to them all, thought Jacques, this labour of the throes of death wherein dying would suddenly become easier, for everything was already unfolding as he had anticipated, he was in his house, he'd been bathed and dressed in pyjamas, and now he was lying in his bed next to the open window, gazing out at his garden, at all those masses of untidy vegetation that he loved, he'd forbidden anyone to clear away the brushwood, it seemed as if the lemon trees, the orange trees, had been twisted by the storm, the bougainvilleas, the roses had over-run the whole garden, collapsing under the abundance of their blossoms onto a carpet of palm fronds as sharp as knives, it was the dense, overwhelming garden that Jacques

so wanted to see again, and so it was true, the time had
come for his friends to perform the unavoidable ritual, just a
week ago he'd had dinner with his students, if they asked
him tonight what he wanted for dinner he would say, something oriental, because the biting fragrance of that cuisine
still stimulated his palate, standing beside him with their
hands on his shoulders, Luc and Paul would say, it was a
long trip, but who was that woman, Jacques wondered,
who'd come to the airport with Luc and Paul to meet him,
that enigmatic being haunted him, was she a friend who was
spending some time on the island, Jacques had often thought
that several times in our lives we glimpse the face that is
the harbinger of our death, but the ambiguity of our
memory won't allow that face to penetrate our awareness,
who was that dignified, kindly woman who had asked if he
was comfortable among the cushions in the back seat, and
the pressure of Paul's fingers and Luc's covering his shoulders at the window, with all this kindness brought together,
the sea, the air, the classic profile of the unknown woman
who had joined Luc and Paul in the ceremony of the final
caresses, the final gazes, he thought, they had been furtively
entwined in the same dance, was it being deprived of
oriental food that was driving him into this tearful sentimen-
tality, soon he'd had enough regrets, he talked about going
out, about lust, about being incontinent with lust, about
violating with his eyes, about carnal knowledge, and as he
said these words a glimmer of doubt appeared in his blue
eyes, as he told himself that thoughts like this occur to all
those who are dying, but they cannot admit them to anyone,
what had he seen on this day that he wanted never to forget
— a young girl swimming with her dog, holding it by its
collar, drifting away, carried along by the waves, the innocence of an image he did not want to forget, and if the

woman driving the car had caused him that unspeakable emotion, it was also because she was alive, because she would go on living when he was no longer there, even though she was old enough to be his mother, as he sank into the cushions an icy fear took hold of him, the sun rising and setting over the sea, the young girl holding onto her dog's collar in the waves, all these movements, vital, imperturbable, and joyous, that would go on without him should stop, the airplane should have crumbled among the grains of sand in its metallic throbbing, he should never have to answer in a disconsolate voice that he was comfortable amid the cushions, in a car that was taking him to the end of his existence, in this paradisal place, he had always despised the Christian delight in suffering, in punishment, it was what he had taught his students in his courses on Kafka, *Letter to His Father* was one of those eloquent literary examples of the voluptuous pleasure to be found in humiliation, since Kafka's cry of distress to the father he accused and denounced had never been heard, yes, but had his students understood the meaning of his boring remarks, those students he would never see again, and Jacques envied the lizards undulating lazily on the stones all day long, with their red throats that swelled amid peaceful happiness, love, the memory of the joyous, imperturbable movement that was life, soon they would announce a scientific development, the disease would regress, ah, how he longed for the birth of hope that would deliver him from his pain, but his work was waiting for him here, he would finally complete his book on Kafka, he would submit it this fall to his colleagues at the university, he would emphasize the hate-filled relationship that joined Kafka to his father, the biological assembly of those two monsters, one of them sensitive and refined, the other perverse, the only outcome of that relationship had been *Metamorphosis,*

through the curse of writing, for it was with that symbol of
the insect imprisoned in a bedroom that Kafka had punished
the father as much as the son, he would deal with the theme
of gratuitous punishment, of the curse, in a tone of bitter,
disillusioned insolence, because until this day he had never
believed that the subject of his study of Kafka was himself
and the unhealthy species that was germinating beneath
his carapace; suddenly feeling drowsy, he gazed through
half-open eyes at one of the reptiles that had jumped onto
the windowsill, the tiny lizard seemed to be eyeing him
too from under his flickering eyelid, he was nothing but
indolence and languor, Jacques thought, and so crippled, so
mutilated in shape was the creature's presence in the sun,
that like the young girl in the waves and her dog with the
collar, or the woman who had driven him from the airport,
the lizard too was becoming one of those unforgettable
figures making its way with Jacques towards the shores of
eternity, he sat up in his bed, trying to see the ocean, but he
could only glimpse a fleeting patch of blue between the pine
trees that had recently been planted on the vast military beach,
perhaps he would fall asleep like that, his head slumping to
his chest as he let himself drop into the pillows on the bed,
then he started, happy to catch by surprise a familiar shadow
in the brush under the lemon trees, the shadow edged its
way inside through a hole in the iron fence, was it Le Toqué
or Carlos, was it the thief or his older brother who used his
pocket-knife to slash bicycle tires, the pastor's sons had
slipped away with their spoils once again, to the other side
of the street, and the snickering that showed their white
teeth, healthy and vengeful, scattered into the air, and who
would dare complain when the fruit was likely to rot soon
on the trees, and despite his lassitude Jacques could feel a
sort of acrid contentment, like the taste of the limes the

thieves had taken, he thought, at having witnessed some illicit scenes, as he'd so often done in his lifetime, was it not the supreme act of disobedience for a black boy to rob a white, he was content too at having had visitors when he was feeling so alone; at the same time a kind of malaise crept over him, wouldn't Carlos and his brother laugh when they saw him walking to the sea with a cane? And what was the faith of Pastor Jeremy, whom did he worship in his temple, that decent man would no doubt tell him as he usually did, Professor, there are those who enter the Valley of the Orchids and those who don't, but we don't see much of you in any of our temples, our churches, so you write from morning to night, then, but you must also pray to God, looking pensive he would cross his pudgy hands on his stomach, ah yes, those who enter the Valley of the Orchids and those who don't, I'm going to water my lawn, there's been no rain for several days now, into the books from morning to night, eh, Professor, I also have to cut my flowers and prepare my sermon, Jacques would quickly tire of Pastor Jeremy's easy-going confidence in those divine forces which he himself denied, he would kick the roosters and hens onto the rough lawn, crumple a blade of grass in his fist, saying, oh no, the Valley of the Orchids is right down here, Pastor, of that I can assure you, I've seen it, or else he would say that whites don't deserve to enter there and Pastor Jeremy would nod his agreement while the silence of evening descended on them. From his twilight bed Jacques set off for the roads of Asia, he ran up the step onto a train, heard the whistle of the locomotives, the Valley of the Orchids is right down here, Pastor, too bad he wasn't allowed spicy food now, too bad there was a throbbing, burning sensation in his throat even when he drank only water, boredom, fetid boredom no doubt had a Christian origin, that was what he'd forgotten to tell the pastor during their conversations on this rough lawn, surrounded by children and roosters, in front of the house painted a green so dark, unhealthy, as if the green colour were tinged with black, and it was that fetid boredom he was eluding by going so far away, the insidious boredom of those cities where you go to bed early in the evening, where you live your life between the university campus and the church steeple, yes, but what was the good of running so far away if it was only to find himself suddenly unable to go out in the street alone without a cane? Dependent now on the heavy intoxication brought by the drugs he took every day, he thought, is it the oil or the flame or the light that is dwindling in the lamp, Pastor Jeremy's words suddenly inhabited his thoughts while he was dozing, when there's no more oil in the lamp, Professor, it goes out, and the birds of paradise close their corollas made glossy by the rain, but there was still some oil in the lamp, hadn't the fire of his senses been stirred by the haunting perfume that projected him onto the desert roads again, the scent of the hashish that his friends were smoking off to one side, in the narrow kitchen, and lifting himself up in his bed, he said, how can you forget me, and it was the first laugh they'd exchanged, he thought, and taking advantage of this moment of sincere elation, he asked for paper and pencil because he wanted to record his dreams, it was so ludicrous, he said, the incoherence of all those dreams he conjured up in a half-waking state, in a sort of trance, but what was miraculous was not so much the strange feverishness of his dreams as the involuntary cascade of laughter that he shared with his friends when they were smoking together in the garden and acrid smoke-rings drifted into the air, the odour gradually mingling with the persistent smell of scorched corn in all the backyards on Bahama Street, he thought, a wayfaring odour

that transported him to the Orient, while with a suddenly
confident hand he recorded his dreams in his notebook, and
the woman who drove the car, in the funeral cortège, he
thought, hadn't he invited her into that same car, amid the
cushions, to race frantically through a city that might have
been Paris during the bombing raids, had he pointed out that
she was driving too fast and she'd replied, giving him the
courteous smile of her handsome profile, I'd promised you
I'd come to see how you were, the car was parked at the
edge of a wood and, as she opened the door, the woman
ordered Jacques to get out, her order was calm and utterly
lacking in violence, she said, come, come into my arms, I'm
strong enough to support you, you're as fragile as a sea-shell,
come, we'll go to the clearing where it's cooler, and then
Jacques realized that he'd probably gone back to sleep as he
was recording this dream, the house and the garden were
empty, Luc and Paul had gone back to the library where they
both worked, he thought the term would soon be over for
his students, thought they might perhaps come to see him
during spring break, that dazzling pause in the monotony of
classroom days, and was it true that Carlos had been sent to
reform school this winter, Jacques would talk to Pastor Jeremy
about it, Carlos, that cottony mass collapsing onto the sidewalk while the family laundry was spilled into a stream of
dirty water, he was that boy who looked like a clown in his
checkered pants, sprawled on the sidewalk in his distraught
drunkenness, and would they bring him that German scholar's
book on Kafka from the library, he picked up the pencil, tried
to describe what was still hazy in his mind about his dream,
he'd taken part in a swimming competition, the anomaly of
that competition required him to dive from a tremendous
height while flying over some oak beams in a swimming
pool, the jump was dangerous but it was as if he had wings,

he sometimes managed to achieve amazing speed while other athletes fractured their skulls on the boards, he conquered the challenge by means of an aerial swim that would hurl him into the ocean waves, he was saved, he thought, his gaze settling gratefully on the writing paper, the notebook, the pencils that had been arranged in front of him, along with the glass of mineral water in which ice-cubes glittered in the sun; as he emerged from his suffocating dream, none of these objects seemed to have been grazed, touched, but were surrounded by a halo of absolute purity amid the light. The earth around the cactuses was cracked and rough, thought the pastor, that was a sign of impending drought, and what had he seen in the temple during the service, those girls smeared with lipstick, his own daughters, their swollen lips, it was the swelling of desire, of sexual hunger, why had God in His wisdom decided that he should have daughters, he had quite enough worries already with Carlos and his other sons, God had created the drought and his daughters, demons who insulted the Lord, two of them, the twins Deandra and Tiffany, were still at their mother's breast, and what would they do later, it was best not to think about it, who knows if Heaven's decisions aren't cunning, you couldn't understand a thing about them, taking advantage of the one jug of water the city allowed him, Pastor Jeremy watered his cactus, and just as he was about to slit the throat of a chicken for the Sunday meal, he remembered that there was sin inside his house, under the roof of his low house, amid the chairs and parasols corroded by the mugginess and humidity that seeped in everywhere, causing mildew, it was not a dream, he really had seen bicycle chains and padlocks in his shed when he went there to fetch his tools, sin and its baseness were inside his house, and it could only be Carlos, of whom he'd been so proud during the boxing match at school, Jeremy shook off the sand that was clinging to his sandals because Mama got angry when people came inside the house with sand on their shoes, his provocative daughters, Venus and her sisters, their lips and faces painted, wearing their starched Sunday dresses, and that bold swelling under their weekday T-shirts on which was written Bad to the Bone, the swelling of desire, of sexual hunger, and as for the bicycle chains, that was no error in judgement, he'd had to put on his glasses to see them properly but he was right, the stolen loot was in the shed, in that corner of filmy dimness where tentacles were lodged, at their age he could no longer tan their backsides with his belt, when they were winning boxing matches and first one white boy collapsed in the ring and then a second, Carlos, again it was Carlos who had flung his worn-out boots over the wire one day and the whole street had been deprived of electricity, a thug, a good-for-nothing, the boots were still there, swaying in the wind, when it cost so much to educate children, Le Toqué was ten years old and still couldn't read, did he really go to school, his right leg dragged behind the other one, what could you do, it was congenital, a second look inside the shed and Pastor Jeremy discovered a wallet, a leather belt, either Le Toqué or Carlos, he was known to tourists for his nimble hand, it was not at reform school that he'd become a boxing champion, they'd have to send him to those white farmers in Atlanta, he would return from there more disciplined, they would beat him black and blue if he didn't listen, the boots flung up there by an expert hand, that Carlos, he was muscular and strong, Pastor Jeremy's chest swelled with pride, Carlos was not just anyone, the pastor had caught his chicken now and blood was pouring from its slashed neck onto his hand, into its russet feathers, Pastor Jeremy would say nothing to his wife about the bicycle chains, Sunday was for relaxing, for playing ball in the backyard, for swimming in the ocean, and the younger ones were learning to walk on the sandy beaches beside their mother, and suddenly Pastor Jeremy remembered that for a long time he'd been forbidden access to the public beaches, he once more saw himself carting earth by truck on his days off, the truck drove through town almost in silence, during the Sunday dinner of the white people hidden behind the mosquito netting on their verandas, the truck in which five black boys stood, their feet bound by chains in a cart, so it seemed, five black boys with their kinky hair, their fleshy lips, their deep-set eyes that seemed to hold no dreams. And Jacques was thinking about the woman who had brought him in her car, why was the face that was a harbinger of his death so seductive, so comforting, even motherly, was her face associated with that of the nurse who would soon arrive to offer palliative care, when he was too weak to eat by himself; from his blood steeped in mourning, which sowed panic and death everywhere, would gush, after multiple transfusions, the ecstasy of clear, purified blood, it was like the time Paul had cooled his face with water from the fountain, the water lukewarm on his temples, why had the face that was a harbinger of his dying been gentle, soothing, and yet, like the woman who had asked him if he was comfortable amid the cushions in the back seat of the car, she seemed to be telling him, I am kindly death, domesticated death, I too am intoxicated by the perfumes of your garden, by its blazing colours, the green of the plants, of their leaves, it is more dazzling than yesterday, such abundance all around you, and Jacques had thought about all those mornings when he'd awakened, his body straining with curiosity, his penis erect, triumphant, awaiting Tanjou's kisses, the languorous body that would snuggle against his, but while he had become enamoured of Tanjou in Pakistan,

now suddenly he no longer knew what to do with him,
either on the university campus or at work, where he was all
decked out in his own brand of professional rigour when
speaking to the professors in his department, the Department
of Foreign Languages and Literature, for he'd thought it all
out when he chose a profession that would require him to
travel. In an authoritative voice he had ordered Tanjou to go
back to his own country, how threatening, how tormenting
suddenly to feel God hovering over you, for that, he thought,
was the meaning of love's domination, the fierce domination
of someone who was a stranger to you, the Pakistani student's
letters had been torn to shreds by the same treacherous hand
that had cherished, caressed, loved, by repudiating Tanjou,
by never replying to his passionate letters, he had experienced that craven delight for which he judged Kafka so
harshly, but even so it was as if a fingernail had caught in
the fibres of his carapace, had prevented him from moving,
had kept him lying on the ground like Kafka's great wailing
insect, his back sustained the insult of rotten apples, he was
relieved and cured of love with Tanjou's departure, furious
that his divine fingernail should have run along his spine,
suddenly cured, yet now he was dying of the same love,
and how threatening it was to feel God hovering over you
when you were defenceless, like a mountain climber who
has broken his back in a fall, and Tanjou repeated amid
his innocent tears, I was just an object for you then, just an
instrument for your pleasure? So you don't love me? And
Jacques replied coldly, that's it, I can't go any further, that's
the way I am, I just want to be left in peace, craven delight
had intervened, he thought, when Tanjou shed his inexhaustible tears, let them flow, let them stream, he thought,
shuddering again at the thought of the cruel pleasure he had
felt at seeing someone, especially such a delightful being,

winning that victory, suffering from love for him. Then
Jacques's head dropped to one side and he dozed off,
wondering if he would have the strength to jot down all his
dreams, because his hand was trembling a little; and again
he saw her, she was suddenly beside him, it was a stormy
late afternoon and the waves were very high, the woman
whose face was a harbinger of his death had changed, the
elegance of that person at the wheel of her car had become
coarse, slack, she was an ordinary woman perched on a rock
by the water, painting, she still had on her beach shoes,
white with flat heels, and well-cut yellow slacks, but you
could no longer see the delicate lines of her features under
the grotesque hat that shielded her from the sun, she was
drawing or painting without looking at Jacques, who had
begun his daily workout on the beach, for that matter was
he not contorting in vain on the pebbles of this beach where
only dogs came, his restless movements on this beach
infested with foul-smelling fish scales would attract them, no
doubt, and his odour, his own murky odour, the woman's
drawing sat on a blue and red schoolbag on which was
written Come Urgent, she was drawing and painting chaoti-
cally, without looking at anything, Jacques began to fear
that she would turn in his direction and spy him in his
humiliating posture, then he woke up, Mac had jumped onto
his lap from a tree, Jacques thrust his hand into Mac's orange
fur, his scrawny flanks, and asked him if that litter of kittens
under the oleanders was his, and what had Mac, terror of
the roosters of Bahama Street, been up to during his
absence, the cluster of kittens with russet spots like Mac's, he
stretched himself in the sun, protect them, you fickle father,
said Jacques, someone might step on them under the leaves,
all the females were afraid of you this winter, and those
stupid kittens, when the exterminator passes by shortly with

his gas nozzle, under the foundations of the houses, what are you all thinking of, and while he was playing with Mac, pestering him until he was ready to bite, knowing the cat wouldn't bite him because he was so glad to see him again, he was disgusted by his skeletal arms and hands, so the affectionate admiration he'd so often felt for himself would not come again; why didn't he get up then, the salty ocean air would be good for him, those nonchalant walks that had so often invigorated him, restored him, no, those hours of radiant and dreamy relaxation on the shores of a sea, of an ocean, would not come again in this world, last year — had it been a premonition? — he'd seen a black sailboat in the middle of the ocean, a sailboat and its crew, have we ever seen that before, a black sailboat? he'd asked his friends, the merciless premonition was suddenly a startling reality, it was the hospital bed transported to the house, to the threshold of the garden, even the part in his hair was getting thinner, he thought, and now the judge was going down to the lobby that would take him to the hotel casino, thinking that one year might have been enough for the pimps but not for the others, the dealers, their network had to be dismantled, there was a telegram for him at the desk, he'd read it later, Renata, he was thinking only about Renata, impulsively she had retraced her steps, kissed him, what were they telling her, that the hotel employees had refused to serve their customers at lunch, the employees had been seen helping themselves at the banquet table in the room at the back, beneath the wrath of hostile suspicion, Renata approved of the insurrection, the strike, Claude had advised her to be careful in her choice of words, she was always on the side of the humiliated, he told his wife she was like quarry lying in wait for the hunter, like the turtledove that hears the shot cracking under the rustling of its wings, Claude, who had often gone hunting with his father in the past, said, the hunter brings down his quarry with a shot, but often he doesn't kill it, it quivers in the grass for a long time, and its consciousness, which has not yet been altered, still reflects the sky in a veil of blood, still hears the hunters' laughter in the distance amid the beating of its heart as it slows down, but already Renata was no longer with her husband, he saw her in the casino among the other gamblers, a group of Asians smoking cigars in a dense cloud of smoke, and Renata seemed to him out of place in this setting where she came at night, her broad forehead lit by a pale light, her hidden refinement close to cold indifference, the domineering timidity that irritated men even as it attracted them, thought Claude, yet now her gaze was fixed, she seemed to be gambling relentlessly, deep in concentration, he doubted that was the case, Renata's mind, he thought, was always wandering in the direction of unfathomable twists and turns, the condemned man in Texas, she would not stop talking about him when Claude was with her, she would turn to him and smile, he could feel her warm breath, her whiskey-scented breath, while the chips rolled across the green baize towards Renata, he thought, these night-time hours among the men belong to her, just like her dark passions for gambling, for alcohol, but how I fear the smoke in those places, with the seventeen she had doubled her ante, the chips kept piling up in front of her but she seemed not at all eager to take them, bothered by the cigar smoke of her companions, she made her way to the bar, and suddenly the judge saw that there was nothing left where Renata had been gambling, the chips had disappeared, and a man whose shirt was open revealing his bare chest had taken Renata's place, he was a poor, scruffy West Indian who had come straight off the street, in a few moments he would receive a huge sum of money that wasn't meant for him, which he'd lose right away, amid the despair that drove him to come here every night and gamble away his starvation wages and his life, and in her haughty detachment — or perhaps it was out of weariness or boredom, or was there some reason for her passion, which was often too charitable, thought Claude — would Renata not be responsible for the man's downfall? Motionless, enthralled, he knew that Renata had seen the chips fly shamelessly across the green baize, and hadn't she also known that the poor West Indian was suddenly the victim of a terrible stroke of luck, which was her fault, the same stroke of luck that could have lightened his poverty, made him rich, those incomprehensible passions of women, thought Claude, what was she trying to find here, in what struck him as an infernal atmosphere, peace of mind or knowledge, she had told him, the stamp of her own mortality, ever since her illness, and Renata's attitude, which consisted of remoteness, of a withdrawal that was at once abrupt and ethereal, awakened in him feelings of failure, of abandonment almost, and showed him how much every one of us is always surrounded by dangerous impulses, whether good or bad, the private hell of criminals was overrun with them. He saw Renata, who was smoking in the half-light of the bar, from the back, sitting on a stool, her legs crossed, was it true what they had read in the morning paper — that these same striking employees had slaughtered the white people's dogs in their villas, had poisoned them — the judge felt the cold touch of the lighter in his fingers, what would he read when he opened his telegram, would he learn that his own home had been devastated, demolished, the greenhouse with its lofty, pan-oramic view of the city, the world was being governed by dangerous impulses, he would leave tomorrow, as his secretary had dictated, his ticket was waiting at the airport, it was urgent for him to go home, Renata would continue her convalescence without him, in the company of her nephew and niece, Daniel and Mélanie, the tropical heat would be good for her, the judge felt the cold touch of the lighter and the gold cigarette case on his fingers, she was cured but she shouldn't smoke, didn't she know that, he could see her solitary silhouette, her broad forehead in the lamplight, against the black velvet covering the walls, soon he would tell her he was leaving, hadn't she reproached him for the overly harsh sentence, and for the risk that someone would seek revenge, Renata seemed hesitant to join the noisy couples in the lighted space of the bar, where musicians were playing jazz close to the sea, the judge mused that while these party-goers, these decadent couples who had come here from seaside resorts, from hot springs, were caring for their radiant health, corpses were rotting in the desert, this January war was never-ending, and how had armed drug dealers got inside the house, it meant that his father's servants in their cottage didn't protect them, Renata took a few steps, stopping near a drunk who pushed his wife backwards onto the piano to kiss her, the man was laughing coarsely, the woman wore a low-cut dress with a bow that her husband had untied, other couples were clustering around the piano, around the woman, laughing and joking, Renata walked by herself to the terrace, under the stars, you could see a pool near the sea where, through some barbaric magic, birds of prey appeared that were missing a wing, a tortoise struggled up onto its front legs and was now swimming against the current, was that, Renata wondered, the incarnation of help-less animal pain, she heard words shouted around her through the din, she felt the words she was hearing were light but contaminated, what were they saying, that she was beautiful, adrift, they were laughing, joking, she looks like a wandering Jew, the turtledove her husband had mentioned hadn't died right away when the hunter shot it, what were they saying as they laughed, joked, she herself had heard nothing, she brought her hand to her brow, stunned by the burst of acute awareness that had touched her, they were saying that the condemned man in Texas had died in the electric chair, and a good thing too, they were glad to hear it, they said, they laughed, joked, during the long days of Renata's convalescence she had suddenly thought about the trials going on again beyond measure, in Europe, the United States, just to denounce a few old men who perhaps resembled these, whose vile past had been buried in a new country, under new citizenship, an innocuous trade such as carpentry, plumbing, residing in the city of Milwaukee like so many others, or somewhere else, after the trial they would be deported, what was to be done with those dejected executioners, with those torturers who were still among us, should they be shut away by themselves in deserted tribunals, alone with the intolerable moaning of their own cursèd brains, Renata thought that despite the stability of her professional life for years now, she was a vagabond running away from fate, that female condition which struck her at times as so weighty, a curse had been inscribed in women for centuries, would every woman one day win the ultimate deliverance from so many injustices? It seemed to her, just now when she was so perturbed, as she met her husband's gaze, he fixed his dark and gentle eyes on her and his manner seemed relaxed as he held out the lighter, the gold cigarette case, the murmur around the piano died down, the musicians were putting away their instruments in the shadowy light of the bar, that you could barely hear the sound of the waves in the night. And all day long they had sung, danced in chorus on the floor of the temple, sung to the glory of God, to His hour of glory that was drawing nigh, the pastor had cried out in a booming voice that continued to vibrate long afterwards in the warm air of the morning, the girls always in the front with their curly hair, their hard lips, at the end of the service the temple doors had been opened, everyone had sung, danced in the street, in all the churches the trumpets of the Lord could be heard, at the New Life of the Tabernacle prayers had been offered for the sick, and at Holy Trinity the pupils had recited terrifying passages from the Bible which they'd learned in Bible school during this period of penitence, as for the Lutherans, it was shocking, thought the pastor, that they offered child care during the service, it was too comfortable at the Presbyterian church as well, what was a body to think about that, when the Lord had died on the cross for the sins of men, for their salvation, and the Episcopalians with their church built of stone, it was too big, you couldn't pray properly inside those walls, and weren't they austere with their hymns sung by elderly spinsters, as for the Baha'i church, did those people even pray to the true God, we love you oh God, in the fear of the flames and the hope of paradise, come, come, all you who are passing by, every one of you is an honoured guest, the pastor had said outside his humble temple, where hens could be heard cackling all day long, they had danced and sung in the temple and in the street, and everywhere the trumpets of the Lord had been heard in all the churches, amid fear and trembling, and now the sun was setting over the sea, Mama was picking up plates spattered with brown beans and sauce, in the bushes in the garden her piercing voice whistled in the ears of Carlos, who was trying to escape to the street, and Mama brought him back, holding him against her heavy breasts heaving with anger inside her mauve cotton dress, her Sunday dress that hung so low on her legs, her ample black legs, her white shoes trampling the yellowed grass, all that overflow of fury was gravitating around Carlos, pursuing him now while he clasped his football, the padlocks, the bicycle chains, his mother lamented, may the Lord have pity on us, and the slaps rained down on Carlos's cheeks, on his heavy, bent neck, was he going to end up like the Escobez brothers from Esmeralda Street, eh, was that how he was going to end up? and in the drone of blows hammering at his temples he suddenly heard — as if those few crystalline sounds, cut off from everything else, had welled up from the earth for him alone — the song of the cicadas and the lapping of waves all around, he saw the Reverend Doctor standing on a cloud in the middle of the sky, he seemed to be upset about something because he was wiping his forehead with his handkerchief and saying in his deep voice, Carlos, one day I had a dream and it was for you, my son, what happened, but the televised message soon blurred before another, this one for the vanilla ice cream Carlos was going to eat, it had been a long time since the Reverend Doctor had spoken to Carlos, standing on a cloud in his robes spattered with scarlet stains near the heart, sometimes he was crying, after all I've done for you, my son, and you spend your time snorting coke with the Bad Niggers, do you remember those thirty-four Black Panthers who were killed in the streets of New York, no, because what you like is vanilla ice cream, made by the whites, because the light, my son, is also the lightning, and the deep voice of the Reverend Doctor in the sky, the song of the cicadas and the lapping of the waves merged with the tap tap of a black orchestra announcing to Carlos the brand name of the vanilla ice cream it was his duty to eat, tap tap, and to the emphatic notes of the tap tap he danced, first on one foot, then on the other, his head nodding under his mother's blows, in a slow movement of extreme indolence, and then, little by little, the drone at Carlos's temples ceased, the strong hand that had shaken him, and slapped him in such an urgent convulsion, dropped in fatigue along the side of her mauve dress, Carlos picked up his football, which had rolled onto the grass, his mother's hand now rested strong and peaceful on Pastor Jeremy's shoulder, it was Deandra and Tiffany's bedtime, the pastor told his wife, and when were they going to get rid of that old icebox in the backyard, and the Christmas tree with its mouldy garlands, ah well, it could wait another few months, why do today what they hadn't had time to do yesterday if it could be done tomorrow, and Carlos ran, hugging his football to his broad chest, because he mustn't be late for the game, and as he ran flags were unfurled, voices were raised in patriotic songs whose religious fervour excited Carlos, for he heard in them words that were addressed to him alone, three cheers for Carlos, three cheers for vanilla ice cream, three cheers for the team champion, for Carlos too had a dream, he was going to be the biggest, the strongest. And why were Luc and Paul quarrelling in the kitchen, it was the soft crackling of ice-cubes in the mineral water that had warned Jacques they were back, they were arguing over the diet he was to follow, tonight rice, fillet of red snapper, in his notebook he observed the fine, tight handwriting that was becoming more and more illegible, rice, fish fillet, Luc and Paul quarrelled because of me, a friend called me from California, had Kafka's period of mental inertia occurred around March 5, 1911? My eyesight is still excellent, in general I'm feeling well, and Jacques, docile, had submitted to the servitude of meals that his liver, his stomach could no longer absorb, over the steaming bowl of rice Luc had served him, he'd shuddered with shameful emotion, with gratitude, perhaps, because someone was

taking care of him, washing him in the morning, bathing him
at night, and this care, for his cleanliness, for his hygiene, was
increasing to the point of derision, he thought, because when
they were changing his sheets he would suddenly be exposed
to the disconcerting coolness of his naked body, before they
imposed on him the nightly constraint of absorbent cloth
under his pyjamas, and then feelings of sour gratitude rose
in him, as they did tonight, of healthy anger too, because it
was time for God to take pity on him, time for this squalid
comedy to be over, for with the sullen temperament for which
Tanjou had so often reproached him, with all his reason, his
pernicious lucidity, was he now about to enter his final
agony? But they took from his hands the plate he hadn't
touched, and fed into the VCR the tape of the film he'd
expressed a desire to see, and it was for them that he displayed his proud smile, his dazzling white teeth below the
fine moustache that his barber had trimmed before he left
the university, it was for them, he thought, that he was still
alive, for he couldn't tear himself away from the mysterious
adoration in all they did for him, nothing seemed more
mysterious to him than this young maleness that was going
to survive him, with its awkward, unpredictable desires, with
the elevation of those desires and the beauty of their sexuality,
when he himself felt so debased; he took Luc's hands in his
own and told him, sighing, you two should go out, go to the
disco, have some fun, and he felt liberated when he saw
them in their white shorts, pulling on their inline skates with
the phosphorescent straps to go out, this night with its silky,
permissive reflections in the bars, on the beaches, belonged
to them, he thought, belonged to the firmness of their brown
bodies in those white shorts, bodies that still shivered beneath
the cold water in the shower, outside, this night belonged to
the solitude or complicity of their pleasures, those desires

they seemed to suppress so well beneath their chaste, reserved appearance, with their thighs, their asses squeezed into tight white shorts, the cocks hard and hot under the zippers of their shorts, but no sooner had they manoeuvred onto the roadway than their finery, shimmering like the plumage of exotic birds, attracted looks from all sides, stirred the curiosity of the lone man, as Tanjou had done in the past with the undulating movement of his hips as he came towards Jacques, skating across a dance floor, an iridescent green ribbon in his short, straight hair, and it was while he was thinking about Tanjou, about the ineffable sweetness with which he abandoned himself, that Jacques replaced the *Amadeus* tape with an erotic film that he kept in the drawer of his bedside table. And if she and Claude had suddenly found themselves close to each other, drawn by the perfumes of a fragrant night by the sea, thought Renata, had they resembled a couple of runaways hastily making love in the anonymity of a hotel room before a departure, a separation, in that feverish clandestinity, a mirror on the ceiling had reflected their audacious demands while they embraced, and suddenly in the silent night the mirror sent back the image of uncoupled bodies that were no longer moving, numbed now in their shared contentment, Renata reminded her husband of the dangers that lay in wait for him, that man was incomprehensibly reckless, she told him, and Claude stood up for himself, saying that with their explosive mixtures the dealers had only destroyed the walls of the greenhouse that housed the tropical plants in the winter, she had never liked the pretentiousness of that greenhouse, he repeated to her, and while they spoke, each caressing the other's face, Renata saw again the vulgar couple shouting themselves hoarse at the piano in the bar, her conscience suddenly reflected all those distressing apparitions in the night, there had also

been the toothless old man dozing behind the dusty coun-
ters of a bookstore in the city, who told her with a look of
resignation, take whatever book you want, madame, I don't
know how to read, myself, I just sell books to schoolkids,
that was when she had experienced a hollow sensation of
thirst, a sensation so uncontrollable that she had turned to a
tourist who was drinking lemonade from a paper cup, the
tourist seemed to be brazenly reading over Renata's shoulder
while she greedily sucked up the drink with her straw, and
now her thirst and the woman's indiscreet presence as she
brushed against Renata's shoulder permeated the lines of
Emily Dickinson she had read in the overheated air of the
bookstore, Because I could not stop for Death, He kindly
stopped for me, The carriage held but just ourselves and
Immortality — for those words written in another language
contained a dense stream of memories, of keen emotions
that Renata felt now, in the present, it was as if, while some
black schoolchildren were jostling her, an unknown woman,
pressed against her shoulder, was savouring a lemonade,
making her thirsty, making her crave a drink as well, she felt
within herself, under the sweat on her forehead, the revelation she'd been waiting for throughout her convalescence
here, in this place where, as she had told her husband, she
felt as if she were in limbo, this revelation of the state of utter
confusion that had inhabited her since the day when she'd
thought she was smoking for the last time, in the dismal
corridor of a New York hospital, at that moment when,
contradicting Dickinson's poem, death had not stopped,
leaving her alone with the whiteness of its passing and the
memorable taste of the last cigarette, its supreme forbidden
succulence that henceforth was part of the material immortality of things, for, she thought, "just ourselves and Immortality"
was perhaps nothing more than the company of those objects

she would find it difficult to leave behind, cigarettes, the gold cigarette case, the lighter, those hollow sensations of thirst that evoked the languor of love, around those objects, objects to which she was connected by the tenacity of all her senses, for nothing in the world had tasted as good as the last cigarette, so that she had repeated countless times the act of bringing the cigarette to her lips, extracting its flavour with a shudder, at once fearful and delicious, of her whole body, for she was suddenly overcome by a despair that led her irresistibly to grasp what struck her as her one chance at immortality on this earth, one in which all her pleasures were marked by a single regeneration, at once exquisite and terrifying, though she knew that sense of immortality in her pleasures was a perishable thing, she wondered how long, how precisely the evanescent sensation of death suspended from her lips, would she come out of it with her courage increased or diminished when she was representing her clients in court on her return, or would she forget that haunting memory of the last cigarette, which really could have been the last, one that was infinitely delectable in her memory, the one she'd smoked in the corridor of a New York hospital, or this other one that she was blissfully inhaling now, taking advantage of her husband's sleep to have a quick smoke at the window, surreptitiously tossing over her shoulders the tweed jacket he would wear for his departure, would she remember her own timid appearance in the bedroom mirror when she'd seen in the lamplight the long, pale scar where her lung had been removed, on skin turned copper by the sun, under the insidious path of the scar that was so perfect, masterly, as she'd told the surgeon, the last breath passed there too, then she had chased away the doubt she could read in his questioning eyes, in the mirror, brusquely she had picked up the gold cigarette case, the lighter, and calmly she had sensed rising to her lips, her nostrils, the odour of damp smoke that brought the sea back to her face, that smell of smoke, hot and damp yet bracing, that came from the ocean. And Jacques had pulled off his pyjamas, removed from his thin waist, his belly, his thighs doomed to the same silent wasting away, the absorbent underpants under his pyjamas, swaddling clothes in which Luc and Paul had wrapped him, with a diligence that was devoted but anxious, before they went out for the night, he shivered as the evening air swelled his chest, for he was finally breathing more easily and he remembered that in raising himself in his bed he had seen the sky, pink between the pine trees, and the glow of the setting sun on the calm sea, on the military beach, deserted at this hour, the football match must be over because he'd heard the cries of the Madwoman of the Path chasing the pastor's children with a stone, heard Carlos's footsteps working their way through the prickly vegetation, behind the barbed wire where captive dogs were howling, police cars were criss-crossing the city, their sirens producing harrowing screams, and Jacques palpated his belly, his thighs, with a clinician's fingers felt his still erect cock, shouldn't he know, even if such curiosity was heavily ironic, how much longer he'd be able to come, to satisfy himself in the shadow of such enormous grief, to accomplish fully the miracles that gave him back his excitable sensual rage, avid such a short time ago, when he cuddled with Tanjou under the blue sheets during those twilit late afternoons in which they both took shelter, at that time when he took offence at Tanjou's modesty, sullenly reprimanding him, when he came here to study he had inherited that disgusting North American puritanism, and why that inquisitorial supplication in Tanjou's eyes, was Jacques not a free man, what he did with his nights concerned only him, at his side he seemed to feel the boy struggling against him with his protests and tears, seemed to hear the voice with its melodious accents telling him, you don't love me then, you don't love me, Jacques would calm him by wearily stroking his brow, his eyes, his mouth, and why the weariness, that was an illegitimate offering to youth, perhaps the stench of that loathsome puritanism in Tanjou had come between them, was the boy confusing sex and noble feelings, what was the shape of his face, Jacques's fingers would slip along Tanjou's prominent cheekbones, over his pulpy lips, silencing them, Jacques was a free man, Tanjou must never ask him any questions, in the silence of those afternoons shut away inside the bedroom you could hear flies bumping into the blinds, the purring of a fan, and suddenly the sententious voice of the professor, expressing the fact that in him the sexual instinct operated like a machine, an engine for his dreams in which risk increased the pleasure, Jacques recalled the glumness of his remarks, he got up, saying to Tanjou, why don't we watch one of my tapes, he fiddled with the knob on the television set, adjusted the contrast, and shyly, modestly, Tanjou looked away from the pairs of boys, from their lascivious impudence, the kind you could see in the film Jacques was watching today, now, while he was still alone; in the parks, the bushes, the bath-houses in every city in Europe, in North America, there emerged from their caves animals who were famished, thirsty, the lethargic lion that was dozing in Tanjou would awaken with a fierce rush of jealousy, what was this latent puritanism he'd inherited from our culture, asked Jacques, I love you, Tanjou replied, still Jacques must go to him, take him in his arms, reassure him with a caress that was slightly aloof, start to fear more than anything that it was true, that he, Jacques, a Kafka specialist the universities were at a loss to know what to do with, yes, if only that were true, that he, Jacques, the inalienable, was loved. Quickly he fled, while the images in the film unfolded, fled to the parks, the bushes, the baths, the ones he had haunted in Paris, New York, Hamburg, Berlin, he fled the nuptial comfort of those afternoons spent lying next to Tanjou in the closed bedroom, for everywhere, both in the open air and in the tainted air of railway and subway underpasses, what awaited him was the complicity of fierce love that does not give itself away, an army of unknown bodies suddenly rose up in the parks, the bushes, the steambaths, the bars, so he would never again see that flirtatious hustler who wore a ring in his left earlobe, or the other one who emerged from the bushes dressed in leather, encircling him in a supple movement, then imprisoning him in his arms, upright against a tree, as he was strolling nonchalantly in the woods at night he had felt around him the invaluable protection of all those bodies that had now forgotten him, how could he live without the acid scent of their indulgent prowlers' lips, without the insistence of their gaze in the parks, the bushes, the baths, in the secret gardens trampled until dawn, surrounded by the smell of leaves or by snow, going home slightly drunk from these raw passions, there came to him the muffled moaning that he'd heard, that he'd often provoked, in the parks, the bushes, the baths, in Paris, New York, Hamburg, Berlin, a TV set transmitted to his still aroused senses the laughing, enraged lament of boys who liked parties, orgies, and who, thought Jacques, for their voluptuous joys, must have shut themselves away together inside the protective halo of their sperm, which spread around them like a bluish-white mist, the colour of their veins, for now that innocent and joyful sperm was tinged with blood, the protective layer of fog no longer protected them, now they derived only hatred and pain from the world into which they'd been born,

only fear and contempt, the parks, the bushes, the baths in
Paris, New York, Hamburg, Berlin were empty, the bushes
deserted, and he, Jacques, with his cock in his hand, was as
isolated as those frail craft on the water that were said on the
radio, on TV, through coded messages from satellites, to be
in peril, even though he received as a favour, a tribute to his
vitality, the feeble tremor that delivered him, the warm dew
that flowed between his fingers and onto his thighs was
restoring him to life, he thought, and it seemed to him that
both in the movie he'd just watched and in life itself, during
those years when for a kiss or an embrace each of them
could founder, perish, could escort into harbour the fallen
craft or a mere ghost of oneself, it seemed that during those
fateful years the hustler with the ring in his left earlobe,
whose memory he had just evoked, as well as the leather-
clad athlete who had kissed him against a tree, in the rain,
that they and so many other silhouettes had already vanished
into the transparency of their own fog, in the bushes, the
baths, the parks of Paris, New York, Hamburg, Berlin, it
seemed that the army of desire had slowly succumbed to
its wounds and was still doing so, that the war was only
beginning, with the loss of countless lives, and he thought
about the roses that turn black inside before the arrival of
winter, under the satiny, velvety petals, those purulent
lesions he saw on his arms, which the sun had had time to
brown since his arrival, and it seemed to him that he could
hear the voice of Pastor Jeremy repeating to him, there's
nothing we can do, Professor, nothing we can do when the
oil dwindles in the lamp, it's night now and there's nothing
we can do, Professor, I'll pray for you in the temple next
Sunday, and one day we shall see the happy valley, the
Valley of the Orchids. The long silent street that ran down
to the ocean in the moonlight appeared to Luc, who was

chatting with his friends from the open window of a bar where he sat swinging his legs, someone asked why he didn't go out every night as he used to, and what had happened to that friend of his, a cultivated man, a little self-conscious, sometimes arrogant, they didn't see him around any more, smoking his hashish all alone at the bar, Jacques, yes, where was he now, caustic, droll too, amusing and seductive, people still remembered his birthday last Easter, the town was still talking about it, surrounded by this din of voices, of deafening music, draped in a solicitude he preferred not to respond to that night, Luc felt a need to leave, and in a leap he spun around on his skates, catching his breath and then travelling almost soundlessly down Bahama Street, over the sparkling asphalt, climbing onto cracked sidewalks where, as he glided along at a nearly fluid speed, he felt dry, thorny flowers raining down on his head; light-headed from the perfume of the bougainvillea, of the magnolias and acacia that were all in bloom at this time of year, he grabbed hold of a branch of crimson flowers, bit it off with an agitated rustling that brought a woman in a nightgown onto her balcony, who is that, she asked, another one of those drug-crazed Negroes, the dogs, call the dogs, Luc raced away on his skates, spitting flowers as he went, at last he saw the ocean glittering in the moonlight and he let himself be carried along to the wharf, in the phosphorescent green wake that emanated from his skates, from their laces, their straps, he listened to the waves rolling under the boards of the pier where the boats had tied up till the next day, and suddenly he came to a halt, scowling, for he hoped to travel far away, as far as Australia, where with Paul he would learn to be a cattle trader, a horse breeder, a farmer brimming with health, the head of a family perhaps, all of it, so he could forget the precariousness of existence, from now on he would have to hide from Jacques the sight of those stains on the sheets, that brownish liquid discharge whose odour soiled everything, but the elegant cruise ships Luc had seen berthing in the harbour that morning were already sailing towards other islands, the fishing boats, like the small sailboats lined up along the pier, inviting the tourist on safaris that would strip the bloom off the lacy underwater fauna adhering to the coral, borrowing its colours, each of those boats, thought Luc, each of those sailboats, with the shadow of its masts wavering in the moonlight on the water, would soon be a house being driven out to sea, a house, a dwelling, perhaps his own one day, where behind the curtain in his cabin he would live among his books, with a dog at his feet, in the company of a faithful love, fishing for shark and dolphin every day with Paul, he would escape the line of fire they heard rumbling in the sky, was it the sound of lightning as it struck the trees near the house, or a bomb exploding in the depths of the ocean, the approaching flames would be their warning, it would keep them awake, coming closer and closer both in the churning water and in the silent bedroom where the sick man was confined, stretching his feeble arms out to the sun at the window, the weather had been beautiful the day they got the news, they were at the home of a writer who was celebrating his belated but magnificent success by having a swimming pool put in, even though he didn't have a house yet, and it was there, around a marble pool, leaning over water not yet cleared of the leaves and debris left by a storm, that they had been sipping their martinis, laughing, when they saw him, heard him, and though the day was glorious, Luc had seen the lightning rend the sky, what was Jacques saying in veiled terms, in a low voice, as he stood next to them, what was he saying with his quiet but feigned assurance, while his blue eyes peered at them with bitter resignation, a dirty business, my friends, it has to end quickly, very quickly, they had seen the nervous tension in his smile when Jacques suddenly left his hosts and went home, the air and the sky were blazing that day, and with a brutal gesture that seemed suddenly to separate him from the rest of the world, Jacques had thrown his still-lit cigarette into the pool, and shortly afterwards Luc had seen him disappear around the corner near the Cemetery of the Roses, Jacques was wearing a short-sleeved blue shirt, light blue like his eyes, buttons open on his powerful chest; determined, hostile, and alone, he would not turn around as he walked, that day Luc had heard the rumble of a storm brewing in the sky, the funereal music seemed to well up by itself, he could hear it in the sound of the waves beneath his feet, in the sky where a cloud veiled the moon, it was the evening breeze that was stirring his soul, he thought, Luc and Paul would live for a long time, one day they'd be seen greeting their friends from those elegant ships that set out every day for distant seas, he was late, borne along by his skates, the iridescent light of their straps and their laces, Luc travelled down the street again, he opened the garden gate that Jacques never closed against thieves, in his celestial flight along the streets and sidewalks, swept up in the night-time intoxication, stretching out his arms on either side of him, Luc had the impression that he was running towards Jacques, that he was unfurling wings around him, and as he pushed the wooden gate before him he could sense in the roots of his hair the tinkling of small oriental bells, the bells purchased after a visit to a temple, when Jacques had walked barefoot through Bangkok because someone had stolen his sandals, for a long time, Luc thought, the tinkling of those bells at the garden gate, the sound of those bells among the flowers, had announced the return of the carefree pilgrim, you could still hear the engaging timbre of his voice when he called to his friends, hop over the wall and come have a drink, and suddenly that voice was barely audible, or was merely a sigh, soon the voice rising from the big hospital bed that had been transported to the bedroom would be heard no longer; as he was taking off his skates on the path that led to Jacques's room, Luc could see the sick man dozing by the window, he seemed more rested, his sleep was calm, the bedside lamp that illuminated his face shone as brightly as the moon, all the way to the back of the room, onto the books scattered over a table, its harsh light setting fire to Jacques's unclothed body amid the sheets that he pulled out all around him every night, as if he was afraid they would smother him, it was true, thought Luc, that he could suddenly hear heavenly arpeggios, because *Amadeus*, the film Jacques had wanted to watch, was still running, and sitting at the foot of the bed with its fetid odours, Luc compared the lovemaking of the young Mozart with his own desires, his passion for amorous adventure, even tonight on a beach he had once again yielded, quickly, he would be more cautious tomorrow, it was as if they'd been at sea on a raft some windless night, Luc and Jacques were sailing far away from the bedroom where they were both prisoners, thought Luc, surrounded by the heavenly music they could hear, one of them asleep, the other awake, his spirits brightened by alcohol, where were they sailing like this if God didn't want them in His mansion, let them drift and sing as they used to when they went sailing with Paul, devoting themselves to underwater fishing, let the sun spread its warmth over them, let them laugh and sing and never know pain, rancour, anger, or humiliation, let them stream through the waves on their sailboards, run along the beaches, the sandy shores of the ocean, until dawn, or let them travel so far into the peace of the waters that they lost their way, with the stigmata on their bodies that were once so beautiful, let them disappear into the waves, fade away without voice or cry, while above them flickered those luminous green signals that guide ships in the night, in his sensual breathlessness Luc had often been touched by the sense of radiant intimacy with another, he experienced it now while listening to Mozart, those few brief seconds of pure, palpable love in the arms of men, those shoulders, those backs sealing a hidden authority, arching with delight under the caresses of his lips, the smell of those rough, voluptuous skins whose fears he untangled amid cries of deliverance, had he known anything more enduring on this earth, the brevity of those seconds, those moments, had overwhelmed his simple soul which asked for nothing more, and soon, perhaps, he would be alone, for he had seen the lights of the final hour flare up on the sea, each of those boats, those sailboats, would leave without him, in the glittering night, with opalescent globes at the summit of their masts, the young captain who had approached him on the beach an hour ago called his dog back to the gangway with a whistle, he had shut the door to his studious cabin, tonight he would open Conrad's book, which he had not had time to read when he was cut off by a storm in the Bahamas, he would listen to Vivaldi while he sailed towards the Indian Ocean, heading for Madagascar, which would be his destination this time, the captain had first gone to sea at seventeen, he had seen Panama, Tahiti, he'd been imprisoned in Australia, in Costa Rica, he'd been wounded in one knee, his dog came running towards him along the gangway, they would all set off again without Luc, without Paul, each of these sailboats, each of these craft in the night, and those fetid odours rose from the bed where Jacques lay moaning, I'm coming, here I am, said Luc, approaching him with all the firmness, the assurance of the movements he had learned with men, Luc freed Jacques of his soiled sheets, he washed him, cleaned him, smiling and chatting all the while, used a towel soaked in cologne to wipe away the traces of brownish discharge from Jacques's thighs, his belly, it's time, said Jacques, yes, the time has come to call the doctor for the shots, I've had enough of this filth, when will it be over? And taking the sick man in his arms Luc said, you should get some sleep now, I won't leave you, Paul will be back soon, it's time to close your eyes and sleep, said Luc, and he began to laugh nervously because it seemed to him that this cascade of warm laughter that suddenly shook him would save them both, would rekindle the green signal lights a navigator followed when he was in peril at sea, and those iridescent globes at the summit of the main masts, and Jacques, who in the past had so enjoyed laughing and having fun with his friends, Jacques in turn laughed a huge laugh, as if he'd been surprised once again by those little pleasures life could bring him, an orgasm — hesitant but serene — a burst of laughter in the night, while a vigorous boy tried to soothe him by rubbing his back and his skeletal shoulders, freshening his soiled flesh with an oily cologne, Jacques thought, when all was lost, all was lost, as he got up to put on the tape of *Amadeus* again he had felt that sudden pain in his guts, the release of the revolting brownish stream that spread around him, so all was lost, and yet celestial music was still coming from the TV set at the back of the room, was it the song of the bassoon, of the oboe he could suddenly hear in the depths, in the obscurity of his suffering, for he knew now that all was lost, tomorrow Luc would call the nurse for the injections, they would summon his sister, they'd let Tanjou know, and meanwhile — how ironic, he thought — Mozart was asking Salieri for a little break; laying down his pen, he was asking for a little break before he finished writing his

Requiem, no doubt the traitor Salieri represented the banal-
ity of fate, the executioner of mediocrity was hounding the
child beloved of God, as he listened to these words, the little
break, with the song of the oboe, the bassoon, he thought
Mozart had felt their notes falling around him like lightning
flashes, as he turned his head Jacques thought he could hear
the prelude to that eternity he was unsure what to make of,
while Mozart's eternity, like his life, seemed to have been
laid out in advance; for hadn't God thought of everything
in his child's chaotic path, the surfeit of solemn notes like
the sarcasm of archbishops and princes, even the yawning
of an emperor who had destroyed masterpieces, the entire
assemblage had been conceived by God alone and, who
knows, for His own glory, the man who was known as Herr
Mozart had never had to look for his birth certificate, any
more than for the common grave in which he would be
buried, the spectre of the sovereign father would follow him
everywhere, and not until it was time for the little break that
was suddenly so long would Heaven's divine buffoon rest at
last, not to sleep but to hear the indescribable song that had
been born in him, upon this earth; Luc and Jacques had
laughed together, for demented though that laughter might
be, it had the spontaneity of misfortune and good fortune
combined, as Luc was still there and Paul would be home in
an hour, and one must bow to divine will when, like Salieri,
one embodies a banal destiny that goes astray, a light that
travels by itself, with no harbour, no attachments, no shore,
when all is lost, all is lost. Luc had remade Jacques's bed,
he had smoothed the sheets left stiff by the laundry, and,
carefully resting Jacques's head against the pillows, he had
entertained him by recounting that night's adventure with the
master mariner sailing alone in the Indian Ocean, and while
he listened to Luc's account, which was a familiar one, Jacques

had dozed off, suddenly in his weakness he was merely a shell rocked by the waves, a plank, a piece of debris, from which a little slimy matter still flowed, and suddenly he saw her again, saw that same woman, the one with the noble profile who had met him at the airport that first day, and as she had on the day of his arrival, she helped him settle into the back seat of the car, asking if he was comfortable in the cushions, with that detached benevolence he also recognized, apologized for dropping in so late to ask about him, and after driving along the ocean, along the gulf that was emerald-coloured in the brightness of noon, the car was now heading towards dark streets, under a heavy grey sky, here it is, said the woman, the place where all separations happen, everything here is inhabited, and Jacques recognized the streets of Prague where Kafka had lived, along with the unknown woman he lost his way in this maze of streets where the brief existence of Kafka and his sisters had unfolded, he'd once jotted down the names of those streets in a notebook while he was travelling, he had drawn a map of the city where were located, according to a German guidebook he'd read, the Geburtshaus, the Kinsky Palace Gymnasium, and even the Geschäft des Vaters, his father's business office where Kafka had perhaps written *The Metamorphosis* in the dread shadow of his progenitor, and when the woman asked again if he was comfortable in the cushions, Jacques saw once more those signs that brought him closer to Kafka's martyrdom, in these austere buildings — the Kinsky Palace Gymnasium, the Geschäft des Vaters — prostrate with grief, he could hear the metallic resonance of those words in their language, and tucked in among the cushions, he felt that he was little by little becoming Kafka's *Metamorphosis*, his human appearance had left him, he was that shrivelled insect on whom rotten apples and insults were raining down, his stunted hands were trembling like the legs of the abhorred animal, while purulent lesions were growing on his back, his face might still be intact but as he painfully touched that face it seemed to Jacques that it was soiled with spittle, like the face of Christ, the place where all separations happen is here, and suddenly Jacques awakened, half opened his eyes, he saw Luc and Paul, who were waiting for the dawn, standing at the window that looked out on the garden, the sun was coming up over the ocean, between the pine trees, Luc's hand was resting confidently on Paul's shoulder, they were alive, thought Jacques, they could hear the roosters crowing very near, in a few hours all the roosters would crow together at the tops of their lungs, among the children, on the rough lawn outside the pastor's house, the scent of jasmine permeated the air, and alive, they were alive. And was it the soft warmth of the air or her husband's departure, thought Renata, though she was used to being alone often, though solitude was the female condition, or was it rather her self-doubt that was prompting her to withdraw, she had never followed Claude to those conferences where women who practised the same profession accompanied their husbands everywhere, self-doubt or pride kept her from doing so, was it his departure or the heat, Renata had often experienced the hollow sensation of thirst that was gripping her chest, clutching her with the poignant revelation that life was merely a passage, when she had read that poem by Emily Dickinson in a bookstore on the island, there was suddenly no more revelation, but the sensation of thirst was still there, along with an urge to smoke which she mustn't give in to, the world seemed inhabited by a white light at the end of a deserted road, like the corridor of a New York hospital after anesthesia, a loss of consciousness, uncaring eternity snatched her up on a road covered with crushed white shells that led to the sea, beneath a blue sky that blinded her even as it revived her thirst, it was just, she thought, that her solitude was as abrupt as the organism's fall into nothingness, when Claude was no longer there to reassure her, what a pity this secret sensation of thirst which was linked to her body's desires also prefigured a supernatural expression that might shed some light on the acts of her life, what a pity this thirst was also her desire for a man, during this separation, could she no longer feel anything without him, for she used to record her daily observations during her convalescence, what a pity her notion that no one was spying on her in this isolation should now overwhelm her with the certainty that she and her husband would always be irreconcilable, like man and woman, now was she discovering that those two beings, inseparable and indivisible both in their struggle to survive and in their mutual greed and curiosity, that they never acknowledged the profound suspicion from which the tie between them had been forged, had they not always lived in worlds so distinct from one another, often enemies, wasn't the woman always there to hamper the man's arrogant progress towards his destiny, the domination or direction of the earthly powers of which he was master, while the woman was quickly thrown back into oblivion, into all the flaws that had led him to abandon her, when the man preferred his warring instincts to her and her children; what woman did not know the unhappiness that was her lot, they were all acquainted with the pettiness of rejection, with the disaster of that condition, all women knew how much they would always be misunderstood, discredited by man, even women who had written the sublime lines Renata had read that afternoon in a bookstore filled with children, while she was experiencing that hollow sensation of thirst, as if the flaw that had led men to abandon, to reject women over the centuries had suddenly struck her down, reminding her how painful her infinite weakness was, but just as it was beneath the sky that burned her eyes, while she listened, as she walked in the silence, to the barely perceptible sound of the shells on the road disintegrating under her heels, the same thirst that was consuming her might have led her to the bedroom, as she stretched out on the bed they had just left, its wrinkled sheets still damp with sweat, she would have felt the slaking of her thirst as she gulped drunkenly from the gleaming carafe of water that sat on a piece of furniture, that thirst had given her a low, rather obscene look, she thought, she could see it on her face when she was searching for her cigarettes, the lighter, the gold case, or when she was gambling at the casino, under her impulse to lose everything, for she'd have had to destroy everything, to annihilate those objects Claude was constantly hiding from her for her own protection, this time he hadn't hidden them, they were with her in the hotel room, she hadn't been able to convince him of the harshness of the sentence imposed on the dealers while he was hastily dressing, shaving, the employees were still on strike, but a driver was waiting downstairs for Claude, he was constantly surrounded by such people to serve him during his imposing mission, he had reserved the driver the day before, he'd said in his practical voice, then added that he had a duty to punish wrongdoings that could become crimes, his voice was kind, you need rest so badly, he said tenderly, suddenly they were closer, they would have rediscovered the same delicious night-time torpor had the taxi not honked its horn a second time, they'd have been reconciled, yes, they would have been loving too, but they'd have had to destroy everything, Renata thought, to wipe out the memory of their greedy lips, their joined hands, she had taken his hands and kissed them as she bade him goodbye, because he was good for her and she

knew it, finally he went down to the hotel lobby, she complained of the cold as she picked up a scarf, though the
heat was dense and humid, her action had struck him as
ungracious when she pulled the scarf from a cupboard, but
that was how she destroyed the exaltation created by living
at the side of this man, he would always be a protective friend,
he would be aware of her strength when she was haunted
again by the suspicion that existed within the bonds between
them, by her doubt regarding her individual destiny as soon
as she was alone, success in her life meant Franz or Claude
when he was the one who told her again that it was she
herself, everything must be wiped out, destroyed, for the
punishment had been too harsh, the lighter, the cigarettes,
the gold case, but carefully, she who was a woman of the
world, she thought, and not in the least ascetic, how would
she get along without the gleam of those objects she so liked
to hold in her hand in the hot, heady dimness of bars, of
casinos at night, yet everything would have to be wiped out,
destroyed, those harmless vanities, those frivolous pursuits
that she held dear, and now rising from the earth, from the
path, there was silence and the resonance of those shocks to
the soul that would change her life, was it true that beyond
this path marking the limit of the land that was part of the
elegant hotel property began the abrupt solitude of a woman
who was suddenly at the edge of a cliff, a precipice, and
began as well the hollow sensation of thirst, for beyond the
path, beyond the road beneath the trees, Claude's car had
already dropped out of sight on the horizon, the taxi in which
he had turned around to offer her a tender, knowing smile;
alone on the water and in the sky winked the blazing light
that burned Renata's eyes. And what was the meaning of this
sudden dwindling of all his senses, what dread was entering
him now that he could no longer see or hear them, for Luc

and Paul had called them and now they were there, along with the nurse, who laid her hand on his, recommending that he increase the dose of morphine, with the help of his timer, and his sister, who must have interrupted her classes to come and see him when Jacques would have preferred never to see his family again, and Tanjou, whose sobs he could hear, like spasmodic murmurs, hiccups, Tanjou's tears that in the old days he had found disconcerting, the roundness of those tears as they streamed down Tanjou's prominent cheekbones when he asked him, don't you love me then, and Jacques brushed him aside for other pleasures, a night in the park, a session at the baths, but above all, let Tanjou stop following him everywhere, and suddenly the sounds of those tears, the murmur of those sobs broken by hiccups, perceived through the forest of tubes and equipment that restricted Jacques's body, during the night those tears, a free man's tears while he himself was in prison, got on the sick man's nerves, it was torture, what fear stabbed him if he couldn't hear Carlos's footsteps as he jumped off the roof of the house to the lemon trees, the orange trees in the garden, if he couldn't see the face of Le Toqué as the boy limped towards the giant lime tree whose green fruits he devoured, in the backyard overrun by cats, what fear if the air he breathed with difficulty, lifting his chest, was dwindling, was merely a frenzied whisper that drummed against his heart, a drumming he could hear as he lay pinned to his bed when everything had fallen silent, he could no longer feel the sun's caress on his arms, no longer hear Carlos's footsteps or the crumpling sound of steel from the objects he stole in the streets, a bicycle pedal, a tire, a chain, some padlocks, because there was nothing to be done, said Pastor Jeremy, nothing to be done when the light in the lamp was extinguished, and what had he done with his life, asked the woman with the noble profile, the one whose face had so many times been a harbinger of his dying, of his death, did she not murmur in a vindictive tone, all those trips to the Orient, the languages you learned, the books you've read, the papers you've written, not one of your actions has ever made us forget who you were, you, who you are, and didn't I get that job in the university after a bitter struggle while you were travelling, while our family was hearing talk about you, about your behaviour, when did you ever come to enquire about my health, my successive depressions, this brother, this curse, and your charm too, and your conquests, my husband, my healthy children have never met you, your selfish happiness, your rage to live, this Tanjou who's not even of your race and whom you loved so much, you could have avoided harming us, what a curse, this brother; stuck there in that corridor from which life was departing in a diffuse mist, the nurse, the older sister, the woman friend, the mother, the woman with a classic profile who had asked him if he was comfortable in the cushions, in the car bringing him in from the airport, the woman who had cared for him, who came back to ask about him again, she had missed him, how was your journey, the crossing, she asked, the woman who said, as she depressed the timer switch to double the dose of morphine, you'll sleep peacefully, the woman whose profile was bitter, distant, for though she stood next to Tanjou she did not look at him, the woman who was jealous or furious with envy, because Jacques had read all the books, his own writing was known in American universities, would that woman be at his side till the end, that sister, that patient woman friend who wouldn't leave him, when Jacques thought he was expected elsewhere, on the beach, it was time for his daily workout, lowly contortions on a foul-smelling beach, when — he was sure of it — he would soon hear Carlos's footsteps in the leaves of the garden, he would

spy Le Toqué's head through the gap in the fence, for there
was still some oil in the lamp, and Jacques could hear that
celestial music, wasn't it the cantata *Davidde Penitente* that
he'd wanted to hear, asked Luc, or the great Mass in C Minor
that Mozart had written as a pious offering to his native
Salzburg, where he would so often be humiliated, a mass
written amid the joy, the effervescence of his heart for the
soprano voice of a woman, of an angel who so many times
would push away the fear of death, the incredible fear of
damnation, of the eternal flames that inhabited Mozart, for,
thought Jacques, there was still some oil, some fire, some
light in the lamp, and he was sure of it, it was that aria full
of exuberance, of bliss, written for Constanze, that conveyed
the melancholy of the Kyrie, the Sanctus, the darkness of the
Dies Irae, for once again, in the song of the bassoon, of
the oboe, Jacques could hear those pleasant sounds around the
house, the scraping sound of steel as a bike travelled along
the asphalt of the street, the sound of snarling cats fighting
on the roof, of muffled footsteps among the faded hibiscus
blossoms on the sidewalks, by increasing the dose, by
depressing the timer button, he would escape this room where
people were weeping over him, for he was expected farther
away, in the middle of the ocean, where, towed by a boat,
he would straddle the high waves on his water skis, the race
was incredible, it was a question of breathing properly, of
not swallowing any water from the powerful waves that were
taller than he was, but the air was light, the sky a thin silk
that a fingernail had torn, had opened to the white wound
of the sun, the sun of blindness that he would henceforth
avoid, the sun whose caress he had known on his arms, on his
bare torso when he used to write outside at his table in the
morning, he had fled forever, and when would the floating
parachute move through the sky to help him along in his

race, his flight, while in the bedroom everyone was weeping and on the beach the rescue workers were waving their black flags, for in the event of peril, of danger, suddenly the sea would no longer be navigable. And Carlos was riding his bicycle down the boulevard along the Atlantic, where nonchalant bathers were strolling on the beaches, dipping their feet in the waves at low tide, he listened to the piercing call of the sirens, telling himself that he wasn't the one they were looking for, because it had been a good hour since early this morning when he'd hopped on the new bike outside the supermarket, it was the latest model on display, the handlebars, the brake cables were the same garish, dazzling yellow as Carlos's jersey, Mama had said it was dirty, and what was Carlos up to now, sprawling on the kitchen table, stupidly watching Deandra and Tiffany drink their milk when he should have been at school, was he thinking about his future, what would the Reverend Doctor who was in heaven say, had he not died for him, Carlos, he would say, my son, you're going to end up like the Escobez brothers from Esmeralda Street, have you thought about your future, my son, and about me, Martin Luther King, whose blood was shed for you, Mama had pushed him out of the house and he hung around outside, grumbling, there were a number of empty bottles, their bottoms smeared with sticky scum, those bottles, like the paper plates they'd used for the Sunday picnic, which Carlos was supposed to have stuffed into the recycling bag, so the pastor said, but did he ever listen to his parents, said Mama, eh, when, and what was he doing sprawling there on the kitchen table, daydreaming, was he thinking about his misbehaviour, the padlocks, the bicycle chains sliced off with cutters in what had become a routine, has anybody ever seen the like of it, hanging out with the Bad Niggers from Bahama Street, young louts, degenerates, watching you in the evening from their lair, drooling and glassy-eyed, did Carlos hear the patrol sirens while he rummaged day and night through the garbage of Bahama Street, those men who were no longer men, on Bahama Street, on Esmeralda Street, the Escobez brothers' street, the next time they'd send him to a farm in Atlanta to cool off, but the Lord in His mercy is better than we are, said Pastor Jeremy to his wife, his voice booming as if he were preaching in the temple, and Carlos's mother replied glumly, padlocks, bicycle chains, he'll go to hell, and could Carlos still hear his mother's curses through the piercing cry of the sirens, the house would be quieter once Deandra and Tiffany were in bed, thought Carlos, flies and butterflies were clustering on the slats of the venetian blinds overheated by the sun, Mama always came out of the house to greet the mailman, who was white, she would straighten up the mailbox, which tilted to one side, it was this excited, laughing young man in shorts who brought the news from other churches, there's been a change in the weather, Mama said, the two of them were chatting about the heat, about the Baptist church choir where Venus sang, at times Mama would mutter that Carlos was a good-for-nothing, again that morning he was lazing around, in the summer they could take him to a plantation in Atlanta, uncharitable souls said Le Toqué wiggled when he walked but Mama had loved him like the others, a lame leg, what could you do, the pastor carried him to the schoolbus in his arms, let them dare make fun of his son, the Lord would punish them, but Le Toqué was a thief like Carlos, if she thought about the black boys who were shot in Chicago every day, Mama was lucky, yes, Pastor Jeremy was right, it was time to get rid of the old icebox in the yard, red ants could make their home in it, near Deandra and Tiffany, Mama was no longer thinking about Carlos, about her disappointment, and the piercing

voice of the city patrol sirens also disappeared, as had Mama's
cries which he'd heard when he got up this morning, Carlos
was happily pirouetting on the bicycle seat, for the gang
of Bad Niggers seemed to be farther away now, in the sinister shadows of Bahama Street, still sitting on their porches,
comatose, yet they were waiting for Carlos to come and deliver
his merchandise before noon, depraved, shifty, they had
fangs that gleamed under disdainful lips, the bicycle with its
new wheels flashing silver would be dismantled, then sold
off piece by piece, but Carlos would keep the puppy whose
name was Polly, Polly whom he'd discovered wrapped in a
bath-towel, at the bottom of the basket on the luggage rack,
with no leash or collar, a long-eared dog, a ball of reddish
fur now panting with thirst in Carlos's big athletic hands, and
too bad for the owner who'd left his bike on the sidewalk
while he was buying groceries, Polly belonged to Carlos now
and soon the two of them would go running along the beach,
that beach where the white heron tucked its beak into its
feathers, they all seemed far away now, the Bad Niggers,
vermin, his mother called them, and the old white man who
had insulted him yesterday by talking to Carlos about his
frizzy hair while he was washing his car at his house by the
sea, as he did every week, Carlos no longer saw any of them
because he had Polly now, and Mama, who had opened up
her newspaper under one of the garden parasols, said what
will become of us if they're being shot down in Chicago
every night, on the Street of Gentle Winds, of Peaceful
Astronauts, on the Street of Warm Breezes, tell me, Papa,
what will we do, and Pastor Jeremy, who was gazing at his
flowers, holding his watering can, said it was time to get rid
of the old icebox in the yard, and to visit the professor across
the street, and to say a prayer, when the time came. That
mass written amid the joy, the effervescence of the heart,

thought Jacques as he listened to the melody of the notes, so pure and solemn, that Luc enabled him to hear, when he placed the headphones on his pillow, what strange act of pity allowed Jacques still to listen with delight on this radiant day when he was hooked up and attached to his humiliating bed, with the faces around him grimacing in pain, he sank into the night, the only night that mattered for him, the one about which he knew nothing, had never known anything, though he was an intelligent man, far from him, far from his persistent senses, this penitent night into which his spirit would vanish in his bruised and humiliated body, which he compared to the bodies of the prisoners in Piranesi's engravings, with their twisted limbs, chained to a post or to the wheel in an ever more violent chiaroscuro, amid the silence of the penal colonies, those stone prisons, those drawn bodies captured by the artist in the stylized, sublimated posture of their torture, when it was so demeaning for bodies to suffer, when outside it was so beautiful that Jacques instinctively turned his face to the sun, had he not written in his essays, as other essayists had done, that these engravings evoked the works of Kafka, *Metamorphosis, The Penal Colony*, had he not bored his students with the interpretations he'd taken from paintings, from prints, from literature, but no more than Piranesi had done, imagining his prisoners with their feet bound, mouths sealed with the ornate stones of ancient prisons, he would have been unable to conceive that one day he would be that prisoner, that some torturer god would be waiting for him in this bed from which he would never again rise to run along the ocean as he used to do every morning, or to swim, to enjoy life, for it was inconceivable that it should be true, that he would soon stop breathing, for a long time he would tell them all that he was still alive, and when he saw Tanjou's face, awash with tears, bending over his own, he was suddenly aware of the words that came to his lips, I'm alive, you know, he said in a breath, insolently, can't you hear me, I am alive, and in the dazzling procession of memories that his memory had stirred, his brief life seemed to be a source of endless wonder, nothing, he thought, could be added to or taken away from the inflexible perfection of that fate which would soon come to an end, even the woman who yesterday had been the harbinger of his death, the nurse, the friend, the sister, the woman who would show him such cruel solicitude by escorting him to the place where he would be the most forlorn of men, Jacques would no longer oppose that sister, that friend, perhaps she had released the pressure of her sharp fingernails around his heart, for now she placed an indulgent hand on his temples, saying that he must be very thirsty, did he want more morphine, and just then Tanjou's hand, which was gripping Jacques's, took him back to where they had first met, a place he thought he'd forgotten, it was as if Jacques were suddenly endowed with piercing sight, though he could no longer see those around him, he saw again the scene in the theatre where Tanjou had danced with other students, Tanjou had stayed longer than the others so he could mark the steps of his choreography on the stage with white chalk, and leaving him unaware of his presence backstage, Jacques had been dismayed by that difference in Tanjou which was his grace, Tanjou soaring into the air alone, his silent leaps, Jacques remembered that he had loved Tanjou for the time-less silence that emanated from him, from his dark skin in the pale lights, the memory was so physically pleasing that Jacques had the impression he was emerging from the wings as he had on that day, winding his arm around Tanjou's waist, and all at once Jacques found himself in his garden with Tanjou sitting at his feet, it was his birthday, Tanjou was painting a watercolour that showed, hanging from a bougainvillea by the sea, an open cage with a red-and-blue-feathered parrot on its bars, Jacques saw the watercolour again as if Tanjou had freshly executed it, from the subtle tones of his brush sprang the sky, the sea, thinned down in water on the transparent paper, and as if the serenity of this day were eternal, Jacques's gaze expanded with happiness into this blue sky, these abundant flowers dropping onto the terrace from the tree, he was the parrot drunk with heat, with sun and freedom, hesitating to escape from the open cage, and against his legs he could feel the erect back of Tanjou, his equilibrium, his harmonious presence while he was painting the sky and sea, the parrot; still wrapped in the silence of a museum statue, compact and silent under his slanted eyelids, he was that indefinable wisdom absorbed in the beauty he reflected, and Jacques had been indifferent to the perfection of that day, feeling irritable because he was one year older, he'd celebrated too hard the night before, and now that day would never come again, nor would the others whose lingering hours had run out far from his gloomy heart, which, for a long time now, had seemed pleased by nothing, when all was lost, all was lost. And the rabbits, the chicks that Samuel and Augustino had been given at Christmas were stirring in the grass, in the sun, still trembling with the shudder of their birth, each of them opening its eyes in the morning light, crying, cheeping, while Vincent was asleep upstairs in the bedroom next to his mother, who had lowered the blinds on the blazing sunlight, for was Vincent not the most beautiful, the most endearing of Mélanie's three sons, of all three marvellous children she was so proud of, she was remembering Vincent's birth amid such moaning in pain, and suddenly he was sleeping in the big bed beside her, for she had lifted him out of his cradle to take him in

her arms and now she was listening to his breathing as he
slept, what was the meaning of that slight gasping, of the
rapid, laboured breathing that had been diagnosed at birth,
Vincent was the most vigorous of her sons, Samuel and
Augustino had been born in Paris, in New York, Vincent
here on this island with its intoxicating perfumes, by the sea,
he was a chubby baby, would he wake up in a torrent of
gurgling or tears, peering warmly at her through his long
lashes, he had the brown complexion of his Italian grandparents, and what was Augustino shouting as he came running
downstairs in his Superman cape, Mummy made a baby and
he's here now, hurray for Mummy, so noisy, Augustino,
when would he quiet down, couldn't Jenny and Sylvie take
him outside, couldn't Daniel take him for a bike ride, it wasn't
a weekday, Daniel would write until noon, the second act of
his play was not yet written because of the children, he was
upset about this delay, Jenny and Sylvie were planning the
party for Vincent, who would be ten days old today, they
had to think of everything, the hors-d'oeuvre, while Augustino
was making so much noise, and Mélanie lingered at her
son's bed, neglecting her duties, she thought, neglecting
Jenny and Sylvie, she wouldn't have time to write that
paper and the meeting of women activists was scheduled
for Thursday, and what was happening now to make her
collapse with fatigue in the midst of the children, she whose
health was so robust, it was shortly after she'd driven Samuel
to school in the van, after she'd stowed his tennis balls and
lunch in his backpack, and the supplies for Jenny and Sylvie,
her arms laden with bags, she had thought with uncontrollable disgust, it was the first time she had felt this way after
the birth of one of her children, this disgust, disgust at his
warm gaze under long lashes, did she love him too much or
not enough, Vincent, oh, if only they could be a single being

in the blazing half-light, said Mélanie to her son as she lay
beside him, listening to him breathe, sometimes placing her
finger under the black hair on the damp little forehead, she
was again dressed in the beige shorts, the wrinkled shirt in
which she'd done her morning workout on the beach, and
her guests would begin arriving at seven, she would welcome them with the elegance that Mère had inculcated in
her, along with her culture and so many vague desires that
went along with her social standing, Mélanie thought, Mère,
Père, indomitable, expecting you to show fierce respect for
their traditions, what would Mère say to her friends in their
tea-rooms, at cocktail parties, my daughter became a leader
very young, she has a brilliant degree in Arts and Sciences
from the university, she went to Africa where she battled
poverty and injustice through demanding community work,
but why did she marry, have children, I don't understand,
when Americans need women leaders so badly, can she aspire
to the Senate now, to lead a political party, our friends could
help her, and while she stroked her son's forehead, Mélanie
was thinking about her overdue paper, she felt as if she
could hear through Vincent's laboured breathing against her
cheek the incendiary commotion in the world, a president's
televised declaration of war on a dark night in January, or
was it at dawn, after they'd calmed the children in their beds,
forgetting Augustino, who had come during the night to be
with them, curled around their legs, he was too big now to
climb into bed at any hour of the night when he was scared,
but what was it Augustino had said that morning, Mummy
and Daddy would never come back, that fire in the sky,
the smell of charred dust that people inhaled in the streets,
Mummy's belly was so big now there was no room for
Augustino, what was Augustino talking about, he had never
seen his parents again, or his black baby-sitters, Jenny and

Sylvie, who were studying at the Virgin of the Sea school, on that dark January morning there was no one in the house, that fire in the sky, on TV a man had said that in the future it would be pointless to brush your teeth before you went to nursery school or school, Daddy had said, take your lunch anyway, turkey sandwiches and an apple, and the tennis balls for Samuel too, don't forget anything, he had insisted on silence around him until noon, Augustino would never see his parents again, or Jenny and Sylvie, and so Mélanie would finish her paper on this dark January morning, her son Augustino who was four years old had asked if today was the day when they were all going to die. Could Vincent, who was asleep in the big bed beside his mother, one fist wrapped around Mélanie's fingers, in the blazing half-light that came in through the blinds, could he hear Augustino twittering as he ran among the rabbits and the chicks in the huge garden where the black almond trees were in bloom, around the pool, the pool that was surrounded by an iron fence so Augustino could romp and play there in peace, all around, it would soon be lit by green luminescence in the night, Samuel would replace Julio at the bar tonight, to serve his mother's guests, Julio who'd been beaten on the beach by some Cubans, himself an exiled Cuban, Samuel, imitating Julio, would like to spill wine into the crystal glasses, the gin, the vodka into glasses over copious ice-cubes misted over with pearl-coloured air, in his uniform, his white knee-length socks, he would ask authoritatively, like Julio, what can I offer you, and his parents' guests would rush to the bar, in the garden under the stars, and because Augustino was so eager he would serve coffee too, it would be late at night but those parties could go on for days and nights, and Augustino would be reeling from sleepiness in the wake of the steaming coffee-pot, between Jenny and Marie-Sylvie whom he would follow step by step, he would tell his mother repeatedly, I did what you said, Mummy, I didn't eat any sugar, and Mélanie would see the thin foam of sugar still sticking to Augustino's pink lips, and his father would say, you'll have to go to bed now, Augustino, since you're starting to tell lies, but Augustino would cry, protest, the crow that had escaped from the storm would hear his cries, the Labrador would trot along beside him, panting in the heat, and Augustino would envy his brother Samuel, whom no one ever sent to bed, who ate sugar and sampled the wine, sometimes with a superior manner, once a week Samuel, who had been given a boat by his parents for his eleventh birthday, more modest than his father's boat but it too was moored at the marina, on a calm day you could see the captain on board his boat, cutting across the waves on the sea, while Augustino never went through the garden gate without Jenny or Marie-Sylvie or his father, how bored he was with all those whimpering toddlers from kindergarten, from nursery school, why didn't his parents see that he was bored with all those toddlers, and the height of his forehead, his high forehead already had a wrinkle, a worried frown above his curved nose, why did Julio get beat up on the beach tonight, he asked his father, why, why, and no one answered, as for Samuel, if he had all the advantages that adults have, it was no doubt because he was already an actor you could see in the movies, the theatre, he went out in the evening on his mother's arm, travelled by plane with his parents, went to New York to attend one of his father's plays, while Augustino wasn't even allowed to eat sugar, because sugar kept Augustino awake at night; Augustino ran through the grass, chasing the rabbits, the chicks, all those tiny newborn animals in their cardboard boxes, and Vincent, who was fast asleep, didn't hear Augustino's cheeping amid the fluttering of his cape, crying hurray for my mummy, hurray for my mummy, she hasn't got a big baby in her stomach any more, I love my mummy, and cautiously getting out of the big bed where Vincent lay sleeping, Mélanie slowly took off the wrinkled shorts and shirt she'd worn for her morning workout on the beach, her heart still gripped by a vague uneasiness, she pulled down over her bony hips the white muslin dress Mère had picked out for her, because she had to please Mère tonight, she donned the gold-trimmed sandals Daniel had brought her from China, it already seemed like a long time ago, before the accident, New York, the illumination that would transform their lives, Daniel's writing; as she placed her hand on the banister, Mélanie had seen Jenny and Sylvie smiling as they looked up at her, their faces expressing an unlimited confidence that she thought was undeserved, she could hear the whispering voices of the guests on the doorstep, Mère was right, haunted by the scourges of racism, of sexism, of the drugs she worried about on Samuel's account, Samuel who was not yet attending private school, Mélanie would have to fight against those scourges for some years yet, then the children would be older, Mélanie could found a political party because — it was true — Mélanie was a leader, she had the personality, the mind for it, as her mother told her friends in tea-rooms, at evening cocktail parties, Mère was often right about Mélanie, except where the children were concerned, what was this passion Mélanie had for motherhood, she asked, and suddenly the shrill voice of the patrol cars' sirens rose in the city, and the cries of Mama who was bickering with Venus on the veranda, while Carlos told Polly not to make any noise in the shed, no, not a sound, he said, while he went to deliver the bicycle, but Venus no longer sang psalms in the Baptist church on Sunday, Mama lamented, the long altercation broken by threatening gestures at Venus, who was sitting listlessly in the swing, the whites of her eyes glittering in the night, Venus who exhaled lazy sighs while she listened to her mother, it was because she'd become a sinner by singing at night with Uncle Cornelius at the mixed club, a fifteen-year-old girl didn't spend her nights outside the house, singing in tourist bars and clubs, a girl of fifteen went to church and prayed, she helped her mother with Deandra and Tiffany, on Bahama Street, on Esmeralda Street, people knew that Uncle Cornelius had been a hero during the Korean War, there'd been an article about his bravery in the local paper, Mama said, but he had never been rewarded for his valorous deeds, Uncle Cornelius lived in a trailer, on a vacant lot near the sea, with his dogs and his cats and always surrounded by women, for those pleasure palaces where Uncle Cornelius played his blues at night, where Venus sang, striking voluptuous poses, attracted lust, sin, what did Venus think about it, sitting list-lessly in the swing, and so arrogant when her mother was talking to her, for didn't people drink alcohol in those places all night long, it was the swelling of the sap that was going to her head, cried Mama, and as she opened her heavy eyelids Venus was thinking about Uncle Cornelius and his sad and haunting voice depicting his longing for friends dead in the trenches, all of them, all, not a single one had survived. Uncle Cornelius played the piano all night long, proudly wearing his veteran's red felt beret, with its sparkling tiny golden eagle, which Uncle Cornelius never took off, day or night, and Mama could hear the melody Venus was humming between her teeth, and when it suddenly grew quiet they could hear the silence, thought Carlos, who was afraid Polly would start barking in the shed, for he could see her, panting with fear, through the cracked boards of the door, Carlos told Polly he'd come back for her, said they'd go to the beach together, but Polly mustn't bark, she must obey Carlos, the

Bad Niggers would kill Carlos if it took him any longer to deliver his goods, the bicycle he'd stolen that morning with Polly in the luggage rack, the bike whose brake cables and handlebars were the same garish, glaring yellow as Carlos's jersey, the bicycle it was so hard for him to part with, as with Polly, Polly who had licked his hands with her rough tongue and who had such a touching way of begging to be petted, cocking her head to one side, and Polly was lucky, said Carlos, that the pastor was in church at this time of day, that he was lighting candles and kneeling to pray for that poor professor who lived across the street who was going to die soon, because in the house they were saying the professor wouldn't make it through the night, at night papa would usually rummage through his tools in the shed or play dominoes with the neighbours in the yard, and you could hear the racket made by all those hands jostling together in the evening air, Polly must stop being afraid, she could get air through the broken pane of the window where the hens came in to roost, Carlos had put down a bowl of water for her and she'd licked his hands as if she were begging him, don't go, don't leave me alone in the dark, in this night where people get rid of dogs that don't have masters, sacrificial animals, and Pastor Jeremy was thinking that the oil had dwindled in the lamp, that the Lord should show mankind more mercy, the poor professor who could no longer take anything in, there was a cotton pad soaked in water on his lips, he was so thirsty, and the night about which he knew nothing was drawing near, the pastor thought the Lord should have shown some pity on this troubled night, would the professor see the yellow hibiscus at the foot of his bed, Pastor Jeremy's offering to the man who was going to die, and he thought they were already waiting for him in the Valley of the Orchids, where all tears, all pain would cease,

Le Toqué had been seen limping down Bahama Street, the
lush plant pressed against his heart, it was the day of the
boat race but it had rained, and the pastor had opened his
black umbrella on the beach to shelter Deandra and Tiffany,
suddenly the pastor had remembered the yellow hibiscus the
professor grew in his garden, and he'd thought, I know, I'll
send him a hibiscus, and Le Toqué, my son whom everyone
laughs at because of his bad leg, will take it to him, a yellow
hibiscus, it was there, under the black umbrella, while the
speedboats were tearing across the lake, that he had heard
the voice of the Lord tell him, amid the breaking waves, in
the rain, you must open a hospice on the island, my son, for
they have no place where they can breathe their last, and
while the candles in the temple were being consumed, while
their wicks were burning down, the pastor learned from the
voice of God that the hospice would be here in the temple
one day, what would they do with all the graves, with that
crowd of young people in the Cemetery of the Roses, would
God in His goodness take pity one day on those lives, and
with faith and hope they would await the end of their martyrdom, those whose families had turned them out by the
hundreds into the streets, they would be seen in the temple,
in the synagogue, where they would attempt to heal their
wounds through prayer, through meditation, would God,
who did not spare the flesh that had suffered such devasta-
tion, take pity, and Jacques thought that in the silky air, in
the exquisite fragrant air, the curtain of his life would be
silently torn, in the yellow glow of a hibiscus held out to him
by a black child who had come in from the street, a child
breathless from running, no doubt what Pastor Jeremy had
said in his sermons was true, that the oil had dwindled in the
lamp, because the air that Jacques was no longer breathing
was now parching his lips, and he could not hear Carlos's

bike scraping along the pavement, the bike he'd stolen that morning, along with Polly in the luggage rack, but where was Carlos anyway, the Bad Niggers wouldn't catch up with him, but the feeble sun of blindness was at last retreating into the darkness, the blinding sun that had moved in the sky, that had whitened Jacques's eyes, amid terror, now he was free of his bonds, the hospital bed that had been transported to the house, the medical equipment that had kept him alive for so long, Jacques's nimble body was drifting now, as it had done in the past, beneath the canopy of his multicoloured parachute, with water skis on his feet he glided through the blue sky, hanging from the rescue workers' parasail, in that exquisite, fragrant air, so high in the blue sky, and he could see the long-haired teenage girl who was swimming towards the shore with her dog, and a small slender boat anchored in the middle of the ocean, so high in the sky, he told himself that this time, this time he would not come back down the rope to the foaming of the waves, he was drawn by the rescue workers' boat, for he was home again and he would tell them all to open up the bedroom, quickly, to let in the perfume of the garden. And Jacques, suddenly set free, had closed his eyes on the glare of the setting sun dropping into the sea, between the pine trees, along the military beach, the rosy setting sun he had watched from his bed so many times, while he listened to celestial music, the cantata *Davidde Penitente* or the great Mass in C Minor that Mozart had written amid the joy, the effervescence of his heart, in the mist of semiconsciousness Jacques had thought that it was over already, that brief pause while one last cloud and its reflections in the water drifted above the ocean, that the touching appearance of the teenage girl swimming back to shore with her dog was disappearing into the darkness, abandoned to the gentleness of the waves,

while the cloud on the horizon was disappearing too, for
there was no more oil in the lamp and the friend, the sister,
the woman who had been the devoted nurse, had sighed
with relief that it was over, while at the same moment her
face with its noble profile had been unable to conceal an
expression of contempt for Tanjou, who was crying beside
her, when was that boy going to leave, on the next train, the
next plane, she wanted to see the last of him, she thought,
as she pulled up her hair and indignantly tied it at the nape
of her neck, hadn't her brother suffered his sordid decline
from associating with those young people of a different race,
she longed to be alone so she could settle the family affairs,
and how were her husband, her children managing without
her at home, it had been several days now, the skeletal man
whom Luc and Paul were holding in their arms, whom they
still held raised from his bed towards the evening light, even
now that it was over, was all over, was that pain-ravaged
man her brother, what was the repulsion driving her away
when she wanted so badly to come close to him, but Jacques
had never felt pity for her, for her shame, her humiliation,
now that he was no longer there how would she be able to
talk about him tomorrow to her husband, her children, the
scent of jasmine, of mimosa from the garden overwhelmed
her, dizzied her with their heady, nearly sickening fragrance,
amid humiliation and shame, for she had always detested the
climate of these tropical islands, the stagnating vegetation on
shores that were stifling in the torrid heat, the humidity, this
climate was unhealthy, and mysteriously intoxicated by the
scent of jasmine, of mimosa from the garden, Tanjou walked
up to the table in the flower-filled space at the window
where Jacques had written every day, piling up the drafts of
his book on Kafka, surrounded by familiar objects, a pen
marking a passage in a German biography of Kafka, some

letters from overseas still in their unopened envelopes lay
there among objects that now would be inert, the watercolour Tanjou had painted the year before, for Jacques's
birthday, which would not be followed by another, and as
he looked at the miraculous watercolour in its frame on the
table, Tanjou saw himself again as he had been when he
painted the water, the sky, his rigid back resting against the
knees of Jacques, who was sitting in a chaise longue, Jacques
would sometimes drop an indolent hand into Tanjou's hair,
again he saw himself happy, painting Jacques a watercolour
in which you could see the sky and the sea thinned down in
ink on the transparent paper, was it true, he thought, that
this sky, this sea, were already clouding over with shades of
grey, shades that the emerald-coloured gulf, the immutable
blue of summer skies would take on tomorrow, when Jacques
was mingled with them, when his ashes were scattered in
the wind, and was it intoxication from the hashish cigarettes
Tanjou smoked, he suddenly felt certain that Jacques was
still there, in the rosy colour of the setting sun he'd painted
in the watercolour, as in the bougainvillea with its blossoms
dropping onto a terrace by the sea, and it seemed to him that
he could hear the words Jacques had uttered insolently from
his bed of pain, I'm alive, you know, I am alive, and the tears
stopped rolling down his cheeks for he had heard the voice
of Jacques, who was speaking only to him, out of the shadows of death, that voice telling him with the inflections of his
smiles and mockery, as if he were there against his pillow,
you know, Tanjou, I'm alive, and everything around me is
rosy, do you remember, rosy like our sunsets when we were
together, and at the bar, on the patio with its acacia-covered
arbour, Samuel was serving his mother's guests, wearing a
jacket borrowed from Julio, the sparkling water bubbled into
the whiskey, the gin on ice-cubes the colour of pearls, soon

they would be asking him to sing, to dance, would it be Elvis
Presley tonight, or Billie Holiday, Augustino was howling as
he thrashed about, no, it's not time to go to sleep yet, he
cried to Jenny and Sylvie, and Jenny told Augustino, not all
little boys have clean pyjamas fresh from the laundry to put
on every night, no, not all little boys, said Jenny, I know
some who sleep on the hard earth, with no pyjamas, said
Jenny, and why had Augustino knocked over the coffee-pot
and eaten all the sugar from the bowl, so much sugar made
him overexcited, and as she cautiously brought her rum
cocktail to her lips, Mère was preoccupied with resuming her
conversation with Mélanie about the greatness of the American
Constitution, Mélanie, her daughter, was the one most like
her, the only person — more than her husband and her
sons — in whom she liked to confide, with whom she
enjoyed getting carried away by discussions about literature
or politics, Mélanie stimulated her intelligence, because of
her probity, because of the integrity of her observations, the
years she'd spent in Ghana had shaped her while she was
still very young, teaching history too, those retro armchairs
they'd brought back from New York were not altogether
appropriate for this Spanish-style house, Mère did not under-
estimate their esthetic sense, but those grotesque leather chairs
in the living room were too much, as was the painting over
the tub in the main-floor bathroom, why did they burden
themselves with those pornographic young painters from
New York, even if they were their friends, as for the toilet, the
gold handles above marble seats, wasn't that rather excessive,
Mère shouldn't tell the children everything that was on her
mind, and with her straw she sucked up some of the delicious
rum drink, upset because her daughter was taking her guests
away from her, into the garden, to the green pool that glis-
tened in the night, not that Mère was obliged to tell Mélanie

that the picture over the tub in the main-floor bathroom was in poor taste, but at least it should be pointed out to her that the crudely drawn position of the two upside-down lovers was inappropriate, especially since Samuel and Augustino always had that picture right there in front of them, and what did she think of the extensive black notes in Beethoven's manuscripts, asked a musician Mère had seen again among her acquaintances that evening, yes, the musician and Mère had seen the manuscripts lacerated with black notes, Beethoven's manuscripts, the untamed, tumultuous writing, yet those big, black, violently expressive notes, or the squat humble letters that still oozed the sour humours of irritation, of fatigue, in his battle against deafness, those notes contained a desperate struggle to set man free and send him towards serenity, towards optimism, what did Mère think about that, she who had specialized in music, who enjoyed having the quality of her mind recognized by the artistic crowd Daniel and Mélanie associated with, Mère nodded, saying, but those few notes, my friend, are sublime, and suddenly she saw Julio running through the garden towards Mélanie, he was pushing aside the flowering branches above the gate, his injured eye was covered with the band placed on his eyelids in the hospital that afternoon, he came closer to Mélanie at the edge of the pool and their two troubled silhouettes were reflected in the iridescent water, what was he saying to her, Mère thought she could hear these words, you must get out of here with Daniel and the children, Mélanie, because they've heard your denunciations on the radio, they've seen you on television, and it won't be long before they threaten you, they're at the doors of hotels, at the marina where your boats are, Jenny and Sylvie have received their vile leaflets in the mail, on Atlantic Boulevard, they hand them out to passers-by. Or had Mère only heard these remarks in her frightened imagination, her husband reproached her for reading too late at the night, and wasn't she being indiscreet, always wanting to meddle in Daniel's and Mélanie's business, after all, they managed perfectly well without her, hadn't she encouraged them too much to preside over the anti-Fascist league in their area, yes, but they were exposing themselves to too much danger with those skinheads, those jobless delinquents who more and more were joining the ranks of the Ku Klux Klan in the South, yet we were so removed from all that here, under the starry vault of the sky, amid the splendours of the garden, in the night, Julio and Mélanie had raised their glasses to Vincent, oh, these festivities would go on and on, and Mère saw with joy her daughter's radiant face under the black almond trees, she approved of the hair-style that bared her forehead, showed off her exquisite high cheekbones, a light breeze from the ocean turned up the ends of her blunt-cut hair, Mélanie was perfect that night, Mère thought contentedly, how sad that Julio had nearly lost an eye when he was attacked by some Cubans on the beach, otherwise the party was getting off to a fine start, and on Atlantic Boulevard Carlos could hear the piercing cry of the patrol-car sirens in the night, swivelling around on his bicycle he saw them, standing on a boardwalk looking down on the sea, yes, that was who they were, just as the pastor had described them in his Sunday sermons, the White Horsemen of the Apocalypse, the ghosts of white supremacy materializing from their invisible hell, they had formed a circle at the end of the street and now they were singing, listen carefully, citizens, we'll lynch them all, there won't be a single one left, you couldn't see their eyes or their faces under the pointed hoods, they were well concealed by their white robes streaked with black lines, by their capes, you couldn't see them, couldn't know if they were good fathers or fine, upstanding citizens, Carlos hadn't recognized the grocer from his street among them, they had already wrecked everything in their path, a black college had been burned down the night before and what would happen tomorrow, they would go to the shed, throw their smoking torches into the yard onto the parasols, the domino tables, through a slit in the hood you could see their macabre eyes rolling, the White Horsemen of the Apocalypse were in town, the pastor had said, and Polly, what would happen to Polly if they covered the yellowed grass in front of the house with fire, if they wrenched Deandra and Tiffany from sleep in their mother's arms, Mama had told him so many times, Carlos shouldn't have been on the road at this hour, because in the shadows of the porches, of the verandas, the Bad Niggers' fangs were gleaming, tomorrow would be a fine day, and Carlos had bought Polly a collar, although it was time for him to deliver his goods, a collar for Polly, when they were together at the beach, and now it was time, thought Carlos, to slip away into the night without even the sound of steel scraping against the asphalt of the street, the cement of the sidewalks, time to slip away under the palm trees without being seen by the choir singing, we'll lynch them all, all of them, and on the veranda Mama, cantankerous, suddenly said to Venus, who was sitting listlessly in the swing, and all those men your brothers see you with, who aren't even from around here, they're so well dressed we'll never see them here, never see them on Bahama Street, on Esmeralda Street, tell me, swear on the heads of Deandra and Tiffany, tell me what you're doing with them when you should be praying at the temple, I'm their escort, Mama, I show them the city, and the old quarter for the slaves who came from the Bahamas, because we can't just live on prayers, Mama; Mama was waving away mosquitoes, her daughter was a sinner, she said, a woman who lazed around with her legs dangling under the seat of the swing, as they passed by, in those hoods with their macabre eyes, the White Horsemen could have taken their blazing torches and set fire to the veranda under the lemon trees, the frightened roosters would have scattered across the lawn, for it was late now to be on the road, it was the hour when you could hear birds shrieking in the trees, the eaglet fell from its nest on the wires, at the top of the trees and houses, tumbling down onto wooden picket fences, regaining its frail equilibrium, stabbing its beak into the brownish down of its broken wing, it was the hour when Carlos's bicycle cast a huge shadow onto the walls and sidewalks and he must flee, for they were all there, in the city, at the doors of hotels, on the boardwalks, in the streets, they merged with Carlos, with the gigantic shadow the bicycle cast on the wall, the White Horsemen of the Apocalypse. And in his white socks, in a jacket borrowed from Julio, Samuel was singing on the patio, among his mother's numerous guests, the voice of Billie Holiday rose up, ripe and deep, from his thin chest, Mère was thinking that the incantation was coming from very far away, from the churches of Harlem, this voice that Samuel had only heard through his headphones as he swirled along, racing on his roller-skates, on his way home from school, or that he'd picked out of the din of rap music that pounded deafeningly at his temples all day long, the voice he was imitating was hers, thought Mère, but was it in the natural order of things that it should be so, that Mère's grandson should sway his hips as he was carried away by this dance that swept him up, that you should hear welling from his throat these guttural sounds marked with an untamed sensuality when Samuel's lips murmured, easy easy living, no, it was not normal for a child to draw so much attention to himself, his parents drove him too hard, no doubt, he had an acting career instead of being a model student, he studied

his parts in the summer, during his vacation, he was being
trained to play Shakespeare at a camp for professional actors
near New York, and his lessons in dancing, in piano, no, it
was too much, Mère would talk to Daniel and Mélanie about
it, but what was the use, she thought as well, no one in this
house listened to her any more, lulled by the hammock that
afternoon, Mère had thought, soon I'll be sixty-five years old,
what will become of me? The question had upset her terribly
in the tranquillity of the hammock, what would become of her,
she who lacked for nothing, wasn't that the thorny question
that was always there while she talked with Mélanie about
the elements of justice that made up the American Constitution, this shadow over her relationship with her daughter,
was it her concern that Vincent slept alone up there, that his
breathing was too rapid because of the winds off the ocean,
Mélanie had gestured impatiently towards her mother and
Mère had been offended, it was as if Mélanie had told her
she was giving in to the drivel of women her age, in their
salons, and Mère, who had always instructed Mélanie about
everything, from how she should dress to the music of Bach
that ennobled the soul, she wondered if Mélanie now
considered her too conformist for her liking, that Mère was
a competent museum director in Connecticut and a committed
activist like her daughter no longer seemed to impress Mélanie,
Mélanie had chosen in her heart a distant aunt, Renata, a
relative she'd met just a few times during her numerous trips,
Renata who'd announced that she was coming to visit, so
Mère's stability was no longer an enviable quality, she had
reproached her, didn't the family know about Renata's instability, Mère had asked her daughter, in a jealous tone, Renata
was constantly starting her life again as if she were still young,
she had lived in several countries with her various husbands,
they'd never known why she was no longer with Franz, in

Austria, now she was sharing her life with a judge in the States, there was the mystery of her instability, though she had practised law in France, practised it still, recently she had refused to put herself forward as a candidate for a judge's position, she was a nomadic soul who never seemed to find a place to rest, and what did it say in that psalm Mère couldn't recite from memory in the hammock that afternoon, something like if your soul resides where it should, you will be at peace, and the soul of Renata, who bowed to no one, was recalcitrant, and under the star-filled sky Mère had been startled when Mélanie's guests applauded Samuel, but it wasn't healthy for a child to be able to sing with such visceral fervour, and when the melody "Easy, Easy Living" had died away from Samuel's lips, amid the shuddering of the guests, for Samuel had the gift of moving them, Augustino stopped crying, he could hear the bird telling him as it did every night, good-night, Augustino, cheep cheep I love you, now they're going to cover my cage for the night, cheep cheep I love you, and the woman who was his friend, his sister, laid Jacques's body across her knees to clothe it, he who now weighed no more than a sea-shell, she thought, she dressed him for the farewell ceremony, which would be strictly private, she announced with feigned detachment to Luc and Paul, to Tanjou for whom she now lacked the courage to feel contempt, begging the others to leave brother and sister alone for a while, for she wanted to choose from Jacques's clothes the most becoming suit, the black tie with the red stripes, the white shirt he wore at the university, that way, she thought, Jacques would look more dignified, and in the austere *pietà* in which her pain held her transfixed, she shed no tears, she laid her hands, her fingers, on Jacques's hair, which was already no longer his, on his face, where thought had ceased to dwell since his eyes had closed, it was not until later that she thought about the blue glow under his lashes, as if the eyes had been poorly closed, or had been on the point of opening for a moment, and then were closed again, the doctor had declared his death several hours ago but that glow, had she dreamed it, she had seen that spark of life beneath the granular shadow of the lashes, that greasy shadow under the eyes, as if Luc and Paul had not washed Jacques's face several times during the night, yet when she had laid her fingers, her hands on Jacques's hair, on his face, she had not been certain he was no longer there, for now the skin of his face, like the texture of his hair, was no longer his, her brother's skin was delicate, his hair fine, and with the departure of life she did not know how to define the rubbery consistency of both his skin and his hair, for to her fingers they had felt like some viscous material of a kind unknown to her, but that glow, that fragment of fire under his closed eyelids, the sudden promise that life was not truly absent from this body that was no longer breathing, that apparently no longer had a voice, a gaze, long afterwards she would think about it again, still unable to account for the significance of that glow, that precious spark which she would not discuss with her husband when she went home, or her children, the glow from Jacques's closed eyes would follow her when she conveyed her passenger along the deserted road at night, the endless road that skirted glaucous marshes near the sea, the swamp where crocodiles wallowed, and snakes, she had come to the airport in this white Cadillac in search of Jacques, asking him if he was comfortable amid the cushions in the back seat, Jacques had enjoyed going out with her in this fluid car from which he could wave to his friends, in the bars open onto the street, resting on his cushions, he had waved to them often, and hadn't seen them again, the car could hold several people but the brother and sister were alone, an unusual seating capacity, but now amid the cushions the package, the wooden box that held Jacques's ashes was weightless, in the past she had thought as she was enduring that abused love, her love for Jacques, that Luc and Paul should have sent Jacques's ashes to her through the mail so that her indifference towards the dead man would awaken sooner, and suddenly that spark of life between the blond lashes stained with waxy sweat under his eyelids had disrupted all her plans, the flash of a secret sweetness her brother was bequeathing to her had torn apart the soul that yesterday had been so tough, and though there was no one to hear her on this deserted road, she felt a lament, a howl emerging from her chest, but her cheeks were dry, she was not weeping, for Jacques was finally at ease in the cushions in the back seat of the car, at ease and serene in the huge white Cadillac where the two of them alone took up so little room, next to Jacques on the seat were some objects that Tanjou had crammed helter-skelter into a beach bag, Jacques's book on Kafka, typed up to page eighty, a biography of Kafka in German cut off for-ever by a bookmark in the middle of the volume, a pair of corduroy pants, a sweater and some unconventional leather boots that made Jacques appear to be walking on stilts, in which he had meditated on the vanity of his conquests, a wet black T-shirt Tanjou had pulled off at the last moment to add to Jacques's belongings, burying his tear-drenched face in it, unstoppable tears that still soaked the shirt, in that odour of air and sea salt that were applied to Tanjou's skin along with sand, and as she undid her hair the friend, the sister felt the shudder of the salt air on her shoulders like a caress, her brother had finally been relesed from his torments, above the seas, the oceans where Luc and Paul had scattered some of his ashes into the warm perfumed night, and all that remained of him were those few words he'd copied into his notebook from one of Pastor Jeremy's sermons: Dear Lord, why must I perish today, on this morning of delights? And now they were advancing towards him while the sirens screamed, was it the White Horsemen of the Apocalypse throwing their torches into the ramshackle framework of those schools near the sea where Venus and Le Toqué had not yet closed their schoolbooks, the fire was creeping up the beams chewed by termites, and Venus, with her hair coiled into braids, seemed to be sleeping between two scorched boards, was it the Horsemen pouring gasoline onto the arrow of fire that would destroy the parasols, the games of dominoes in the yard, or the Bad Niggers, whose livid fangs shone beneath the caps turned backwards over their greasy hair, while they paced the sidewalks dangerously in their boots, Carlos was thrown off his bike and into the wall by those vindictive hands, in a burst of that cruelty to which the innocent are subjected, Carlos saw again a cat that had been run over by a truck that morning, its paws still twitching on the blazing pavement, a black woman had grazed Carlos with her car, rolling down her window she'd shouted, go home, nigger, go home or I'll run you down, he saw her drunkard's face again behind the smoke-coloured glass, and now those hands that had come from a sky of darkness, those weak, limp hands were holding him above the void, his body swaying hatefully in the position of a hanged man, Polly's fur, silky in the sunlight, no longer cheered him, the bicycle with its yellow handlebars, a yellow as garish as his jersey, had been demolished in a dark corner of Bahama Street, hadn't Carlos always known that he was on the wrong road, that the Bad Niggers were waiting for him on these paths where dogs and dealers prowled, they delivered punches with their boxing gloves, they circled him in a crazed dance until Carlos began to stagger under the blows, only letting him go when the patrol cars took off after them, criss-crossing the streets, the sidewalks where frightened passers-by got out of their way; sprawled on the grass at the edge of the sidewalk, Carlos heard the patrol cars' strident sirens at his temples, and had Mama, had Venus, who was singing in the Baptist church, heard the footsteps of the White Horsemen of the Apocalypse as they marched through the city, flinging their torches into the ramshackle framework of houses, of schools, of colleges, setting ablaze those flat shacks like huts on Bahama Street, on Esmeralda Street, long afterwards a scrawny dog would wander around lawns razed by fire, they would all be massacred, all of them, Grandfather Davis, Uncle Lee, Uncle Cornelius who at the age of seven had played piano in the streets of New Orleans, that was how in the past the Wood of Flowers had disappeared into the flames, while Uncle Lee was playing the organ in church for the whites, the fire had climbed up house-beams chewed by termites, and opening his eyes in the morning sun, Carlos ran his hand over his bloody lips and nose, it was the hour when all the bells in all the churches rang, a hen and her chicks were clucking and cheeping on the lawn, Carlos held out his hand to them while he went on rolling in the grass, the voice of Venus singing in the church, let my joy endure, Carlos got to his feet, dazed, it was the hour when all the bells rang together in the churches, and Carlos had Polly, Polly who was thirsty, hungry, Polly whom he'd left alone in the shed, in the dark, Polly, he had Polly, and in the church Venus was singing, let my joy endure. No, thought Mère, it wasn't good for a child to draw too much attention to himself, and Mère remembered Samuel's party costume last year, what would he dress up as this year, Mère remembered the adults gathered around Samuel with his paint-daubed face that day, some school-children had been sent to reform school for slaughtering foxes and killing a deer, Samuel had protested that massacre, was it his face, his lips that he'd painted black, the red marks on his face like marks left by bloody claws, the effect of Samuel's mask had been studied, thought Mère, he'd known he would shock, frighten, Mère was convinced that Samuel had wanted to scandalize the adults with a burlesque depiction of the head of someone who had been crucified, for his paint-daubed face was that of a man on a cross, and it was as a man who had been crucified, with that face, Mère thought, that Samuel had danced in the crowd during the festivities, and why had Mélanie and Daniel not said anything, was everything permitted then, Samuel's picture had been taken in that costume, and what was happening to children's education nowadays, it was her memory of Mélanie's impatient gesture towards her mother that caused this disagreeable reflection from which the haunting face of Samuel emerged, thought Mère, for otherwise the festive evening had been a success, and amid the hubbub of the guests interrupted by the song of the cicadas, Mère could hear Maria Callas singing the aria from *Orpheus and Eurydice*, the Greek singer's voice tore at Mère's soul, and didn't that cry or that lament, I've lost my Eurydice, come from the singer herself? Mère had lost Mélanie, she thought, she would soon enter her sixty-sixth year but Mélanie would conserve her flourishing youth for a long time yet, Mère's energy would decline, Mélanie would take her place as president of the Union of Women for the Defence of Workers, on committees against racial discrimination, Mélanie would be an adviser to battered women, I've lost my Eurydice, Callas sang in a cry of keen disillusion, and that voice shattered the evening air with its quavering and its modulated tremors, no one asked Mère what she thought of Gluck's music, she would have talked about the renewal of the musical style, of the psalms, the passionate "De profundis" Gluck had composed, but Daniel and Mélanie's guests barely spoke to Mère; Samuel was at the bar again, in the waiter's jacket he'd borrowed from Julio, and Mélanie, standing close to him, would sometimes run her hand affectionately through his hair, I've lost my Eurydice, thought Mère, and they all raised their glasses to the health of Vincent, who was ten days old today, and if Gluck's sacred art was to be believed, thought Mère, Vincent, barely emerged from his Creator's hands, already contained the seed of immortality, and shortly after the plane took off, the judge remembered a face he had spotted as he was leaning out the window of his hotel room to see what was going on in the street, pushing aside a curtain while he was shaving, from the second floor where he'd thought he was alone and invisible, he had met the gaze of the chauffeur who was waiting for him down below, under the trees, a young Arab dressed in the beige uniform the hotel employees wore, he had tipped his cap in the already hot morning air, signalling his presence with a nod towards the second floor where the silhouette of a man was moving behind the curtain, and that man was Claude, a judge who was in the habit of looking at others, of weighing their acts, within the rigid structure of a court, and suddenly the eyes of a man unknown to him, a man he'd exchanged a few words with the day before, while he was touring the city, those eyes had latched onto his own with a laughing, almost teasing expression, and he had responded to the eagerness of those eyes on him with his own expression of guilty docility, as if there were some obscure tie between the man and himself, he had thought about the sentence he'd given the drug dealers, for which his wife had reproached him, if she was right, had he caused some irreversible damage, like that American judge who had sentenced a black man to death by lethal injection in a Texas prison, the offences, the crimes weren't comparable but an unjust sentence was a crime too, if he had been mistaken, what was the good of all the police vigilance around their house, Claude's eyes had also confronted the chauffeur's when the young man, smiling at Claude from the distance, had solemnly caught up the scarf that was slipping off Renata's shoulders, that scarf, thought the judge, like the mockery in the chauffeur's gaze, all of it had suddenly united the two men with a violent tie that for a moment ended their disso-ciation from one another, set apart as they were by race, by the inequality of their chances in life, the chauffeur's eyes seemed to be saying to Claude, the same blood, the same water, are we not all of us mortals, the powerful and those who serve them with devotion, the hasty confidences of the driver the previous night implied an alert, a danger, in the words he murmured into the judge's ear, they are killing our children, driving us from our mosques when we're at prayer, we're too noisy, they say, we're too noisy, we make too much noise with our children's crying and our own prayers: the airplane was going through some thick clouds when Claude had seen again the chauffeur's face as he tipped his cap in a sign of respect, even if his intentions were hateful, the chauffeur was a polite man, the same water, the same blood, the judge had thought in the airplane, given over to the collective weight of his body in the immense sky, or weight-less, he thought, his body apparently held in its seat by a belt, its passive needs to be filled by attentive hostesses; he had also thought about the condemned flesh of men, it was this flesh the chauffeur had perceived with his insistent gaze raised in Claude's direction, he had surprised the judge in the middle of his surges of happiness, of satisfaction, a man shaving in a hotel room in a luxurious suite after making love, and now he was surprising him again as he opened some files on a tray in the first-class section of an airplane, giving orders around him with his usual ease, the chauffeur had heard the imploring voice of a woman carved inside him, he had perceived, thought the judge, something all men could share among themselves, the secret of an unspeakable fear amid the turmoil of their guts, the turmoil of flesh under threat, under sentence, that nothing could allay, and then, glancing at his documents, the judge thought he had been right to bring down that sentence on the dealers, his wife was always sentimental when it came to young men, to their lives, he read the statement by an American judge, telling himself that one day he would make such a statement and Renata would congratulate him on his tolerance, the liberality of his think-ing, legalizing drugs would cut down on crime, a retired judge had declared, anything that was prohibited, as alcohol had been in the past, contributed to a wave of murders, but still, thought Claude, minor offences have to be corrected before they degenerate into real crimes, and just then he saw again the chauffeur's face as he drew attention to his pres-ence in the hotel courtyard, the same blood, the same water, the face told him, and yet they're driving us from our mosques, we're too noisy, they say, and so is our children's crying. And that hollow sensation of thirst had never stopped debasing her when she took the West Indian's hand to give him a sum of money he'd held onto while gripping Renata's fingers in his own, lowering her eyes, turning her head, she had tried to get away, thanking him in a vague voice that he probably judged, she thought, to be falsely timorous, still too strength-ened by his insolence, she had thanked him, her gaze shifting under her eyelids, for having so kindly helped her bring her suitcases to this house she had rented, still gripping Renata's hand in his own strong dry one, the West Indian told her she was a woman he'd been observing for a long time, alone at night at the casino, among the men, then, suddenly embrac-ing Renata, reproaching her for having witnessed his own destitution that evening, when he had lost everything and the other gamblers had thrown him out on the street and beaten him, you, you're a rich woman and you did nothing for me, he seemed to be saying, but he was taciturn, quick-tempered, pressing his lips against Renata's forehead, the proximity was so embarrassing, she could feel the West Indian's teeth bite her forehead, his panting breath on her neck, born to lose, he said, furious, or while he was holding her captive in his arms could Renata read these thoughts in the man's haunted eyes, to ravish this woman, with one angry movement of his arm he had thrown her down on the bed, the bed where he had respectfully placed the suitcases a few moments earlier, he looked all around, bewildered, while he was stripping off her scarf, her silk dress, and it was there that the hollow sensation of thirst had kept debasing Renata, the scarf, the silk dress that barely covered her shoulders, any elegant fabric, any clothing touched by blood or sperm would adhere to her shame as it did to the membrane of flesh exposed to all the blows while her clothes were being torn, those organic secrets of the body trampled, struck, even the circulation of her blood whose turmoil, whose agitation she could feel, the man still bending over her, with all the determination of his muscles, his weight, pinned to her, to relieve the shame he had suffered, the man was wreaking vengeance for the baseness of his own life, which was telling him, through the effects of the drugs, to destroy her, to possess her, as if this unleashed violence made him able to be suddenly enamoured of her as he said, who are you anyway, with that haughty attitude towards me, what is your race, and that attitude, those jewels, that stream of pearls, what do they represent to you, and what about your sensual expectations as you saunter through the frozen smoke of casinos, of bars, alone or with your husband, I saw you smiling at me, haughty, contemptuous, in that smoke near the water at night, with the glittering of your bracelets, the gleam of your gold cigarette case, from now on everything in you must be debased, destroyed, and then the West Indian had thought he heard a sound in the bushes through the wide-open windows and like a coward, he had fled; in the morning she saw the white underwear, the tear in the elegant fabric, the spongy tissue stained yellow by sperm, a piece of white cloth on the bed whose sheets had been pulled out while their bodies struggled, when the light of an incandescent day, warm and humid, spread over Renata, now that she was alone, she remembered that she'd decided to go to the rented house at dawn, as he was furtively leaving the casino her gaze had ordered the West Indian to follow her or help her with her bags, in his confusion he had obeyed that authoritarian gaze, that peremptory look, for he had suddenly seemed to her to be in danger at her hotel, and she was still imbued with that hollow sensation of thirst when he followed her, she would place a quick call to Claude, tell him she was truly in limbo, would not tell him exactly where she was, she was going to take the time to write, to think things over, she would tell him, and he would express his concern, ask her how much longer, tell her to come home, he would admit his error about the judgement he'd handed down, but eager as she was to hear the words of their reconciliation she would not call him right away, fearing that he might be distracted, might be less loving or too preoccupied, the hand on the green clock she'd taken from her suitcase showed nine o'clock, as if she had been immobilized in mid-ocean and the hand of the clock had shown her some ordinary hour in eternity, the hour when she had been born, the hour when she would die, the one mystery that holds us all in thrall, then she would fall again, stripped bare and lost, onto this mattress where she would sleep for a few hours, alone, as she had often dreamed of being, swimming in her dreams in slack, green water, the sea was calm, Renata stared at the green paint of the walls and ceiling, the heavy decor matched the lushness of the vegetation outside, she thought, and why was she thinking about Franz at this moment, about what he had told her when he came home from one of his concerts in Vienna — that during his absence she, Renata, had aged a little, or was it just that she was old now, and she told herself she must find that man again, in the street, the one who was staggering towards the deserted casino, who had fled at the sound of a dewdrop melting onto a palm frond cracked by the lengthy drought that had preceded the storm, it was the dull sound of the drop of water that had made him run away, but she would find him again, she would denounce him to the city authorities, if there hadn't been that overwhelming evidence against her, the look she had darted at him on the way out of the casino in the pallid glimmers of the neon lights on the water, but the evidence did exist and, still imbued with the sensation of thirst, she would tidy up the rented house, a famous poet of Scottish ancestry had lived here, within these walls he had written the bulk of his books, but if she had rented this house swallowed up by dense vegetation of cactuses and tropical shrubs, it was because a woman had come here too, to be by herself and write, she had written her books and then disappeared in Brazil, it was that woman, whose name was not well known, whom Renata was seeking in these places, though there was no tangible sign of her presence, while they knew everything about the male poet, even when he was still there, so they said, his preference for austerity and the pastoral life in this country house in the city, the hand on the green clock face told Renata that the poet would set to work at nine in the morning, that his timetable followed rigorous rules every day, that his disciplined spirit watched over her when she was often totally disordered and dismayed, rigid too, while she refused to be submissive it was an illumination that had brought her here, reading a poem by Emily Dickinson in a state of fever and thirst, it was the hour to swim in the ocean now, but she was still forbidden to do that, soon it would be time to dress for going out that evening, to her nephew and niece Daniel and Mélanie's house in the bay, it would be all lit up for the festivities, there would be the blaze of light from the lamps, from the candlesticks on the tables in the garden, and from the garden would come the scent of the lime trees, the acacias, the pointilias all in bloom, a party in honour of Vincent, who was ten days old today, days and nights of festivities, Mélanie had said when she begged her to come, and Vincent, said Mélanie, would be fast asleep on the pillow, with all this noise, and Renata had thought about the rivalry that linked women, the rivalry between herself and Mélanie's mother, she told Mélanie on the telephone that she would come later that night, she had talked to Mélanie about the operation forcing her to rest while an important trial was waiting for her on her return, and how that long and trying rest was called limbo, I'm unsteady, Renata had told Mélanie, a little unsteady, then she'd hung up abruptly, thinking she would say nothing to Mélanie about that night, that dawn, already she was holding back some disconcerting secrets and confessions that were on the tip of her tongue, for she thought that if the sorrows of which the female condition was woven were insidious, then was she too responsible, for men liked her, the law, the rule said she was supposed to attract their gaze, it was a secular law, but she modified it to her liking within her own rules of misconduct, of confrontation; the sorrows that burdened the humiliating female condition were insidious, Franz, suddenly capable of grave insults on that day when he had spoken to her in French, confused by alcohol, but didn't he speak all languages after a night of partying with friends, you, didn't you age a little while I was gone, for my concerts in Vienna, and was that the same day a humble manicurist told Renata she was beautiful; with Franz's kiss a breath of nothingness passed over Renata's mouth, flattened all her expectations, one after the other, with the exception of Claude, who was a precocious man and judge, they had banished her to the limbo of rejection, of dispossession, stopping-place for those childish souls whom God refused to admit to His kingdom, and in that clandestine place, as in the rented house to which a woman had withdrawn to write her books, the creeping sensation of that limbo amid the heat, amid the high, dense vegetation, was as real for Renata as for the woman from Brazil, whose books were dominated by such painful omens that few people had penetrated, had read them, and the woman who was the sister, the friend, slowly opened the drawer where Jacques's possessions were kept, her husband and children must not see her when she was absorbed in contemplating these revered objects, they had all gone out and wouldn't be back until evening, the husband and children were all reprimanding her, scrutinizing her, for henceforth she belonged to Jacques, they said, to him alone, a hand clutching her skirt, who was he, who was that uncle, that brother, didn't he have a bad reputation, who was that man, their uncle, their mother's brother, whose ashes had been scattered so quickly to the bottom of the sea, had dispersed into the mugginess of the air, she heard those voices endlessly asking for her, intransigent, threatened, they all said, we need your help, we depend on you, how could the door of the cozy Victorian house inherited from their parents close in on her that way, how could those shutters, that wood panelling suddenly shut up her life while in the meantime her brother was travelling in Asia, writing books, reading, dreaming as he breathed the fluid air of his garden, he was alone yet he was loved, when his sister's proud stability, her domain, had been taken over, when in the presence of her husband, her children, all of them temperamental, she was never alone, and it wasn't clear that they even appreciated her, these petty thoughts had occupied her mind in the past, but the friend, the sister no longer felt them as she slowly opened the drawer in the secret cupboard, those objects with their imperishable marks, she thought, Tanjou's black T-shirt, the corduroy pants, the boots whose leather hadn't had time to wear out, she would sometimes spread out all these objects at the windows so that, after the winter, the sun would come and warm them with its rays, like the potted geraniums she'd just taken out, she breathed in the sea smells from Tanjou's black T-shirt, all at once it caught her attention because of the drawing printed on it, in which she could make out acrobatic forms on the black background, it showed skeletons dancing in a variety of amorous poses, whoever had designed this ballet of bones on a T-shirt possessed an ingenious perversity, the tiny fresco on a T-shirt expressing love, which in our time was shot through with lethal radiation, those embraces were as true as the embraces of kings and queens carved in the stone of fifteenth-century cathedral tombs, she thought, but the porous flesh, already corrupt, had been illuminated here by the artist so that you could not see it waste away and die, but this was that same T-shirt, with its salty odours, its sweat of health and well-being, that had covered Tanjou's upright torso when he ran on the beach at dawn, this T-shirt had travelled among the grains of sand in a beach bag with the rubber balls that Luc and Paul still bounced above the water, the soft towels with which they dried their bodies after swimming, Tanjou had entrusted the salt of his tears to that T-shirt, and underneath the ghostly white of each precisely drawn skeleton on the T-shirt was still frozen the dazed sensuality of the movements of love, necessary and urgent, as if the woman who was the friend, the sister, that woman who was above all reserved and prudish, had taken part in those games of Jacques's in a closed room, games that she had always found unimaginable, reprehensible, but that were now suddenly appearing to her with all the clarity of a child's drawing on a blank sheet of paper, and the melody of "Easy, Easy Living" had fallen silent on the lips of Samuel, who, imitating Julio, was serving at the bar, moving between the tables with the wine, in the fragrant garden; what was Julio saying to his mother, Mélanie, the White Horsemen of the Apocalypse are here, I saw them on my way home from the beach, Mélanie, listen to me, they've covered Samuel's boat in the marina with indelible red paint, that's how in the olden days the hangman marked the shoulders of people condemned to be branded, and the brand could never be erased, tomorrow, in the sunlight, we'll see their insignia, we'll see it appear at the tiller of Samuel's boat, at the helm, we will see the Nazi insignia surmounted by an arrow, and that arrow will strike at the heart of your son Samuel, I've seen them, run away, they are at your gates, run away, Mélanie, you must run away, but when he tried to listen to what Julio was saying in his mother's ear, Samuel could hear nothing but the murmur of voices in the garden, Mère had taken Julio's arm as she sighed her regret about how Julio had been savagely attacked on the beach, what was the world coming to, she said, but fearing that Julio would confess the reason for his nocturnal walks on the beaches, Mère quickly changed the subject, wasn't it at one o'clock

tomorrow, she asked Julio, that the boat race off Atlantic
Boulevard would start, she would be there with her grandsons, it was too bad Mélanie had so little interest in sports,
there would be several women captains tomorrow and Mélanie,
whose notion of family responsibilities went a little too far,
would not be among them, and then Mère held back a yawn,
it was still too early in the evening and the festivities would
go on so late, already she was feeling tired, at my age, alas,
one goes to bed early, she said to Julio in a peremptory tone,
already her eyes seemed to be seeking out the room where
she would sleep, it was outside the house, at the end of a
path in the garden, you got there along a bridge that was
thrown like an arcade over the gushing fountains, across a
pond filled with pink Japanese fish, that was another of the
children's costly fantasies, she thought, and an invention of
that architect they'd brought with them from New York, like
the indecent painting in the main-floor bathroom, the gold
handles in the bathroom, those were pointless expenditures
on which Mélanie hadn't consulted her, and what was she to
think of those sculptures that blocked the space near the
pool, and as for the antique Mexican furniture in the guest
room, that was unquestionably the most discordant note in
the entire decor, for you couldn't combine ancient and
modern art in a single arrangement, it was an aberration, but
Mère was thinking most of all about her sleep, which would
be agitated because of all this noise around her, suddenly
she felt as if she were made of porcelain, she crossed her
hands on her compact, heavy bosom, thinking it was already
past her bedtime, she would need at least six hours of sleep,
unbroken and without memory, if she was to continue these
festivities for nearly three days, for Mère did not dream much
and hadn't Julio told her that a rock group would be coming
around midnight, was that any way to welcome the newborn

who was sleeping upstairs, with such a noisy party, but the
children hadn't consulted her on this either, and you could
hear Augustino's strident cries in the evening air as he
escaped from Jenny and Sylvie's supervision, once again
he was running through the garden in his Superman cape,
Mère moved out of his way under a tree, Augustino might
push his grandmother into the acacias as he ran, and ridicu-
lously she was still holding her glass, she thought, though it
was empty and the straw was soft from the meticulous
pressure of her lips, and then Mère thought it would be even
later before she could go to sleep because wasn't that Renata
arriving at the main entrance of the house, why couldn't she
just come through the garden gate like everyone else, thought
Mère as she hooked her glasses over her ears to observe the
woman who was turning up so late, her shoulders bare under
a satin jacket, perhaps she wasn't wearing anything at all
under that jacket, thought Mère, it's true that the heat is
suffocating, Mère found it very annoying that Renata should
have changed so little over the years, that she looked even
younger, she had retained her goddess-like appearance for
so long, thought Mère, her neck and head were rather
powerful, masculine almost, but there was such dignity in
her bearing, who was Mère beside this woman, Renata was
well known for her pleading in defence of women's rights,
while Mère defended no one aside from her children, her
role as museum director was rather an honorary one, both
her scholarly knowledge of painting and her patronage of
the arts had won her the respect of her city, and there was
nothing surprising about that, she thought; in decadent
circles where ignorance ruled, Mère, like her daughter, was
unique, and her uniqueness, her exceptional value would
only have been recognized, she thought, if Mélanie had
considered a career in politics, everything pointed to Mélanie

sitting in the Senate one day, and then suddenly she was just a mother, of course she was still a young woman, but if she was to live her life to the full she needed to make herself indispensable, and Mère's worried eyes were seeking that room, beneath a canopy of oleanders at the end of the garden, her eyes were observing Renata's shoulders, bare under the satin jacket, the harmony of form was not perfect, thought Mère, Renata's nape, her neck, were too powerful for a woman, at least Mère's plastic surgeon husband had never seen her as a model of prettiness, of flawless beauty, anyway overly beautiful women were so conceited, why were others so envious of them, and with her hands crossed on her compact, heavy bosom Mère suddenly felt as disparaged as she'd been that afternoon in the hammock, when she was talking with Mélanie about the American Constitution, along with the appearance of Renata baring her bronze-coloured shoulders under a pale satin jacket, around her, emerging from the same golden, mysterious night, was an entire procession of young people, the musicians invited for the festive nights, yes, they were the ones showing up at this late hour, thought Mère, in their white evening clothes arranged to please by their sophistication, thought Mère, with the grungy stylishness today's young people are appropriating for themselves, with their insolent actions, with the luminous accompaniment of their youth they seemed to reinforce Renata's mature charm, her inaccessible supremacy in this tableau, her cold indifference, the instantaneousness of this tableau had just been formed, thought Mère, when the young people who were hurtling down the streets with their instruments under their arms had suddenly spied Renata and brought her along with them, laughing, and the mad wave was still murmuring on the threshold, Renata's face raised, glacial, wearing the shadow of a smile, a somewhat terrified smile, thought Mère, but in spite of everything it was a smile of victory, and it was diminishing Mère's soul, just as it had been diminished in the hammock that afternoon when she was talking to Mélanie, who wasn't listening, Mélanie who was worrying about the effect of the powerful Atlantic winds on Vincent's breathing, while Mère was explaining the grandeur of the American Constitution, only those words that went with Gluck's melody were true, forsaken, abandoned by her own people, now Mère was being deprived even of her hours of sleep, she had lost her Eurydice, and now Renata looked up, fearing him, dreading him, who knows, what if the West Indian had decided to follow her here, to surround her on this festive night, was he hiding behind the musicians, for he would always be there, she thought, she would never be able to banish him from her flesh, in her shame she had to distance herself from these young people who were all around her, at whom she was smiling kindly, for these young people were amused by her discomfort at being in limbo, this limbo clung to her life like the climbing plants around her rented house, constantly renewing the sensation of unquenchable thirst, what was to be done with these magnificent young people, was she to shut herself inside with them, under the roof with its climbing plants, for a series of nuptials, but as with the Venetian gondoliers who had approached her when Franz no longer desired her, she knew it was too late, still, she thought how enchanting, as she gazed at all these faces, these virile bodies, the languorous musicians, like the mocking gondoliers in their small Venetian craft, all had provoked the same sensation of thirst, it was in Venice that Franz had been applauded for his oratorio while she was content with exciting men's desire, walking up to the gondoliers alone, fleeing him, Franz, creator of a grandiose composition, a childlike man whom she had often trained, directed, in preparation for his concerts, whom she had tried to prepare amid his setbacks, his shyness, his madness, and all at once Franz's music was nothing but an orchestrated racket when the voices of the gondoliers spread across the coolness of the water, the rippling of water and sky, in a languid melody, she was only passing through, living with a musician, in apartments, in luxurious hotel rooms, she was a woman abandoning the duties of her profession to take care of Franz, that was Renata, an incomplete being, she thought, bearer of doubts, a woman who enjoyed pleasure, the happy company of a man still youthful and sincere, still light-hearted, and suddenly that company was hovering around her in vain, detecting her thirst, thirst that was so hollow and helpless, they were all there just a few steps away, they took her by the waist, their hands settled on her shoulders, inside the satin jacket, the gondoliers in their Venetian craft on the water, the rippling water in the evening, and yet Franz had said to her, haven't you changed while I was away, she was ephemeral but still burdened with the years, with knowledge, because she was a woman, and with a death that was just as ephemeral as her life, now it was time to hear that music, to listen to it, when the young people were returning to their places in the orchestra under the trees, near the pool that was iridescent in the night. And stepping nonchalantly, Venus descended the steps of the veranda, she was on her way to the beach when Mama grumbled from the swing, why, she asked, why was Venus going out so late in the evening, the night, was that any way to dress for going out, in a transparent pale pink dress that fit so tightly around her hips, her bust, and that provocative pink hibiscus blossom in her hair, the hair Mama had braided that morning but that now hung loose, a wisp of straw and hibiscus blossom twined together in her thick abundant hair, and Venus said to her mother, laughing, her laughter close to a snicker, that she had been invited to sing during the festive nights, three days, three nights, tonight she would sing "Let My Joy Endure," and Mama could hear Venus's muffled laughter through the sound of the waves, her lascivious way of walking, said Mama, and her impudent expression, it's the influence of Uncle Cornelius and those whites at the mixed club, Venus was going towards those houses where blacks were forbidden to walk, said Mama as she closed the kitchen door on the glare of her Sunday shoes, Mama was disgusted to breathe in the aroma of barbecued meat from Bahama Street, a stench of rotting meat from the grills where Carlos and Le Toqué hung around among the depraved dealers of crack, of cocaine, and on Street of Warm Breezes in Chicago they were being cut down by bullets, one by one, when would peaceful life return to Bahama Street, to Esmeralda Street, it was time now to pull down the mosquito netting over Deandra's and Tiffany's beds, families of riffraff, of lowlifes dozing on their porches in the evening were complaining of an invasion of red ants, when would peace return to Bahama Street, the ocean, the evening air were intoxicating to Venus's soul while the waves caressed her bare feet, the sea, the sky, it all belongs to me, Venus was think-ing, and in those houses by the sea, in their air-conditioned bathrooms, their pools and saunas, she lent her body to the whites, some day one of those houses would be hers, and images passed before her eyes which she brushed away, was it true what Mama and Pastor Jeremy said, that the White Horsemen were back, that in their houses by the ocean they tested their skill at video games in which, like throwing a metal ball, like aiming at the long wooden pins in a bowling alley, they symbolically bashed in the heads of blacks, and those heads caved in with no bloody explosion on a television

screen veiled in darkness, behind the slats, behind the panels
of lowered blinds, was it true then, what Mama and the
pastor said on their verandas at night, or were Mama and
Papa jealous of Venus, of her youth, her beauty that excited
the white men, men to whom she yielded one by one, in
public toilets or at the mixed club, while Uncle Cornelius's
rickety fingers crashed down on the piano — Cornelius who
for so long, starting when he was a child, had played in the
streets of New Orleans when the temples and churches were
still burning, the flesh of those men was insipid, Venus was
not afraid of them, neither the men nor the bite of their teeth
on her skin, under the transparent dress, the world had changed
a lot since Uncle Cornelius and Mama were children, and
Mama, who was pious, knew nothing about progress, Mama
and Uncle Cornelius could still hear that rumour in the
distance, while Venus heard nothing but the movement of
the warm waves on her feet, while on Atlantic Boulevard,
she was thinking, the air was perfumed by the yellow
jasmine blossoms scattered along the sidewalks, near the
beaches, and as Venus had told Mama this evening, giggling,
she'd been invited to a party, Venus would sing tonight as
she had sung in the temple this morning, her voice as clear
as crystal, oh, she would sing as she thought about all of
them, about Carlos, Le Toqué, Deandra, Tiffany, Mama, let
my joy endure, for like Mama and Pastor Jeremy, Venus
loved God and the ocean, loved the sky, the air He had created. Mère had lost her Eurydice and whenever she felt
belittled in that way, whenever she felt that sense of failure
with her daughter, she was ashamed of the opulence in which
her family lived, she was such a comfortably serene woman
who lacked for nothing, not even the non-essential riches,
when the Polish cousins, as Mère designated them, though
she had never known them, those cousins, distant cousins

who for generations had been unable to flee to Canada, to the United States, had all perished in the village of Lukow, in the district of Lublin, you could see them still in photographs unearthed by historians, by journalists, their hands thrown up as if the scene were eternally alive, towards their butchers, their murderers, in an ultimate and panic-stricken movement of surrender, but not of revolt, for the Polish cousins had known they would never be able to flee, their ranks were incalculable and they were standing beside some sheds from which a smell of gas and carrion was rising, and kneeling in the same row, the rabbis prostrated themselves as a sign of their acceptance of a spiritual law that they had chosen but that suddenly was betraying them, under their skullcaps each of them was shaking his head, a *danse macabre* of terror in the cold and snow where all those widened eyes, all those gasping bodies were desperately begging to escape, when the silent, grey sky was soon to close around their laments, around the cries of children separated from their mothers, all had perished, while Mère was living amid opulence, while her daughter, her sons, were the joy of her life, though it was never without shadows; was it the sight of Renata coming through the front door that had suddenly conjured up the Polish cousins for Mère, or were they always present in her thoughts, she wondered, lost for ever, at the edge of her awareness, like Mère, Renata knew these relatives, these Polish cousins whose memory Mère would have preferred to push aside for ever, only as faces seen in photographs and newspapers, but neither Mère nor Renata could ignore the existence, so brutally ended, of those who had been unable to flee the village of Lukow, in the district of Lublin, indeed Samuel bore the name of a great-uncle who had been shot down during that same winter of 1942, Samuel, the child who had imitated a black voice as he sang with studied sensuality, easy, easy living, Samuel, and all that should have brought comfort to Mère, should have gladdened her in her sorrow, with Samuel, Augustino, Vincent, those faces from Lukow in the district of Lublin should have become a little more distant, for out of death life was reborn, Samuel was the glorious phoenix reborn from his ashes, like leaves that grow back after a fire, it was no doubt Renata's appearance through the main entrance that had awakened these exhausting memories, this complicity in the secret struggle between them, between adult women, the ineradicable memory of the Polish cousins, as for the youngest ones, who knows whether they thought about them often, for out of death life is reborn, why had Mère thought just now about the sweet taste of strawberries on the fresh fish that had been served at dinner, she had wept in grief when she thought about the Polish cousins whom Renata's face brought back to her, it was an ineradicable memory, the intelligence of that face and her own permanent, nearly ancestral concern, and now suddenly she was giving in to memories of delight, of the taste of strawberries on fresh fish, it was time they let her retire to her bedroom, but now the musicians were starting up their racket and everyone was listening, glass in hand, so this was what that bizarre music, choppy, nearly disintegrating, sounded like, the music Samuel listened to through his headphones after school when he was zooming towards the house on his inline skates, skates whose wheels gave off iridescent green flashes, with their skates and their bikes Mélanie's sons were growing accustomed, too young, to a way of life that the future might deprive them of, for who knows what the future has in store for each of us, driven off on Sundays by their father in his car, an Infiniti, they set off, buried by their over-abundant toys, for beaches, outdoor cafés, restaurants where they were served copious meals, banana pancakes swimming in black currant syrup and heavy cream that would soon drip off their fingers and onto their white shorts, their tennis balls and racquets at their feet, weren't these princely sons collecting the share that others had been deprived of, backed up against the barracks of hell, and the writing of justice through time was illegible even though it was inscribed on every life, thought Mère, for out of death life is reborn, what did Mélanie, think about it, weren't those doubts, those moments of discomfort between Mère and Mélanie, like the black spots that cloud the clarity of water and sky on a fine day, she had achieved her dream of being alone with Mélanie, without her husband, for a few days, a pity Mère did not feel she could help with decorating Daniel and Mélanie's spacious house, but she had experienced a *joie de vivre*, a highly unexpected feeling, she thought, as she walked along the pier at daybreak with Samuel and Augustino, close to the port, ecstasy was defined as a burst of joy so vibrant that by casting you outside yourself, towards a sky filled with bliss, that same ecstasy would cause irreparable pathological disorders, but Mère didn't believe a word of it, she told herself that was exactly what she'd felt this morning; leaving her alone in the middle of the high causeway built over the tumult of the waves, Samuel and Augustino had run a long way towards the end of the pier, until Mère could no longer see them though she still heard them, that was the comfort of solitude rediscovered, or the sea air with which Mère filled her lungs till she was euphoric, for no more than a few seconds Mère had been submerged by a sense of immeasurable vitality, overwhelmed by an exquisite grace, she had called to her grandsons, stirred by the echo of her voice in the wind as she leaned into the rolling of the waves, she had thought she was merely a speck of dust on which the eternal winds soon would blow, but that was as it should be, the dust would travel on its elusive journey far from earthly roads, her life had been fulfilled and she had seen the white heron who was alone, he too, ecstasy was the blinding quality of that image of the heron, still and calm, suddenly taking flight, slantwise and slowly, over a stormless sea, that was how Mère would leave the world, she had thought, in that same silent flight, with no commotion, amid silent dignity, but who knows what the future has in store for everyone, for Mère as for Samuel and Augustino? And Renata thought the orchestra musicians were as charming, as attractive in the garden that evening as the gondoliers in their Venetian craft on the rippling water, slightly apart from their group, she could now see them without being seen, a grizzled man had placed his arm under hers and she had instinctively accepted the casualness of this gesture that took her away from the rest of them, from the rapture they stirred in her, that hollow thirst, henceforth unquenchable, she would have liked to silence the voice inside her that reminded her of the remorseless ride of eleven young men, the same number as the members of the orchestra, whose parents had brought them up equally well no doubt, charming, attractive, and like the musicians they were between sixteen and eighteen, they had entered a kibbutz dormitory and for several nights, with no remorse, no dismay over their acts, they would rape a young girl, for seven days, seven nights, she was fifteen years old, she would say nothing for many years, for a long time she would say nothing, fearing she would be hospitalized, so charming, so attractive, all of them, how could she have denounced them to her parents, to their friends, to the educators, how could it be, they all lived together on the same kibbutz, and suddenly the dormitory where the sensible student was asleep in her bed was occupied by the invaders' footsteps, by the cavalcade of young predators, they were so charming, so irresistible, the student in a state of stupor, of appalled disbelief, at first had smiled at them distractedly, as Renata had done under the pressure of the West Indian's fingers when he suddenly pulled her close to him to kiss her, and after many fears, after much hesitation, the student had finally confided the facts to the police, yes, all eleven of them had come, for seven days and seven nights, to the dormitory, and at times she would break off her account with sobs and disjointed words, they had come into the dormitory, all of them so charming, irresistible, though she had been devoured, torn by the fury of their penises, yet she was still alive, all so charming, irresistible, like the musicians this evening, during the lawyers' indecent cross-examination in court, the student had known the eleven young men would not be accused, condemned, for she, like Renata, had been guilty of an absent-minded smile, a guilty smile, when the young men, rushing into the dormitory towards her bed, had started their attack, but the lawyers had declared that, through lack of sympathy on the part of the jury, the public, the case had been dropped, didn't the young girl suffer from mental problems, she was confused, no infraction of the law had been attributed to the young men, who had returned to their work on the kibbutz, for seven days, for seven nights, they had prayed, lit candles in the evening, they had joined their families on Saturday for the sabbath meal, and the judge, who was a man, had told them, go in peace, you're innocent, remembering the young girl raped by eleven young men in the tranquillity of a kibbutz, Renata had regretted her refusal to apply for the judge's position, an arrogant act, for she did not want Claude's support, to say nothing of that of the judges in his family, was it this act of self-doubt and self-abnegation that imbued the entire humiliating condition with the same shame, was it that movement of arrogant suspicion in the face of men exercising their power, of their authority, that had kept her from denouncing those same eleven young men, regardless of where they are, of where they come from, as a judge she would have hauled them into court, would have revealed the hideous nature of their crimes, over seven days, seven nights, on the kibbutz, she would have accused them, they'd have been punished, and the memory of it would have been long-lasting in their consciences and in the conscience of the world, but who was she, a being and bearer of doubts, of concerns, was this nightmare, the thought of that rape in the kibbutz dormitory, the image that had tormented her during those few moments when she'd been asleep, shortly after the West Indian made his escape, when she had heard the dull sound of rain dropping onto the palm frond, during that brief lethargy she had dreamed that a black spider was spinning its web on her left breast, and when she woke up she thought, that's how the student felt the stretching of the web formed by those eleven young men, all those fibres, those foreign membranes on her body, it was within the dreary walls of the rented house, when the flowers of the luxuriant vegetation were sparkling in the first light of day, the black spider again spinning its web on her left breast, and Mère thought an Erté print would have been attractive in this art deco house, and a few bronze figurines in the overly dramatic black and white decor, but would Daniel and Mélanie listen to her advice, and what was she to think of those marble tiles in the dining room, wasn't there something pretentious about them, and why was Samuel always at Julio's side, what kind of friendship could exist between Samuel and Julio, who was twelve years older, an ingenuous admiration, perhaps, what a sad fate for Julio, who had watched his sister and brother, his mother Edna, his brother Oreste, his sister Nina drown before his eyes, and on the raft, where he had long been delirious from thirst and fever, he had barely managed to reach our shores, what a horrible fate, when Mère was living amid opulence among her family and friends, giving in to her frivolous thoughts, when she would have liked to replace the obscene painting in the main-floor bathroom with an Erté print, Samuel also had a friend his own age and that reassured Mère, Jermaine, who would soon be going to private school with Samuel, his parents were remarkably refined, thought Mère, the father was one of those rare black senators elected since the new government had come to power, Jermaine's mother, a Japanese journalist from an aristocratic family, was an activist along with Mélanie, they were a courteous and discerning couple, Jermaine had the oriental grace of his mother, her blazing eyes under long lids, but Samuel didn't play with Jermaine the way he used to, evening rehearsals kept him at the theatre too late, was that any life for a child, the life of an actor, a singer, and all that questionable company, Mère intended to take Samuel to Europe this summer, and during the trip he'd forget about the world of actors that was his father's world, soon Daniel would be directing the play on the civil war that he was writing these days, yes, this summer Mère would take Samuel to Europe, where there were still some relatives, you could hear the refrain of Samuel's song in the evening air, easy, easy living, Mère suddenly remembered with regret that Mélanie wouldn't let her replace the painting in the bathroom with the Erté print. Then Mère noticed Julio sitting alone by the pool, he seemed lost in thought as he brushed the surface of the water with his toes, it was iridescent under the lights illuminating the garden, Julio sometimes brought his hand to his forehead, his headband, as if he had a shooting pain in his eye, and Mère reproached herself for being so insensitive towards the dramas in other people's lives, Julio's hair stood up in brown spikes above his forehead, there was a ring in his left ear, he was a young man like any other, the sensual movement of his feet brushing the surface of the water, was this the same Julio who had drifted for two weeks on his raft, with his mother, his brothers and sisters, on the waters of the Atlantic where the storm, the blast of wind rose up that wrenched away the provisions, snatched from the raft its inhabitants and their frail masts, and they couldn't swim, that floating tableau, no, Mère was not imagining it, but she remembered one detail from Julio's account, it was during one of those devastating storms between the sky and the sea of fire that Ramon, that Oreste had swallowed salt water, as she thought of Vincent who was asleep upstairs, of his tiny infant heart, Mère could hear in the silence those hearts that had suddenly stopped beating, Oreste, Ramon didn't breathe again after they'd taken in the salt water, their tiny hearts had stopped beating, or were they still beating when Julio saw a helicopter in the sky, had the pilot shouted through the obscure density of the air, we'll be there soon, the helicopter *Homeland* will be there soon, how had the helicopter and its brave pilots dissolved, along with the hope of the *Homeland*, of the land regained, between the sky and the stormy sea, how could that vision be erased for Julio forever in the thick fog of his fever, the duration of that two-week crossing, yes, Mère remembered that detail in Julio's account, it was the salt water that had caused the heart of Ramon, of Oreste to stop irreparably, while the motor of the helicopter *Homeland* was still rumbling in the sky, homeland, we'll be there soon, but for a long time Julio appeared to be sleeping, in the sun as in the rain, for two weeks on his raft, and when he regained consciousness he recognized them, recognized Oreste, Ramon, Edna, Nina by the colour of their hair amid the flotsam hanging from the raft, Oreste, Ramon, Edna, Nina who had not been saved, though the motor of the helicopter *Homeland*, land regained, was still rumbling. Julio looked up towards

the second floor, from where Samuel was diving into the
pool, into the shattered waves, Mère felt a slight shock, the
red of Samuel's swimsuit was electrifying, Mère was annoyed
that they let Samuel dive so late at night, it was unwise,
thought Mère, Samuel was scarcely out of the water, amid a
burst of laughter, when Jenny and Sylvie were beside him,
swaddling Samuel in a silky, flowered dressing-gown, one of
the silk kimonos Jermaine and his mother, Tchouan, had given
him on their return from a trip to Japan when Jermaine's
father, on mission there, had been honoured for his writing,
the silk kimono on Samuel's body streaming with water, Jenny
and Sylvie's hands running furtively over his shoulders, that,
Mère thought, was a tableau of lazy sensuality, Samuel's senses
were too keen, with those perfumes of jasmine, of acacia,
under the arbour where the vigorous sound of Samuel's
singing had come from his round mouth, but the senses of
all children nowadays were too keen, and below the dark
spikes of his close-cropped hair, his expression sadly cheerful,
Julio had applauded Samuel's excessive dive from the second-
floor window, and suddenly Samuel's aquatic frolicking under
the lanterns, in the pool with its iridescent glimmering,
displeased him, for now that the silence was spreading across
the raft, the barely audible voices of Edna, Oreste, Ramon
were swallowed up one by one into the sound of the waves,
telling their brother, come to me, quickly, for here, far from
the land regained, from the homeland, I am dying, oh, come
to me quickly, Julio, and when would they arrive in the port
of Brest, thought Renata, how had they ever reached the
shores of the Atlantic in that storm, why had the waves
subsided all at once, if a single wave had swept the deck of
the yacht they would all have been lost, Renata had known
she would be the first one swallowed up by the murderous
wave, suddenly, but her life had not ended on the deck of a

cruise ship, death had breathed on her when the wave passed, twisting and turning, the one who would have escaped with his children was Franz, whose oratorio was to be played in a cathedral in England at Christmastime, Franz who was expected in Brest, in a humble church at Finistère, the Church of Saint Louis, and through the mist, when would Franz and Renata, when would Franz's sons see the glow of the lighthouse at Brest shining on the rocks, he, Franz, would have escaped with his children, it had to be him, Franz, whose music could now be heard in cathedrals and churches, he had written a psalm that had been translated into Hebrew, for the soprano voice of a child, O thou who art our shepherd, deliver us from the scourges, the curses of war, those waves where blood flows every day, guide us, O shepherd, away from the fierce storm, and those words were heard during these nights of shadow, during these dark times, they were heard in a church in Finistère and in a London cathedral, when Franz entreated God, in a lament that a boy soprano's voice sustained in its flight towards a paroxysm of joy, O thou who art our shepherd, deliver us from those scourges, lead us away from the curse of that storm, because Franz had composed that music, only he and his should be saved from the destructive wave that was surging over the deck of the yacht little by little, amid an outburst of wind-loosed lines, Renata was only the second wife of that great man, one of his mistresses, she had begun studying law in France but her studies were constantly interrupted by her need to think only of him, of Franz, no doubt overwhelming him with an irrational, insane love, like a beggar woman who knocks at a closed door she felt only abandonment, but the man was Franz, that narcissistic man, and all his children who would have been saved, who would have escaped, as in the poem by Emily Dickinson that would often be evoked, thought

Renata, in other perilous circumstances during her life, with the sudden awakening of a storm on a motionless sea, would the ship or the carriage of death stop for her here, though she was in no hurry to climb the steps bringing her to its threshold, but was it not her destiny to know that the man would always be right, even at the moment of survival, for she was merely a woman, a being who is a bearer of doubts, of uncertainties, and why should death not stop here today, during a storm on this yacht, when she was smoking in the cabin she'd retired to this morning, when for some hours, as they moved across the barely navigable water, the boats had already been sending out whistles, the sound of bells foretelling danger, and when she opened the cabin door she would receive the wave and its silvery thunderbolt right in her heart, a thread of grey water had already seeped under the cabin door where the wind was tugging, in this cabin she had retired to this morning, she would say nothing to anyone, she had known that insatiable desire to be far from any gaze, smoking her cigarettes one by one with a stabbing pleasure, displaying by the stormy light from the porthole the gold cigarette case, an ironic object, if she thought she might be living her final hour, for the thread of water would expand as it moved under the door, it would seethe up to her neck, to her temples, only let them leave her alone that morning, as she had been alone yesterday, amid the secrecy of her insatiable desire. And when they had all seen the glow of the lighthouse on the coast of Brest, the sea had grown more gentle and the sky had been lit by a red light, they who could have been nothing but debris, bones under the water, the empty hull of a boat, they were saved, Renata had looked for a long time at Franz, who stood on the deck with his children, all of them bent beneath the rain in their hooded slickers, if they had all been shipwrecked in this winter storm, if the lights of the lighthouse had never shone again, it would have marked the end of the years of magnificence and success for Franz, the destruction of that feverish face, that body, those hands that had perhaps lived only for music, and she would have retained of him the memory of his weather-beaten face crowned by hair like black flames, the memory of his long hands, he would have enveloped the children, would have defended and protected them with his male faith in life, a tense and powerful figure against the red sky like Goya characters facing up to the torturers of the Inquisition and the catastrophe of war, a revolutionary figure among them, with small figures of men standing nearby in the expectation of gunfire, characters with their hooded slickers all in a row, in the rain, a sign of innocence in Goya's paintings, that figure, that character was dressed in a white shirt, like the white shirt from the yacht club Franz belonged to, which clung to his torso, with a spot like a burst in the middle, that white, that whiteness before the ordeal, but in its whiteness and innocence it was already the shroud, the garment of death. Mère thought it was too late now to go to sleep, and it seemed to her that her existence would be curtailed by this sleepless night, other guests, the younger ones, were arriving, among them a young black girl, impudent, who proudly displayed a crown of pink hibiscus on her braided hair, she was bold enough to pour herself a cognac at the bar, thought Mère, then she made her way to the musicians' stage where Mère looked for her, this festive night, these nights would be too costly, thought Mère, the number of eccentrics among musicians always amazed her, but Daniel and Mélanie would ruin their parents, and Julio climbed soundlessly up to the bedroom where Vincent was asleep, was it true what the family doctor said, or was he misinterpreting a symptom, the thin breathing of Vincent who was ten days old today, Julio approached the big bed where

Vincent lay sleeping, listening for a long time to his breathing, Vincent was breathing normally and his breath, barely
expressed, filled the bedroom, behind the closed blinds, with
its reassuring sound, Ramon, Oreste, Edna, Nina, my little bees,
my little flies, you're all gone, murmured Julio, as if he were
still suffering from fever on his raft, but the flies, the bees,
like those translucent insects burned by the flames of tallow
candles, of beeswax candles on the tables in the garden, the
diaphanous victims in the light of the fire were dispersed for
ever before the party had even got under way in the night.
And Vincent's thin breathing, Daniel was thinking as he stood
welcoming his guests at the garden gate, questioning their
gaze with the golden, penetrating gleam of his eyes, in
their lives wasn't Vincent's faintly laboured breathing like the
menacing sound, drawn out and deep, that announced an
earth tremor, under the brevity of that breathing their lives
flickered like flames in the wind, what did the New York
publisher say in his letter that had come in the mail, that the
manuscript of *Strange Years*, on which Daniel had worked
so hard, had been turned down, the publisher praised the
author's poetic style but the account of Daniel's strange
years, of his years of cocaine addiction in New York, did not
suit the publisher's list, the account hadn't held the attention
of their readers, and when Daniel heard the words Julio
whispered into Mélanie's ear, get out of here and take the
children, the White Horsemen are back, he recognized the
Shadow that brushed against the fence, up against the orange
tree that yielded bitter fruit, where Augustino was circling in
his Superman cape, the Shadow was that of an old woman
with a flushed face and stiff white hair, the old woman was
not the itinerant she could be mistaken for, in her dress like
a pouch sewn to her body, the dress was one of the disguises
that belonged to the cursèd clan, the White Horsemen were

back, the Shadow of the woman went back and forth behind the fence, very close to Augustino, who was playing under the orange tree that yielded bitter fruit, the woman was not the itinerant she looked like, no, thought Daniel, when she went home in the evening, it was to paint slogans at her husband's side, dipping her brush into paint the colour of blood, slogans that would be seen the next day on the white walls of the new houses along Atlantic Boulevard, that indelible red mark, and its inscription of hatred, would also be seen encrusted on Samuel's boat at the marina, for the White Horsemen might be back, as Julio said, he'd run into them on the street; the mayor of the city advised Daniel to calm his young activist's fervour, here in this place that Daniel called paradise in his books, laws were imposed that always brought victory to the rich, in his writing Daniel aroused the anger of reactionaries, incited the black community to revolt, and as he listened to the mayor's words Daniel thought there was no paradise for man except in silence and cowardice, he reproached himself for his happiness, but was he still so happy, from now on there was the problem of Vincent's laboured breathing, the mayor moved away towards the pool in an intoxicated waltz, what did he care about that riffraff from Bahama Street on their porches, thought Daniel, and the Shadow was coming closer to the other side of the fence, you could hear its hissing under the heavy branches of the orange tree, you could hear its clamour, its sinister voice, you entertain too many black activists in your house, said the nurse Mélanie had consulted about Augustino's earaches this winter, and those girls, Jenny and Sylvie, who are they, why do you let them into your house, Marie-Sylvie, Julio, they're refugees, aren't they, those rafts that run aground on our beaches, they should be sent back to the sea; in their own country they bear the name traitor, worm, insidious, and the words, the speech, prowled around Daniel with their portents, they distilled a toxic venom into the fragrant air that Daniel breathed cheerfully, for how could he not enjoy his happiness with Mélanie, with the children, here in this oasis, some time after the torments of the strange years, years without faith, without hope, before the revelation of writing, and it was that same nurse who each day would dilute in warm water, in the warm milk for his bottle, the drug Vincent was to take every four hours, it had been when they changed positions while making love that they'd sensed Augustino's presence in the bed, wasn't he a little too old now to be getting into bed with them at night like this, under Père's presidency of the marine biology laboratory, a black commissioner would be elected to replace that mediocrity who was spouting his inane remarks by the pool, Daniel thought, the Shadow was brushing against the fence in front of the house, Augustino running in his cape, and every day there would be that medicinal smell in the bedroom with its closed blinds, there's no cure, said the doctor, but if the medication is taken every four hours it has preventive properties, the child will feel better, were the Strange Years that penetrated hearts and brains with their poison still surrounding them, the bottle, the spoon, the contents of the medication would be diluted in the bowl of the utensil, who knows whether there had been an error in the doctor's insolent diagnosis, how moved they all would be, later on, thought Daniel, who had filmed the birth of his son, to see again the strong, happy baby, plump-cheeked, the baby they had made, an achievement of nature, like a flower, a butterfly, the world had been so beautiful until Daniel and Mélanie witnessed among the recorded images and sounds an imperceptible distortion of the image, slowly Vincent's smile was erased, that smile even through tears, that suddenly accelerated breathing they thought they could hear in the fog, that sound, roaring, drawn-out and deep and low-pitched, announcing a seismic tremor to the inhabitants of the earth, yes, how moved they would be later on to see again the chubby-cheeked baby, the healthy baby they had made; Tanjou's black T-shirt, his corduroy pants, the boots whose leather hadn't had time to wear out, Jacques's sister held all those objects on her lap, along with the sheets from a book of notes on Kafka, in the notebook she'd taken from the pocket of the cords some German words had been transcribed, for an unfinished translation, it was as if Jacques had barely managed to jot down those words, as they had been felt by Huldrych Zwingli, in the time of the Plague, Tröst, Herr Gott, tröst! Die krankheit wachst, we und angst faßt mein sel und leib, Comfort me, Lord, comfort me, the pain is growing, sickness is striking me down, my body and my soul have been taken; the words had been crossed out and replaced by others, seized by dread, by horror, by fright, help, O Lord, help, had Jacques written, translated these words, thought the sister, the friend, before he was completely altered, while Luc was cutting his hair he'd had that vision of the hospice Pastor Jeremy would open soon, for the Cemetery of the Roses was overflowing with all those young men for whom the pastor lit altar candles in the temple every night, during prayer vigils, Tröst, Herr Gott, tröst, Jacques had repeated those words while he thought about the foul sores in the groin, in the armpits of the poet Zwingli during the time of the Plague, when religious wars divided peoples, when no one knew that a flea transmitted to man by a rat would decide the fate of them all, and what was that insatiable thirst, in the cabin of a boat or in a Paris hotel room, where, even when she was travelling with Franz and his musicians, she preserved that secret isolation, in the hope that she would be able to study, to read by herself, the hope of gaining herself

some time that was not merely idle time, drifting, numbing
her with a sensation of futility, of a dizzying void, they were
always celebrating, from one country to the next, one city to
the next, with Franz reading to his friends during dinner the
laudatory reviews of a brilliantly executed piece by Schubert,
even in the solitude of a hotel room, or a cabin on a boat,
Renata would hear that piece of music as if it belonged to
her, or to Franz, *Death and the Maiden* or an excerpt from a
Stravinsky concerto, the hotel room and the cabin were the
extension of those works in which, for Renata, the sounds
suddenly expressed a melancholy, a helplessness that had
become her own, she was Franz's hand as he conducted an
orchestra in a Paris concert hall, the fear of an error in the
score would waken her at night, but she was not Franz
conducting an orchestra, she was only the background of
melancholy and helplessness from which his music burst,
when she found herself alone, getting up to smoke a cigarette at the window, there were times when that window, in
Paris, opened onto people who didn't see her, those
deprived lovers in the street who moved exquisitely in a kiss,
in love, like Rodin's lovers, for them the edge of a street, a
sidewalk in Paris, in the deserted city, served as a bed or, a
few moments earlier, as a table, when they'd shared with
their dog a piece of meat they cut with their knife, suddenly,
in that dance of love on a sidewalk, against a wall, before the
fruit vendor and flower-seller returned, under the wan light
of a streetlamp, in their poverty, their destitution, they were
the splendour of youth; from her bedroom under the rooftops
Renata could see them dancing wildly with heavy black-laced
boots on their feet, and while they were kissing, the music
from *Death and the Maiden* came back into the silence of
the room, and the lovers on the street were like the lovers
who had posed for the bodies sculpted by Rodin, Renata

thought, they had the savage ardour and the vehemence of those bodies, and who knows whether, like those attractive young people of long ago who posed for Rodin, they would not become toothless and destitute old people, those models of Rodin's who, with the beauty of the hands that had sculpted them, had merely taken a step towards degradation and death, while *The Kiss* depicted them as eternally beautiful and young, Rodin's *Kiss* in which the bodies of deprived, indigent lovers were frozen in time, they were the kiss of eternal youth, and Renata, participating from afar in their fleeting embrace, could hear the voice of Franz telling her he no longer desired her, or was it her own obsessive fear that, for a woman, old age was always too close at hand; from the angle of the window where she stood smoking, she could also hear *Death and the Maiden*, the song of her own helplessness, of her melancholy in the deserted night inhabited only by some gasps of pleasure; and why was she thinking about him, about Franz, in this enchanting garden, close to her nephew and niece, Daniel and Mélanie, just as she'd been close to those destitute lovers, why was she again seeing the West Indian at the door of the casino, or seeing his brown back as he fled, his hair, on which, as on his arms and hands, there was a kind of dust, a dusty patina under the sweat, those grains of dust, that sprinkling of dirt and sand adhered to the West Indian's destitution, they were his skin, his odour, his fatigue as well, for he had gradually started sleeping on the beaches after he'd hung around the casino all night, a pathetic shadow, he had stopped removing the sand, the dust from his hair, his eyebrows, Renata would again see him being slowly petrified under those scabs of dust, of sand, on the beaches where he would protect himself from bad weather with a blanket when the nights were cold, and the length of fabric or wool would be saturated with salt water, it would be the colour of sand, or the poverty-stricken colour of the West Indian's face when he'd told Renata that she was an insolent woman, she would sometimes see him lying in the middle of the elegant streets near the harbour, when magnificently dressed people were heading for their hotels, for the casino, he would be lying in his own vomit on the pavement, the length of fabric or wool would be saturated with water, with sand and urine, people would walk past him without seeing him, in his hair the grains of dust would accumulate, the scabs of filth and sand, as she walked past him Renata would avoid lowering her gaze to his degradation, his disgrace, but the taste of that dust, of that sweat, would be on her lips again like the words of hatred the West Indian had uttered as he rested his face against hers, amid the tension of struggle, of anger, and now, in the garden with Daniel and Mélanie, she was afraid he would suddenly appear to her under that powdery brown blanket, a length of fabric or wool, stolen cloth in which he would array himself at night so that people who were leaving the casino, walking past him, couldn't recognize him, and Mère wondered when Mélanie would come out on the veranda on the second floor of the house, as had been planned, carrying her son Vincent in her arms and saying proudly, here is my son, see his fingers, like petals, see his little fists that open like the corollas of flowers, here is my life, that was how the scene had been planned, Mère thought, Mélanie would be charming among the orchids, on the high veranda above the garden, with Samuel, in the waiter's outfit borrowed from Julio, pouring champagne into glasses, but his breathing, Vincent's breathing, Mélanie wasn't telling Mère everything, why was Vincent having trouble breathing? Franz, one of Renata's husbands, Mère was thinking, was a composer and pianist whom Mère still remembered, born in

Kiev into a family of musicians, he'd started studying music at the age of five, but he had not gone on living in Kiev for his destiny was not that of his Polish grandparents and cousins; born in Kiev into a noble, educated family, at thirteen he had made his first concert tours in the United States, it was surprising that Franz's compositions were religious since he had been brought up in his parents' atheism, but the mystery of his parents' exodus to the United States, to Canada, had perhaps kept alive in him the doubt, the false hope that with music a divine power was brought to bear on his life, was it some limitless hope in his bride, or the doubt that gnawed at Mère's soul, there were some who could suddenly believe they were loved by an unbending God, shortly before he met Renata at a Chicago university where he was completing his studies, Franz had composed a symphonic work inspired by the psalms, the psalms in the Scriptures that Mère read, not without fear that the Divine Wrath would swoop down on her and on her people, Mère thought that perhaps what Renata had loved in Franz was his mystery, the mystery of the exodus that had taken him and his parents out of Kiev, and what a fragile wonder was that child, Vincent, still so fragile beneath his downy hair, Mère was sure Mélanie wasn't telling her everything about Vincent. And this extreme heat, during the afternoon, the tendency towards indolence that Mère had experienced while she was reading in the hammock, her failure to persuade Mélanie to care passionately about a career in politics — senator, governor, she was very competent — those cruel moments of failure when the sky was blue and the day was superb, yet the heat was oppressive, listlessness did not go with Mère's personality and she had felt so listless at three o'clock this afternoon while Augustino was taking his nap, and wasn't that listlessness, that tendency to drowsiness, because of Jenny, because of her jazzy voice while she was putting Augustino to sleep ˙on the upstairs veranda, go to sleep, little angel, Jenny sang, or had he eaten too much sugar again so he couldn't sleep, Jenny sang, it was Jenny's voice that was the cause of Mère's drowsiness, that jazzy voice, the warm cadence of that voice, and Mère had thought that a swim in the pool would be good for her, and at last she would be alone there, she wanted no one to see her flapping awkwardly in her swimming exercises, and after she'd taken off her plain culottes, her blue-flowered blouse, the traditional straw hat she wore when she had lunch with friends in outdoor cafés or restaurants, when those friends were women she would try to steer them into politics because women today should take part in the country's destiny, Mère had drifted towards the sparkling green water under the blazing sky, seeing again the white heron taking flight above the waves on the pier, how calm, suddenly, was the sound of the water around Mère, had it not been for Jenny's lilting voice as she told Augustino a story, Mère would have heard in the silence the piercing cries of cicadas and catbirds that began at dawn in the oleanders by her bedroom, the green water was as cool as a stream, as if she were alone in the woods, how calm it was, except for Jenny's voice in the oppressive air, and Mère stopped swimming in the middle of the pool, she had been struck with dismay as she looked at the marble shores, as if she had been captured in the pool in this ridiculous position, her arms and legs flailing in awk-ward flapping movements, what would Daniel and Mélanie have thought as they darted down towards the underwater fauna of the Coral Coast, would they have thought Mère deserved mockery when she looked like that, touching the water with her polished nails as she flapped, and Mère was no longer thin like Mélanie, her bosom was too generous, Mère saw the pile of clothing laid carefully on a chaise longue in the garden, how pathetic, she thought, what was she doing in the middle of this pool, in the restful coolness of the water at three in the afternoon, she could have told Daniel and Mélanie that she was enjoying life to the full on this wonderful day, in this garden, this pool among the flowers, they were like those paths that open onto paradise, Jenny's recitation, her voice filled the air, suddenly her lament was that of her ancestors in the cotton fields, Mama was rocking me too, Jenny sang to Augustino as she was putting him to sleep on the upstairs veranda, my mama told me, pick the rose from the thorns where it grows, pick the cottonseed, pick the fruit of the coffee tree, because this is the time when the master comes by with his whip, but such stories shouldn't have been told to Augustino, Mère thought, Daniel and Mélanie were rushing their children's education, Jenny, Marie-Sylvie, Julio had all grown up in the street, and when Jenny's voice fell silent on the upstairs veranda, Mère heard the creaking of the wooden chair in which Augustino was still being rocked, little by little Jenny's sighs, her sleepy yawns, faded away, and Mère advanced slowly in the water, swimming cautiously, returning to the middle of the pool, moving helplessly, she was not advancing now, she thought, her husband, her children, the fulfilment of their careers, Mère was advancing on her own, without them, she was incapable of action, would she make further progress into life, she wondered in the middle of the pool, or would her hopes for progress, for personal development henceforth be merely plants growing in the dark? Mère looked at the sky and asked herself why Mélanie was staying so long with Vincent, could she be worrying about the contrary winds that would blow over the ocean during the night? It was normal for a mother to be struck by that almost carnal emotion for her newborn, but Mélanie was too worried about her child, and Mère, a captive of the marble shores of the pool, 'had thought about the words her French governess had once spoken to her, isn't mademoiselle getting too worked-up? Mademoiselle wants to be the centre of attention, Mère had enjoyed hearing those words again in all their severity, words that were so intolerant of a five-year-old's errors, but they were fair, it was true that Mère had always wanted to be noticed for the intelligence of her rejoinders in the family house where, she already knew, they were considering sending her brothers to Yale, whereas for her, though she was just a little girl, they were talking already about marriage, she was getting worked-up again wanting Daniel and Mélanie to see her as a woman avid for life, for experience, as long as it was within the confines of a well-ordered life where she would be allowed to sleep more than five hours a night, the French governess had had to come back to prove to Mère that she was a real person, that she would take care of her as she'd done in the past, that she would fix afternoon snacks on the grass for her and her brothers, on those tables where Mère had tasted delicacies she still found it hard to resist, so much so that she had even written an article on desserts for a newspaper, the chocolate cake with apricot liqueur had been one of Mère's suggestions, as for pastries based on flour, sugar, and eggs, Mère no longer enjoyed them quite so much since her husband had reprimanded her for indulging in too many of them, the elasticity of Mère's weight-loss plan had little to do with the laws of nutrition, and why should she revel in such insignificant thoughts when her daughter hadn't been the same since Vincent's birth, Mère had been very familiar with that pain verging on disgust, that incapacity, but what was going on now, Mélanie confided nothing of her uneasiness, and why had Mère never seen the French governess again after she'd come back from a trip with her parents, the governess's absence, or her dismissal, had never been explained, Mère had never bidden her goodbye, never showed her appreciation after all those years, instead, like her brothers, who had died prematurely while they were at Yale, who had succumbed to diseases as benign as chickenpox, to some lung infection after swimming in icy water, the French governess had gone back to her own distant road in her black cloth coat, suitcase in hand, among the brothers she was a silhouette snatched up by the fog and heading for another passage where Mère would not see her again, and so that was the music Samuel was listening to through his headphones, on his way home from school on his inline skates, the music the orchestra was playing at the back of the garden, deafening, its volume stepped up by the mikes, with the sound of the drums, of the cymbals being struck one against the other, Samuel could hear the ocean waves, he was doing his lessons, the languid strumming of the guitar disturbed his hours of study, of sleep, but where had Samuel been since Mère saw him get out of the pool and into the rustling silk kimono, lifted up by Jenny's arms, by Sylvie's, how languorous was this night with its tumultuous rhythms created by the drums, could Mère hope to be restored to life, to dance, imitating the young people, but it would never be anything but an imitation, how languorous was this night, these paths under the trees, these gardens that opened onto paradise, in the intoxication of the air, and Renata remembered that hollow, that latent sensation of thirst, even on this very hot afternoon in the city streets, when she stopped at a foreign exchange counter, she was sending her husband a telegram, it was an airy office that opened onto the street and the curious passing crowd, a makeshift stand for tourists, perhaps, where behind a screen stood a grimy-faced man, withdrawn into himself, collapsing over his paperwork, that hollow sensation of thirst had come

to Renata when she noticed that the man did not deign to
look up at her, from his piles of paper, why should he pay
attention to her, even to send a telegram, when she was merely
a woman, the man's grimy face sank deeper, a dark mass
among the papers in the brightness of a yellow wall too
harshly lit by the sun, and the man himself, insignificant-
looking, with the black stubble on his cheeks, wasn't he stuck
in the grime of that yellow wall, among the mosquitoes, the
insects squashed there during the daytime, and suddenly
Renata had heard the nasal voice of a parrot in its cage, it
seemed to be repeating the words hello, how are you, hello,
the presence of the perching bird rubbing up against the bars
of its cage as it pecked at a cuttlebone with its beak, the
bird's abandonment, as if it were merely a clump of threadbare
feathers forgotten by its master and not the splendid bird it
had once been in its jungle paradise, no doubt it had been
the presence of the mistreated bird that had made the hollow sensation of thirst intolerable, and Renata had brought
her hand to her heart, as if she had stopped breathing in the
stifling air, the parrot, its feet attached to a steel wire, repeated
again, hello, how are you, hello, I'm fine, and Renata saw the
words she was writing to Claude, their separation wouldn't
last much longer, she wrote, but why was this solitary woman
measuring the degree of knowledge, of ideas, that would be
acquired by her alone, that was no doubt the reason for this
disgraceful, often humiliating journey into the limbo of a
woman's condition, so unsure of herself, on her own, the
woman felt ineffectual, her body was under threat from all
sides, but she wouldn't write those words, about the grimy-
faced man collapsed over his paperwork on the other side
of the street, about a woman singing in the shadowy cavern
of a bar, hush little baby, don't you cry, I'm feeling better
every day, Renata wrote to her husband, Daniel and Mélanie's

son is doing well, but would the hollow sensation of thirst vanish here in this garden, on this festive night, the orchestra musicians were all so charming, seductive, they were like the gondoliers in their Venetian craft on the rippling water in the evening, what was the source of those cries Renata thought she could still hear, the students' mouths had been gagged, their hands tied behind them so that no sound, no cry could be heard in the neat and tidy houses on a Florida campus where a group of young girls, a few boys, applied themselves to their studies, having very little fun during this exam season, how would the troubadour of death, wearing his suit and tie as if he were a smooth-voiced businessman, come into their midst this evening or tonight, to charm them, seduce them with the fatal melodies of his voice, what could they fear from the amusing, charming troubadour, from his voice, his songs, in one hand he held his camera, in the other his guitar, with sadistic pleasure his fingers in the pocket of his suit jacket stroke the blade of his knife, an army knife, he strokes it with one finger, with the palm of his hand that slips around it, at first they listen to him, he approaches them, and then come rape and crime, murder and mutilation, and while he was raping them, killing them, each woman, each man could hear his voice, the fatal melody of that voice marked by the blows of the knife, the wailing, the moaning, the laments of victims whose mouths were gagged, tomorrow the singing hangman will remember nothing, the sordid details of his rapes, of his murders, will only come back to him when the film rolls in his camera, as if he had dreamed the gory theatricality of his acts and their location, a campus where female students lived in neat and tidy houses beneath the trees, the stage on which he would be the actor in episodes, in dramas, each more squalid than the rest, who knows if he had seen in a dream the knife that once belonged to a soldier, with that same knife, in the rice paddies, a hapless soldier who was also guilty of great massacres had sliced open the bellies of little girls and their mothers, the assassin singing, killing a student as he lay asleep, to the rhythm of his own silky voice, then turning him on his side the better to see the profile suddenly so pale in the moonlight, afterwards raping five young girls, and killing them all, the murderer had the rapid flight of an angel as he took his knife and planted it right in their hearts, backbones shattered, necks, already long and reedlike, snapped, necks that for a long time would be bent over books whose pages were covered with blood, on students' desks, on tables where reading assignments were piled under a lamp, though none of them — so arduous had been the struggle with the angel — would obtain a graduation certificate while parents, professors looked on with emotion, only during the days of his trial would the singing murderer remember his acts through nerve-shattering nightmares, for the meticulous camera would show him the blown-up images of his crimes, here a leg dangling off a bed, there a mouth that still seems to be breathing like a rose, curls of hair veiling their gazes like those of watchful does, the bouquet of young lives plundered, cast out, in the sheets, on the wood floor, next to overturned chairs, against the work-table, and even the coffee, the cup of coffee consumed during a two o'clock break would preserve the greedy imprint of life, the foam of the lukewarm coffee still wetting the cup but, Renata thought, the case of the singing killer abandon-ing himself to the carnage of young girls on a Florida campus was one case among so many others, for from birth to death a woman's life was doomed to immolation, now the judges, professional examiners of conscience, were trying to comprehend the reason for that immolation on a Florida campus, and they would not understand, any more than the murderer, how it could have happened, these disasters weighing on the conscience of one rather ordinary man, a man lacking courtesy who walked into houses, into kibbutz dormitories, a humble singer and his guitar, here, and the jury asked for the death sentence, would it be the electric chair or lethal injection, as in the case of the prisoner in Texas, so seductive, so charming, those young people in the orchestra at the back of the garden, Renata thought she could hear those cries, those moans issuing from the bound lips, from the breasts of students lacerated by a knife on a lovely night in June, if she had been the judge, forgetting her own principles, she would have condemned him too, but it would have been in vain, the students would never get their graduation certificates, and with their faces hidden in their hands, in the courts, in the gatherings of judges, the inconsolable mothers were mourning those daughters they'd given birth to, and amid cries and lamentations, amid tears and sobs, Renata could hear the liturgical music of *Death and the Maiden*, on each of the corpses, on those lips where the colour vermilion would well up no more, the music spreading like a funeral pall, the liturgical music of Schubert, death and the maiden, der Tod und das Mädchen, death and the maiden. And during the night Franz suddenly entered the secret room in a Paris hotel to which Renata had retired, he seemed to be squeezed into his conductor's outfit, the jacket, the black trousers, the dazzlingly white shirt, his hair fell untidily over his black eyes that gleamed in the shadows, furious that she had thus distanced herself from him, he'd gone drinking with his friends, had lost a great deal of money gambling, but that was how he was, he explained to Renata, an uncivilized man with a volatile temperament, he mumbled apologies, telling Renata he loved her, she pushed him away, told him to leave the room, der Tod und das Mädchen, Franz's concert had been praised by the critics, received an ovation in the hall, wasn't Renata familiar with her husband's outbursts after a concert, why had she felt no pity for him, he tightened his embrace, he was a savage, she thought, even when he was conducting the orchestra with all the expressive shading of his art, he still had that Berber look, the black flame in his eyes, if he'd come into this room, Renata thought, it was because he'd heard the cries of pleasure from the lovers in the street, the cry of the young woman standing against the wall, a sustained cry whose echo flooded the deserted city in the mist from the quays, it was that appeal, stimulating desire, exciting the senses like the swirls of hot wind, that had brought Franz, intoxicated, running to Renata's hotel room, but no more than he had come to the cabin of the yacht, she'd often told him, and never when she was alone, should he come and annoy her with his insistence, but he was responding only to his own excited desire, he wasn't listening to her, his imagination was bringing back to him, as to Renata's memory, the swelling cry of the lovers in the street, and when she had given in to the savage nature of her love for Franz that night, was it because the humble manicurist had told her she was beautiful, when she was making herself elegant to go to the concert with Franz that evening, as she thought about what Franz had told her the previous day, wasn't she a little old for him, she had wept, letting the tears roll shamelessly down her cheeks, as if she were thus giving up her secret to a woman who knew nothing about her, who would never see her again in this city, suddenly, amid the nakedness of her tears, her pain completely filled the space of the secret room while Franz was bringing his face close to hers, stunning her with the black flame in his eyes, der Tod und das Mädchen, he said, that music, though it expressed such reverence for the sacred, was sensual, and his fleshy lips kissed Renata's neck, she could see his white teeth gleaming, she remembered how he had talked to her about Schubert's syphilis, about the six masses he had written during the same years as *Death and the Maiden*, afflicted by a venereal disease, wizened by destitution, by poverty though he was still young, Schubert had been worn out by persistent fevers during his walks in the gardens of Vienna, he had heard those celestial voices that would help him forget how the syphilitic chancre was working away inside him, der Tod und das Mädchen, Franz said to Renata, so close to her, in a voice that hardened when he was talking about those women, young but already withered, whom Schubert had perhaps been with in houses of debauchery in Europe, did Schubert's music not betray a sublimated impulse towards the pleasures of love that had perhaps been the only joys in his life, a life marked by poverty and lack of understanding, der Tod und das Mädchen, now he was suddenly remote, speaking another language, so that she could not comprehend that the portrait of Schubert he'd drawn for her was in some measure a portrait of himself, she recognized in it the solitude, the poverty of the exodus from Kiev with his parents, the taverns in those European towns where he'd started playing the violin at the age of twelve, even those houses of debauchery where, for him, love was associated with death, sexual pleasure with the fear of syphilis, when like the young Schubert he had seen in a mirror, above the cool, laughing mouth he was kissing, the reflection of his own mortality, death and the maiden, der Tod und das Mädchen, and so it was that on that evening, she thought, she had been unable to defend herself against the savage nature of her love for Franz, for she had not sent him away from the secret room where, mingling their destinies, they had heard the cries of the lovers in the street, the woman's sustained cry gradually lost in the mist of the deserted city.

And the lighted lamps in the garden, the music and this glittering festive night had wakened Augustino, and Jenny caught hold of him by the tail of his Superman cape, under the orange tree that yielded bitter fruit, Augustino's shrill cries irritated Mère's ears, what was going on, it was past midnight and they hadn't put him to bed yet, he ran even as Jenny came around the tree, its long branches bending under the heavy fruit, Jenny was rather inattentive when it came to watching the children, Mère thought, she was playing with Augustino more than she was keeping an eye on him, now and then touching his cheek, his tiny temples under his sweaty hair, he wasn't going to sleep by himself up there in that bedroom without his parents, Augustino cried, no, not any more, two more days, two more nights, he would jump up and down on the grass in the garden under his floating cape, ever since Mummy had that new baby she didn't think about Augustino, but I still love you as much as ever, said Jenny as she stroked Augustino's temples, his forehead, look, here you are, I think I can feel Augustino's forehead and his eyes under my fingers, I think his warm face is pressed against my hand, is that you, Augustino, Augustino's shrill cries started up again, I want to sleep with my mummy, my mummy, cried Augustino, it was the same thing every night, Mère was thinking, since the birth of his brother the child refused to go up to his bedroom at night, and suddenly a laughing Augustino told Jenny that she couldn't see him because he was under a tree, Jenny carried Augustino away amid the sound of his floating cape, she hoisted him up very high, as high as her shoulders, she said, so he'd stop thinking about running away, again Augustino let out cries that rang in Mère's ears, even if she was some distance from him, taking quick looks in the direction of the path under the fountain's spray, which would bring her to her room and her well-earned sleep, she thought,

Augustino's cries, full of the vitality the very young possess, reminded her that she had a duty to stay up, at least until the end of this first night of festivities, but what was that across the street, beyond the gate, that seemed to be holding Jenny's attention, Mère could see no one, only that Jenny, who was standing motionless in front of the garden fence, seemed mesmerized in an attitude of fear, there was a shadow on the other side of the fence, said Jenny, who was that shadow whose sly head was hidden inside a hood, who was it, and Daniel saw Jenny running off with Augustino, he remembered the Shadow on the other side of the wall, the aggressive hissing in the night, as soon as they were alone on the broad veranda Jenny resumed the story she'd been telling Augustino to put him to sleep in the wooden chair, sleep, my angel, Jenny sang, as at the feet of Jesus, from here, as Mama used to sing to me, we can't hear the nasty shouting any more, let the song of the cicadas rock you to sleep, sleep, my angel, sleep at the feet of Jesus, and as she uttered these words Jenny could see the hooded spectre whose breath she had thought she felt on her shoulders, they were all dancing, drinking beside the pool, she thought, while the spectre was there, was it a woman with a red, puffy face she'd seen on the other side of the fence, Augustino would be playing under a tree and an iron hand would close on him, no, Jenny had seen nothing, it was a memory from Mama's past, the blood she saw everywhere, in her thoughts and in her dreams, ever since she had denounced the sheriff, was she too visible, especially with this animal sensuality that was revealed with every move she made, she could be picked out anywhere, even when she was rocking Augustino on the broad veranda, passers-by did not even know that it was she, this black woman, who had denounced the sheriff, he would come here, he would emerge from the swamps, from the bushes

where he killed the eagle and the stag, he would take her
off again to his plantations, his land, oh, sleep my angel, as
at the feet of Jesus, and don't let that horrible shouting come
to us, murmured Jenny's voice in the evening air humming
with sounds whose strident din covered the song of the
cicadas, who was that shadow, its iron hand stretched out
towards Augustino's neck, his cape swelling as he ran beneath
the orange tree that yielded bitter fruit, was it the shadow of
the sheriff, the awe-inspiring shadows of his friends, of the
sailors, the hunters, the hooded phantoms who used to haunt
the swamps in the woods, decimating black men, hanging
them from trees, a muddy corpse bleeding in the sun amid
a cloud of mosquitoes, the Shadow reached out everywhere
under the burning sky, had the Shadow come back now, no,
even though Jenny was still quaking with fear, she carried her
fate like a banner, hadn't she had the courage to denounce
the sheriff, even though she was just a servant in the house,
for his despicable attacks on the decency of black girls, and
when she complained the officers of the law had told her
that a sheriff is always right, wasn't Jenny provoking acts of
revenge from a man who was respected by his people, Jenny
had no regrets, she thought, she'd had the courage to
denounce the sheriff and she'd do it again, watch out for that
girl Jenny, said the mayor to Daniel, because of her a sheriff
was put in jail, but Jenny was still quaking with fear, for they
emerged from the swamps, from the bushes, carrying rifles,
and suddenly a shadow appeared, gigantic, at the side of a
child who was busy at his games, and under the Shadow was
the outline of an iron hand ready to strike, to lacerate, the
hand of a predator, a human hand that would indiscrimi-
nately strangle a fox, a rabbit, that would decapitate a man,
later on Jenny would be one of those heroines whose stories
of defiance she often read in her illustrated book, though as

far as the whites were concerned these heroines were only vestiges, Jenny thought, their photos in the newspapers were surrounded by a line of ashes, they had been returned to the limbo of segregation, of oblivion, where they had always lived, Mélanie had told Jenny their stories, Mary Ann Shadd Cary, born in 1823, was the first black woman journalist on the North American continent, she had published the first anti-slavery newspaper in Canada, she had called on the heroism, the love of justice of the whites, but beneath the face of Mary Ann Shadd Cary, the first black woman journalist, as beneath the photographs of Crystal Bird Fauset, a specialist in race relations in 1938, leader of a democratic party in Philadelphia, or of Ida B. Wells Barnett, publisher of a newspaper advocating freedom of expression, of Nina Mae McKinney, the first black actress to perform in New York theatres, of Ida Gray, the first black woman dental surgeon in Cincinnati, why were all those faces surrounded by a line of ashes, still being assaulted on the other side of death as they had been during life, for insult and rejection still moved over them, so recent was the memory of their crusade against lynching, those assaulted faces demanded compensation for the insult after all these years, how much blood had flowed under the line of ashes, as it had in Jenny's dreams, even if she was safe here on the broad veranda, singing Augustino to sleep with Mama's inno-cent songs, was there a place for her in the whites' paradise — aside from here in Daniel and Mélanie's house — for the prowling Shadow was back, you could hear the words whistle, hiss as someone spat, as a woman, a man, a child said from the other side of the gate, through the branches of the orange tree whose bitter fruit would soon be blackened by the sun, those words, that hissing Jenny could still hear, go home, we're going to lynch you all, but sleep, my angel, Jenny sang, and don't let that horrible shouting reach our

ears, for he who died on the cross died for us too, and amid
the sighs, the lamentations of that jazzy voice, Augustino
closed his eyes, for it was night and soon Mère saw Jenny
climb the outside staircase with Augustino sleeping languidly
in her arms, he'd been so boisterous all evening, it seemed
unreal for him suddenly to be so calm, his arms dangling on
either side of Jenny's neck, in the position where sleep had
caught him by surprise, alone, Mère walked towards the
pool, when she was swimming this afternoon, she thought,
it had certainly seemed to her that the happiest days of her
life were those from the rather distant time when she had
been so eager to get up in the morning, at Augustino's age
or a little older, when she was still on the lap of her French
governess, from that stern woman's mouth she heard that
she would have a fine future, with her gift for languages, her
parents would send her to France one day, to the Sorbonne,
for graduate studies, or else the governess had wanted to
pass on to a little rich girl the hope of her own dreams, born
of an enslaved existence, yes, the governess had said in a
voice that was suddenly very confident, Mademoiselle Esther
learns so quickly, one day she may go to study in a great
university, in my country, and then I'll be able to see her
again, but I shall be very old, retired, or else, like many
people when they get old, I'll no longer be in this world, but
Mademoiselle mustn't get overexcited, she mustn't snitch her
brothers' cream cakes, Mère could hear the governess's strict
voice, would that loss leave her disconsolate forever, but
the boat trip with her parents had seemed to her too long,
suspiciously long, she should have anticipated, from the
slowness of that journey with her parents, that some tragedy,
some heartbreak was about to darken the dawn of her life,
and the governess's notion that Mère would one day be an
independent woman, that she would study at a university in

France, for a long time had nourished Mère's hopes, delighting her with the prospect of freedom unimaginable for a woman in her circle, but what did a diploma matter, it's true that in her student days Mère had been passionate about political science and later, about engineering, but what did obtaining a diploma matter when Europe would soon be set ablaze by the madness of dictators afflicted with senility, when thousands of young people were preparing to die for them, was it not foolish that at the time Mère had thought only of returning to America to start a family, for life would always be more powerful than death, and for a long time she had borne in her heart the dream of conceiving Mélanie, Mélanie, a new birth in a purified world, should she not wait until that world was less blood-soaked before she conceived Mélanie, and today Mélanie was over thirty, the mother of three sons, she had studied political science, what did a diploma matter when Mère had suddenly experienced the shame of resignation, like the breath from some far-off decomposition, over the joys of her life, always on the edge of her awareness, the vague memory of the Polish cousins had saddened her, they too would have liked to study in France, to attend some institution of higher learning, but the imponderable madness of those men had led them close to the swamps of the Dachauer Moos where, in camps that had been built for them, they'd been deported, exterminated, who was Mère in the face of the mystery of those dramas, the immensity of those tragedies, had she thought while she was walking with Samuel and Augustino on the high pier, above the tumult of the waves, that she was merely a speck of dust soon to be blown away by the eternal winds, and that dust, that life had been regulated by an invisible power, for that was as it should be, no doubt, gradually that speck of dust, that life would succumb to a progressive decline, such was the will of the power that regulated all humanity's movements, was Mère not bereft of answers in the face of the mystery of her life and those of her children and grandchildren, like the faces of handsome natives in Gauguin's paintings who turn towards the rose-coloured sky of their paradise saying, where do we come from, what will become of us, why are we on this earth, for a long time now those sleeping faces from the warm islands, those unclothed bodies brushed by the perfume of the tropical breeze, had no longer been lulled by the sensuality of our world, were they still asking themselves that question, who are we, where are we going, each of them, like Mère, only a speck of dust blown by the eternal winds, drifting towards the horizon, and every morning, every night, from the high pier, the white heron took off obliquely with the slow, majestic unfolding of its wings, from the platform of a pier, of a raft, onto the waves, Mère experienced then the indescribable joy of a life without boundaries, unlimited, that was what lay before her now, and to feel the joy, the appeasement of harmony restored, she had only to spend some time in lonely silence, and suddenly, whether it was night or day, alone, at the edge of the ocean, it seemed to her that the gods were coming to meet her, to murmur those lies in her ear, I recognize you, I know who you are, for I am or we are the authors of your life, the thought of those taciturn gods left Mère to muse on the brevity of life, the sweetness of the air that intoxicated her with its sugary fragrances as when she was in Daniel and Mélanie's garden, savouring the perfume of ripe oranges and lemons, and the clinging odour of the tree they had planted for Samuel, a fruit tree from another island that bore the name Lady of the Night, for its flowers opened only at night, was that not the perfume she was breathing now, telling herself that some exotic Japanese plant would have brought a note of calm here, to this garden setting which she was forever perfecting, completing, as she did the inside of the house, which struck her as much too heavy, there, on the patio, they should have had the finery of some birds of paradise in a vase on a table, and the brilliant flowering of bougainvillea against the door of the pavilion by the pool, but who in this house would ask Mère anything, she was merely a speck of dust soon to be blown away by the eternal winds, yet she had seen the white heron unfold its vast wings towards the sun setting on the sea, and she had thought, when everything is finished all will be as it should be, all will be well, suddenly she was not so tired as she'd been at the beginning of the night, no doubt it was because she could no longer hear Augustino's cries; a strange young man had just come through the garden gate, Daniel had not seen him entering, who was he, a beggar with an ambiguous smile beneath a Mexican hat, his skin was a dull brown, the expression in his eyes was vague, but as soon as his eyes were fixed on you, they were marked by a solicitous cruelty, who was he, Mère wondered, another of those creatures reduced to deceitful begging to whom Daniel and Mélanie would offer lodging, though neither of them would have noticed the individual lying in wait among their numerous guests, the young man's clothes were the same dull colour as his skin, he was holding a stick that had a thin silvery blade at its tip and the stick, its tip adorned with red paper garlands, could have looked like an elegant ornament had Mère not spied the silvery blade sparkling in the night, under the weight of the garlands that stirred in the warm breeze, Marie-Sylvie, who was also called Sylvie, walked surreptitiously along the patio wall, she handed the man a package that he stuffed into a brown pouch hanging from his shoulder, from that partly open pouch came a stench of rotted food, of embarrassing smells, Marie-Sylvie, her expression pained, said a few words to which he did not reply, then she ran towards the house, avoiding being seen, who was that individual, Mère wondered, Sylvie's husband, a brother, a friend, a refugee from far away like her, she who yesterday, in her own country, was called Marie-Sylvie de la Toussaint had been the only one that night to see what the expression in those staring eyes under a Mexican hat wanted to take in, the friend, the brother, he was as familiar as those White Horsemen of death, soldiers or young armed men who would soon be killed in their turn by the black gangs lying in wait for them under the palm trees, in Cité du Soleil, the city of mourning and sorrow when, piled up in the harbour, near beaches caressed by the waves, between two mounds of filth, streams of raw sewage, there were the corpses nobody had had time to collect and bury, the husband, the brother, the friend, the man who had been able to escape by boat was here, very close by, in this garden, Mère was thinking, that fixed expression in his eyes, which Sylvie had recognized at once, was that of his madness, he belonged — this brother, this husband, this friend, this ghost of a man — to a sect that was dreaded on the island for sacrificing animals in graveyards, and without blinking the young man's eyes had immediately seen, seized all of them, those he'd have liked to destroy on the altar of his sacrifices, on tombstones laden with roses, prey so tender it would be easy to cut, to open up Samuel and Augustino's parrots that were asleep now till morning in the birdcage under the roof of the broad veranda, the chicks, the rabbits, the cats, the dogs of the house, all those pets that were kings while men were to be pitied so, dying in the sewers, the scorching sun, Jenny was, who knows, the only one in this garden to recognize the all-consuming expression in those eyes over which was falling the veil of madness, a diabolically fixed stare that only adversity could explain, Marie-Sylvie had recognized the starving ghost of the young hunter who was, perhaps, her husband, her brother, her friend, bowed down by sorrow, she herself had fled, for the Cité du Soleil had lost all its light, never again would it be radiant, its children would laugh no more, shed no more tears, and she had been unable to do anything more than give the remains of the still-warm banquet to the man whose behaviour was suspicious, as if she wanted to make him forget his evil plans for the night, this young man who was her friend, her husband, or her brother and who suddenly had a terrible fixed gaze in his eyes, as on his dull face, Mère saw again the blade gleaming at the tip of the stick, under the red garlands, the young man left through the gate and Mère sighed with relief and wondered if she had been dreaming, her thoughts returned to the decoration of the garden, the house, to the preparation of vanilla desserts for the grandchildren, her husband had brought her a vanilla plant from a journey to Panama, she would extract the precious perfumed essence from its beans, the yellow blossoms of the climbing orchid would soon overrun the gardens, the fences around the yards, and the scent of spices, of vanilla would be even more abundant with the greater humidity of spring, and the heat as summer was approaching, one could only marvel that there were seventy species of vanilla and that Mère knew only the one plant with its aerial roots that her husband had brought her from Panama, the children would mainly enjoy the chocolate and vanilla cakes served with freshly picked raspberries, or did they still like dessert now that they'd grown, and Mère saw two little girls jump from a dormer window under the roof of the house, Jenny told them to come down, told them they'd wake the baby, and what were they doing up there, and when Mère heard Jenny speaking firmly to the little girls, she remembered her governess again, like Mère these children were obeying their mother, their governess, dressed in their Sunday best, so this was just the beginning of the festivities, thought Mère, with all these children turning up so late everywhere, in the doorways, the windows, wearing dresses adorned with jewels, all of them as pretty as their mothers, you could see that these children were wealthy and already insolent, they'd been prompt to obey Jenny's order though, one of them said that Samuel had a girlfriend called Veronica Lane, she'd read his love letters, how exuberant, how healthy were all these children around Jenny, these flowers that would only open at night, like the flowers on the tree they'd planted for Samuel this year, which resembled white lilies, Mère saw the young man again, saw his eyes, his frozen smile, those unhappy thoughts, why, she wondered, was it because of the emptiness she'd felt this afternoon, in the middle of the pool, while Jenny was rocking Augustino on the broad veranda, and was it true then what the child was saying, that Samuel was in love with a little actress who performed at the theatre with her father, it was Samuel who had taken the little girls to the dormer window under the roof of the house, Mère caught sight of him swinging his legs under the roof, through the dormer window, just a short time after he dived into the pool, he was shivering inside his short silk kimono, was it the coolness affecting him or were they shivers of a private and discreet pleasure, when would the girls' muffled laughter stream into the garden, those shivers, thought Mère, inside the silk kimono, the tapping fingers, the clapping hands of all these little girls on Samuel's neck, his chest, Mère had sensed the awkwardness of this first love-play, this timid touching, how soft Samuel's skin was, they said, laughing, too bad he was only eleven, would he take them out on his boat with him next Sunday, and one of the little girls had put on Samuel's sailor cap, saying, Samuel's in love, Samuel's in love, and in the bedroom with its lowered blinds Vincent was asleep, his breathing seemed calm, Mélanie came up often and bent over him, running up the stairs, asking Sylvie, Jenny, is there enough fresh air, it's time for his medication, all the women were listening to that quavering inside Vincent's ribcage, they could open the blinds but only a little, certain kinds of pollen could be fatal, and Jenny put her hand on Mélanie's shoulder, go back down now, Jenny said, he's a good little boy, Jenny said, he's sleeping now as if he were at the feet of Jesus, you shouldn't let your concern show, Mère had said to Mélanie, to her guests and her friends nothing should show, and Mélanie had a natural elegance and it seemed to her that none of her grave concern could be seen by her guests, and so Samuel was in love with Veronica, thought Mère, but she was a good ten years older, she was playing Ophelia, there were phone calls to Veronica in New York at night, love letters written on his father's computer, all this, in the garden the little girls had told Mère all this, and speaking to them as if they were grownups, Mère had asked why they felt the need to give away Samuel's secrets, because we love him, replied the one wearing Samuel's sailor cap, as if she were a woman, because I love him, she said, and Mère saw Samuel swinging his legs under the roof, cheered up by the chattering but locking up his secret, Ophelia, as he had seen her in the theatre, drowning on a bed of flowers, Veronica playing Ophelia with her father in the role of Hamlet, magical sets were put up for Samuel, the castle at Elsinore, the forests of Denmark, mazes of water and stone, reefs around the islands, the peninsulas where Ophelia sailed on her raft of flowers edged with snowy dunes, ah, why were they all living in this insular country when yesterday Veronica was still close to Samuel, at the theatre, hadn't she come to the house for lunch before a rehearsal, her car speeding through the streets of New York, hadn't she introduced Samuel to Maximilien, the twelve-year-old acting prodigy appearing on screens everywhere, whose salary was more than a million dollars a year, and one day that will happen to you too, Veronica had said, more than a million dollars a year, and Papa had decided they'd all go to live somewhere else, would Samuel, like Veronica and Maximilien, also become a victim of the acquisitive materialism of our time, they would all go to live on an island, was it for him, for Samuel, or was it on account of Vincent, of Vincent's breathing, that they were all living here, far from Veronica, was that what Samuel wondered, Mère thought, when would they be seeing him on the screen every evening, like Maximilien, Mère had seen a photo of Maximilien, the twelve-year-old acting prodigy, on his bedside table, what exuberance, what health, all those children in the doorways, the windows, Mère no longer regretted spending time with her children and grandchildren, this was as it should be, she thought, as it should be. And on the arm of that grizzled man, Renata had agreed to dance tonight, to the rhythm of those slow steps, bestowing her confidence on the unknown man while her gaze, impatient with desire, settled on them, on that chorus of young men in their sophisticated white suits, on those orchestra musicians who continued to stir in her the same rapture, the same sweet ecstasy, excited by the heat, by the humidity in the air, they were like the sparkling blue sea where she had not been able to swim this afternoon, after leaving the foreign exchange office where she'd encountered the grimy-faced man collapsed over his paperwork against the yellow wall of his kiosk, they were that blue, slack, triumphant sea that all at once she could not even walk towards without feeling a brand-new weakness in her body, during her convalescence, although she knew that the scar would heal

over, that the operation had been a brilliant success, she would
be forbidden to swim in the sea for a long time, she thought,
just as she was forbidden to smoke, and they, the orchestra
musicians in their white suits, were that incredible taste of
water and smoke, of a fire at the edge of your lips that makes
your gaze flicker, towards which every nerve in your body
strains, they were agile while the man she was dancing with
encumbered her with his weight, with his emphatic presence,
but she had accepted him as he was, saying nothing when
the grizzled man slipped his arm under hers, she would say
again as she'd said in the past, I want, I desire, with the same
body that in the past had been home to so many feverish
desires, although the doctor's success had been brilliant,
although all that was visible now was a small star-shaped scar
above where the lung had been removed, she had already
noted that the decline in her life forces was beginning, because
she was forbidden access to the salty water, just as she was
forbidden the taste of the cigarettes that burned away in her
fingers, while the orchestra musicians, like the whistling
gondoliers poling their Venetian craft, would be changeless,
or would change only to become more perfect, more virile,
as if they and the attributes of their youth were covered with
a thin coating of gold, like statues, they would not decline as
they worked their poles in the rivers, the waterways, what
would they ever know of those stabbing pains of desire that
women suffered for them, indifferently they would sail for a
long time on the sea-bound rivers, the seas, and Renata would
watch them, would watch one of them standing in his craft
and greeting her as he passed beneath the arch of a stone
bridge, or nodding to her between two low brick walls to
which prickly wild roses clung, but when they went away in
their boats, passing under other stone bridges, under the
vaults of other low rose-covered walls, she could not shake

off her desire to see them again, to have them close to her, and now their hair was still waving in the wind, an imprisoned swallow was flying low, as if it might brush those temples, that hair, and changeless too was the sky above them, a liquid azure in which were reflected the sea-bound rivers and the seas to which they would sail, singing, where on feast days they would cast off their boats to enter glorious competitions on the Adriatic, carefree, making their boats glide towards the winding roads of lagoons and beaches, above coral reefs, above muddy marshes, far from the temples, from fortresses and citadels, from cloisters and abbeys that would have weighed too heavily on them, and with the same smile, the same grace they would all disappear and Renata would never see them again, and the most charming gondolier of all, the one who stood as he poled and who had waved to her as he was passing beneath the arch of a stone bridge, among the rosebushes, would leave behind him in the warm wake of the water nothing but the memory of a hollow sensation of thirst, henceforth unquenchable, and whom did she suddenly see, while she was languidly dancing in the arms of an unknown man, he seemed to be coming towards her, carrying his violin across the raised platform, laying the instrument against his cheek with affectionate indolence, he had been looking at Renata with a playful expression as if to say, don't you recognize me, I'm the son of one of your friends, the boy was perhaps just a familiar figure she'd encountered in her circle of friends, he was seventeen, dressed as Samuel had been at the bar, in white Bermudas and knee-length socks, his hair fell straight, it was brushed and combed as if an attentive mother had cared for it, had burnished it, his face was healthy and tanned, he was perhaps something like a son of one of her friends, she wouldn't want to run into him standing near his mother, hadn't this adulated youngster looked down on her, this woman who was so much older than he was, like his mother, but here in this sensual garden the boy's cheerful smile, his mocking eyes that sought hers as he lovingly laid his violin against his cheek, this surprising apparition, like the gondoliers in their Venetian craft in the rosy light of the sun setting on the water, invited Renata to some fleeting moments of eternity, to some melancholy, piercing regrets that these moments had already existed, at a time when she had not hesitated to keep near her whatever pleased her, but now she was entering an unlit night, the man with grizzled hair had brought his heavy head close to her, he was leaning on her shoulder heavily too, already she could no longer see the cheerful smile of the boy who had resumed his place among the orchestra musicians at the other end of the platform, no doubt she would never again see that tender, still innocent child, and she thought that what sometimes brought her into such fierce opposition to her husband was the fact that he, who was himself a judge, judged the misdemeanours of youth so harshly, she could not believe — nor could he, no doubt — that these children born of woman, who were beautiful like the one she'd just been gazing at, surrounded by their mothers' affection, would be capable tomorrow of raping and killing, but he, Claude, knew that beneath the fingers that burnished their children's beautiful hair slept sinister dreams, dark acts of treachery that were hidden from generation to generation under their unsullied brows, the first wrinkle of cruelty, the mark of shameful victories could be read on their thin lips, from what had looked like a flower at his mother's side was born man, eager to destroy those close ties of blood, of tender pity that still joined them to a woman, Renata was fiercely opposed to everything Claude set forth in the courts, the judicial author-ities, the burden of judging others was men's business, but it seemed to her that a woman should have seized that power, with all the pity she felt for those close ties of blood, the flesh of man from which she could have extirpated, like roots, the terrible evils, the gangrene of the heart and senses decreed by ancient laws, but like other women she had yielded to the feminine tenderness that was filled with wonder before a male child, when the young musician had settled his laughing, impudent gaze on her, for it required little, she thought, to make her identical to all the others whose condition she shared, the humility of their sentiments, the mother burnishing with her fingers, with her vigilance, the hair on the heads of these men when they are still very young, the tanned shade of their skin, everything that for her was still so nearly the ardour of the senses, but was also the maternal love that had not been disappointed, when under that same brow, that same hair, Claude would have guessed at dark acts of treachery, at sinister dreams, none of the inevitability of those signs was visible to Renata, who had been born a woman and a mother and ennobled, she thought, by this single paramount aspect of her condition, she saw no perfidy on those pure profiles, those childlike profiles, and Julio bent over the silky pillow, already damp with tears and drops of sweat, where Vincent was sleeping in the big bed, his sleep peaceful now after the panic over his breathing in the twilit bedroom, Julio heard the gentle exhalation of Vincent's regular breathing and he thought that Ramon, Oreste, Nina, and his mother, Edna, would have breathed like this if they had lived, in twilit bed-rooms with lowered blinds, in the afternoon and evening they would have inhaled the strong scent of the jasmine whose yellow flowers dropped off into backyards, into gardens, deserting their country, their city, they had left so hastily on those rafts that were carried away by sudden blasts of wind from the high waves, with few provisions, a

lifebelt, a lifejacket would have saved them had they not all
been so poor and without a guide, alarmed by the urgency
of their departure, Edna went to wrap a modest shawl, some
cotton underclothes around Ramon, Oreste, concerned about
their dignity when they all arrived in port she would put on
their white shoes, for God watched over them all, she said,
someone would be waiting for them in that land of milk and
honey, towards the shores of paradise, let them just set sail
on the fragile raft and soon they would be provided with
water and light, far from the stench of their pathetic hovels,
when they arrived in port in the land of milk and honey, they
would be given something to drink, to eat, and so the lifebelt
or lifejacket had been forgotten, neglected, in the litany of
prayers for her children that Edna offered up to an implacable
Heaven, but in vain, resolute, daring pilots had long searched
the sky without seeing them or hearing their calls for help,
those whom the wind snatched from the frail masts of their
raft, homeland, land regained, it was over there, said Edna,
in that lush paradise where milk and honey flowed abundantly, the coast guard were awaiting the arrival of small boats
and rafts on their sunny shores, oh, only let her children not
lose courage, said Edna, for God was with them, but while
she was praying to Heaven for her family, wrapping up her
few possessions, covering Ramon, Oreste, Nina with her
rumpled shawl, slipping on the white shoes she had bought
with such difficulty, the land of milk and honey shone on the
horizon, but none of them would be saved, it would be too
late when Julio stole the lifebelt from a drowned man floating on the water, his face turned towards the bottom of the
sea, in his swollen rags, when the motor of the helicopter
Homeland rumbled below the thick clouds nothing would
be found of them but one of Oreste's white shoes, Edna's
shawl, Nina's doll, for they would never reach port, never be

provided with food or with water to quench their thirst, or with light, and Julio thought he could hear those winds raging on the waves around the raft, the growling of the water and the winds that swirled around him amid the thunder and lightning of hot nights, under the burning sun by day, the thirst made his lips sting, it tasted of the salty sea that would never quench the refugees' thirst, anyone who inadvertently swallowed that water would die from it, like Oreste, Ramon, Edna, whose heartbeats had fallen silent, other dark silhouettes lashed to the frail masts of their boats, their rafts, the short-lived manna of oil and antibiotics that brave pilots flung from their planes as they criss-crossed the sky, Ramon, Oreste, Nina, their mother, Edna, would not have survived even for an hour if they had been transported to other islands bathed by the Gulf Stream, never would they open their eyes on those archipelagos, those islets of prison camps that would be their brothers' fate, Edna's prayer had been granted, the merciless sky had saved her children from the stabbing thirst, thought Julio, for the flame of a stormy night had consumed those flies, those mosquitoes as they flew, Ramon, Oreste, Nina and their mother, Edna, specks of dust still swimming on the surface of the water, Oreste's white shoe, Ramon's hair, Edna's rumpled shawl caught in a fisherman's net, Nina's doll and its blind eyelids beneath a firmament of steel, others would gain this lush paradise where milk and honey flowed abundantly, Nina, Oreste, Ramon, Nina separated from her doll, all were sleeping now, far from the blue glimmers on the shore where the coast guard had been waiting for them during so many nights, so many days, they were sleeping now in the troubled waters of the oceans, that was how God had answered Edna's prayer, Edna who had been forgotten, neglected, she who was so alone and without a guide, the lifebelt, the lifejacket, for they would all be clean, shod in their white shoes, when they arrived in port, when they arrived in their new homeland of grass and of milk and honey, and sitting close to Vincent on the big bed, listening to the respiration of life reaching up to him, Julio had felt Jenny's hand touching his, it was unreasonable for Julio to keep wandering along the beaches at night, said Jenny, what good did it do to look out for beacons shining on the water, no small boat, no raft would come in at night, into the glittering green lights, except for the small boats of seafaring drug dealers, Julio would bring too much violence on himself if he kept wandering, they would not come back on those small boats, those rafts, what was he looking out for, for Ramon, Oreste, Nina, Edna, like so many others they were dead, and now they were at the feet of Jesus and his mercy, and if Julio had been saved it was to help his brothers, said Jenny, and as she lifted Vincent's head from the silky pillow Jenny saw drops of sweat, Vincent was having trouble breathing, she told Julio, soon it would be time for his medication, it was the night air, the damp night air, the moisture in the air that came in through the blinds, and pollen from the flowers, could Julio go down to the garden and call Mélanie, above all the poor angel mustn't be disturbed in his sleep, with his heartbeat speeding up beneath flesh that seemed as delicate as the petals of the roses whose pallor it shared, no, they would not come back, on those small boats, those rafts, for the currents of the tropical storms, said Julio, had carried them elsewhere, so far away, with the fishermen lost at sea and the adventurers killed by rival gangs, mosquitoes, flies that could no longer be distinguished, they were lifeless, buried in the light of the lantern, but Julio, stubborn or insanely dogged, would go to wait on the beaches every night, Ramon, Oreste, Nina, Edna, he was going to lose sleep, did he want to lose his sleep, lose his mind, when his brothers needed him so badly, said Jenny, every hour a horde of the living hoped they would be fished out of those unfathomable oceans whose shores they could barely see, and once the medication had soothed Vincent, Jenny saw again the nonchalant summer days when they had all been serene and happy, they never thought about that happiness, as if it were eternal, and perhaps it had been, for the duration of those days, standing on a terrace by the sea, a warm breeze scarcely brushing against her, under her swimsuit, Jenny saw Augustino, who was learning to swim with Mélanie, Samuel swimming on his back, and the clear, smooth water all around them, it was one of those days when the sea was calm, delightful, and Jenny could hear laughter and cries of joy, had it been yesterday, she thought, when Augustino, under Mélanie's admiring gaze, though he was already too boisterous and too fond of sugar, took his first steps along a beach, in the grass of a palm grove, a park, where Samuel was playing tennis, oh, had it been yesterday, before the birth of Vincent, his mother's sorrow when she had heard his laboured breathing, the sea air would invigorate them, weren't they always outdoors, with Jenny and their mother, loved too much, perhaps, but they would grow up quickly, let them enjoy themselves and sing as at the feet of Jesus, let them dance, for it was summer and it was a year now, with Mélanie and the children, since Jenny had been a servant in the sheriff's house, no white man debased her now, and the sheriff had had to appear in court, oh, had it been yesterday when Jenny could hear the children's joyous shouts, from a terrace, in the warm summer breeze, their laughter as they frolicked in the waves, when the tropical summer winds came up, the pastor's daughter Venus, that brazen child, at the hour when rich families walked their dogs, Venus would grab one of them by the collar and swim in the ocean by herself for a long time, nonchalantly, Jenny would listen to the snickering echo of the laughter that seemed to split the vast expanse of water, of sky, with airs of triumph, hallelujah, she thought, hallelujah, I shall be one of those who has nothing to fear on Judgement Day, hallelujah, hallelujah, had it been yesterday that Jenny was singing, dancing on the terrace in the warm breeze, before the children came running up to her, she promised to hold them so high on her shoulders, as high as the rosy tinges of the setting sun, until their father had finished writing in the bedroom with the blinds drawn, amid the humming of the fans, but sometimes night would come before he was ready to see the children, to sit with them at the table for the evening meal, what on earth could he be writing up there that made him so gloomy, so unfair to Samuel, oh, had it been yesterday, Venus, the pastor's daughter, sitting astride dogs with magnificent fur, white dogs, slender black dogs, the snickering echo reverberating in the sun, in the middle of the smooth surface of the water, when everything in Jenny's life seemed all at once to be so calm, so serene, had that happiness been only yesterday, Venus, the pastor's daughter, swimming among the guard dogs, the German shepherds, the dance of her arms and legs as they emerged gracefully from the water taming those wild beasts that had ferocious teeth but also gentle black almond eyes, the children's laughter, their cries in the water around Mélanie, and she, Jenny, who lifted them so high onto her shoulders, the milling of the waves, of all these lives, while Jenny stood on the terrace, let them relax, she thought, as at the feet of Jesus, for soon, like those explosive storms on the sea in the late afternoon, amid the dense, violent rains, would come those dark January mornings when Augustino asked his father if today was the day when all life on earth, the plants, the birds, would end, and Jenny, who was dressing Augustino for nursery school, heard the words Augustino had uttered, a very old man, he was saying, had said on television not to get ready for school or nursery school, it was pointless now, because a cloud of smoke was coming loose from the sky and in that smoke Augustino would never see his parents again, or his house, or Jenny and Sylvie, Papa as usual had asked for a little quiet until noon, when Samuel left for school he hadn't forgotten his fruit for recess or his tennis balls, but in this January dawn Augustino had understood that, just as fire devours the wings of butterflies, an underground flame was going to set ablaze the wings of schoolchildren, their clothes, so short on their bare legs, their schoolbags, the food they brought for lunch, a cloud of wings would swoop down on the world, of wings and blood like those Jenny saw in her dreams, oh, let them play in the waves with the dogs, let their mother give them loud kisses between water and sky, for the merchant of mourning would pass and how many more times would Jenny see her family and friends wounded, insulted, afflicted by all the misfortunes down here, on the dry red earth of Baidoa, their eyes devoured by flies, vainly huddling against their mother's empty breast, their skeletal shadows piling up the way their corpses would soon be stacked, in trucks, in common graves, on this arid land with no rain-clouds, they had been so thirsty, holding out their beggars' bowls, they who could not run away or who would die as they fled, would someone today give them the corn, the soya that would save them, would they walk in the sun, amid this torpor and this thirst, as far as the Red Cross canteen, numbed by heat, by hunger, they would wrap themselves in the envelope of their bones, of their crumpled flesh, as if in a coat, suddenly they would feebly refuse the rice that a few emaciated mothers could still offer them, the cattle had been killed, the earth of their ancestors, laid waste by the war, was now dying, and through the ranks of those corpses the hyenas would feed on strolled a general protected by his armed supporters, he wore civilian clothes and carried a silver-headed stick, indicating thereby that he was master of an undivided power, he was waiting, while the corpses rotted, for the return of the imminent sowing season, for the fall of an enemy dictator whose place he had taken, oh, how many times, Jenny wondered, would she see those women holding their bowls above their heads, above their eyes devoured by flies, above their half-starved children, how many times would her own family and friends be piled into trucks and then flung into common graves, for that was how the blood flowed in her dreams, amid a cloud of wings, of mouths, of hair, of flesh that was crumpled, melted in the ashes, flee or die, should she too have gone and joined some international rescue team as Mélanie had done in the past, let them enjoy themselves, let them play in the waves, for one dark January morning they would suddenly waken in the silent house, still in bed, and they would cry out for their mother, their father, who would no longer answer them, a passing general in a cloud of his own smoke, in civilian dress, surrounded by his armed supporters and carrying a silver-headed stick, would have killed them all without a sound, so that he would be master of this silent universe, absolute master of an undivided power, while to Jenny, who was standing on the terrace, the world had seemed so beautiful in the presence of Mélanie and the children swimming in the clear water, oh, may Augustino, may Samuel shout for joy, for those dark January mornings would soon be here when, waking, they would weep endless tears, tears like those butterflies adorned with all the rays of the sun, bursting open, golden, at birth, their wings would crumple silently in a candle flame, in lethal dust that would issue from the sky, let them hear the joyous echo

of their voices and their mother's loud kisses because, for
Jenny, each day was stamped with the memory of that happy
eternity she was living at the feet of Jesus, and she prayed
every day in the temple when her friend Venus, the pastor's
daughter, allowed herself to be corrupted by men, or followed
Uncle Cornelius into clubs of ill repute in the town, yet it
was for her, as for Jenny, that Jesus had been tortured on the
cross; and Luc's boat was pitching and tossing in the rolling
of the waves, so close to shore that Luc and Maria could still
make out the narrow boats lined up on the water, the small
floating houses and their balconies decorated with sirens,
with red and blue lanterns, where their festive friends were
still celebrating their marriage amid joyous euphoria that
would last till dawn, before they tirelessly went back to sea
on their small craft, their sailboats, for as they swung back
and forth in their hammocks, on their balconies, touching
the sea air as they stretched their feet out over the ocean,
they loudly proclaimed their freedom from land, where they
would never return to live, no one could dislodge them from
their ramshackle houseboats, never would they live anywhere
but on the water, they shouted, and Luc and Maria need only
do the same for their marriage to be perpetual enchantment,
but they must be cautious, for the patrol ships would shoot
to destroy these luxury liners that islanders would rent for
one festive night, they could smell hashish from a distance,
sniff the cargo of crack in the shape of ice-cubes hidden in
the jump seats, the benches in the cockpit, where the occu-
pants of the boat lounged around with phony expressions of
innocence, the soldiers of the sea were everywhere, but now
the boat with its noble and fluid lines was fading into the
starry night, thought Paul as he leaned on the railing of his
lonely balcony, and so Luc and Maria were married, were
going away without him, Luc and Maria, soon they would

cross the bay where Jacques's ashes had been scattered, it was as Jacques would have wanted it, a festive day, with balloons thrown up into the sky, a night for drinking champagne on the water, from a nearby fishing boat a fisherman had shone his lamp on them, saying, we've never seen so many ashes in this sarcophagus of the sea, and the wind won't carry them back to where they came from, what a stubborn person your friend was, and the fisherman's boat drew nearer and they prolonged the party, laughing wholeheartedly as they smoked their hashish-scented cigarettes, and now the boat was fading into the night, Paul would be alone, ah, what were the hopes of this couple, Luc and Maria, who were stunned by their own youth, their lack of experience, she a Cuban refugee and Luc, whose ashes would one day, in a year from now, in two years, for he knew the doctor's verdict, be mixed up with those of Jacques, beneath the water of the bay where tonight, at the rear of the swimming platform from which the boat's instrument panel had been moulded, he was making love with a woman, but let them love one another, let them sail so far away, over the peace of the water, thought Paul, with their secret stigmata, like their hero, amid gusts of wind, amid the giant waves, let them complete their tour of the world in eighty days, let them make it around the Equator, a slight couple, unfaithful, let them capsize, perish, it would take a mere marble to destroy the hull and keel of the boat, a marble, let them come back, let them escape those dangerous crews, they were not vigorous sailors proud of having sailed around Cape Horn, overcoming all obstacles, so healthy, so strong, they were only Luc and Maria, already the hull of their boat had been damaged by some serious cracks, but Luc had dreamed for so long on the piers as he watched the boats come in from the open sea, on the piers where he stood by night in the green, phosphorescent wake of his skates, he would go to Australia with Paul, he'd be a farmer, a cattle merchant, a horse-breeder, a family man, for he must conceal from his sight, as he had concealed them yesterday from Jacques's sight, those brown spots on his face, and all the silent pain the others couldn't see, let alone feel, for so long now Luc had been gazing at the elegant cruise ships moored in the harbour in the morning, but now let them love one another, let them sail through the peace of the waters, Paul would be waiting for them with Mac the cat on his knees, listening to the tinkling of the oriental bells at the gate to the garden, he would remember Jacques's words to Pastor Jeremy, come to my place, for the Valley of the Orchids, the paradise you talk about incessantly, is here, and they would come back from those storms at sea, for Luc and Maria were just a young couple stunned by youth, two fiancés, one of whom had released black balloons into the sky among the multicoloured party balloons, for that was how Luc drove away the evil omen, concealing it from his sight. And as he moved along the beaches at night in the green and phosphorescent wake of his skates, Luc would observe the fleeting light of beacons on the water stirred by breezes from the south; when Jacques had closed his eyes, he thought, the sun had been setting over the sea, between the pines on the military beach, Paul had removed from the emaciated face, from the hollow-seeming head, the head-phones whose wires still dangled from Jacques's ears, and the great Mass in C Minor that Mozart had written amid the joy, the effervescence of his heart was the music to which Paul in turn listened while he was roller-skating down the streets that lined the sea, that day Jacques had complained that he was thirsty, the day was blazing hot and no one seemed able to find shelter from the heat, it was as if the thirst consuming Jacques were drying the earth in the gardens,

curling the leaves of the Spanish laurel and the scattered
blossoms of the frangipani whose heady aroma Jacques had
breathed in even through the tremors of his vomiting, after
all the tremors, all the quavering, he had listened to that sublime music as his head fell back onto the pillow; complaining
of thirst, at the time of day when the turtledoves seemed to
be flying so low over the fences that Mac was chasing them
with dreams of munching them, with his drawn-out, gentle
meowing in the heat, from grotto-like bars where everyone
was seeking shade came the music of trumpets and drums,
the plaintive elegy of a woman's voice before the long silence
of these afternoons when the earth was blazing hot even so
near the water, on Bahama Street, on Esmeralda Street, while
fighting cocks dozed off on the lawns, it was the time of day,
thought Paul, when the doves and turtledoves flew away into
the blinding sky, and as Paul opened the cage of Jacques's
captive dove, whose neck was adorned with a pink ribbon,
he saw it fly away with the others, towards an endless horizon of blue and glittering seas, and he thought that in this
way the soul of Jacques was departing, irrevocably, was it the
Mass in C Minor he'd listened to so piously, or the Beethoven
oratorio, *Christus am Oelberge*, Christ at the Mount of Olives,
Paul was moving along the length of the beaches, in the
green and phosphorescent wake of his skates, henceforth, he
thought, surrounded by that sublime music, the Mass in C
Minor, Christ at the Mount of Olives, he reproached himself
for never having appreciated that music before today, how
absent-mindedly he had been living, falling asleep so many
nights to the sound of music that cast a spell over his senses,
how could he and Luc have spent the fever of their youth
otherwise, but now at the age of twenty, without warning,
without realizing it, they had fallen into a leprous old age,
before they'd had time to realize it, while they were trying

not to fall off their sailboards amid the blustering waves, or lulled by dancing in the discos, the baths at night, no, without realizing it, they were entering the final age of their lives, the age of cynical renunciation with its visible, purulent traces, they were handsome, they were young, if only this tragedy that was dogging them would cease its foul deeds, those affronts to their innocence, let Luc and Maria love one another, let them sail far away upon the peaceful waters, let them be free and proud, let them hear the low-pitched throbbing of the drums that the blacks played in the night, hear the plaintive elegy of a woman's voice on the water, Paul was moving along with them, in the green and phosphorescent wake of his skates, along these streets that skirted the sea, when the sun had tanned them too much, had turned them the same dark and fiery brown, like the fire that was devouring them, no doubt before they could abandon themselves they would have to take poignant precautions, thought Paul, those gentle touches must avoid contact with living flesh, Luc would dream about other similar kinds of languor, in attics, in the shade of the venetian blinds, when, to soothe the burning, the caresses were mixed with the bitter resin of aloes picked in the garden, the balm of that African plant could heal all wounds, Mac would hunt along the shore of the Atlantic, for doves and pigeons, with the tails of lizards between his teeth; the hibiscus would stay in bloom all year long, you would hear the tinkling of the oriental bells when Jacques came home in the evening, no, was it not rather the cantata *Davidde Penitente* that Jacques liked listening to, did he not know that in a few moments he would be washed, changed, and he asked candidly, isn't today the day I'll walk to the sea, tell me, isn't it today, and they would say, tomorrow, it will be tomorrow, and we'll go to the harbour together; and together they all would go, whether

on their own two feet or confined to bed, towards the light
that was shining on the beach, through the pines, and with
their headphones stuck to their heads that were getting thinner and thinner, they would listen to the Beethoven oratorio
some boorish critic had been dissatisfied with in the past,
claiming that the musical structure lacked some expressive
rigour, they would hear the angels' aria, the recitative by Jesus
on the Mount of Olives, how his Father Who was in Heaven
would banish from him the fear of death, whether on their
own two feet or confined to bed, the same light would guide
their flock in the direction of the night, already they would
see the soldiers' spears at their side: how would their father
banish from them the fear of death, only let this tragedy
cease, thought Paul, these foul deeds that were dogging
them, Luc would return, disappointed, from his savage
wedding, they would set out for Australia, they would be
farmers, cattle merchants, horse-breeders, heads of families,
for they would be healthy, young, and alive, happy everywhere in this land of milk and honey, their paradise; the
great Mass in C Minor that Mozart had written amid the joy,
the effervescence of his heart, now Paul in turn was listening to that sublime music which praised the beauties of the
earth, it was the time of day when doves and turtledoves
flew away into the blinding sky, the cage had been opened,
thus would Jacques's soul fly away, irrevocably, after a day
when the earth had been so dry and blazing hot, when he
had several times asked his friends, Paul and Luc, why, dear
God, why was he so thirsty, when would the fountain's thin
thread of water flow in the garden again, under the baking
sun, then he had closed his eyes, thought Paul, because at
last the sun was setting over the sea, they had all heard in
the distance, was it on Bahama Street, on Esmeralda Street,
the low-pitched sound of the drums, later they heard the

drawn-out notes of the trombones that, on the Mount of Olives in the Beethoven oratorio, had heralded death. But, Mère thought, the party was just beginning, with all those children in the doorways, in the windows, and the adult couples drawing in around the pool, under the starry sky, it seemed to her now that Mélanie had been listening patiently during their conversation on the swing that afternoon, when Augustino was still asleep on the broad veranda, Mère had feared that she was just a tiresome old woman like so many of her friends, what was she saying to Mélanie, while the warm air vibrated with a duet by Puccini to which they had listened together, he was so brave to have composed that music, Mère had said in a knowledgeable tone that her daughter bowed to, and Mère had gone on to express her delight with what she was currently reading, it was then most of all that she worried about boring Mélanie, when she talked about some books by a Japanese psychiatrist who recommended that his patients feel gratitude to life rather than self-deprecation, they could all translate into a written reflection their gratitude for benefits received, that Buddhist ode to life troubled Mère, who, like the psychiatrist's patients, had undertaken an epistolary relationship with herself, gratitude contained a clear equilibrium, a harmony, what had we given our parents in return for life, for good fortune, now Mère was enumerating all her own chances for happiness, and her children's, at this very moment, and while Mélanie was looking silently at her mother, several scenes had unfurled in Mère's mind, it had seemed to her that she was reliving a trip to Egypt with her husband, it was shortly before a difficult period of betrayals or infidelities, when Mère had retreated into a shadowy chill that had lasted for several years, never would she speak to her husband in front of the children at mealtime then, no grief could have brought them back together, at the death of one of their parents they confronted each other at the graveyard, how sad for the children was this spectacle of her affliction, today Mère no longer thought as she had in the past, it seemed normal to her that men should have mistresses, why not see it as an accommodation for the legitimate wife, who could gradually resign herself to her duties towards the children, Mère had been seen at her husband's side in the white limousine, they had been going together to take their sons to the colleges, the universities they were to attend in the fall, Mère remembered them sitting in the back seat of the limousine, it had been her husband's idea, not hers, for them to attend those expensive universities, quickly applying her makeup in a miniature mirror she held at eye level, Mère read in her sons' gazes, reflected in the surface of the mirror, the capricious disdain they felt for their mother since her husband had been deceiving her, yet it was she who every year had dressed them in their elegant green sweaters under navy blazers, before returning them to the gymnasiums of their colleges or universities, where they excelled at all the sports, it was while thinking about the two boys in the back seat that she would write to herself, as the Japanese psychiatrist recommended to his depressed patients, her ode to life, her gratitude for having received so many benefits from life, but her sons would never console her for her shame, her ode to life would be for Mélanie, her only child, it sometimes seemed to her, too bad she'd gone to Africa shortly after the journey on the Nile and her grandmother's funeral, during that period of malediction when Mère had retreated into a shadowy chill, too bad that Mélanie too had thought she would marry, have children, of course she must thank God for the benefits she had received, that Puccini had composed *Madama Butterfly*, had understood the drama of the woman, the pitiful drama of the bourgeoisie of which Mère was part, she who had lost the love of her French governess and then that of her husband, over some question of debauchery, he was a plastic surgeon of some renown, what a weakness in a man who was otherwise flawless, she must feel gratitude rather than anger, rather than self-deprecation, didn't the Japanese researcher denounce the blasé ills of the West, guilt, depression, the colds and flus of our day-to-day lives that would kill us eventually, he said, nirvana on earth could be attained only through good, in a cycle of repeated rebirths, would Mère relive again the same life, would she see again in her mirror the hard gazes of her sons, sitting in the back seat of the white limousine, asking herself, what have I done to deserve this hell, was it the duet from Puccini's opera that brought back those moments when her sons had judged her; although a non-believer, Mère was a follower of Buddhism, she was thinking, that trip to Egypt with her husband suddenly seemed like one of those benefits received from life, the temples in front of which their cruise ship was moored, the tombs of the princes, the peaceful waters of the Nile, the night they'd spent together on the boat when Mère still had the illusion that she was a woman who was loved, who was lusted after, when night fell little by little over the temples of the gods, over the silence of the night, and their boat furrowed the river, they seemed to love one another still, to appreciate the restful hours of the siesta, amid the whistling of the boat's engines, it was on the waters of the Nile, lost in the sumptuous capitals of a thousand-year-old past, that they heard at night the monotonous drone of the muezzin's call to prayer, it seemed to Mère that nothing emerged from the ruined princely tombs of ancient civilizations but a crowd of slaves, figures of women doing the laundry, thin peasants bent over their ploughs under the red rays of the sun, near these dirt roads, near these hills of sand where rice or sugar-cane was grown, obeying the imperturbable cycle of rebirth that would bring them to the nirvana of the humble builders of temples in the past, they had inscribed upon the walls of temples, of pyramids, the offerings of their sweat, of their blood, and today, still at the feet of those crowned heads they had served, they were hauling stones down the congested waters of the rivers, unloading their portion of stones onto the wharfs for their brutal masters, what would Mère have done if she had been that woman doing the laundry among her children, that exhausted man unloading stones onto a wharf all day long, was it during a stop at Esna, on the outskirts of the desert, that Mère had experienced her first doubts, for any woman who was still young and beautiful would attract her husband's gaze, an uncomfortable inflection in his voice had betrayed his impatience, in his profession he was constantly in the presence of pretty women, he said, she shouldn't bother him with those misgivings, he was a man, and Mère had known that after the restful hours of siesta on a cruise ship, she would live through that distressing phase, she thought, one that was compromising for her family and friends, for what would she say to Mélanie when she returned from her mission in Africa, how would she tell the boys that their father would not be with them this summer, for their vacation, was it a duet from Puccini's opera that was taking her back so far, the music of Italian composers always produced these heart-breaking recollections in Mère's soul, Mélanie had listened silently to her mother, hands crossed on her knees, in the swing, it was not until later, Mère thought, that, holding out her hand in the hot, humid air, Mélanie had made a brusque move towards her mother, as if Mère had become the tiresome old woman she didn't want to be, who resembled her friends at tea-time, idle, chattering women

smoking on chaises longues at the end of the day, in gardens
maintained by their servants, was it true that for her daughter just now, she was a faded flower to be tossed onto the
sidewalk, whose petals had only to decompose, to wither,
along with her reminiscences and the phantoms of a life
that had now vanished, the heart-breaking memory of a duet
in Puccini's *Madama Butterfly* or *Tosca*, didn't everything
belong to Mère, the pyramids of Upper Egypt and Puccini's
harmonic audacity, the dogmas of Buddhism, the religious
music of Vivaldi, they were countless, the benefits Mère
had received from life, the great Japanese therapist would
have urged her to begin her hymn to life with the names of
Daniel and Mélanie, her beloved children, the names of her
sons Édouard and Jean would be inscribed on the paper
next, but how embarrassing was the memory of their presence
in the back seat of a limousine, wasn't Mère very satisfied
that they were both in good health and so successful, yes,
on the swing Mélanie had listened patiently, showing concern, agitation only at the approach of bad weather, for
contrary winds were rising over the Atlantic, but it was an
apprehension Mère dared not acknowledge, for wasn't there
suddenly, in the way Mélanie moved, in her hand held out
into the hot, humid air, in the brightness of her brown eyes
under her pageboy haircut, in her wilful profile, something
of her father, a hint of him that still weighed on Mère
through her daughter, as if she were still merely a faded
flower to be tossed onto the sidewalk, a woman to be lied
to, for Mélanie didn't tell her everything about Vincent, why
should Mère's love for her daughter be tinged with that
shadow, the breath of a new life, and would there be a new
life for a long time still, Vincent's breathing, but the benefits
Mère had received from life were countless, countless, with
the appearance of all those children framed in the doorways,

the windows, the party, the festive nights were just beginning, and wasn't it always like this, Mère thought, the old generations did not resign themselves without pain or disgust to the coming of the new ones, for the petals of those who had been flowers were decomposing, withering, and in the palm of her open hand Sylvie could make out the heartbeats of the parakeet, it was Augustino's parakeet, the one whose orange plumage around the eyes and beak were shaded with a rosy colour, fly, my angel, you must fly, Sylvie was saying, the bird fluttered its wings feebly but did not raise itself up, the pulsations died away in Sylvie's hand, the orange plumage shaded with a rosy colour was icy now like the heart beneath the feathers, it was as if they were stiffening under a freezing rain, and Marie-Sylvie de la Toussaint could see the shadow of her brother at the garden gate, let him go away with the still-warm banquet food and never come back, let him be driven far from here, she thought, and she was also beseeching God to have pity on the man who was known in his village as He Who Never Sleeps, for her brother had been responsible for watching day and night over the shores of the ocean where the enemy would appear amid bursts of machine-gun fire, what sobbing, what weeping there would be at dawn when Augustino ran through the grass towards his parakeets, his chicks, he would see the chick house, the roost, empty, and masses of orange and blue feathers shaded by a rosy colour stuck to the compartments of the cages, their wings and their pale gold feathers would drop away from the silvery blade at the end of his stick, and at night, in the silence of the streets, they would hear that stick which belonged to Sylvie's demented brother, hammering at the iron gates, at the fences with its silvery blade beneath the garlands, for heavy with blood was the shadow of He Who Never Sleeps, of the Watcher of the Dead on the shores of

Cité du Soleil, curled up under his Mexican sombrero in the peace of a cemetery, laughing foolishly, he now was grinding the birds' hearts between his incisors, their tender flesh, the fibres of the rabbits and piglets he had sacrificed, no longer remembering that peaceful time in the village of God-Is-Good by the ocean, with Marie-Sylvie and his brothers, when he had been a naïve fisherman and salt worker, stretching out at night on the beaches, a pious child in the village of God-Is-Good, where he attended the priests' school, it was one of the priests who had been their saviour, coming to their rescue in his motorboat, Marie-Sylvie de la Toussaint had heard her name in the burst of machine-gun fire, come with me, the priest had cried, the sea is your only refuge, and so they would head for the Bahamas and all those who didn't leave would succumb to the machetes, the sabres, under bursts of machine-gun fire, already the putrid smell of the corpses dug up by half-starved dogs and pigs filled the village of God-Is-Good with a foul smell, had it been the hunger or the thirst on the boat that had sickened the mind of He Who Never Sleeps, or was it the dysentery that had carried off three of his brothers, he saw them again, crawling through the sand, soiled with excrement, delirious from thirst, thirst as painful as the cramps from their red diarrhea, or did he suddenly have no memory of them all, the skin of He Who Never Sleeps, thought Sylvie, that olive skin beneath the broad sombrero, was made of animal tissue like that of the beasts he hunted for food, it was old leather tanned by the sun, the blade had drawn some lesions there, the blade at the end of a stick from which the wing of a chick came away, a pale yellow feather under the impulse of a macabre ritual celebrated in a graveyard, what tears there would be at dawn tomorrow when Augustino saw the empty cages, and what would Sylvie say to Augustino's mother before he wakened, Jenny and Sylvie would fix everything, for on Easter morning they would buy from the merchant the most sought-after birds on the island, the parakeet, the hummingbird, with their fingers they would smooth the wing of the topaz colibri, the red ibis, the Cuban couroucou, the pelicans and the green-feathered peacocks would stay in the garden, along with the fish in the pond, for children's tears are an insult to God, said the priest who had been their saviour, and from now on the sea, only the sea, would be their refuge, but how many murdered bodies had been pulled out of the laguna in the village of God-Is-Good, how many rebels had been executed, victims offered and carried away by the water that rushed in with the waves of the sea, for soon they had to run to the sea, board boats only to collapse under the trail of fire roaring from the beach, was it the fever of a contagious disease that had sickened her brother's mind, was it hunger or thirst, while as for Marie-Sylvie, she remembered the voice of the priest pronouncing her name, Marie-Sylvie de la Toussaint, amid the burst of machine-gun fire that assailed them from all sides, in the distance they would see their goats, their sheep wounded on the yellow grass of the hills, the killers would have murdered their parents and grandparents in their houses, for a long time they had sailed this bloody sea, along the shores of the once luminous city, Marie-Sylvie, listening to the beating of Augustino's heart, in her arms, her hands, he was as small as the parakeet, the rabbit that belonged to her little brother Augustin, had that heart stopped beating under the bursts of machine-gun fire, Marie-Sylvie dared not open her hand for fear she would see blood streaming there, but he was alive, Augustin was alive, that was how the coast guard would lift him in their arms when they washed up on their shore, O paradise of milk and honey, Augustin is smiling and full of life, his sister would hold him to her breast as if he'd been brought to her from his cradle, in his swaddling clothes, Augustin would have miraculously survived and was making his way towards her above the ship's lines, paradise, a land of milk and honey, for it would all be fixed, thought Sylvie, the grief and the sorrow, Jenny and Sylvie would buy from the bird merchant the topaz colibri, the parakeet with the orange and blue plumage, the red ibis, the bird of paradise, the Cuban couroucou, and later, when the junta's soldiers had finished looting and massacring the village of God-Is-Good, when the carcasses of its last goats and sheep lay rotting in the sun, Marie-Sylvie would hear that voice on the sea, would it be the voice of the priest who had saved them, or that of her demented brother pounding the iron gates, the fences around the houses with the blade at the end of his stick, amid the night-time silence of the streets, Marie-Sylvie de la Toussaint, the voice would say, now that everything has been looted, destroyed, go back with your brother to the village of God-Is-Good, go back to your country with He Who Never Sleeps. And Mélanie saw her mother, who was walking alone by the pool amid the twinkling lamps in the garden, their conversation on the swing this afternoon, thought Mélanie, had been darkened by the acquisition of the Greek painting during a visit to the antique dealer, had Mère insinuated that Mélanie lacked taste, discernment, in buying that painting, I don't understand, she had said, as strict with her daughter as always, why you chose that painting when so many works of art exist that inspire serenity, the subject of that painting is upsetting, and isn't the painter an unknown, his signature in Greek characters is illegible, of course it was a naïve and deeply moving picture, but was it worthwhile seeing it on the walls of Daniel and Mélanie's house from now on, was it the approach of Mère's old age that was complicating everything, thought

Mélanie, where was their sweet complicity of old, when they would go walking together, hand in hand, visiting the Louvre, travelling together to the most beautiful cities in the world, all the museums, Mère said, they must see all the museums, they would never separate in summer when her brothers were sent off to board in Switzerland, or to summer camps where they would practise horseback riding, water sports, and then, grabbing her glasses, Mère had studied the painting from close up, sighing with a pained expression, ah, those poor women, those poor women, but when did this happen, she suddenly asked Mélanie more sharply, was it at the time of the Turkish invasion of Greece, or during the intervention of the Egyptian army, and silently Mélanie had looked at the picture, her eyes seemed riveted to the scene depicted there, seven, eight, ten women, so many, all the women depicted in the Greek artist's picture were standing in a row, leaning against a low stone wall, each of them hugging an infant in a shawl to her breast, awaiting her turn against the background of the city in flames, beneath a smoke-filled sky, waiting to hurl herself into a gorge with her small child, it was that unbearably real scene, during an occupation, that had upset Mère, Mélanie was thinking, as if Mélanie herself were not a mother too, like every one of those women fleeing the insurrection, the mutinies, it was, said Mère, a time of wars succeeding one another, war after war between Greece and Serbia, and so many other occupations would follow in our time, the poor women, all of them so young, preparing to die with their first-born, without a struggle, their forms swayed one by one towards the gorge, and the child knows nothing of what is happening, he is trusting, he won't even feel the fall, his skull will be quickly crushed against the branches in the gorge, the stones, Mère was reciting these words, thought Mélanie, like a lesson learned by heart, she was not affected by them, for the subject of the picture offended her taste, her sense of what was beautiful, the blaze of the sky and the burning city seemed to her too purple, a vulgar dark red, and as for the poor women leaping into the gorge, Mère could only pity them, was it not their maternal duty, she said, to fight for survival whatever the cost, and under the smoke-filled sky, behind the low stone wall where the women were standing in a row, Mélanie could see the humble peasant women's looted land, the merchants had deserted the harbour, in the ruined streets the shops were closed, how would they be able to feed their children when, as in any insurrection, any mutiny, the town notables, the high clergy had left with whatever belongings they could bargain away, hadn't the world and the jewel that was Greece always belonged to them and to their cavalry, but Mélanie knew she would no longer share these thoughts with her mother, for Mère was upset by the real scene in the painting, it was too distressing, she said again to Mélanie, and where did Mélanie intend to put the painting, and that duet in Puccini's opera, the duet they used to listen to together, sitting side by side on the swing during Augustino's nap, that duet, those voices were wonderful benefits received from life, said Mère, did Mélanie sometimes think about everything she had been given by life, for life itself, said Mère, was a benefit, Mère had read a Japanese psychiatrist who urged his depressed patients to feel gratitude, appreciation, and Mélanie saw the sky filled with smoke, and Vincent, Augustino, Samuel flinging their arms around her neck, clutching at the folds of her dress, as it passed over the republic of Ukraine, through the hair of small children, the cloud had transformed them into a multitude of hairless youngsters with leukemia, on the edge of the grave, the plutonium cloud gliding across the Atlantic with the contrary winds, an infinitesimal drop on this January morning and Augustino coming in from his nursery-school games without his blonde curls, with no eyebrows or lashes, the terror in that naked gaze under the eyelid, the unspeakable fear Mélanie would read in the gaze of her sons would already have hurled her into the gorge in her turn, for the occupier was nearby and the sound of his cavalry had been heard, early on this January morning when the children were still in their beds, was it the approach of old age or the nerve-shattering recollections that the music by Italian composers stirred in Mère's soul, Mère no longer paid attention to Mélanie's concerns as she had in the past, the music, like the works of art in a museum, seemed to have been created only for her amusement, she was frivolous, all taken up with outings and diversions, she denied the apocalypse of that infinitesimal drop of plutonium above the Republic of Ukraine, gliding with the contrary winds onto the Atlantic, into Augustino's hair, into Vincent's breathing, which it had perhaps caused, Vincent's laboured breathing which that drop of plutonium had suspended, and that naked gaze beneath the eyelid with no lashes — how would Mélanie bear it for one moment, the young peasant women in the picture had lived for a long time in a paradise of blue water and sky, picking cotton in an abundance of fruits and veg-etables from the earth, they would never have believed, thought Mélanie, that one day they would be without fresh fruit and raisins, until one of them saw that flame in the sky, it was above the port of Piraeus, she ran to warn her sisters and her friends and they took their children with them, many of them would stay together that way near the gorge, lean-ing towards the grave, during every occupation, Bulgarian, Italian, or German, every time they saw that fire in the sky, they were drawn, dry-eyed, towards the gorge, for all was lost, all was lost, Mélanie saw her mother walking by herself amid the twinkling lamps on the tables in the garden, she was sorry she had allowed herself to gesture impatiently towards her, in the afternoon when the contrary winds rose over the ocean, what Mère, who had perhaps only a few years to live, thought Mélanie, hated about the painting purchased from the antique dealer was the reminder of her own end, it was a lapse in judgement, in taste on Mélanie's part to have chosen that picture, to have talked with Mère about it while Augustino was asleep on the broad veranda and the birds were cooing, when Mère aspired more than anything to have Mélanie hear her music, a love duet from an opera, Mélanie had her father's strength and independence of character, but his insensitivity too, she thought, and now that duet from an opera by Puccini haunted her soul, Mélanie admired her father, who had come from a modest background, he'd never had the arrogance of the ruling classes even though little by little, because of his harsh nature, he began to resemble those he disliked, what would he have been without Mère's generosity, and what would Mélanie have been, was Mère guilty of the cloud of radiation gliding over the Atlantic, gliding around Augustino's hair, around Vincent's breathing, poor Mère, thought Mélanie, may she preserve the naivety of those whom time wears down slowly, without damage, and perhaps leaves intact, over a book, over some bedtime music, Mélanie was not of her mother's time, the time of the exodus and the Polish cousins, of Great Uncle Samuel, shot up against the barracks of hell, whose name Samuel bore, she belonged to the time of a January war, when the president of a country spoke on the radio, on television, before the children were wakened in their beds, in these days of spontaneous wars and environmental exoduses, the towns, the villages in the Republic of Ukraine had been stripped bare like their hairless children, like the leaves on their trees, tourists came from far away to see those ghost towns, ghost villages, where irradiated peasants in their isbas would offer them vodka to drink beside a fireplace whose flame seemed to be burning the snow, its extent visible from the dwelling built of fir, and yet that city, that snow were quite dead, as were the peasants and the vodka with which they warmed themselves, for without the tourist business, which would have rescued them, it was called the dead city of Chernobyl, tourists would come there with their guides, nothing could be seen now of the lethal cloud that had contaminated the hogs and the cattle, and in the spring, the summer, in the dead city of Chernobyl, new divinity of tourism, each of those who were deceased continued to eat the pumpkins, the potatoes as they'd done yesterday, in the festivities of a rural life that was also dead, and they invited one another to the isbas, laughing at the risk of radiation so high that everything in the city was bald and dead, like the trees with no sap, with no leaves, under snow or sun, in summer as in winter, but Mélanie thought, how could Mère be guilty of those contrary winds on the Atlantic, of the existence of that drop of plutonium mingled with the air, the water, the light above the Republic of Ukraine? Mélanie was reassured to see Mère in conversation with an architect friend of the family, she was about to design a new decoration for the house and garden, and what was that pavilion near a fountain under the oleanders, a luxury, to the murmur of voices was added the applause that met Samuel's daring dive from the upstairs window into the pool, the crystalline laughter of very young girls burst out in Samuel's direction from all sides of the garden, from the veranda, these festivities were for him, thought Mélanie, everything would be a celebration for Samuel, his boat moored at the marina, the silk

kimono he'd received from Jermaine's mother, which Jenny
would wrap around his dripping shoulders, this party, this
banquet, and he was always happy, thought Mélanie, sometimes, when he emerged from the water, from the pool, the
ocean waves, amid the spraying perfumes of water and air,
he would press his body against hers, in silence, but now his
brown cheeks flushed more readily, she stroked his long back,
Samuel had grown some more, he who was so handsome by
day, as Daniel was by night, though she must stop Augustino
from climbing into their big bed before morning, for a long
time the young peasant women in the gorge depicted in the
Greek painting had lived in a paradise of blue light and
water, never lacking fresh fruit, and like Mélanie they had
experienced the exaltation, the joyous sensuality of life with
their husbands, their children, in their fields while their
flocks grazed, they were intoxicated by the perfumes of the
eucalyptus, like Mélanie they had gazed out at the sea
sparkling in the light of the setting sun while their bodies
gave off dizzying desires for love, for life, before the cloud,
the flame, the combustion in a summer sky froze them all on
the edge of the gorge, their newborns now as heavy as
lead weights at their breasts, before Mélanie became aware
that contrary winds were rising over the Atlantic, but from all
sides of the garden, from the verandas, the sounds of cheerful voices rose up towards Samuel, thought Mélanie, and
hadn't she been promised that in a few months Vincent would
be more robust, Mélanie would have only strong and healthy
children, how impatiently they would all look forward to
Vincent's first steps on the beach where the egrets landed, on
Thursday Mélanie would read her paper to the city's women
activists, Julio needed a new suit, Jenny would take Augustino
to the dentist in the afternoon, that duet from an opera by
Puccini was haunting Mélanie's soul and when, during this

dawning century, would Mélanie hear the works of Anna
Amelia Puccini in a concert hall in New York or Baltimore,
the works of all those forgotten Anna Amelias, the compositions by Anna Amelia Mendelssohn that her brother Felix had
sometimes appropriated, for Anna Amelia's father hadn't
liked his daughter's works to be performed in public, who
knows whether Anna Amelia was a virtuoso violinist like
Vivaldi, an orchestra conductor obedient to the obligations of
her charges, she had been choirmaster in convents, in monasteries, rigid institutions that took in orphans, she had been
restricted to the quick composition of music for the Divine
Office, to syrupy, more powerful music for vespers, she had
been an abbess during the twelfth century who composed
entirely liturgical music, a princess of Prussia insisting that her
compositions be played at court, where she had written
marches, compositions for the court's parades, she had been
poor, she had taken her music away with her to be buried in
the ditches and gorges, where her own compositions slept as
did her children, her music still dissonant from the tremors
of her time, from the gallop of the black horses of plague
and cholera over entire cities, but in what new century, in a
concert hall in Baltimore or New York, would Mélanie hear the
music of Anna Amelia, a fragment rediscovered in a monastery,
a convent, a fragment so tenuous it would barely be audible,
opening an encyclopedia on the arts Mélanie would see the
name of Anna Amelia among the six thousand names of female
musicians, composers, although Anna Amelia Mendelssohn's
father hadn't liked his daughter's works to be performed in
public, although her brother Felix had appropriated their
lasting quality, suddenly that fragment would be a symbol of
bruised echoes and fractures, who knows whether Anna Amelia
had been a virtuoso violinist like Vivaldi, of the fifty pieces
she had composed since her childhood in the monasteries,

the convents where she'd been choirmaster, nearly all had been taken away with her and her children to be buried in ditches and gorges, where, stripped of everything because of her burdens, her obligations, she had also thrown away her soul, thought Mélanie, it was the Puccini duet that was now haunting Mélanie, while bursts of laughter and happy voices came from all around her, and Venus's alto voice humming the rhythms she'd sung in church that morning, it was a disrespectful voice, slightly drunk, that rose up, solitary, from the stage during the musicians' break, Mélanie listened to the syncopated modulations of that voice, which showed so little respect for the music written by whites, and she thought that the song expressed an irrepressible rage between Venus's clenched teeth, she could hear in it the clanking of the chains of slavery, and against the background of the starry sky could be seen as well the burning houses of the black community of Bois-des-Rosiers, for a delegate, whom no witness had seen get out of his car during the fire, had given the order to wipe out this town and its thorny rosebushes, for all time, among the perfumed flowers in the copses, Sylvester and his dog, Polly, and Sarah, Sylvester's mother, had all fled through the woods, the forests, while their houses burned, looking between the branches, frightened, at the onslaught of fire and men in the town of Bois-des-Rosiers, a mob of men and their dogs sniffing at their footsteps on the paths, Sylvester and his dog, Polly, Sarah, they would all see, through the torn veil of winter foliage, in the cold, they would see the boards of their shacks collapse, see their town collapse in the smoke, under projectiles, under loads of gunpowder, a delegate had given the order to acquire all that ammunition, although he remained very calm in his car, waiting for the massacre to end, smoking his cigars, and very close to them Sylvester, his dog, Polly, and his mother, Sarah, saw the black man everybody was looking for, accused of having talked to a white woman, the panting of the pack of dogs, the pack of men, filled the night, and beneath the cold starry sky Sylvester saw the man being whipped against a tree, among the thorny bushes, they were whipping him with a rope while asking him to confess his crimes, at what time had he spoken to the woman, was it in her house, the muscles in the man's face, in the night, had been lacerated, the tendons of his neck torn by the fibrous threads of the rope, by the men's leather belts, and suddenly the muscles, the tendons were no longer shuddering and the woods, the forests howled with the cries of men and their animals around the man tied to a tree, one held a rifle, the other a rope, though no muscle, no tendon was shuddering now on that face in the night, that night Sylvester and his dog, Polly, his mother, Sarah, had all watched their town burn, hidden, buried in the woods, in the copses, and for a long time to come they would remember, while Venus's voice rose up, disrespectful of the whites' music, thought Mélanie, her song of irrepressible rage still rattling the chains of slavery, the ashes of the fire deliberately set in the town of Bois-des-Rosiers, the syncopated modulations of Venus's voice would haunt Mélanie's soul, would it be tomorrow, tonight, that the descendants of Sylvester, of Sarah, would emerge from the woods and in their turn demand justice, redress with whip and rope, Venus's voice rose up, lascivious, laughing, on the stage, an irrepressible song of rage. And they alone were still sitting around the same table, amid the twinkling of the lamps, the night wind lifting the tablecloth under their nervous, nimble fingers while they talked about their work, about translations of Dante, of Virgil, a work in verse or prose that one or the other had written, the era and the literary reputation of Charles, Adrien, and Jean-Mathieu had made them venerable, thought Daniel, all three had without a doubt achieved the highest levels of acute awareness, existence and its trivialities seemed to them like heavy armour they would lay down without a struggle at the gates of eternity, and what were they thinking, they were so comfortable with the words they had chosen for their numerous books, what did they think about Daniel, about the new generation of writers now offhandedly appropriating the language to deconstruct and reconstruct in their own manner? The manuscript of *Strange Years* had been turned down, had it been, Daniel wondered, by that New York publishing house, by a transcendent circle of poets who understood nothing of the chaotic way men cohabited with the past, new men worn down before birth by their own fathers' pasts, thought Daniel, young people who were also searching for paradise, as was Daniel, bursting with life and sensuality, Charles said one had to admire the exuberance of young people who alone were right, Charles, Adrien, and Jean-Mathieu, said Charles humorously, each resembled old Schopenhauer making ready to leave the world, and their expressions, their suspicious eyes, were those of Schopenhauer, for there was nothing sadder than being inflexible and irritable in old age, making everyone suffer, even the mosquitoes dying in the flame of the lamps, which they brushed away, mosquitoes bit through the fine sweat on the backs of their necks, they transmitted to the delicate, nearly transparent skin the germs that caused fever and malaria, was it not surprising that what had been a paradise was, with the touchiness and intolerance of age, now becoming a purgatory, and with the penetrating yellow light from his eyes Daniel looked at the silhouettes of these three frail men against a dark blue sky in the night, where you could hear the song of the waves as if it were coming closer, would this henceforth be the site of all the sharp pains of love now lost, of the regrets of a lifetime as they were described by Dante in the *Purgatorio,* said Charles to Adrien, "the hour that pierces the new pilgrim with love if he hears from afar a bell that seems to mourn the dying day" e che lo novo peregrin d'amore, punge, s'e' ode squilla di lontano, che paia il giorno pianger che si more, Charles recited, in a lyrical voice, and Daniel thought, was it like this, as he supposed, that each of the three poets imagined for himself the Divine Comedy that inhabited him, each suspecting that hell was threatening to expel him from the secluded bedroom where he thought and wrote beginning at dawn, what harm was there in writing in his bedroom, said Charles, if the world, the earth was declining now, this young man, Daniel, might not believe a word, but it was true, everything would vanish, disappear into the bluish tinges of the water, Charles, Adrien, and Jean-Mathieu, like Virgil, like Dante Alighieri, had played their parts, had written their essays and treatises, but year by year, when they were photographed together, standing against a background of rocks by the sea, often someone would be missing, this year it was Jacques, barely a year ago he had been there, at Adrien's side, dressed despite the heat in grey cords and high boots, and now suddenly his place was empty, where was that smiling figure who had posed for Caroline, whose expression changed so quickly from sweetness to mocking insolence, Adrien, Charles, Jean-Mathieu now heard only the sounds of distant bells on the sea, Caroline had brought them all together, lined them up like schoolchildren to photograph them every year, and suddenly the space that Jacques had occupied was empty, his ashes had been scattered to the wind, each of them, said Adrien, was coming to the end of his own role around a table, at a banquet, although during the time they played that role, they had never been invited, like Dante, like

Virgil, to change the unsettled politics of their native cities or their country, they alone had been given over to the perils of their overflowing imaginations, as they had to the madness of those who possessed power in this world, what did the three of them hope for now, didn't each of them secretly dare to believe that he was expected somewhere else, where — as they did during those long afternoons when they conversed together in the shade of parasols, or played chess in the humid heat of the verandas, under the mosquito nets — tomorrow, in this select club of the immortals, they would discuss the linguistic problems that preoccupied them or a particular sonnet that Dante had written for Beatrice, the vision of Beatrice that had appeared to Dante when he was a child, was it not, in all its brilliance, the great Shadow of God pursuing the poet to the end, those who had not known Beatrice, who had never experienced a virginal passion with such force, had written that from the land of shadows, with no light or beacon, their words, like they themselves, were liable to vanish with Jacques into those bluish tinges of the water, of the sky that had so delighted them, for just as on this festive night everything was distilled into the fragrant air, the dark voice of Venus surrounded by the musicians on the stage, singing, let my joy endure, just like the racist remarks of those who listened to her as they strolled arrogantly by the pool, just like the sublime verses of a poet, e che lo novo peregrin d'amore, all words were distilled into the fragrant air, from the waves some blue smoke that had been the body of Jacques rose into the night, his body made of water, of salt, and which of them was soon to be a pinch of ashes beneath a flowering tree, and had they not, all three of them, also heard, when the headphones were taken from Jacques's ears, from the gaunt shape of his head, the mass that Mozart had written amid the joy, the effervescence of his heart, that celestial music, when the doves and turtledoves flew away, and later an oratorio by Beethoven, no doubt they would be together for some time yet, as they were here this evening, tonight, with Daniel and his wife Mélanie, who was so charming, and their children, tomorrow, in the shade of parasols, with their books, when it was hot on the beaches, or in the humid heat of the verandas where they played chess, it would be strange to find themselves all together in the same Eden, under the same palm trees, in the same sea breeze, breathing in that delicious air, Charles, Adrien, Jean-Mathieu would see Virgil and Dante, whose biographers and eulogists they had been, from each in turn would be heard the most beautiful verses of their poetic epic, like Virgil before he met Maecenas in Rome, Jean-Mathieu had had a poverty-stricken childhood in the port of Halifax, or would Charles, Adrien, Jean-Mathieu be considered by their sublime masters to be poetic novices, not yet polished by the cycle of the ages, and would they still remember the verses they had written? A mountainous city in Italy would appear to Jean-Mathieu, emerging from weightlessness, he'd had a drink at noon, in the sun, how tasty that Cinzano or vermouth had been, and now he was forbidden to drink, so many echoes, of water noises and voices, in this city he'd come to by train from Milan, he'd slept badly the night before, then came those mornings of pure light that drove away the pale night-time glimmer of the streetlamps, a family was sobbing in the smoke of a bus outside the train station, in a quick burst of saliva a priest spat out an apple core, what meaning should be given to those words in the new kingdom, on this island where all languages would perhaps be forgotten, the Cinzano at noon in the sun, the fat priest spitting out an apple core, or say it was the same city but the shutters were closed, a dog and a man selling pencils in a shady corner, and watching them

from a terrace while he wrote, Jean-Mathieu had heard that
question in his mind, how old am I, isn't it much too early
in this day and age to ask oneself that question, where was
the dog going, his companion, the man selling pencils in the
square of shade, as well as the remainder of a circle of
pigeons fluttering at his feet, those images, confined for a
moment by Jean-Mathieu's thoughts, now seemed to him
alive as they once were, above the city in the mountains, a
hand was closing the shutters, in the evening silence, alone
on the terrace of that café, surrounded by snow-covered
peaks, Jean-Mathieu asked himself what he was doing here,
after he'd read the morning's letters, there would be no mail
at the hotel until the next day, no rain on these mountain
peaks, today or tomorrow, when Jean-Mathieu would never
go out without his umbrella, and already his glass was
empty, the scrawny dog and the man selling pencils had
disappeared, what was missing then in this place that overwhelmed him so, some atmosphere of hidden piety was
choking him, who knew if suddenly, from the churches,
from their panels of glass, some delegation of saints and
apostles would emerge, dressed in green like the grass on
the hills, no, night was falling, tomorrow Jean-Mathieu would
climb the mountain, how old was he, how stupid to ask himself that question when he was going to climb a mountain
the next day, said Jean-Mathieu to himself now, and he
could see clearly the young man of another time in his
forsaken mountainous landscape, he had, as he did today, a
bald head and an enigmatic dimpled smile, he wore trousers
and a jacket buttoned over a necktie, his complexion was
fresh and pink, how stupid to have thought today about the
problems of old age, among delegations of saints, of green
apostles in the churches, the circle of pigeons fluttering at
his feet, the young man was henceforth in a stained-glass

window, where he inspired violent emotion in those who
visited him, what bracing air he had breathed in the mountains, what bracing air he still breathed on the balcony of
his apartment by the sea, beginning at dawn, with the sky
casting its powerful light over the water, feeling euphoric
and rested after his morning shower, Jean-Mathieu would
spend a long time writing at his window, wearing his khaki
shorts, later he would have lunch with Caroline, in the afternoon he would write to his former students of English poetry,
oh, all the same he would have to wait until tomorrow for
the mail to be distributed, the soft drink he sipped would
taste insipid, for a long time the glass would glisten in the
sun with his inadmissible, languorous thirsts while Caroline,
with the bright and mischievous eye of her camera, again led
him towards some joint book project, my dear, he would
say to her, and his voice would be reasonable, I don't have
enough time left to write that book with you, though I have
no objection at all to the idea, what do you want, you'll have
to go away, she said, peremptory, to go away, but that's out
of the question, my friend, I need you for this book, you
know all those poets whose pictures I took when they were
young, only you can write about them, only we, Jean-Mathieu
would say calmly, because we were there together, my dear,
you, your camera, and I, and he would turn his gaze towards
the splendid wintry summer of the flowers on the terrace, the
emerald-coloured water of the Gulf of Mexico, all that is still
ours, he would say quite simply, while he felt himself a
captive of the way that eye of Caroline's would operate on
him, the eye, or the camera, which recorded everything about
himself that he would have preferred not to see, the face
of a writer, a poet, well cared for in old age, was it really
necessary to entrust it to film for the future, an umbrella, a
hat would have shown him to good advantage, but now that

bright and mischievous eye was confusing him with the flowers on the terrace, as it did with the glittering water, capturing him in a way that stripped him of all his possessions and left him passive, motionless, hypnotized, he would think he still loved that woman, Caroline, even though she struck him as too nervous and possessed of inexhaustible energy under her straw hat; in this winter light that was still a little cold, she would order him not to move while she took a better camera from her bag, this time the image would be filtered, shaded, she would say, the sun was so strong that day, Jean-Mathieu would not have been satisfied at being only a spot of shadow in a patch of light, and with each of Caroline's shots, her eye glued to the camera, he would see again the faces of those friends, those companions who were now merely photographs in books, impressions of men and women on the black-and-white paper of a page in a book, an album, were those poets who had been called modern already part of an earlier, bygone era, some of them among the dead, oh, how brief their lives had been, some had been war heroes, remarkable physicians on the battlefields, others had founded poetic protest movements in North America, one had associated with the greatest poets of his time, some had been art critics, spending their lives between Paris and New York, others had been destroyed by cancer, depression, or suicide, how brief their lives had been, and now, feeling euphoric and rested after his morning shower and wearing his khaki shorts, Jean-Mathieu would spend a long time writing at his window, for he knew the unchanging order of his days, life was irresistibly long when it was harmonious and serene, he would wait until tomorrow for the mail with the same impatience, as he finished his poem, he would write as he'd done in the past, among the snowy peaks, why this uneasiness, what was missing in this place, hadn't Adrien put his king in check on the chessboard, it was the suffocating heat that had distracted Jean-Mathieu, the situation of the queen was provisional, Adrien was so quick-witted when he was playing chess, as when he was writing poetry, Jean-Mathieu would be more alert tomorrow, still, it was embarrassing to have been beaten by his opponent, his king put in check, each of them so irritable as the languors of the scorching summer approached, it would be better for all three to separate shortly, Jean-Mathieu dreamed of the bracing climate of the Alpes Maritimes, Adrien would play tennis with Suzanne all summer, oh, that couple's superb independence, Charles, disdainful of social life, of festive evenings with his friends, no longer had an appetite for such pleasures, he would take refuge in a monastery to write; the situation of the queen was unstable, that was how Jean-Mathieu had been beaten by Adrien, the situation was provisional with Charles, whose nerves had been on edge for some time, what was the meaning of Charles's fits of irritation, was it the sultry air in the bedrooms where each of them spent the day writing, or the suffocating heat behind the blinds, or the mad wind from hurricanes on the Atlantic, Charles could no longer bear the sea or the islands, in his eyes those vast liquid expanses were now sources of pain, of tribulation, or had his vision been changed by a secret distress that would thus bring to a close his image of the sea, to see it no more, he said, to see it no more, he had written in one of his poems, the seas, the oceans had lost their sovereignty, their monumental grandeur, opening his window in the morning what could he observe that had not gone out to sea, pitiful objects unrescued by the ocean waves, they were there, on our shores, mired in the wet sand of the beaches, like a child's toys in an empty bathtub, there were inflatable tires the water had gnawed at, a yellow life-belt still tied to the mast that had snapped off, an entire uncertain flotilla drifting away with its rafts, its wooden or rubber craft shaped like small coffins, sometimes an oar would appear on the beach among these tubes and sad assemblages, pleading for the memory of the human arm that had made it sail this far, to these shores where poorly built boats, formless things, had survived longer than a multitude of men, women, and children who had sailed with them against the reefs, into the fringes of coral, as he opened his window in the morning what could he observe that had not gone out to sea, a little girl's dress hung from the rotten planks, the yellow lifebelt sparkling like a sun, still at the peak of its mast was the cross of a drowned pilgrim looming from the water, so it was true, thought Jean-Mathieu, that the sea, as Charles had written, Charles whose nerves were on edge, who suffered from headaches, that the ocean Jean-Mathieu looked out on in the morning while he wrote was a sea that we should be ashamed of, or was that the vision of Charles, who was fenced in now by so many hazards, by ambushes that blurred his sight, his thinking, the poet had also written in the same flights of prophetic delirium that his funeral mass would be sung in the New York cathedral where he had received honours, was Charles so tormented by an ineluctable death, while Jean-Mathieu devoted so little time to such thoughts, why bother, didn't that make him lose his freedom, his nobility of spirit, when Jean-Mathieu, incorrigibly sociable, was still going out for lunch every day, in the same way Adrien and Suzanne, with the gusto that would characterize the bonds between them until old age, loved one another with the same touching love, they wrote and published their books together, walked hand in hand as soon as the sun was shining on the water, to the pool, the tennis court, their slender sun-browned feet in leather sandals now ready for their morning run, how cool the water and the sky were when Jean-Mathieu rose so early for the conquest of a uniform and peaceful day, why, in this paradise that was as ordered and harmonious as heaven must be, why were Charles's nerves always on edge, no doubt it was because of his frequent visits to monasteries in Mexico, in Ireland, because of those forced retreats meant to purify his writing, retreats into the spiritual life, where was Jean-Mathieu's charming friend whom Caroline had photographed at the time of Charles's first books, he seemed to be smiling his sensitive smile of resignation at Jean-Mathieu in the black-and-white print, in the book Jean-Mathieu had published long ago with Caroline's photographs, it showed Charles with his back to a piano, a musical score, in a study or music-room, beneath the beams of an ancient house, oh the pedigreed adolescent whom all the gods adored, was this the same boy who today compared himself with old Schopenhauer, who, unlike Virgil and Jean-Mathieu, hadn't had to suffer the aberrations of material life, Jean-Mathieu becoming head of the family in almost the same year he learned to read, in a humble section of Halifax, yet what sweet light had bathed his childhood during those foggy mornings on the harbour, born into a wealthy family of brokers, immersing himself early on, like Dante, in philosophical reading, for a long time Charles hadn't needed to be concerned about his fate, independent in his thinking, he had grown up among his parents' servants in their huge mansion, he had not been that child begging by the roadside, let alone that unemployed worker during a global depression in which Jean-Mathieu had struggled as in mud, solitary and mystical among his people, from his isolated room beneath the beams, had he not had a serious approach to life, O Charles, beloved of the gods, thought Jean-Mathieu, intellectual, theological, although he was alone and unhappy, Charles was a born moralist, fleeing any form of decadence, he was not searching for his happiness on earth, embarking early upon his vast literary production, avoiding the mud, the silt that, as it weighed upon the manners of the poor, marked them with manners so uncouth, on Charles, on Beatrice, the "happy and beautiful lady," on himself, on art, before writing, before the university education which came late, Jean-Mathieu had had the rough hands of a worker, of an unemployed man who had endured years of deprivation, his face with its ravaged features under a cap, the youthful faces of the damaged miners Caroline had photographed during a period of severe economic slowdown, and these eras of anxiety, of struggle, must never come again, thought Jean-Mathieu, had he not finally earned the right to a life free of those worries, an orderly life, how annoying this king that Adrien had put in check, tomorrow Jean-Mathieu would be more vigilant. But on this festive night everything was distilled into the fragrant air, both the drunken song of Venus, who had pulled off her espadrilles and was dancing barefoot on the stage among the musicians, and the crystalline laughter that exploded in Samuel's direction from all sides of the garden, from the verandas, would it be tomorrow, when he wakened, thought Samuel, who was standing near his mother, the silk kimono barely covering his shoulders streaming with water from the pool, that he would come racing towards them, waking Julio who was prostrate with grief on the beach, saying to Jenny and Sylvie, to Augustino, here is the ark for animals with no masters, and the engineering officer from a military base, who had gathered up Augustin from Sylvie's trembling arms, would tell Samuel, yes, that's the raft we've been expecting for several days, we were able to make it out tonight in the bright light from the lighthouses, it's definitely the ark for the animals whose masters are being held in the camps with the iron fences, like Augustin whom we just have to wash and feed, they have been saved, their skin, their fur is streaked from being burned by the sun, by the salt, now they have crossed the peripheral zone where the small boats that sink so close to shore suddenly come to a standstill in the eddies, so close that we can see the victims' tear-filled eyes, from the boats where we hold out blankets for them, and water and rice, but in vain, they moan, we won't go any farther, here is the offering of our lives, the end of our exodus, Samuel would waken Julio, are they going to make a sea landing, have they arrived, asked Julio, didn't the officer recognize them among the others, a second raft had been lost on the horizon that day, beneath the clouds, was that the raft that had been unable to go up the Santa Fe, as they called the zone of the waters of death, so near the coasts and docks, said the officer, that you could see the eyes, the faces of those who would soon be asphyxiated by immersion in the waves, among the others the officer had recognized Oreste, Nina, Ramon, his mother, Edna, a few moments earlier they had been there and suddenly they could no longer be seen, nor was their sail, made of sheets and rags stirred by the wind, that Santa Fe zone, so close to shore, had already swallowed up so many lives, a stirring and sad endeavour, said the officer, had Augustin got over the swelling brought on by the sun, a thousand miles from home, the engineering officer had held in his arms the swollen, puffy little body of Augustin, who was hungry and thirsty, and had thought about his daughter, Casey, back home, calling his wife that evening, he had come so far, a thousand miles from his home, he would tell her that he had saved Casey today, when would that child, that poor child, recover from his swelling, his puffiness, for was it a limpid love that had guided him to Santa Fe, these

waters that held so many ruins, where the double faces of
Casey and Augustin would suddenly be one, and Julio would
say to Samuel, they're still there, on the raft being flattened
by the clouds on the horizon, my mother, Ramon, as for
Oreste, as for Nina, Julio thought he'd forgotten them, then he
would see them again in a clothes closet, lying on a shelf in
some piece of furniture, or in the refrigerator, where Julio
had sheltered them from the scorching heat, tomorrow
Samuel would tell Julio to wake up, why sleep that troubled
sleep on the beaches when today the raft of animals would
slip over the smooth water, among the fishing boats, and later
some of their masters would come to meet them, in the
kennels, the campgrounds where their cages would be set
up, among the red-flowered mangroves, under the blue sky,
the animals' ark would arrive, the one Samuel and Augustino
had been expecting for some days now, with the canary, the
white kitten, there would be more than nine of them on this
crossing, with a fawn called Pine Needle and a piglet called
Charlotte, survivors of the arduous odyssey, and starting this
evening they would jump up and down with gratitude on the
linoleum flooring of their prison, some would be suffering
from internal hemorrhages, or broken limbs, veterinarians
would rehabilitate them in their shelters, the chihuahua
beside the giant Doberman, the canary and the white kitten,
it would be Samuel and Augustino's Noah's ark, why was
Julio sleeping a troubled sleep on the beaches at night, and
now, suddenly cheerful, still dressed in their rags from the
rafts, dazed by the rhythm of the waves, they would go,
holding cellophane envelopes to show that they were the
owners of an old, dehydrated dog with his rough coat, a
woman would recognize Toki, Kikita, would anyone dare
forbid them to take their pets, they would rather go back to
sea, Linda, Toki, would go away, content, joined to their

masters by a blue rope, a collar bearing their name, with no place or destination, wandering from a transit centre to an encampment by the sea, surrounded by iron fences, but now they would no longer be alone, forgotten as in the nightmares, those nightmares Julio had on the beaches, forgotten in a closet, on a shelf, in a refrigerator to keep them from the scorching heat, from being annihilated by his fevers, by the dangers at sea, now they would no longer be alone as Oreste, Ramon, Nina had been, entangled in the powerful roots of mangrove swamps, under the flowering trees of the lagunas, in the forests of mangroves, in the silt of the calm waters, having wandered so deep into the foliage, into the vegetation that grew in the saline soil, into the reddish glow of the flowers, while above them flew eagles and slow-flying pelicans, protected from hurricanes by the ephemeral wall of the mangroves, like the panther, the crab, the untamed dolphin, they too had buried their powerful roots in the bay, the curls of their hair in the seaweed, in the complex ocean plants, and they in turn were metamorphosing into that microscopic food from the depths of the sea that would nourish birds of prey, the jaguar, the shark, entwined so far away in the moving roots of the forests of mangroves, they went through the canal among the insects, the dolphins, the turtles, in the waters of the canal that gave off mercury vapours that had killed the deer, poisoned the golden eagle, they had wandered so deep into the foliage of the marine soil, Julio had long ago stopped seeing them, who could have escaped from those impenetrable forests of mangroves, no small boat, no raft, even though everyone had seen them, Nina, Ramon, Oreste, and their mother, Edna, so close to the shores of the Santa Fe zone, the mangroves seemed to Julio to light up the night with their reddish signals of menace, of danger, warning anyone who was lying on the beach, on a pier, watching,

that here among the mangroves that filtered the fresh rain
water from the salt water were filtered the lives of Ramon,
Oreste, Nina, Edna, whose small craft had run aground so
close to shore, in this flowering, sandy bay of the Santa Fe.
And Renata raised her head, still filled with dread, perhaps
the West Indian had decided to follow her here, to hem her
in on this festive night, when she saw Mélanie and Samuel,
who were walking towards her, what a pleasant sensation of
coolness to see them here again, it was like the hope that
she would soon swim in the green, slack water, on a day
when the sea was calm, they were there, close to her, under
the almond trees, why, asked Mélanie, had she taken a
house isolated in the climbing vegetation of the town when
there was a pavilion for her here under the oleanders,
Renata brought a cigarette to her lips, Mélanie seemed still
fragile to her so soon after the birth of her son, this festive
night, these nights, as people said here, would take her away
from the throbbing pain of her convalescence, how Renata
loved being suddenly close to them, to Mélanie, to Samuel,
and far from the insular limbo of her status as a woman on
her own, in a rented house where the clock on a table beside
the bed indicated that it was nine o'clock, and a man had just
come in with her, he was breathing his sour breath onto the
back of her neck, after a night of gambling when he'd lost
everything, a night of drunkenness and anger, a humiliation
Renata would not talk about to Mélanie, who was a happy
woman, the cold touch of her lighter, of her gold cigarette
case, the light smoke of her cigarette in the jasmine-scented
air — more than any human presence these pathetic objects
of her thirst were beneficent, soothing, she would give them
up when she went home, tomorrow, tonight, for these objects
were associated with a loss or an irretrievable surfeit, she
knew all that, her husband told her so, repeatedly, and

Samuel had grown so much over the winter, said Mélanie, that when he stood on tiptoe he came up to his mother's shoulder, his dive had been audacious but now it was time for a few hours' sleep, Samuel had grown so much, repeated Mélanie, who could see the bombed communication towers, bridges, and oil refineries of Baghdad, thinking how she would tell the women activists to what extent the January war had already been pushed back in people's memories, for like trees swept away by tornadoes the world's dramas were swept away at the same irascible speed, suddenly this island, this paradise, was as strategically important as the city of Baghdad for the vacationing Europeans who postponed living here, imagining recumbent images adrift everywhere, in the streets, as if they had been vines climbing along the walls, beneath the palm fronds, curled up on the beaches, even more unpleasant to contemplate were the wrecks of all those rafts, they were thinking, on the seashores where they used to bask among so many comforts, in the indulgent light of the sun, Samuel had grown so much, said Renata, who was watching Samuel punctuate Venus's song with movements of his pretty head, with a supple dance step that was barely perceptible, like the underwater dance of a snake, her song, her music, her voice that tore the air, the night, with their trances, with their pious, unbridled incantations, with lamentations of joy and fury that Renata thought she heard erupting deep inside herself while Venus sang, dancing barefoot on the stage among the musicians, and it was that music Samuel reflected as well, discreetly repeating her gestures, her movements, one might expect that like Venus he would gradually become boisterous, be carried away by the music, dancing barefoot, he had so often seen Venus sing for the whites at their parties, their weddings, in their stores at Christmastime, for their children, in their churches and temples, that same wild dance compliantly took hold of Samuel, who let himself succumb to its rhythm, and wasn't this the return of the sensation of coolness Renata had felt when she was admiring the teenage violinist on the stage, she admired Mélanie and Samuel's pure resistance to being what she herself would not be tomorrow: marvellous creatures of the future like the teenage violinist, Samuel and Mélanie's resistance to life's worst ugliness, to its most appalling ills was a resistance that seemed to be fashioned as much in the flesh as in the granite of their thoughts, for must they already learn how to resist anything that might offend that purity, but so sharp, so markedly the same were they both, that firmness rather than softness would be more help to them in living with the faith they had imposed within themselves, just like the waves in the sea rolling in nearly at their feet, under the window-shutters, in the grass of the garden, a warm wave, Venus's voice, the thrill of that voice, seemed to spread all around them along with the warm glow of the lamps, the iridescent night around their profiles, around their faces that were so much alike, they who were ideally suited for a fruitful survival would be here, on this earth, when she no longer was, unless, as an image in their memories, they preserved her until their own resplendent and lethal immortality, and what would Renata be in their memories, a family member passing through on a festive night, they would be more familiar with her dignity during an ordeal than with the fissure, for she had insisted to all of them that she was cured, hoping it was the truth, but since she'd been with them she no longer doubted it was true, and Mélanie told Renata that Vincent was asleep in the room up above, if they didn't make a sound they could go up and see him, wasn't there still too much humidity in the air, asked Mélanie suddenly, uneasily, and to Renata none of Mélanie's uneasiness showed through, she was so full of praise for the newborn, for his charm, already, for Vincent's fingers that opened like petals, for his exquisite smile, didn't he have his father's features, his long eyelashes, the eyes were still a remarkable colour, neither brown nor blue-green, his Italian grandparents adored him, but the air was laden with an unhealthy humidity tonight, Mélanie observed, or was she tired as she'd been this afternoon when she had to lie down, no doubt she had done that so she could lie next to Vincent for a few minutes, in the indulgence of her love, now and then stroking his downy hair, his fingers, those petals, all of that, which was Mélanie's life and work, she had written to Renata that the child was strong and healthy, already exceptionally vigorous, now in the room where Vincent slept Renata and Mélanie were bending over the child and Mélanie had thought that it was true, yes, her child was beautiful and healthy, his breathing was regular, Mélanie, Jenny, and Sylvie, who took turns watching over Vincent, had perhaps become alarmed too quickly over some symptom that lacked foundation, Vincent, Mélanie, Samuel, Augustino, their father — all would be the prolongation of Renata when she was no longer on this earth, and it had seemed to Renata that such thinking was not without happiness or glory, then she had thought that Mélanie, a woman like her, was already mutilated, even if it did not show, like that Brazilian-born poet who had disappeared, thought Renata, whose house she had rented, a woman was not born to endure, to establish herself, unlike her husband, her sons, Mélanie was not permanent and solid on this earth, like Renata she was a creature marked by fissures, by the same condition, the same servitude, even if she had given life, and Renata felt for Mélanie the tenderness that animals sometimes experience among themselves, suddenly she said, my dear Mélanie, seeing Mélanie's hand as it brushed against

Vincent's forehead, his eyes, his downy hair, for Mélanie had betrayed the inner fissure, the weakness of woman, by mentioning something that concerned them both deeply, she said, a compilation, a report that had been published in an American university journal, about rapes of women between the ages of five and eighty, committed in former Yugoslavia, during the winter, in their computers some female students, law students, had the confessions of the victims of these rapes, these assaults, there would be a war-crimes tribunal, now they were searching through those archives where the atrocities were still so recent, said Mélanie, a war-crimes tribunal as had not been seen for years, and Renata had shocked Mélanie by saying to her that the work, the search for the truth by those female law students and volunteer lawyers was admirable, but that the perpetrators of the five thousand murders and rapes would never be punished, those blood-soaked records would sleep among countless other records of cruelties committed throughout history, and those murderers, those rapists, would never appear before tribunals organized by women, they would continue to rape, to kill, any hope of prosecution would be vain, for the women, the little girls only recently born, had been mutilated for ever, if they had to be represented to the mind by an image, they would be shown holding their breasts, their wombs in their hands to offer them, all those organs ready to be tortured and raped, to be mutilated by men, or else they were doomed to disappearances of all kinds, demeaned in silence by a rape, a crime, at their birth they held in their hands the organs of both their life and their destruction, often it was their humiliated spirits that disappeared before their bodies, through rape, through torture, during this new century, said Mélanie, the paths will all be found again, Mélanie would go with her sons to the meeting of the international tribunal, she would hear the victims' voices, she would see the murderers incarcerated, no, said Renata, none of that can happen, our records will always be stained with our own blood, with blood and organs always new, ever newer and younger, human rights will be respected more and more, said Mélanie, of that she was certain, and in his sleep one of Vincent's fingers was entwined with Mélanie's, in the future, said Mélanie, women, men, children will no longer have to suffer such serious violations of their moral rights, no, for women would govern and they would change the mentality of men, in their own country, women today lived as if they were in a totalitarian country, but that would change tomorrow, said Mélanie, when men have been killed in a war, said Renata, their widows are cattle for the surviving men, they are there to be killed and raped, in military barracks in Peru they are tortured for months with electricity, or attempts are made to drown them, in many countries they are held without charge as soon as there is a military coup, they are deliberately mistreated and detained under terrible conditions, political prisoners are beaten, tied up before being executed, I see no end to those rapes, those violations for women and their children, said Renata, when I plead for a woman, I know that she was born and will die in pain, even in the cases of infanticide I've had to confront, I have doubts, I've had doubts about the women's guilt, although they are capable of killing and mistreating others too, I will always have doubts that they are truly guilty, we know the most dangerous, the most criminal women, who are still being sought in Canada, Mexico, Montserrat, Bertha, Sharon, Valérie, they had killed a hotel doorman to rob him, they were drug addicts, they'd escaped from correctional institutions, from prisons where they had seemed to be making progress along the path to good, they had attained the rank of warden but they had the personalities of liars and hypocrites, they were said to be perverse, often psychotic, like Bertha from Guatemala, who was engaged in fraud, who dealt cocaine, she was working for a man, and those were the reprisals for lives of misery, said Renata, we'd have had to know the story of every one of those women, go back to the roots of the true tragedies of their childhood, before all those crimes escalated, they had been little girls raped by a father, a brother, blindfolded by their assailants, and their souls, their spirits had evaporated, and all their crimes, the accumulation of those crimes, were the signs of that disappearance of the spirit, of the soul, a disappearance so common, each of these women had suffered sexual cruelty, abuse, an act of torture that had defiled her, Renata doubted that any one of those women was guilty, often she was unable to sleep at night when she thought about the infanticidal mother, Laura, whom the judge had sentenced to the electric chair, Laura, mother of a child known as Sugar Candy, must die, it was rare for a woman to be sentenced to capital punishment, but Laura Nadora had killed little Sugar Candy, her crime had been premeditated, said the judge, Laura Nadora had heard those words in court at nine twenty-five a.m., after a night of anguish and fear in her cell, Laura Nadora, you are sentenced to die, leave this courtroom, criminal, she had also heard, while she murmured in a faltering voice, her eyes bulging with terror, Your Honour, listen to me, as she struggled against those who were holding her under guard, she had said repeatedly, the judge has to listen to me, I have to talk to him, as if she were expecting, with this pitiful appeal, the assistance of a confessor, of a friend, being in a foreign country, at first she had not understood what the judge was saying to her, Sugar Candy had been whipped, beaten to death, it's that man's fault, she had cried out, that man and cocaine, but it was the man who had buried him on the beach, a cruel and hateful crime, the judge had commented, an unpardonable crime for a mother to commit, while Laura Nadora continued to cry out that she was innocent, she was not innocent of the crime she was accused of, she said, but only let them listen to her, a man had forced her into those terrible deeds, a man who didn't want his child, the eyes bulging with fear in the young Cuban woman's face saw — beyond the judge, beyond his sentence, the courtroom, the grandiose hostility that would be fatal to her — the act of damnation, of torture, committed in the darkness of her life, it was a long time ago that she'd been wounded, it was inconceivable that, after she had immigrated to this country to know freedom, an unpitying judge who spoke not her language but the language of freedom, of abundance, a man of good faith and a Christian, no doubt, should send her to the electric chair like this, she was wearing a flowered dress that day, she had washed and styled her hair, she had prayed in her mental distraction, but did no one know she needed help, needed her little boy to pardon her for having lost her mind, needed, above all, her son to preserve her life, he who had died because of an accident, she thought, for she felt cowardly and frightened, Sugar Candy who was always sucking a candy, people gave him candies all day long, not having time to look after him, Sugar Candy, who had died from the blows he'd received, again laid his hand, sticky with chocolate, against his mother's hand, his cheeks were smeared with blood, although too young to talk, he told his mother that everything would turn out well, for he was the angel of love, and the angel of vengeance had just died, and Laura no longer remembered him, had he been buried under the sand of a beach, under the lagunas of the sea; he had fled, now there was only a good little boy with her, not the one she'd never wanted but another, his only flaw was being overly fond of sweets, he was always smeared with candy and now he was saying to his mother that with her clean hair and her mauve-flowered dress all would be well, all would be well, sentenced to die in the electric chair, the judge had said, and she could not believe him, repeating until she was taken back to her cell that there'd been a mistake, that she wasn't guilty, that she wanted permission to speak to the judge alone, but the judge was a man, said Renata, it was death for the accused woman because the judge was a man, there was no doubt that she would die in the electric chair, in this country, a foreign country, in exile, in this place she had come to, at the price of her own crimes against herself and of her child's innocence, to win her freedom, and she would die thinking that it could only happen to her; it was a nightmare, and the smile of God, whom she had invoked, would open heaven to her, for in her soul that had vanished, had been murdered, little by little, along with her grief for her child, a naïve soul was awakening, God must exist, she thought, as she'd been taught in childhood, so that the criminal injustice of her death, of capital punishment, would be put right, said Renata, and Mélanie could hear that low, slightly hoarse voice in her ear while she walked along the paths in the garden, and she thought about Augustino, who also loved sweets, about Vincent, who was peacefully asleep upstairs, Augustino was her son, and Sugar Candy, who hadn't even had a proper name, who had been born only to be extermi-nated, was the son of Laura, an infanticidal mother, a guilty mother, thought Mélanie, no rape in Laura's childhood, no wound could have justified an act so hideous, the woman was guilty, profoundly guilty, thought Mélanie, looking up, determined, in the night. And there's a shadow on the other side of the gate, of the garden fence, said Jenny, running towards the house with Augustino, don't you see that shadow, its treacherous head concealed by a hood, don't you hear the hissing of hatred, Daniel remembered the grey shadow when he was sitting next to Charles, placing his big hands on the white tablecloth like Charles, in the twinkling lamplight, the athletic Adrien, who was burlier than his friends, had got up to join Suzanne, who was the same height as he, they had to get up early tomorrow, to go to the tennis court, said Suzanne, an unbreakable agreement, there's an unbreakable agreement between them, thought Jean-Mathieu, who was looking at the abandoned chair beside him, gleaming white like the tablecloth and the white flowers in a vase on the table, in the night that spotless white suddenly struck him, the roomy garden chair that Adrien had just left, everything on this side of the garden was white, but I want to talk to that young author about his manuscript, Adrien told Suzanne, the style, I want to talk to him about the style, he has to make a few corrections, it should be entitled *Approaches to the River Eternity*, the black waters of Dante's rivers are very much present, the circles of hell are all packed with accursèd souls, with disasters, tutti son pien di spirti maladetti, he quoted in a powerful, dramatic voice, tutti son pien di spirti, yes, but we also have to pick up our son at the airport, he told Suzanne all at once, in a tone of private complicity, we both know how absent-minded the boy is, he's probably forgotten his arrival time already, no, said Suzanne, he won't forget, true, he's absent-minded, but he's an excellent mathematician, and what kind of life is that, mathematics, asked Adrien, yes, a few corrections are essential, Adrien added, I must talk to Daniel about his *Strange Years*, and Daniel watched the united couple formed by Adrien and Suzanne, thinking, one day Mélanie and I will be like that, will we be inclined to quarrel, where will the children be, *Approaches to the River Eternity*, wouldn't that title be more relevant, Adrien asked Daniel, *Approaches to the River Eternity*, and Daniel could see the shadows, the Shadow with its crimson face concealed by a hood, along the garden fence, the gate, around Jenny, Sylvie, shadows whose faces are crimson like the monsters reddened by the cold flames of Dante's Inferno, or was it Daniel's, no, he told Adrien, those monsters weren't there, so far from the approaches to the River Eternity, in any abstract manner, they were here, close to us, I don't see anything, I confess that I don't see anything, said Adrien, shrugging, and Daniel thought of the indelible insignia Julio had described to him, on Samuel's boat, the Shadow and its hissing, thought Daniel, tutti son pien di spirti maladetti, those shadows were climbing up the walls of the house, up to the room where Vincent was sleeping, with the hurricanes of Dante's Inferno, Samuel's boat had been painted with the red paint of their hatred, the boat clove the waves on fine sunny mornings, with a child on board, Dante's circle, the circle of the damned, also stirred up waves around Samuel's boat and Samuel was happy, innocent, he knew nothing about it, nor did his brother, Augustino, in his Superman cape, but no doubt, as Daniel had written, at those stages the circles of hell were circulating in the black waves stirred up by innocent souls, those waves and those rivers and the rivers that ran to the sea Eternity, the manuscript of *Strange Years* was brimming over with those disturbing souls, wasn't it a little awkward to see them all again, Adrien had asked Daniel, was it even in good taste to remember them all, but Daniel was a writer of his century, though still very young he had a long memory, and was his heart not too tender, too vulnerable, offering no protection, said Adrien, between Daniel and his circle of the damned, when with his talent, his astonishing family, his life could only be very agreeable, sensual, and sweet, why not, asked Adrien, but the unfortunate man had a conscience, he who possessed everything for a comfortable life, and wasn't it a shame, at eight a.m. tomorrow, on the tennis court, we have to be ready, Adrien had told Suzanne, alas, the manuscript of *Strange Years* was brimming over with them all, with those who had been turned away from the gates of hell, for a number of souls would not enter there, said Daniel in his book, and for eternity those souls, those spirits who had been turned away would inhale some unbreathable substance, Daniel had described those beings as if he'd known them, in a bunker a woman and her children had been poisoned, what had they done to be brought there, by a parent who had been damned, who had died along with them, in the bunker were the corpses of well-dressed children, involuntary suicides, what was to be done with Goebbels's children or with Hitler's dog, their hell had been to be born into the hands of their executioners, no one took pity on the innocent souls born of damnation, could an infant, a young child be guilty of destroying entire populations? Yet in the judgement of men they were, and it was from all of them — and they were multitudes, like the multitudes in Dante who were driven to the gates of hell — that Daniel extracted laments and cries, for it was to be feared, he had written, that having been barred from both the threshold of hell and the threshold of the paradise that could never be conquered, those souls, the souls of the dog, of the children who had witnessed those atrocious events, would return, in their chagrin, and that we would begin to encounter them today among the avenging shadows, initiated into crime before their birth, poisoned before they had grown, weren't those souls, those bodies, Daniel had written, the bodies, the ruined souls of whom Dante spoke, but through what curse, a divine curse perhaps, had those souls thus borne the catastrophe,

they who were innocent, for around Samuel's boat cleaving
the waves were other black waves heading out to sea, to the
estuary, the gulf was overrun with them, those souls were
the same angels of the past who were stifling beneath the
dull waters of swamps, of marshes, in the stagnant waters of
muddy ponds, innocent souls, they were demanding the
right to the innocence of never having wanted to be born,
their laments were laments of eternal thirst in this air of some
unbreathable substance, those circles held the accursèd
spirits whose laments were those of barking dogs, tutti son
pien di spirti maladetti, children of fathers and mothers who
were damned, in this circle of waves where they had drowned,
the shore would never appear to them from so far away,
and never would their thirst be quenched, how could this
modern writer be described, Julien wondered, this writer,
Daniel, had undoubtedly composed his *Strange Years* under
the influence of some noxious substance, heroin perhaps,
hadn't an ambulance come to pick him up, his back broken,
in his vehicle on a bridge near Brooklyn, thought Jean-
Mathieu, scrutinizing from behind his glasses the yellow light
in Daniel's eyes, saved by writing, he had written that
apotheosis from the black depths, to art, beatitude, for we
shall leave here, Daniel will replace us, and is not illusion,
dream, the essential part of life, Jean-Mathieu would see
sitting in the Senate of the Immortals, Gertrude Stein flanked
by Virgil and Dante at the banquet table, Caroline and
Suzanne would be there too, listening to praise of their
merits on earth, women writers, writers' wives, what martyrdom, thought Jean-Mathieu, women poets, women translators,
had their books been read properly, would they be in the
sphere of the sun or of the moon, the majestic light around
them would now be without shadows, Caroline had been
one of the first women of her generation to pilot a plane,

she'd had to give up architecture during the Depression, they would all occupy the places of the saints in Dante's churches, at the side of the lion and the leopard wreathed in fire, they would have the elastic gait of Suzanne as she passed through those rings around the sun, rays that, we are told, are blinding us, each would dance in a more and more exuberant joy, come, da più letizia pinti e tratti, Gertrude Stein would resemble Picasso's portrait of her, her autumnal colours would be the same, Picasso had often stopped painting that portrait, questioning his model, starting again, painting and brushing his canvas, the pale face of the writer beneath the black band of hair had the religious intensity of an El Greco, Picasso, who at the time was living in poverty, liked those sun colours, the tones of light that had been set on fire and then cooled, signs of an inner maturity, on his work-table Jean-Mathieu kept a reproduction of the Picasso portrait that inspired him every morning with its rigorous laws, waiting for sun in autumn, in winter, the Invader, the Occupier was at the gate but the writer in her apartment on the Rue de Fleurus had been imperturbable, art, language, literature would triumph over all, she seemed to tell the painters who visited her, and what was even truer, thought Jean-Mathieu, they would triumph over those hateful and petty disturbances of men, over the debauchery and corruption of their wars, come, da più letizia pinti e tratti, let their dance be joyous and exuberant, Gertrude Stein would sit in the Senate of the Immortals, between Virgil and Dante, Suzanne and Caroline would be there too, what was a man's life without the essential part of illusion, of dream, and thus would ruined souls leave and dissolve into the air, thought Daniel, those souls that were turned away from the gates of Dante's Inferno, from the gates of cities assailed by epidemics, the multitude of contagious orphans whose mothers were already dead prowled there, uncared for, homeless, in the cities of New York, of San Juan, Puerto Rico, what was to be done with so many condemned orphans, dead among the living, like the murdered dog, the rigid corpses of children in their fine clothes in a bunker, they would no longer attract men's pity, their skeletal ghosts could be seen at the windows of houses, they would be legion and hospital doors would be closed to them, who would ensure their survival on an overpopulated earth where only hunger grew, confused with other silhouettes shrivelled by famine, they would be neither fed nor clothed, the cotton, sugar, asparagus, peanuts, would not be for them, for those who were banished, let their cadaverous forms melt in the sun, among the stones, the garbage cans of shantytowns, for they were the wretched of the earth, and the souls of those orphans would disintegrate in the foul air of all disasters, thought Daniel, how many had perished already on this festive night; Daniel must have written those mad prophesies under the influence of heroin, of cannabis, thought Jean-Mathieu, he was the pampered son of his father, Joseph, who was president of the marine biology laboratory, Daniel had begun studying science in New York before his collapse into drugs, it was Joseph's past that had shattered Daniel, yet how had he, the son of a good family, with a promising future, how had he seen, how had he known what was Joseph's secret from them all, the number on his father's arm, perhaps, though Joseph had never talked to any of his children about the past, oh, let them know nothing about Great Uncle Samuel who had been shot down in the ghetto, but they had known, Daniel had had an inkling about all of it, suddenly, while he was experimenting with hard drugs, Mélanie had seen him screaming as he stood on a rock by the ocean, during vacations on the coast of Maine, what was he screaming in

the panic of his ecstasy, that he was standing on one of
those emaciated heads from Dachau, standing on those
skulls, those livid faces looming from the seas, the oceans,
screaming, possessed, standing on Great Uncle Samuel's
bleeding head, a car accident in which Daniel nearly died
had cured him of his addiction, of course writing *Strange
Years* had required a certain courage, thought Jean-Mathieu,
reflecting that it would soon be time to go home, those
young people in the orchestra were too noisy, although it
went with their age, you couldn't blame them, what time
would the mail arrive tomorrow, the young people are rather
pleasant and well brought up, but I wouldn't want to show
them that I need a cane to go home, I'll leave through the
gate without being noticed, a good thing Mélanie is seriously
considering going into politics, there will be a new party, she
could well get elected, she's an intelligent woman, thought
Jean-Mathieu, leaning on his cane to go out, would she be in
the sphere of the sun or of the moon, in a continuous wave
of light, rather that of the sun than that of the moon, Gertrude
Stein seated among the Immortals, and this time Suzanne,
without Adrien, what could they be saying to each other in
such a thoughtful manner, was it true that they were still in
love, how would esthetes like them accept the withered state
of old age, its inertia, its slow paralysis of the brain, and the
blemishes, the bacteria that would defile the beauty of their
bodies, the decay that leaves us no choice, will they have a
pact, a secret pact, like some others, a shameful agreement
they can't speak of to their children, but don't parents have
the right to be silent, why should they tell their children
everything, parents in the past had more authority over
their families, the dark colours of Daniel's *Strange Years*
leached onto you, he wrote with chlorine on the fabric, on
the protective layer of his readers, Hitler's dog had to be

shown as innocent, of course, like the child Mussolini, for
want of evidence, but the boy was undoubtedly a little crazy,
thought Jean-Mathieu as he graciously bade Mélanie good-
night, what an unforgettable evening, madame, he said,
looking out towards the street, which was dark and deserted,
it's so late, soon we will hear the song of the doves and the
turtledoves, and Veronica Lane will be my girlfriend, thought
Samuel, who was dancing close to Venus on the stage, they
would be married in their diving suits at the bottom of the
Atlantic, twenty-four feet below the surface of the seas, like
Rachel and Pierre, that other couple of the seas, other underwater weddings would follow next to the statue of the seas,
the Christ of the Rocks that sailors had carved in wood, a
statue flying as Samuel and Veronica themselves would fly,
among the rocks and the fish, the lively, quivering blue
fauna, the striped spider-crabs, jumping from the sailboard's
float or from Samuel's boat, diving so deep with their air
hoses, their waterproof flashlights, their harnesses and their
weightbelts, like Rachel and Pierre, beneath their masks, with
flippers on their feet, Samuel and Veronica would be reunited
when she came back from New York, a hot, humid wedding,
they would have many children and they'd drive them
around in a carriage sitting comfortably on roller-skates that
gave off translucent flashes, like Samuel's skates on the pavement at night, an umbrella against the sun in the daytime,
over their heads, skating without stopping, rolling along
amid the incessant buzzing of flies and bees, Samuel and
Veronica, and Samuel had also sung psalms in his alto voice
with Venus in the school choir, and was it true what his
parents said, that no compensation, none, could bring relief
to those who had lost their houses, their temples, their
churches in the village of Bois-des-Rosiers, long afterwards,
Sylvester, his mother, and his dog, Polly, who had been shot

down behind the trees, a rifle to their heads, their prayers could be heard through the partly open door, come and dance, said Venus, for this is our dwelling-place, there was also the sound of hollow laughter, of the gnashing of teeth, the hot, humid wedding of Samuel and Veronica among the beetles, the frogs, at that very moment astronauts were beginning their days of flight, perhaps a researcher, Samuel's grandfather, Joseph, who had been launched into the space station, would experiment on himself for the doctors in his laboratory, how did the human organism adapt to space, he would need a probe to determine the heart-rate during the days spent flying in a state of weightlessness, some mice would go with them, how would the tiny animals in orbit react to the tests to which the American and Soviet crews would subject them, there was no promise of landing with such spacecraft, yet there would be landings on Mars through migrations, each person from so far away would remember the sweet world, the sweet earth, after a number of years in flight space-shuttle pilots would suddenly be earthsick, Samuel and Veronica, soon to be married twenty-four feet below the ocean's surface, like Rachel and Pierre, themselves a flying statue like Christ of the Rocks, arms reaching towards heaven beneath their masks, for on these festive nights when the jasmine blossoms, the mimosa, were distilled in the fragrant air, and Venus sang, let my joy endure, what a sensation of freshness to find them all here, thought Renata, Daniel, Mélanie, Samuel who had grown so much over the winter, Daniel and Mélanie, a luminous couple who did not yet know the painful findings of conflicts and rifts, what freshness, like the hope of soon swimming in the green water, avid for water, for rain on her burning body, why had she not postponed her departure, suddenly she was very sensitive to the discrepancy between her ideas and Claude's, the mystery of that unknown woman who had written a book, beneath the vegetation that climbed over the rented house, should it not be revealed to her, a woman's writing was often impenetrable, each of them imposed on her audacious feelings of rebellion the armour-plating acquired through an archaic education, what confusion though, what giddiness to go to bed and get up alone here, with no sensuality, deprived of strength in this insular limbo, the clock showing that it would soon be dawn, morning, and that she would be no less alone, hearing Claude's voice in the evening, how many times had he spoken to her reproachfully about her cigarettes, her gold cigarette case, objects of a satiety beyond redemption, O light smoke in the jasmine-scented air, soothing objects, beneficent as the green ocean water would be on skin set ablaze by a gentle fire in the sluggish heat, when she walked to the beach, permeated by the sultry air, the heat, and the vague desire to be somewhere else, at liberty, dissolved into the life of that other woman who had gone away, now so remote, the ghost of a woman's existence on which the wind had breathed, even though she was said to have written some wonderful poems, in the solitude of this dense, abundant vegetation, having disappeared into these places as she would do elsewhere, she had chanted the lament of her soul, she had learned Hebrew, ancient Greek, she had written "into this room where tension, disorder, and discord reign, behind this door, my illuminated spirit withdraws," was her spirit secluded and walled up, whom had she waited for, loved, against what man, what love had she defended herself, alone, with the tension of her preoccupied and fervent spirit, she had been incapable of living without waiting, without hoping, the study of ancient Greek, of Hebrew, had been her treasures buried in the drowsiness of the heat and, little by little, of abandon, like Renata she had feared the sentinel behind the door, had been startled when someone sneezed in the street at night, a few steps away, so near, there was always a shadow, the black sentinel behind the door, the opaque presence of the West Indian suddenly slumped against a wooden fence, or on a sidewalk, like that other woman who had also written poetry no one could decipher, in the deportation centre of a ghetto, she had left only a few words that were legible, help, help, before she was taken to a train, the train would go to Treblinka, to this room my illuminated spirit withdraws, none of her poems would be read, to this room where tension and discord reign, behind the door, help, that existence had been merely a phantom breathed on by a wind of madness, and rather than run away to Brazil where she had died, the unknown woman who had written wonderful poems had been illegally confined by a brother, a friend, in the name of Christian faith, of silence, of oppression, in a psychiatric hospital where she had suddenly stopped writing, dazed, numbed, within the walls of her white cell, in Hebrew, in ancient Greek, she had tried to write letters on those walls, help, she had chanted her soul's lament, in the chamber of disorder where her voice had been lost among so many cries and lamentations, around women, even when they were scarcely born, were the mysteries of their disappearance, in India, in China, their mothers still laid them down two by two, in holes in the earth that would be their graves, those same mothers had gently choked them with balls of rice, and now they lay entangled, dolls with silken hair, the cut sheaves of their lives, with their hands joined under the veil of dirty, dusty earth, unproductive, with no dowry, their mothers had held them against their own bodies, as if they were nursing them with murderous milk, the final weaning of the constrictions in their throats, holding them so close to their breasts, and who heard the words those mothers spoke to their daughters while they choked, wept, O unproductive, choking, weeping with their daughters while the balls of rice sank deeper, these mothers whose fingers were scissors cutting into their children's mouths, their throats, snipping the veins in the gullets of those small birds, in other countries those same mothers, assisted by the same accomplice, abandoned the passengers in their van beside a beach, a girl, a boy, toddlers with a shovel, a bucket, now long ago, when night fell shortly they would wait for the new car to return, its low-slung, gleaming profile, that woman at the wheel of her car who was their mother, during the long, long journey from the house to this beach far from their city they had slept safely, the door locked, and suddenly they were alone, with their buckets, their shovels, on a sandy beach, the van driving very fast along other roads, without their mother, who was at the wheel, what would become of them, the night wrapped itself around them, murmuring with hostile sounds, a mother, Laura, a mother who could never be dissociated from her crime, the mother of Sugar Candy or of the orphans on a beach, a woman threatened with being disappeared, with being taken away by the abductor, had betrayed them, had abandoned or killed them, some of these women remembered their disappearance, their abduction, schoolgirls skipping rope, in the parks, a boy, nearly a man, had invited them to lie down with him in the grass, on those days in May when the earth was perfumed, they recalled their disappearance from that park, from that garden, sometimes they had been taken away, as if by the evening breeze, from the bed where they were napping, they had scarcely been deflowered, then returned to their beds where their mothers would discover them and dress their wounds, oh, the pleading on her return, Renata's pleading would be tireless, for those lives, victims or criminals, alone or with Claude, she would be tireless, Renata told Mélanie, and seeing the two women so close together in their passionate discussion, Renata's hand clasping Mélanie's in a burst of protectiveness, as if Mélanie were one of those young girls, again, whom she had just described, taken from their beds while they were napping, by some thoughtful seducer who had come in through a window, climbed down the face of the wall, Mère remembered her solitary reflections during the afternoon, in the pool, Renata's bare shoulders under her satin jacket, the way that proud, beautiful woman attracted young men to her suddenly offended Mère, and most of all the influence, however discreet, that Renata seemed to exert on Mélanie, who listened to her with respectful attention, but if they were discussing politics or motherhood, Mère's daughter would lose her temper finally, for you could no longer bring up those subjects with Mélanie, could she be pregnant again, was she going to have a fourth child, as Mère had asked Mélanie on the swing that afternoon, let Mère be preserved from all those grandchildren, she had so many to visit already, to bring up, to educate, when Mère was so often alone with her husband's infidelities, when Mélanie had so much to do, she was so gifted, it's true, as her architect friend had explained to Mère, that a pond by the pavilion beneath the oleanders was a charming idea, Mère remembered a castle, the Château de Marconnay in the Loire Valley, details of the fifteenth- and sixteenth-century architecture, the Loire Valley, said Mère, the châteaux, the caves, the snails and tasty mushrooms raised there, the dried apples cooked over a wood fire, Mère's gastronomic fervour was stirred along with her memories, it's been a long time since I saw that château, I was with my French governess, Mère told the architect, the keen scholar listened to Mère, repeating, ah, you were there, you've been to the Loire Valley, but Mère's emotion when she talked about her French governess did not touch him, Mère's eyes settled again, sorrowfully, on Mélanie and Renata under the black almond trees, on Samuel who was dancing next to Venus, just a few hours ago Mélanie had been angry with Mère over some observation she had made, saying she didn't approve — the observation was mainly a moral one — of models in bikinis displaying the advanced state of their pregnancy on magazine covers and on television, in the past models withdrew from public life when they were expecting children, what about this display on magazine covers, in illustrated periodicals of bodies deformed by motherhood, and now these young women were exhibiting themselves ostentatiously, sometimes in the seventh month of their pregnancy, their hands exposing the indecency of their rounded stomachs, naked or in a bikini, what was this rage for making children, for displaying them before their birth, the couturiers, the clothing industry shouldn't let those young women humiliate themselves like that, said Mère, and why should those young women have to interrupt their careers, Mélanie had replied to her mother, they had quarrelled, argued for a few moments, the children of those progressive mothers, Mélanie had said, and Mère thought her daughter was something of an idealist, those children whose mothers were awaiting them so proudly would be born into a world that had been disarmed for them, as you saw on the covers of magazines, the great powers were signing peace accords, never again would genocide through nuclear weapons be contemplated, and while Mélanie was talking to her mother, Mère had imagined those technicians of death camouflaged by their gloves, their aprons, their laboratories, carefully they would dismantle the bombs they had built, bombs that were their children and that they referred to in tender terms, they would put them to bed after knowing them in the cradle, they said sadly, they would get rid of the atomic material, the arsenal of destruction, in the laboratory elevators a halt in the music had long since announced an ultimatum, an emergency from which there was no way out, the technicians were dismantling their toys, armed convoys would transport the dead bombs along winding roads, where would they be buried, interred, so close to the sand, to the earth, the explosive cargo would be positioned, put to bed, not without regret, the music in all the elevators would fall silent, four dazzling young women displayed their rounded bellies on the covers of magazines, in newspapers, where would the defunct bombs be buried, under what hills, what mountains, under the sand of what California desert, those children would come into a world that was united, disarmed, and Mère had announced these stupid observations to her daughter and there was a sudden misunderstanding between them, yes, Mère had been happy in the Loire country, it was a long time ago, she told the architect, who was a family friend, she had been with her French governess. And Jean-Mathieu, leaning on his cane, made his way towards the dark, deserted street, Daniel and Mélanie are absolutely adorable, he thought, what was that murmur of cars and the shouts coming from the main avenues all about, the festivities were getting under way, festivities that struck an old man as so noisy and carnival-like, everywhere there was too much noise, too much agitation, sensations perceived by the ears are amplified by our internal sounds, by the waves inside us, whereas the poet had always liked to live amid silence, on Atlantic Boulevard there was too much noise, the motors of boats, of cars, all those motors revving, Jean-Mathieu had forgotten that the festivities got under way so early this year, one just had to avoid the main avenues, to go towards the harbour, in the past, of course, when they first came here,

Daniel and Mélanie had had numerous reasons to be
delighted, it was paradise, we were ruled by liberty and
poetry, or both at once, the island was the Athens of our
Socratic mayor, Plato's Athens, we were the city of liberalism
with Martin and his companion Johann, everywhere, on the
terraces, the poets would read their works, the artistic
Johann opened art galleries, the young people's hair rippled
to their waists, they weren't always clean, they slept on the
beaches at night, and this Athens in America, this oasis of
peace had seduced Daniel and Mélanie, it was like them,
of their time, the "ever-changing world" was here, said
Martin, and when he fell sick a poet took over from him,
Lamberto, who was equally imaginative and determined, he
was a gourmand who loved good food, women, with them
the current of ideas expanded, a few women, a few black
judges were elected, Martin's Athens, Lamberto's epicurean
island, and suddenly they came, no one knows how they
were able to slip in among us, at first we barely saw, barely
heard them, ah, and now it's too late to think of being useful
to society, who wants to listen to an old man's protests,
some day, who knows, perhaps he will be heard, and now,
with one hand on his cane, Jean-Mathieu stopped to look at
the ocean as he approached it, poor Martin, he thought,
holding his breath, when I saw him in the hospital, those
tumours, those things in his head, he said, in the city of the
"ever-changing world," and suddenly here he was, all in
white, in his bathrobe, with Johann at his side, Martin asked
Johann for a glass of water, and when he came back from
the bathroom Martin was no longer with us, Martin had
always said he didn't believe in those things that were gnawing at him like worms, he didn't believe in death, he said,
tomorrow he would be the first light of dawn, for, as you'll
see, no glimmer of light is ever lost, Jean-Mathieu had walked

too quickly down the dark, deserted street, avoiding those sounds, so close by, coming from the main avenues, already the sound of drums could be heard, poor Martin, he had said, you have to dance with death, poor Martin, thought Jean-Mathieu, leaning on his cane, he had never realized that the vultures were among us. And Tanjou's black T-shirt, the cords, the leather boots that hadn't had time to wear out, Jacques's sister had put those objects in order, along with the book of notes about Kafka, the unfinished translation of a poem by Huldrych Zwingli, one of whose lines, Gsund, herr gott, gsund! offered hope, good health, dear God, good health, Ich mein, ich ker schon widrumb herr, would it be the return of good health, I am no longer afflicted, those objects, those words, shouldn't she put them in order, weren't these verses addressed to her now, Gsund, herr gott, gsund!, from these objects she had held on her knees for so long, Tanjou's black T-shirt, the cords, the boots that hadn't had time to wear out, out of their reach, for she was healthy and alive, she was Jacques translating the words of his resurrection, emerging victorious from the humiliating passage, she was Jacques writing in his notebook, Gsund, herr gott, gsund!, good health, dear God, would I be out of their reach, she was the gaze directed at the notebook, the industrious hand that was writing, oh, good health, dear God, would it mean the return of good health, for after the humiliating passage, the complete debasement of the body, what had suddenly happened: the improvement, the perfecting of a life, a glimmer of light, a solar light in the night, each object had been put back in order, thought the sister, the friend, on those mornings, those dawns that were soon to be reborn around Jacques, there would be a harmonious link between them, all anger would have vanished with his ashes, Gsund, good health, dear God, all anger between them would have vanished when Jacques had indicated to his sister in a dream where the key would be found, it was in the drawer where she stored the children's school things for fall, their scarves, their woollen hats, let her quickly open the compartment in the drawer, there would be no more secrecy there, only good order, and what a radiant impression struck the eye from what she discovered there — paintings her brother was bequeathing to her, pictures that were imprecise but gave off a rosy light, what a radiant impression the paintings made on the soul, she drew courage from looking at them, from the rosy light came pale drawings of their faces as children, at the time when they had been gentle to one another, without anger, before Jacques was despised by his family and friends, it suddenly seemed that she drew some comfort from her brother's presence, he was standing near her, showing her the way, there, take this key, open this compartment, the paintings are for you, the light of dawn had wakened her, had she slept, what had she dreamed, about those objects, Tanjou's T-shirt, the cords, the boots that hadn't had time to wear out, she had put those objects in order, Gsund, good health, herr gott, gsund!, she was beyond their reach, she was becoming Jacques's industrious hand, his gaze directed at the notebook, and the light of dawn shone beneath her eyelids. Marie-Sylvie will go back to her country, Jenny will be a doctor in the swampy bush where white masters no longer kill their slaves on their plantations, thought Mélanie, for Jenny had the courage to denounce the sheriff, and she, Mélanie, would be alone with Vincent, alone, without Jenny and Sylvie, what would Mélanie be to Vincent, bending over him in the big bed, would it be tonight, tomorrow, every day she would ask Daniel, the incursion of the wind, both of them bending over Vincent, when would they be shaken by masses of air from every direction, so close to Vincent, to his suddenly more rapid breathing, in the room filled with vortical winds, the windy room, but the air would be pure, would be endlessly cleaned, in the room resonant with all the storms, all the tropical storms, sometimes they would have to rush the child, wrapped in a blanket, to the oxygen tent, but shouldn't they thank heaven that Vincent had been born in paradise and not in some infernal part of Mozambique, Daniel and Mélanie were members of the Association of Child Survivors, those children too were called Vincent, Augustino, Samuel, let us save the children who can no longer be saved, thought Mélanie, but it's too late, for by the age of eight or sometimes less they've become officers, guerrilla commanders who have learned to execute, to loot, in the adults' guerrilla warfare you would think it was a school assembly, Vincent who slept in the big bed would not be with them in Angola, in Cambodia, child soldiers like war, kidnapped from their families, from their villages with no ransom, they perpetuate the atrocities of their elders, obeying orders, it was said that they learned quickly, sometimes they came back home to loot the very villages from which they had been taken, with their submachine guns the child soldiers made excellent assassins, they would be told, kill your father, your mother, chop them up with your knife as you'd chop an onion, and they would obey, their reward some cigarettes, a piece of clothing, a few paltry provisions, they would go into battle among the rebels, the patriots, but from what country, Mozambique, Afghanistan, in the camps, among their rifles, they could have been a gathering of naïve school-children, they were kidnapped, stolen from their mothers, they would die at the front in their thousands, die of starvation as well, they were familiar with AK-47s, they could storm the enemy, but what was to be done with them afterwards, when they were found by some volunteer association, in a few months Vincent would take his first steps on the beach, Mélanie would talk about the AK-47 in her presentation, Mozambique, Cambodia, would it be tonight, tomorrow, thought Mélanie, the irruption of winds in the room, winds lashing the blinds, the shutters, the rumbling of those winds, the long lugubrious note as they raced under the black clouds, they would circulate in the room, and from every direction, suddenly, even on sunny days, would come the gushing of water, of rain on the roof, but Vincent would be close to her, in the big bed, there, under the oxygen tent, she would watch over his sleep with Daniel and the nurses, night and day, they would neither sleep nor eat, they would hang on the breathing of Vincent, who would be saved, in the room resonant with all the storms, when Jenny and Sylvie were far away, when Mélanie was alone, but what's the matter, why this sudden sadness, asked Renata as she took Mélanie's hand in hers, and Mélanie said she was worried about Jean-Mathieu, he had refused her husband's offer to take him home, the streets are dark and deserted at this time of night, but these are festive nights, said Suzanne to Adrien, see you later, our prison, my friend, is that we go out every evening, said Adrien, every night even, I'm asleep on my feet by afternoon, over my dictionaries, Adrien sighed, and with our son coming tomorrow, the mad ecologist, we won't be allowed to smoke, let alone drink, not even a five o'clock martini, though he didn't learn that from us, I'd have preferred a dissipated son, said Suzanne, now, now, said Adrien, restraining Suzanne's outburst, she often seemed overexcited to him, too passionate, now, now, I know you prefer your daughters' company, that's because they're more interesting, said Suzanne with conviction, they're young journalists who are already being noticed in New York, I must have a word with Daniel before I go, said Adrien, how will the boy describe us in his books, perhaps he intends to put us in somewhere, among the shadows on the way to the River Eternity, our small craft isn't ready for such a departure, said Suzanne, laughing, we must tell the boy that we have a long life ahead of us, plenty of parties and outings, what a child, I'd gladly let him in on some of my youthful follies. Above all, we mustn't give him anything, said Adrien, he already remembers too much, but doesn't it bother you that such young people are writing books, didn't we start later? No, said Suzanne, we were thirty too, I'll take him out to lunch, said Suzanne, and my amusing stories will damp the fires on the shores of his inferno; Mélanie heard Suzanne's laughter in the night, dawn has not yet broken, thought Jean-Mathieu, it's the time of day when the sick do battle with their illness, perhaps I could visit Frédéric, isn't he here, near the harbour? It's tiresome listening to the background sounds from over there, like the clamour of a crowd, and Jean-Mathieu was walking towards the paths where only giant palm trees could be seen, their trunks half-uprooted by storms, they seemed to be drifting on the water, thought Jean-Mathieu, Frédéric's house was buried under the palm trees, Edouardo, I'm back, said Jean-Mathieu, knocking on the door of the yellow-painted house, I've come for a short visit, Jean-Mathieu followed Edouardo into Frédéric's bedroom, dear Fred, I knew you wouldn't be asleep, we had a date on the roof of a café yesterday, with Adrien and Suzanne, I think you forgot to join us there, wasn't that date a month ago, said Frédéric, now then, come and sit on the bed, Jean-Mathieu, Edouardo's bought a TV set, a new Walkman too, would you like to listen to the Grieg concerto, Edouardo is neglecting his work as a gardener to take care of me, why is he so concerned about me? It's because you're forgetting your appointments, said Jean-Mathieu, Edouardo reminds you about them, of course, but you never forget the Grieg concerto or a single image on your TV set, Edouardo pulled Jean-Mathieu into the corridor, what can I do, he said, Frédéric won't eat properly, he's lost more weight, Fred is getting thinner, thought Jean-Mathieu as he approached his friend lying on his bed, in front of his television set, you look more and more like a Giacometti sculpture, Fred, he observed, I see you're all dressed up to go out, as if you wanted to spend the night with us, we even saw Charles, who goes out so seldom, and Daniel and Mélanie are absolutely adorable. I forgot to go to their house, said Frédéric, eyes glued to his television screen, Edouardo even wrote me a note, I've forgotten everything, was it a week ago, last Monday, on the roof of a café? asked Frédéric, his voice suddenly filled with anxiety, this is the fourth time in three days that I've forgotten an invitation. The people are all in disguise, and in the streets we can already hear the drums, yes, said Frédéric, I can hear them, and Jean-Mathieu said that the beginning of these festivities would be exhausting, they would have to be wary of vandalism, and all that noise, all that noise, he repeated, and now look at you, said Jean-Mathieu to Frédéric, so skinny that your belt can't hold your pants up, and I'm dizzy too, said Frédéric, oh, if it weren't for Edouardo, what would become of me? The question hung in the fragrant air, unanswered, Frédéric was breathing in the cool evening air, the night air on the orange trees, the lemon trees, I'm so comfortable here, he said, his voice was broken by his use of tobacco, what torture, said Frédéric, all those hours spent rehearsing Grieg's "Lyric Pieces," which I used to play in concert when I was twelve, and the Mendelssohn concerto, we must have pity on child prodigies resting their foreheads against their pianos, their violins, as for me, I was right to give it all up, my younger brother and my classmates were all so jealous, what torture, all those hours of exercises,

Grieg's "Lyric Pieces," the Mendelssohn concerto, now I have to watch the screen in silence, my friends, where is that street, tell me, how does one get to Daniel and Mélanie's place? And is Charles in a monastery already, has he forgotten we were friends for nearly half a century, has he forgotten the portraits of him that I painted in Greece, in Germany, it's true, said Jean-Mathieu, close to half a century, it's true, what old soldier doesn't remember his wounds, said Frédéric, Charles was my war wound, my defeat in combat, he's a genius, Charles, I was just a young virtuoso with my forehead pressed against the keyboard of my piano, pity those boys and girls collapsed on their musical instruments in fatigue, Charles, why doesn't he live with me now? It's my music, perhaps he doesn't like my music any more, or the sound of my TV set all night. He's an ascetic old bachelor who can't live with anyone, said Jean-Mathieu, and the love of God is a battle, said Frédéric, nodding, his head seemed to be adorned with downy white feathers like a bird's, God, a battle against the cold, I've always told Charles, God is too cold for me, I thought you were an atheist, Fred, said Jean-Mathieu, what does God have to do with it, we were talking about Charles, God and Charles resemble each other, said Frédéric, has Edouardo shown you my book, it's a marvel, again it was Charles's idea to bring together what I've written, a gift from Charles, a marvel I had so little faith in, such a beautiful book inside its midnight-blue covers, and did I really do all those drawings, all those portraits, it's essential to live and create, even if, as in my case, everything is suddenly forgotten, even if I forget everything, you know, Jean-Mathieu, those portraits and drawings really are my work, even if I often forget every-thing, God, no matter how cold He is, said Jean-Mathieu, though I'd rather not talk about Him, what's He doing in our conversation now, God didn't deprive you of any of His gifts, music, painting, like Charles, oh, if you'd wanted you could have been the poet of your generation, yes, but the writing, all those hours of exercises, even during the recital of Grieg's "Lyric Pieces" I already couldn't take any more, what was my brother doing, he was playing ball, going to dances with girls, when I was sixteen I had definite proof of the cold indifference of God, He made that pianist go ahead of me, the one who unleashed the audience's enthusiasm, a pianist who didn't have to work, despite the difficulties of the pieces he played with diabolical ease, he was the Paganini of the piano, his name was Frédéric too, he hadn't even reached puberty, I was amazed that his child's fingers could stretch across all the notes, my studies had been thorough but his weren't, he only had to appear in public and he was applauded, yes, there was that portrait of Charles in the red velvet music-room, somewhere in New England, in one of those houses the two of us shared, I also remember "Flowers on Christine's Table," in Sicily, and "Bust of Charles," we used to play bridge, how I miss those winter evenings in Greece, even if we used to quarrel all the time, how young we were then, thirty, thirty-two perhaps, the candelabrum had six branches, the ceiling of the study hall, the ceiling that I painted, in a watercolour, it was red too, wasn't it? The Paganini of the piano, a phenomenon, a genuine prodigy, when I got that uncomfortable proof of the cold indifference of God I renounced everything, though I still remember Grieg's "Lyric Pieces" and Mendelssohn's concerto by heart, but how is Charles, is it true he intends to become a monk? Is he still so gloomy, does he still care for me a little, even though I lost my memory first, does he still remember me? Tutti son pien di spirti, thought Jean-Mathieu, and as if he had suddenly forgotten what questions he'd asked, with Charles's face growing blurred in Frédéric's mind amid the mist where God cast His cold indifference over men, the TV screen again consuming all his attention, Frédéric was describing how the pilots flew under the bridges in Munich, I was with them, he said, in those airplanes, how terrible for all those people who were dying in the smouldering wreckage, others ran away, ordinary people like all the rest, and how terrible for them, for all of us, when we flew under the bridges, you'll never see me in one of those planes again, never, I came to remind you that we're having dinner at Suzanne and Adrien's on Sunday, said Jean-Mathieu, I'll pick you up at seven, you'll have to write it down, Edouardo, otherwise I won't remember, said Frédéric, Sunday night, dinner at Suzanne and Adrien's, were we thirty or thirty-two in Greece, two men, so young, meet in a bar, both of them waiting for someone else, and two weeks later they're living together, for an eternity of time, though they hardly know each other, was it madness or the generous inspiration of youth? Tutti son pien di spirti, thought Jean-Mathieu, what noise, what noise, those planes flying under the iron bridges, the poor people leaving with no baggage, Vincent would grow up in paradise, thought Mélanie, but there would always be the predators' shadow, the Shadow with the crimson face under his hood, that Julio had talked about, but hadn't Julio been delirious with sorrow that night on the beach? Vincent would take his first steps on an airy beach, the crimson-faced woman with her children, they were obese, like their mother, they wore the same clothes, resembling sacks, their bodies were never subjected to any healthy exercise, they were envious of Samuel, Augustino, Vincent on the beaches, playing in the ocean waves, envious, cruel, the Shadow's sons, fed copiously on the carnage of cattle, those sons whose bodies seemed to have a gelatinous consistency, the Shadow's massive children, a people so undeveloped they were not human, they would all roughly attack the beauty, the grace of Samuel, Augustino, Vincent, killing Mélanie's children would be their revenge for the disadvantaged world into which they'd been born, they who had never been loved or desired, who were ugly and fat, their obesity making them repugnant to themselves, while fat accumulated around them, they, the sons of the Shadow, crimson-faced beneath his hood, neophytes of hatred, of racism, how they loved throwing stones at the slim legs of Samuel on his skates, they would grab hold of the cherubic Augustino, their hands hungry for stones, for blows with a stick, to rape, to kill these children of Mélanie's, their hungry hands would strip them of their Sunday clothes, they had to brutalize these beings from a different class, a different religion, they would maintain their coarse cruelty even before the courts, they would all attack the grace of Samuel, of Augustino, attack Vincent's frailty, they were the predators, their Shadows were prowling near Samuel's boat on the sea, they were prowling past the gate, everywhere they were free, and as they grew they were unrecognizable inside their hoods, painting the walls with their insignia in the colour of blood, was it true what Julio said, what Jenny and Sylvie said, but the children must know nothing, let them enjoy themselves, let them sing beside Venus on the stage, oh, was it true what Julio whispered very softly into Mélanie's ear when they were alone, was it true that the White Horsemen had arrived? Suzanne is a serene woman, thought Mélanie, I too was a serene woman, and it seemed that Mélanie's serenity before Vincent's birth had dissolved, like those cruise ships whose decks were decorated with all their lights in the night, suddenly, at the end of the horizon they could no longer be seen, and always there was the memory of that hollow sensation of thirst Renata had felt when, beneath the flight of swallows, the laughing boatmen glided across the water, and when they came in contact with that thirst, when it was present in their lives, all living creatures trembled, they understood the extent of their mortality, there was terror on all sides, the animals that could not defend themselves as well as we could were destroyed by it, thought Renata, among the world-famous palaces in Venice, their marble façades, under the basilicas, in the density of its coloured houses on the water along the Grand Canal, a humiliating detail reminded Renata of that appalling thirst from which one could die, behind an iron gate where men released their urine, amid the Gothic architecture that was so precious, a thirsty cat was wandering, its flanks plastered against its bones, it went behind the iron gate, crawling towards the excremental water of life itself, so alone in the vast light of the Venetian afternoon when the bells no longer announced the arrival of those rich travellers who had perhaps given it food and water in the past, alone in that grandiose landscape it might perish from this aching thirst, this hollow sensation of thirst that affected the senses, that was for each of them the sign of a slow debasement of the vital forces, of a sly decline towards mortality, and holding in her open hand an iguana just a few days old, which would be a present for Samuel, grazing the iguana's prickly crest with her sensual fingers, Venus sang, she danced on the dais among the musicians, higher than the sound of the trumpets, of the alto saxophones, thought Mélanie, that voice of Venus's, its pitch, its range transported her, had she forgotten, thought Mélanie, that back home Deandra and Tiffany hadn't been vaccinated yet, that Mama was barely able to read and write, Uncle Cornelius was languishing at night on his piano, at the mixed club, he had tuberculosis and he never rested, oh, but it was the fault of all those women in his life, said Mama, they took all his money, they devastated his health, when Uncle Cornelius had all those children, where were they all, on Bahama Street, on Esmeralda Street, Venus was the skater whirling across the ice who would take the bronze medal, a reward for her dazzling technique, now she laughed at the competence of white people, she was Mary McLeod Bethune, born after the abolition of slavery, she founded the first school for black girls in Florida, a friend of Eleanor Roosevelt, she played an important role in the fight against racial discrimination, in her country's government, for so high was the range of Venus's voice conveying joy that the old world and the darkness of years past crumbled against its freshness, thought Mélanie, the abolition of slavery, the snowy beach of a century on which no step had left its mark, no echo, no voice, only the voice of Venus, and Tanjou had walked along the beaches all night, along the piers and their wooden pavilions, he was walking towards the tennis court, holding his canvas shoes, towards the gardens of the Grand Hotel, their shimmering greenery under the rosy line of dawn where he headed every morning, in his shorts and brightly coloured shirt, today his game would be aerial, soaring, he thought, he would return the ball across the net with decisive precision, would suddenly see Jacques's silhouette against the rosy whiteness of the sky, when would this player stop flying, his partner would say of him, he kept himself in the air with the wing of his racquet, a sardonic winged figure, when will those Orientals stop outdistancing us, they were too skilful, how precisely Tanjou in his light tennis shoes would return the ball, from the city the modulation of voices still rose through the sound of the waves, a clamour, the second player would soon be here, or should Tanjou admit that he too could lose, smiling through his tears at a ceremony where he was receiving flowers like Martina Navratilova, you could try to suffer this defeat with a smile, the desire to win gripped him even more as he approached the court, how alertly, how precisely he would send the ball to the other side of the net, thought Tanjou, but where was the second player, was he still back there parading through the streets during the festive nights masquerade, and Renata said to Mélanie, soon it will be dawn, could we not drink a toast to Vincent, wish him happiness with all our hearts, for one couldn't live without serenity, thought Mélanie, yes, as day broke they would all raise their glasses to Vincent's health, from the second floor of the house, on the veranda shrouded with roses, with Daniel at her side, and Jenny, Sylvie, surrounding the couple with their vigilant presence, as this night drew to an end would it not be too humid, would the air not be too hot, they would say as they inhaled the flower-scented air, Mélanie would take her child in her arms, she would be triumphant, happy, for at this dawn of a new century Vincent had just been born, and she would say to all of them, here is my child, my son, what she had seen, the cruise ship *America*, its decks decorated with so many lights, no longer merged with the darkness of a long night at the end of the line of the horizon, it was a cruise ship flickering with light but for a long time it projected luminescent beams onto the water, like those of the moon, Vincent's life was this beach where no step had yet left its mark, no, who could live without serenity, without happiness, hope, thought Mélanie, so high was the range of Venus's voice that the old world crumbled against its freshness. Charles's nerves had been on edge for some time now, was it the muggy air in the bedrooms where each of them spent the day writing, or the suffocating heat behind the blinds, I must go home now, thought Charles, enough of this social chitchat, he said, getting to his feet, Adrien and Suzanne were chatting about literature with Daniel, when would they go back to their houses, all these outings, all these trips, Charles was expected at one of those far-off universities where he was to be given a prize, an honorary doctorate, it's time now for meditation, for silence, he thought, for so long our existence consists of such triviality, then death comes unexpectedly, and we haven't even kept a little time for it, such triviality, thought Charles as he looked at the straw-bottomed chairs in which they'd been seated, all four of them, during the night, now dawn was colouring the backs, the seats of the unoccupied white chairs with its vivid light, a few more years and there will be nothing but the white of our empty chairs around a table, white as the white flag of our shared surrender, for in this garden filled with the voices of children and the young we, Jean-Mathieu, Adrien, and I, will have left nothing but the white of our chairs, chalk white, in the hesitant rays of dawn, has the time not come, thought Charles, to shut ourselves away, to submit to the rule of silence, far from the follies of the world, that chitchat, those never-ending conversations, for they went out for dinner every night, when everything would soon be white, like those four chairs now coloured by the vivid light of the dawning sun, though to Charles it still seemed like night, and for him a starry sky always inspired some comfort, an illusion of well-being, white, nothing but white, on the walls of a cloister, of a secluded convent in Ireland, in a Buddhist retreat in Michigan, what would Charles do in Chicago, deliver a pompous speech to some students, and Adrien said to Daniel, believe me, my friend, it's the critic in me speaking, there's too much excess in your description of chaos, my friend, sobriety of phrase, you need more sobriety and more restraint, my friend, your manuscript, *Strange Years*, is an overexcited product of our time, enough, thought Charles, I think I can hear myself in Adrien's voice, that way teachers purr to their students, we have the conceit that we know everything, and as we approach the hour of our death we are as ignorant as at the hour of our birth, Charles's nerves had been on edge for some time now, he could no longer tolerate the sea, would have had it fenced in so he could no longer see it, no longer hear the tiresome lapping of the waves beneath his window while he wrote, or the scraping of his pen on the paper, for he would never own a typewriter, a computer, and what about that white mane of hair, growing older, people said, absurd, it was the white of chalk, that white at the summit of a brow, a head, the white of the four vacant chairs around a table, when the joyous uproar of the children, of the young people, rang out in the garden, even tucked away in a monastery in Ireland, Charles would still hear everything, the pen scraping on a sheet of paper, like Grieg's "Lyric Pieces" which Fred was listening to as he lay on his bed in front of his TV set, old people had the ability to hear the slightest breath in the night, to be alerted by every sound, they tossed and turned in their sleep, he would hear the Beethoven oratorio Jacques had been listening to, his wasted head between his headphones, secluded behind the walls of a monastery, a convent, a Buddhist retreat, he would hear the tumult of prayers in a mosque, the commotion of voices praying to God interrupted by automatic-weapon fire, the praying, the Intifada that had risen gently from hearts, from chests, suddenly became a contrite and poignant song of war, so many bodies lowered, kneeling before the deaf deity amid so much commotion, from those knees, those chests, those hearts all swallowed up in prayer, what bloodshed when the sweet lament of the Intifada rose up, and Jean-Mathieu told Edouardo and Frédéric as he was leaving them that he'd be back on Sunday, soon we'll see the doves and turtledoves, he said, I'll continue walking along the beach to the house, but Fred must remember that they were all going to dinner at Adrien and Suzanne's on Sunday, Edouardo's hair was always neatly combed, falling down his back in a heavy braid, thought Frédéric, and wasn't Edouardo saying to Frédéric, who was listening abstractedly, always, at this time of year, I think about the aroma of the scorched tortillas I used to eat in my mother's house, and about the gardens of Oaxaca, of Puebla, of the Sierra Madre, but my place is here with Frédéric, said Edouardo, the turtledoves with their collar of black feathers, their piercing eyes, I see them on my terrace when I'm writing, said Jean-Mathieu, the delightful spray of cold water in the shower, so many wonderful hours before I meet Caroline at noon, thought Jean-Mathieu as he descended towards the calm shore of the sea, telling himself he had done the right thing by going to visit Frédéric, in the past we complained when our trash cans stood close together on the sidewalk, when our tree branches were tangled in the branches of our neighbours' trees, and suddenly what we regret most bitterly will be the exact opposite, the absence of invasion on those cracked sidewalks, the branches of the fig trees growing wild, with no one to complain to, neither Charles nor Fred nor Johann, ah, we'll have plenty of regrets one day, thought Jean-Mathieu, putting his cane in front of him as he walked, he felt that his gait was still assured and dignified, what would he have done if he'd suffered dizzy spells like Fred, who sometimes woke up to find he'd fallen out of bed, nor was he irritable like Charles, his health was stable, serene, ah, who was the swimmer arriving so early to break the peace of dawn, Jean-Mathieu moved closer to that form on the water, it was a fair-haired young man outfitted with a diver's mask that he held with his right hand, he was swimming almost silently as if he were floating, in the blue sea glinting with grey, then he straightened up and only his right profile could be seen as he appeared to be shaking the water from his shoulders, one of those blond gods devoted to athletics, to swimming, to scuba diving, but the young man didn't seem concerned that someone might surprise him here, thought Jean-Mathieu, who was he, a strength so compact and solitary emanated from him, and suddenly Jean-Mathieu saw the left side of the young man, an arm was missing, part of the damaged arm was still attached to the shoulder, among the scars of the amputation, like the stump of a bird's wing, there was grandeur in that body that lacked its left arm, a fierce independence in the swimmer's entire person, he expressed such flexibility with his right hand in the way he handled the diver's mask, no, the crushed god had no need to know that an old man was trotting along a beach with his cane, for even though damaged he was still a perfect creature as Jean-Mathieu, with all the weakness of age, no longer was, and what a pity, thought Jean-Mathieu, that blond god struck down on the shores of paradise, swimming by himself among another species that all at once he seemed to belong to — pelicans in search of food, turtledoves with their collars of black feathers and their piercing eyes, white-feathered doves, in that blue water glinting with grey, was he like all the birds taking flight, and thus a poem was born, thought Jean-Mathieu, would it be a prose poem on Fred's broken divinity as he listened to the Mendelssohn concerto he had played in concert when he was twelve? From the boy standing in the water emanated a force so compact and solitary, until that vision disappeared into a vigorous rippling, like that of a tremendous beating of wings under the water. And all is well then, thought Mère as she gazed at the sun rising above the tall pier, next to Augustino whom she was holding by a fold in his cape, the child was wriggling a little, he was agitated, it was true he hadn't slept much last night until each of them raised a glass to Vincent's health at dawn, how proud Mère was of her daughter when she appeared under an arch of roses on the veranda, all is well then, thought Mère, leaning out towards the rolling of the waves, it was here, close to the pier, that she had seen a woman this morning who lacked all of Mère's scruples, and weren't they superfluous, a woman older than Mère decked out in a ridiculous hat as she swam energetically, like a joyful animal, with a gaiety that had struck Mère as infectious, it was time Mère lost her scruples, it was not too late for Mélanie to run in the local election, thought Mère, suddenly experiencing a sense of immeasurable vitality, and who can you see out there, Mère asked Augustino, you can't see the stars any more, said Augustino, they're all gone, no, you can't see the stars or the moon, said Augustino, could Augustino see the ships that would dock soon, and the white heron alone on the high causeway between the sky and the ocean, both of them too vast, already you can't see the stars any more, said Augustino, it was the same white heron rising slowly in his oblique takeoff over a stormy sea, that was how Mère would leave the world, in the same silent takeoff, with no agitation, mutely dignified, she thought, and let Luc and Maria love one another, let them sail far away over the peace of the waters, let them hear from afar the grave drumbeats of these festive nights, Paul skated along with them amid the green, phosphorescent wake, along the streets that lined the sea, from Pedro Zamora, an activist who had died at twenty-two, Paul had received illumination, grace, he thought, Pedro, who was being mourned by his seven brothers and sisters, and hundreds of demonstrators on a beach, during a religious service, so many candles were being consumed for Pedro, the hero whose brown eyes were so gentle under

their heavy brows, had he not been born to save lives, had
he not told them up until the end, in schools, in universities
everywhere, each time he gave a speech, it can happen to
you too, this tragedy, this viral contamination, Paul could
hear the voice of the gentle Pedro, let us live for today,
let's not suffer for tomorrow, Pedro who had been loved,
venerated, God loved Pedro, his friends and his brothers said
of him, God despises you, said his belligerent opponents,
why didn't they put you in jail in Cuba, put you away in one
of those camps filled with people with AIDS from which no
one returns, Pedro, Pedro Zamora, how many candles consumed, how many songs and prayers for Pedro, dead the
same year he finished university, suddenly, the educator of
crowds, a hero mad for love who had been born, like Paul,
like Luc and Maria, only to lose his life, God loved Pedro
Zamora and candles were consumed on the beach during a
religious service, how many tears, how much laughter at the
evocation of the tender-hearted Pedro, whose very
gentle brown eyes under heavy brows could be seen on a
videotape, for it can happen to you too, he said, and a
minister told the demonstrators, let his spirit guide us, let
Pedro's spirit guide us, there are days when we go to the
mountaintop and cannot come back down, that is the story
of Pedro, of Pedro Zamora, and Augustino saw Samuel's
Noah's ark, a boat moored at the pier that was pitching
and tossing on the green water, he told Mère that they were
all in the boat Samuel had seen, the marsh deer, even the
tortoises that had fled during a tropical storm, the cat beside
the duck, the greyhound with the hen, all of them, they were
about to leave, but with no moon, no stars, said Augustino,
it will be colder, it's as if we were at a window open onto all
sorts of wonders, said Mère, and with the vision of the white
heron it seemed to her that the tumult was subsiding in Mère,

the painful feeling that she was at the mercy of all perils, as when she had discovered in her mirror the offensive smile of her sons sitting in the back seat of the limousine, or when she had learned from her parents that her French governess had been dismissed, let us live for today, let's not suffer for tomorrow, said Pedro Zamora, and his spirit guided Paul, he too would go into the schools, the universities, Paul moved with Pedro's soul, his grace, his gentleness, amid the green, phosphorescent wake of his skates, and Luc and Maria were sailing far away, towards the peace of the waters. And Carlos came running at top speed through the parade for this festive night, this night that would last three nights, three more days, and it seemed to him that he could hear the resounding voice of Pastor Jeremy in the hot, humid air, a voice Carlos had often imitated as he strolled with Le Toqué along Bahama Street, Esmeralda Street, shouting to everyone on their porches, on their balconies, O lost sheep who have been unfaithful to your pastor, I say to you, you will all go to hell, for when the oil dwindles in the lamp the life of a man also ends, you, Carlos, said the resounding voice of Pastor Jeremy, haven't you forgotten your dog in the shed, haven't you lied to your mother, those who forget their dog in the shed will go to hell, for the sin of negligence, she would have suffocated to death, her pink tongue lolling under the hair of her muzzle, asphyxiated, if Mama hadn't released Polly from the shed in time, turning her over to the roosters, the hens, on the yellowed grass, and where was Polly on this festive night, without her sliding collar, alone in the crowd and frightened, Polly whose leash Carlos was no longer hold-ing, for three days, three nights, Carlos would devour meat from all the outside grills on Bahama Street, on Esmeralda Street, and spicy rice, he would be drunk from dancing, from beer and rum with the Bad Niggers, his nose bloody from

the last times he'd been punched, and woe unto him, said
Pastor Jeremy, he had forgotten Polly in the shed, a dog, a
stolen animal he was abandoning to suffocation in his father's
shed, in the bush garden, with the icebox, the gambling
table, some ancient Christmas trees with their tinsel, he
would have to clean up the garden, replace the icebox, but
what's not done today, said Mama, will be done tomorrow,
and Carlos had seen the giant sphinx with its crown of pearls,
its lion's head, as it passed under the verandas in the parade
of chariots drawn by the pharaohs; everywhere, hybrid beings
were advancing under the sky, while the moon and the stars
grew slowly fainter and Carlos ran, ran, calling out to Polly,
while others who were staggering and raving under the palm
trees said, me too, Carlos, I've lost my dog, Sunbeam, where
are you, they asked, answer me, and mine was a tiny little
thing, dressed in a hood for Christmas, his name is Lexie,
Lexie, and mine was dressed like King Arthur, I wore him
around my neck, but Polly, where was Polly, her lolling pink
tongue, her wandering eyes, Polly, where was Polly, Uncle
Cornelius's musicians were all there, sitting on narrow chairs,
their instruments propped against their knees, they looked
lugubrious during the procession, all of them shaken up in a
truck that jolted along Bahama Street, Esmeralda Street, and
Mama had said, what's not done today will be done tomorrow,
what can I expect from these good-for-nothing sons, Le
Toqué and that boxer, Carlos, people who steal new bicycles
with bright yellow handlebars will go to hell, said Pastor
Jeremy in his resounding voice, O lost sheep, why do you
not listen to me, it was the night of princes and queens, of
nymphs and coral whales on chariots drawn by pharaohs,
the night of sovereign fish, the night that rules the seas, and
Carlos wasn't dressed up like the others, there were blood-
stains on his yellow T-shirt, a T-shirt that yesterday had sparkled

with the garish yellow of the bicycle handlebars, the bicycle
that held Polly in a basket, and the way Polly understood
everything when Carlos told her, sit, Polly, sit, Polly, on the
sandy beaches, let's go into the waves together, Polly, zigzagging through the crowd, Carlos called to Polly, charged with
fever was the crowd, with intoxicating fervour, drawing the
floats with their sphinxes, their rams, their sparrowhawks,
dragging on its moving back all the monsters of the seas,
moulded from cardboard, from plastic, from plaster, among
the lions with women's heads beneath their feathers and
their crowns of pearls, so many nymphs emerging from the
water to drift through the streets, from the hotel verandas,
the vast balconies, everyone leaned out to look, dazzled, at
all these depictions of myths, of sea legends, the marvellous
coupling of beasts and forests propelling itself everywhere,
down Atlantic Boulevard, and how sad Uncle Cornelius
seemed, sitting among his musicians in the truck that jolted
along under the palm trees, the Bahamian trees on Esmeralda
Street, he was very sick, said Mama, he who had lived the
life of a fisherman, but he was a war hero, a great man
whom his nation had not rewarded, said Mama, in the past
playing the piano, dancing in the streets of New Orleans, his
fingers gnarled, his back bent, so tired, Uncle Cornelius, all
of them dressed in black in the jolting truck, as if their hands,
their feet were still in chains, staring vacantly, what was
Uncle Cornelius thinking about, Christo Salvo, cried a voice,
Christo Salvo, red airplanes were hovering noisily in the low
sky, Christo Salvo, cried a voice, where was Polly, was she
frightened, alone in this crowd, thought Carlos, and Sunbeam,
where was Sunbeam, according to the legend of this festive
night an entire island and its inhabitants had been lost, swallowed up, and it was this Atlantis at the bottom of the ocean
that was springing up from the waters of a catastrophe, a

disaster, with its stone columns, its treasures that everyone
looked at from the balconies, the verandas, where was Polly
in this zigzagging crowd, had she been swallowed up with
the thousands of inhabitants of lost Atlantis, and the path of
Memory is here, thought Charles, who was pedalling along
calmly on his bicycle, so many deafening noises there, so
close, but here, along this path of Memory, of Remembrance,
you could hear the isolated knell in the temples, the
churches, in Pastor Jeremy's hospice, the death-knell tolled,
its tolling repeated in the temples, the churches, amid the
joyous cries, the hubbub of the festivities, announcing the
death of Jacques, of Pedro, of so many young people, said
Pastor Jeremy, there was no longer room for them in the
Cemetery of the Roses, so many tearful grandparents who
had been entrusted with all those grandchildren, with the
children of their daughters, their sons, after their sudden
departure, for Atlantis would be swallowed up by the living
strength of Pedro, of Jacques, at the bottom of the Atlantic,
and against the rosy whiteness of the sky Tanjou could no
longer recognize Jacques's silhouette, the second player was
walking towards him, his partner for the tennis tournament,
why was he so late, asked Tanjou, and hadn't he been drinking, they don't have our discipline, thought Tanjou, no doubt
Raoul would tell him again that Orientals were too strong,
spiritual athletes, he would say, Raoul was wearing his tennis shoes but he had not yet taken off the costume he'd worn
that night, what's the meaning of that costume, thought
Tanjou, when he saw Raoul dash across the court towards
him, his entire body drawn, marked by the framework of a
skeleton, similar to the drawing on a black T-shirt that
Tanjou had worn for a long time when he hung around on
the beaches, I didn't have time to take it off, said Raoul, I just
grabbed a sheet and drew a skeleton on it, said Raoul, lots

of other people had the same idea, and suddenly, at dawn, the city's full of us, all decked out in our skeletons with the green light glimmering on our skin, and Tanjou looked anxiously for Jacques's silhouette against the rosy whiteness of the sky, telling himself that he wouldn't win the tournament, the frail skeleton moving in the air on Raoul's torso bothered him, tears of rage filled his eyes, we're going to lose, he said, and it seemed to him that he could hear Raoul laughing on the other side of the net, whispering some contemptuous remark, his face very pale, Raoul picked up his racquet from the grass, everything's fine, he said, but I feel like vomiting, and the festive night, the festive nights will be extended, two more nights, two more days, Tanjou heard the trumpets and drums, and Polly, where was Polly, Carlos thought, so many puppies lost in a few hours with their ribbons, their sequined collars, so many parrots taking off from their masters' shoulders, in the crowd that had trampled them, and who were all these people coming after the others in the procession, treading heavily, under the wave of their white sheets you could see their eyes through the holes in their hoods, in their hands they held crosses of fire, flaming crosses, they would set fire to the school, from these blazes the village of Bois-des-Rosiers would once again be destroyed by fire, and Polly, where was Polly, was it true then what Mama and Pastor Jeremy said, or were those eyes under the hoods, under the white sheets, merely disguises for a night of masquerade, thought Carlos, running at top speed, sniffing the aroma of the fragrant dishes on the tables set up along the sidewalks, inside him was the growl of hunger, a hunger in his guts that he could satisfy for two more days, two more nights, with spicy rice, with beans and honey, the growl of his hunger which would be satisfied, he would have his fill of beans with honey, of sugary bananas, tutti son pien di spirti maladetti, said Adrien to Suzanne, in his powerful and dramatic voice, those circles of hell contain the accursèd souls, the catastrophes, in that book of Daniel's, really, you're obsessed with our friend Daniel's manuscript, said Suzanne, it's his eyes that fascinate me, coal-black with yellow highlights, I'll invite him to have lunch with me this week; they were pacing back and forth along the seashore, suddenly anxious to return to their house, which resembled a Japanese teahouse with its brown wood laths, their slender feet in leather sandals, their hands enlaced, they were anxious to take off their clothes rumpled by the heat, to lie side by side and nap, friends were expecting them on the tennis court at eight, the sea was sparkling at their feet, in the first rays of the sun, am I not just as beautiful, Suzanne asked her husband, laughing, or don't I have the same regal, defiant attitude as Renata, Mélanie's aunt, whom we've seen surrounded by young men all night? But the style is incoherent, Adrien went on, the style follows the mad slope of a train of thought that is never rational, said Adrien, and it seemed to him that he could hear Suzanne singing softly, it was singing that expressed her satisfaction, her joyful mood, thought Adrien, musing that their son's arrival would inevitably change their indolent habits, champagne and music in bed, Antoine would undoubtedly be displeased to learn that his parents were inseparable accomplices in all their pleasures, and so close to the approaches to the River Eternity, thought Adrien, I think that as Charles suggested tonight, the Inferno section should be structured quite differently, of course I too have seen the prominent shadow on Joseph's arm, but I understood why he never said anything to his children, let us leave what belongs to the past to the circles of hell of the past, tutti son pien di spirti maladetti, was that not Joseph's reaction even when a skinhead had insulted him recently on the bus to Hamburg, all the while deploring the fact that nothing changed, Joseph's reaction at first was one of forgiveness, tutti son pien di spirti maladetti, said Adrien, a pity that Daniel's writing sometimes seems totally incomprehensible, but why did Charles and Jean-Mathieu leave so early? Those chairs suddenly empty at noon, the siesta, Suzanne's soft singing, a little champagne, some music, the sun appearing through the blinds, paradise, said Suzanne, and Adrien was afraid that Suzanne would suddenly undress to go swimming in the sea, he heard her soft singing which expressed her satisfaction with being alive, and Suzanne was right, he was obsessed with Daniel's manuscript. And the path of Remembrance, the path of Memory, thought Charles, as he pedalled his bike beneath the palm trees, here only the repeated tolling of a knell in a church, a temple, could be heard, a fifth straw-bottomed chair was unoccupied, it was Justin's, a chair drifting down a river in northern China, thought Charles, had anyone described the nobility of the human spirit better than Justin in his books, Justin who had in his turn become a painter, a Chinese philosopher like the characters from his childhood in northern China, his soul was somewhere between the high mountains of a village where his father had once been pastor, sad to think that amid the noise and din of the world Justin's compassionate heart made so little sound, that he was so modest when his book questioned the most devastating conflagrations, the bombing of Hiroshima, of Nagasaki, beneath the destroyed cities he had seen men, women, children, dust extirpated from burned flesh, under the metal of arms, it was Justin's chair, unoccupied now in the garden where his large family held their reunion every year, and so he had returned to the rivers, to the mountains of northern China, that humble heart exclaiming that it had not beat enough, a heartbeat and his novel about modern China would be finished, and he would delicately slip away, pen in hand, thought Charles, like a Chinese painter, an old philosopher, the unoccupied chair drifting down one of the rivers of China, and Renata thought that the orchestra musicians in their white suits were the incredible taste of water and smoke, of fire at the edge of one's lips, that causes one's gaze to falter, the fire towards which all nerves strain, they were nimble, racing down the streets with Renata, taking her home, spreading in their wake the music of their guitars, their violins, she would remember this mocking laughter, these songs at dawn, they would continue to stir the same enchantment in her, the same sweet ecstasy exalted by the heat, the dampness in the air, her arms overflowing with the offering of blue orchids and birds of paradise, they were all just undulating forms in the light, she thought, against the slack sea, its tranquillity, its immensity, but like those boatmen standing in their small craft, greeting her as they passed beneath a stone bridge, or inclining their heads in her direction between two low brick walls to which thorny wild roses clung, when their small boats moved away she would stop seeing them, would hear only the few sustained sounds they still drew from their instruments, their mocking laughter, and so, little by little, the hollow sensation of thirst would be dulled, and on the path of Remembrance, of Memory, where Charles was alone, a woman came running from the bushes, telling Charles he wasn't allowed to ride his bike on this path, Charles recognized the Madwoman who tormented the pastor's children, she was constantly dismantling the framework of her fence, preventing people from having access to their houses, the Madwoman of the Path, thought Charles, she always looked respectable in her striped navy sweater, her white slacks, and her one concern was the cleanliness of the island, she would say as she dismantled the framework of the fences or wielded her broom on the sidewalks, sweeping up trash, all those thugs, and was it true, as the Madwoman said, thought Charles, that this city belonged to her, every house, every path, the streets, you see, sir, I can buy them, and the city will finally be cleansed of all those young people, of the Jews and the Chinese, I can buy it all, I have four cars and two chauffeurs in my twenty-two-room house with its closed shutters, but no one goes out, I forbid it, or was Charles imagining the Madwoman in the exhaustion of the end of this night, and I have several black servants too, like your hundred-year-old mama, did you visit your mama this year, sir, how can a famous writer like you, who has won all the prizes for the glory of our country, though you defend blacks and homo-sexuals too much, social parasites who spread disease to everyone, on the ocean waves, sir, they should be sent back on the ocean waves as Dr. Freud said, how can a writer from your social class, with your wealth, give away everything he owns to those indecent unemployed youths who beg in the streets, outside our most respectable buildings, hat in hand, and in particular how can a writer like you travel by bicycle, what would your mama say if she could see you, this island was once our paradise, the paradise of your hundred-year-old mama and of my family, at fifteen my sister was already sec-retary to a banker, we had only bankers and distinguished people here before the arrival of that horde of criminals, of thugs, see how they defile our sidewalks, our paths, with their trash, like you, always on your bicycle on our paths, I nearly fell when I saw you, you knock over everything in your path, this island is an inferno, Mr. Charles, that mob of thugs, Sodom is living within our walls, haven't you read what's written in the Bible, Sodom is within our walls, and it's your fault, sir, your tolerance has brought them all here,

those degenerates, those transvestites who only go out when
night has fallen for fear they'll be killed, but they all will be,
they all will be, the Ku Klux Klan will burn down their
houses with their fiery crosses, you'll see, sir, you'll see, oh,
this infernal city, island of the dregs of hell, Inferno, Inferno,
said the Madwoman, brandishing a red picket from her
fence, but was he not imagining it, he who heard everything
those perfidious voices said, did he not still hear the
Madwoman's mocking voice, which was accepted everywhere as normal, sowing her reactionary doctrines, thought
Charles, O, the Republic of Lamberto, the Athens of Plato
could only be repudiated by that Lady Macbeth who represented the mass of citizens, Lamberto was like the Scottish
king she'd had assassinated by her husband, the Republic of
Lamberto, the Athens of happiness having fled, with the
domination of the new mayor no black commissioner would
be re-elected, perhaps Lady Macbeth had made that decision
in her twenty-two-room home where she'd locked up her
serfs, the phony black commissioner, that ambitious boy,
why not suggest to him a sea voyage from which he wouldn't
return, the young and handsome princes, the kings who ruled
amid innocence and goodness kindled aversion, rage, they
could not survive the ephemeral success of their reign, they
were assassinated like the Kennedy brothers, thought Charles,
he looked around him, there's no one here, I'm delirious, no
one, only a rustling of lizards and cats under the foliage
lining the footpath, after the Republic of Lamberto, the Athens
of Plato, won't the Madman or Madwoman of the Path, who
appears to be such a conformist, triumph over us? And the
nearly hundred-year-old mother of those sons, who are still,
in her mind, young people, says, it doesn't matter if I die, I'll
see them this evening, tonight, we shall be together at the
same celestial table, at last I'll be with them again, with both

of them, the path of Remembrance, the path of Memory, thought Charles, pedalling his bike beneath the palm trees, here all that could be heard was the repeated tolling of a knell, in a church, a temple, at times a wise old man like Justin would manage to express some wisdom gained amid unspeakable pain, it was the mayor of Nagasaki, who had survived being shot in the chest when he opposed the emperor, bringing down nationalist vengeance on himself, who said long afterwards, nothing was ever as cruel as the bomb dropped on Hiroshima, no act of destruction can be compared with it, for under a layer of ashes and coals every-thing entered into nothingness, the churches and those who were praying in them, kindergartens, cats, dogs, and Justin too had written and said that no act of destruction could be compared to that genocide, the shot in the chest had been for him, that piece of steel, the lungs, the heart, that piece of steel, guilt, from which he had finally died, the path of Memory, the path of Remembrance, thought Charles, pedalling his bike beneath the palm trees, here could be heard only the repeated tolling of all those knells, in churches, temples, gardens, under a beautiful August sky, its light the light of autumn, where under a layer of coals all of life, without a breath, had entered into nothingness. And it's as if we were at a window open on all sorts of marvels, said Mère to Augustino, whom she'd brought to this white sand beach where, in a few months, Vincent would take his first steps, you can play in the waves, said Mère, but stay close, don't go out too far, I'll keep an eye on you from this rock, Augustino's clothes on Mère's lap were no bigger than a handkerchief, she thought, let him play, let him frolic, what pretty features that child has, the curved nose under the curly hair, already so stubborn, wilful, like Mélanie, and naked under the Superman cape he played, frolicked, how pretty, while his clothes were no bigger than a handkerchief on Mère's lap, but what piercing cries of joy to Mère's ears, today's children make a lot of noise, she thought, with the sight of the white heron on the pier Mère's tumult and the painful feeling that she was at the mercy of all perils had subsided and suddenly, amid the silence of dawn broken by Augustino's twittering and the soft succession of waves, Mère thought she had heard her name, Esther, said a voice, Mama, we've been looking for you, Esther, it was as if Mère were going to turn around and cuddle up against the heart of her French governess, all rigid in her black dress, and to hear her name lovingly pronounced as in the past, against her cheek, into the long hair her governess brushed every morning, Esther, said Mélanie, Mama, I was looking all over for you, for Mélanie was there, standing by her mother on the white sand beach, she's finally found me, thought Mère, most likely it's Renata's presence that has mellowed Mélanie, and moved by the memory of the heron on the tall pier, Mère thought, she loves me, Mélanie is my daughter after all, and Sylvie saw the shadow of her brother on the garden gate, was he not, all at once, in the image of his country, bloodstained, bowing to dictatorships, so many massacres in the land of milk and honey, don't let this brother approach her, opening the birdcage with his stick, the blade stroking the wings of the parakeets, of the chicks, she must protect Augustin from him, little Augustin whom a priest had rescued from the shipwreck; under his broad Mexican hat, amid the peace of a graveyard, he was grinding between his incisors — laughing stupidly, no, let this never happen — the fibres, the tender flesh of Augustin, and in the silence of the streets, at night, she could hear her demented brother's stick hammering at the iron fences, the gates; for heavy with blood was the Shadow of the man who yesterday had watched over the dead on the shores of Cité du Soleil. And as he stroked the rough back of his iguana, Samuel said to Venus that he would wear a costume for the festive nights that would go on for two more days, two more nights, all those nights for singing, for not obeying his parents, a few musicians had just gone off towards the streets, the gardens, two more nights, two more days, but a ceaseless music droned from the back of the garden, the voice of Venus accompanied by the grave and isolated sounds of the guitar, the double bass, how many more of these long festive nights, thought Samuel, who was dancing up the stairs to his bedroom; Samuel, to whom Venus had given on this festive night an iguana whose back was rough, coarse to the touch, like a thistle or the stiff spine of a cactus, an iguana for Samuel's Noah's ark, for Augustino's, it would be among the foxes, the tortoises, the doves, the turtledoves, and Daniel saw that the Shadow was still there, the Shadow who was brushing against the fence, very close to the orange tree that yielded bitter fruit where Venus was singing, was the woman with the crimson face in costume, no, she was not an itinerant, she was the wife, the woman of one of those White Horsemen, she was no longer alone, and wasn't he there beside her, he too, a child was between them, his appearance was misleading, in the robe that seemed sewn to his body, under the white hood, he was a child dressed up for the festivities, like those who could often be seen parading, singing in old streetcars, and under the hood, like the children in the trains and streetcars, in the streets, wasn't he wearing a crown of luminous seashells on his head, but why, despite the enchanting appearance under the white hood, was Daniel so afraid of these three characters, or were they merely fictitious characters from his book, all three of them went back and forth — the man, the woman, the child with his heavy tread — very close to Venus, who was singing, close to the two black musicians next to her, why was Daniel so afraid of them, there are three shadows on the other side of the fence, said Jenny, their deceitful heads are hidden by their hoods, don't you hear the hissing, the words whistling as they spit, said Jenny about a woman, a man, a child, niggers, we're going to lynch you all, they say, or else, weren't all of them, and their numbers were growing, merely fictitious characters in the novel Daniel was writing, they were there, for Jenny could see their three distinct shadows under the hoods, the mother, the father, the child with the heavy tread, and Carlos saw the giant sphinx, his lion's head was moving under the verandas, in the parade with its thousand splendours, and drawn on chariots by a multitude of black schoolchildren there appeared to Carlos the ship *Henrietta Marie*, her three masts, her mountains of gold and silver that had sunk beneath the sea in an eighteenth-century shipwreck, the great ship with her three masts and her treasures buried in the coral of the Marquesas, but then where were the jewel-hunters sailing towards the New World, they had been able to identify the *Henrietta Marie*, whose name had been written on an iron bell, a bell sleeping in the water with the other objects, the bar that held the prisoners' feet in its traps, where did they all come from, from Nigeria, Guinea, what tortuous route would they take across the oceans to the Gulf of Mexico, to the New World, where the African cargo would be torn to pieces, sold off along with the heaps of gold and precious stones, so many feet still caught in their iron traps, a bell that lamented for a long time on a foggy night, so much mourning on this tortuous road, so much ocean all the way to the New World, Carlos saw the *Henrietta Marie* which had been found again, but then where were its treasure-hunters, where was the Atocha treasure hidden from her captains, among the iron bars of the shackles on bruised feet, what night of mourning for the *Henrietta Marie* sinking with her captains into the sea, beneath the verandas passed the *Henrietta Marie*, towed by a multitude of schoolchildren, Christo Salvo, cried a voice, and Carlos came running at top speed, where was Polly, frightened, in this crowd, and how sad Uncle Cornelius seemed, seated among his musicians as the truck jolted along Esmeralda Street, along Bahama Street, the truck dragging along the schoolchildren and the *Henrietta Marie* rediscovered at the bottom of the sea, its heaps of gold and silver in the coal bunker, the ship *Henrietta Marie*, her three masts, by what tortuous route across the oceans had she sailed, those men, those women whose feet were still encircled with iron had been devoured by barracuda, by sharks, and in the light of dawn, on this beach where Julio came every day, he saw above the waves a multicoloured banner, so vast it could have covered half the city, its fabric embroidered with all their names — José, killed on March 11, Pinar del Rio, Candido, victim of police violence on November 4, Ovidio, killed in clandestine fighting, Andrés, shot down as he tried to flee his country — all of them drowned or killed, José, Candido, Ovidio, Ramon, Oreste, Julio's mother, Edna, their names were embroidered, sewn into the transparent fabric of a banner that was moving above the water, thought Julio, and suddenly Julio was tearing the patch from his injured eye, he was running through the waves towards the banner of his martyrs, calling to them one by one, Oreste, Ramon, Candido, José, Nina, his mother, Edna, in Havana, Miami, that banner, he thought, could have covered fifteen streets with its names embroidered in blood, fifteen buildings, the immense banner testifying to so many disappearances, drownings, crimes, I believe in God and in human goodness, that had been the last message from one of them, and Julio was swimming towards that multicoloured banner on the waters, swimming in his fever while the shore moved away, Christo Salvo, cried a voice, come back, Julio, and Julio swam back towards the shore where a boy was trying with frenzied movements to raise the anchor of his boat, where were you going, he asked, there's a storm in Jamaica, it's unwise to venture out so far, at this time of day Mélanie and Daniel always went for a long run along these shores, this strip of land, was it that thought that had promptly sent Julio back towards shore, suddenly, he had swum towards them as if they had been there, running beneath the pines, wearing their beige shorts, in the already warm light of the dawn, of that multicoloured banner so vast it could have covered the entire island, the names of José, Candido, Ovidio, Ramon, Oreste, their mother, Edna, covered him with the waves of their shrouds, the marks of their struggles, for all of them, didn't Julio have a duty to live, for Ramon, Oreste, Nina, it would have taken almost nothing, though, if the boy who was raising the anchor of his small boat hadn't called him, hadn't pushed him towards the shroud of all those lives, it would have taken almost nothing, Julio thought, to make him slip into the depths of a sea, an ocean, towards that multicoloured banner on the water, and Tanjou could no longer recognize Jacques's silhouette against the rosy whiteness of the sky, he was holding the head of Raoul, who was vomiting into the shimmering greenery near the tennis court, angry tears rose to his eyes, what disgusting drugs are you on, he said to Raoul, shaking him, and still two more nights, two more days of festivities, murmured Raoul, I don't remember, two more days, two more nights, it's a mixture I tried, look, I'm shivering with cold, and under Raoul's funereal disguise Tanjou saw on his brown, muscular shoulder the ritual tattoo, a death's head pierced by a dagger, and his repeated vomiting alarmed Tanjou, you see where that's taking you, said Tanjou to Raoul, can't you see it now, undisciplined, confused, we won't win the tournament, Tanjou understood too that the tattoo on Raoul's shoulder perhaps revealed his membership in some dangerous gang, they were handsome, young, let the tragedy that was dogging them all cease its foul deeds; Tanjou could no longer recognize Jacques's silhouette against the rosy whiteness of the sky, but suddenly he thought he could hear, even though Raoul could not hold back the convulsive sounds from his body bent over the grass, Beethoven's oratorio *Christus am Oelberge,* Christ at the Mount of Olives, which Jacques had piously listened to, he could hear the angels' aria, the recitative of Jesus on the Mount of Olives, how could His Father who was in heaven keep death away from Jesus when the soldiers' lances were straining towards his flanks, that's better, said Raoul, give me my racquet, seven-five, he said, getting to his feet, let's go back to the court; and in good form, cool in their sports clothes even though they hadn't slept much, thought Adrien, didn't Suzanne say that three or four hours' sleep a night was healthy and enough for them, wouldn't too much sleep be indecent, Adrien and Suzanne were walking hand in hand towards the tennis court, the gardens scented with flowers open under drops of dew, today, I'm sure of it, said Suzanne, Tanjou's game will be as light as air, doesn't he always surprise us with his courteous volley across the net, I'd rather come and play between noon and three o'clock, when no one can see me, said Adrien, this morning I feel exhausted, as if I've been riding forever, and those young people play so aggressively, come on, snap out of it, said Suzanne, who was thinking that her husband was worried in particular about the article he intended to write when *Strange Years* was published, for it would be published, Adrien suddenly seemed to decide, the manuscript must soon become a book, a concrete, tangible work, so that Adrien could be one of those who would write a brilliant review of it, an article he'd already started, his idea, he confided to Suzanne, glad of this discovery, was that Daniel depicted the world as had Hieronymus Bosch and Max Ernst, absolutely, he said, Daniel doesn't have the fluid control of those great masters, but his book abounds in their visions, you plunge with him into the Ship of Fools or the Garden of Earthly Delights, Adrien had been wrong to think that the young writer was haunted like certain southern writers by the crushing weight of sin in a puritan society, Daniel was first and foremost an unbridled painter, at times his pity was a caricature, his writing lavishly symbolic, which was barely noticeable on a first reading of the manuscript, very gently he led us down to the dizzying regions of hell, he dealt with human folly, that theme so dear to Bosch, with death, his delirious compositions juxtaposed the ancient world and the modern, throughout was a theatrical milling, a strange procession of human fauna, of flora, the Ship of Fools, the Garden of Earthly Delights, and, at times, the Last Judgement, a pervasive esotericism, like Max Ernst he assembles objects into collages and *trompe l'oeil*, he too has studied psychology, he is a writer of the occult, I assure you, Suzanne, it's all very disturbing, especially on first reading, but as I told Daniel, there are too many troubling assemblages. There was also a painful omission from Daniel's *Strange Years*, one that Adrien would point out, if hell and its outskirts were present everywhere, Daniel seemed unaware — and this was the sin of youth, youth did not know everything about the sojourn of souls in the melancholy limbo of life, about the uniformity of actions — that these were the limbo of the most sensual pleasures, the paroxysm of sexual pleasure or losing oneself in material pleasures, a man like

Adrien knew, even as he was intoxicated by his most delectable and satisfying possessions, that with an ejaculation or an
insolent appetite that transcended the measure permitted,
the brief immortality that was his, like that of the birds and
the flowers of the fields, would be arrested, those intolerable
sojourns in a futureless limbo would be repeated during
Suzanne and Adrien's daily walk to the tennis court, the
gardens with their greenery shimmering in the sun, Daniel
seemed unaware that one day this enthusiastic stroll would
not be repeated, pleasant though the habit had become over
the course of a lifetime, God would suddenly let you drop
in your fresh morning garments, like a moth in a flame or a
flower in the turbulence of the wind, what serious omission
would Adrien point out in his criticism, the muggy paradise
apparently distributed to all was not given to anyone, that
was something he must above all not discuss with Suzanne,
women suffered less than men from the lassitude that
secreted self-absorption, selfishness, they were totally
absorbed in their children, such violent possession of life
was unknown to them, O baneful melancholies of man, of
the male avid to invest his authority in every matter, thought
Adrien, and Suzanne astonished him with a declaration of
her difference, by expressing as she did so often her faith in
life after death, she had no doubt, she told Adrien suddenly,
her face illuminated by that supernatural certainty, that in the
past Charles and Frédéric had communicated with the spirits
of the dead, during their nights in Greece, around a table
under the chandelier, they had seen and heard the signs of
those spirits, read their inscriptions in the registers on the
table that seemed to be moved by underground hands, such
communication between the living and the dead would
always exist, said Suzanne, those followers of spiritualism had
understood it in Greece, at midnight, under the chandelier,

when a voice said, sailor, aged seventeen, still lost at sea, come to me, O torments of the taverns and the harbours in the mist, of ships that are foundering, come to me, aged seventeen, name, Thomas, born in England, an orphan like the poet Keats, my friend, I too have written sonnets, O torments of the taverns and the harbours, the year 1818, an orphan, already lost at sea, the letters, the words printed themselves, lost at sea, a fog, like the London fog that greeted the birth of Thomas or the romantic poet John Keats, at a time when death could follow so soon after birth, that same fog, that mist in which all the cries and all the signs would suddenly sway, would suppress any sign of the impudent deceased fellow the Shadow was taking back, Tho-mas, Tho-mas, Keats, and the exalted Charles, Frédéric would retain the ultimate sign, around the table, under the chandelier, and Adrien, aware he was a reasonable, level-headed man, disappointed Suzanne's hope for a dry phrase by saying, what we have here in Charles and Frédéric are some very imaginative individuals who not only affirm the survival of the spirit after death, but dialogue as fluently with John Keats and many others whose verses about beauty and truth they confuse with their own, O torments, O taverns, wrote Fred, in those days, in Greece, during his marital tribulations, they are the spirits of poets, of story-tellers, of writers of fables, what have they not seen and heard around the turning table under the chandelier at midnight, what have they not seen and heard, the poets Keats and Shelley, what noble soul stamped with lyricism does not come to confide in them, amid the sound of breathing around a table, and Adrien regretted that as his dramatic voice grew, so did his jealousy, but still, said Adrien, I too am a poet, only I have my feet on the ground, or was it some jealous feeling of a different order, thought Adrien, regarding those invisible, mysterious ties uniting Suzanne, Charles, and Frédéric, it's true they all were together so often, suddenly on both sides the same passions, the same imperfections developed, wasn't too much imagination a flaw, it's just that I too believe in that doctrine, said Suzanne softly, and Adrien thought a poisoned arrow had pierced his heart, three, there were three of them getting to the heart of the same mysteries, three of them the elect of God's mysteries, and what did you hear or read around that table, didn't you have a meeting at Charles's place, after many efforts, many illusions and interpretations, what were you able to hear or read, Adrien demanded of Suzanne in an urgent voice, the word deleth, we saw it being written before our eyes, deleth, a Hebrew word that means door, you see, you don't know if that door is open or shut, said Adrien, irritated, deleth, said Suzanne slowly, or was it with her stubborn languor, thought Adrien, deleth, it's a question of walking towards that door from where one can see, even from far away, a wall that reflects the light, deleth, said Suzanne, while that face lit up with impenetrable certainty was turned towards Adrien, that's it, that's all, it seemed to be saying, repeating the word, pronouncing it so that both syllables stood out clearly, de-leth, a door. And would it be tomorrow that Suzanne finally wrote to her daughters, tomorrow or later, they were still so happy, about their pact to obtain the right to that door, deleth, without causing their children any sorrow, was it not simple and per-fectly normal, when someone had lived serenely in paradise for a lifetime, to go towards that door, deleth, while still in good health, to its luminous opening, to walk there while still sound, with honesty and frankness, as if going to the tennis court in the morning, in the blazing sunlight, she should have talked to Jean-Mathieu as well, but he would judge them harshly, my dear daughters, Suzanne would write, this evening, tomorrow, in ten years, five years perhaps, I am writing to you from behind the Chinese screen that separates my workroom from your father's, the white lotus drawn on the screen, you'll remember, represents Chinese Buddhist philosophy, which has always fascinated me, with its calm elevation, my dear daughters, I've been considering telling you about our decision for a long time now, you know that even in legal terms it will soon be true, assisted death is not suicide, deleth, a door, an opening onto the bay, the sun, the greenery, was it wise to write to them, Suzanne thought, had they not always kept their secrets from their children, on that day we'll be on a cruise ship, Suzanne would write, her gaze sometimes settling on the Chinese drawing of the white lotus, no, she would say nothing to them, or to Jean-Mathieu, why disturb them all with the same dread, in his icy limbs could Jean-Mathieu still feel the cold that oozed from the walls of the factory where he'd worked as a child, in Halifax, no, she would have to cross out what she'd written and write, though it's the subject of much debate these days, assisted death is not a crime, I confess that I'm afraid though, my dear children, that Dr. Kevorkian will be condemned by the courts for the twenty-one deaths of which he is accused, what worthy being can fail to sympathize with the suffering of those who cannot obtain the right to a serene death, how I pity them all, my daughters, all those who ask for that right in their deadly pain, Ruth, aged ninety-two, afflicted with bone cancer, such torture, so many destructive drugs absorbed, intruders that at the end blight the beauty of lives, their harmony, we have lived a marvellous life with you, all those who ask for it, who wait, deformed, are we not, all of us, born responsible for ourselves, no, that thought was too arrogant, thought Suzanne, she would not write the letter tomorrow, at least, or tonight, my dear daughters, the

greatest medical experts don't know our bodies as we
ourselves know them, don't listen, you who are radiant and
so young, to whatever you've been told, no, her daughters
would never have tolerated such advice, my dear daughters,
Suzanne would write, I think that when we grow old, unless
we take care of ourselves, others will mistreat us, think of
those survivors of a cruise ship, all old people whose cruel,
cynical young crew nearly let them perish during a crossing
to Kenya, or the five hundred white-haired passengers in
their small boats on the Indian Ocean, waiting for their
laughing captain to rescue them, there were no motors in
those small boats, no drinking water, no blankets, the
captain laughing and chatting on the bridge while fire crept
towards the cabins and his passengers, no, my dear daughters, we will not share that fate, but it wouldn't happen
tomorrow, for Suzanne and Adrien were still so happy, it
was a simple pact they had not signed, but how sweetly
scented, how fragrant was this day, thought Suzanne, and
how reassuring it was to see the couple playing in the
golden light, Raoul, Tanjou, Tanjou whose game was ethereal.
And the others, the orchestra musicians in their white suits,
thought Renata, they were the astonishing taste of water and
smoke, of the fire at the edge of one's lips that causes one's
gaze to waver, but suddenly she could no longer hear anything but the tenuous sounds they were still drawing from
their instruments, their mocking laughter as they ran towards
the festive diversions in the streets, her arms still overflowing with their floral offerings, she watched them move away
and she saw that he was still there, she should have kept
away from the grimy mass on the sidewalk, was it the fallen
West Indian, intoxicated, opening blind eyes in her direction,
or one of the many others who might resemble him, an
itinerant knocked out by a car driven by a drunk in the harsh

light of the first hours of the New Year, wandering from the prisons of California, Nevada, Michigan, abandoned on a sidewalk, on a highway, an orange-picker who had no relatives or friends, how would he be cremated tomorrow and buried, or was it he, under the blackish matter covering his face, was it his debased body under his sooty rags, this man surrounded by packages and string, littering the street, the sidewalk she should have avoided, her arms laden with flowers, she did not know what visceral pity had made her bend down to him, for those remnants of humanity clung to her as they did to everyone, in the place she would return to she would be loved, esteemed, while he would only be further diminished, a contemptible black stain against the whiteness of a wall, under the radiant sun, or seated, his torso stiffened by the cold, a cold that would materialize just for him in his damp rags, but that was just a disturbing urge, she would step rapidly around that mass on the sidewalk, the glaucous glimmer of the gaze beneath the eyelids of the man who was still pursuing her to her cave of vegetation, to the rented house, a dubious mass that would always oppress her with that pleading expression, that link of shame, that she no longer saw him amid the throng of half-starved animals that followed him, animals, women, or children, their tumultuous crowds would scatter on the fine sandy beaches, across the grass of gardens outside churches and schools, at times young people clad in black leather, decked out in felt hats and hobnailed boots, would join them, a ferret or a rat on their shoulders, when they doffed their hats you could see the scar among a few hairs where the rat spent the night, under the hat, nibbled at, nibbling, gnawed at, gnawing, rodents, all of them, they were tangled in that blackish mass against the white wall that she was passing, that she no longer wanted to see, it was as if her vitality had already dropped, while the echoes of the festivities still reverberated within her, and those thin, light-hearted sounds the musicians drew from their instruments in the distance, and Adrien was thinking about his critical paper on Daniel's *Strange Years*, he was not so easily influenced, he thought, as to accept that the boy's writing would rub off on him, enough of this, a little self-restraint, instead he would be invincible under the critic's shield or under the shields of critic and poet, invincible, if only that young author would stop tormenting him as he stretched his elbows in front of his computer, so inspired that he was unable to silence his voice, if only he didn't have to hear it any more, only let the manuscript be published, at this hazardous curve where Adrien and the clairvoyant tools of his analysis lay waiting, a strange procession of human fauna, flora, the Ship of Fools, the Garden of Earthly Delights, like Max Ernst, Daniel assembles objects, makes *trompe-l'oeil* collages, approaches to the River Eternity, the title would be more relevant, yes, but so awkward to see them all again, Hitler's dog, the unwitting child suicides in a bunker, Goebbels's children, whom he showed to be innocent, nowadays we encounter those vengeful souls among us, he wrote, carried off by the black waves in spite of themselves, no, that had all been written, dictated, under a dangerous, malevolent influence, the air between those lines was made of some unbreathable sub-stance, he was no doubt one of those depressed writers, how dreadful, thought Adrien, that it could rub off you when you went to play tennis with your wife and the weather was so fine, and yet life, as the visionary painters had seen, was an enigmatic collage or a troubling construction, Fred had painted flowers in Munich, flowers that bore the title *Eve's Flowers*, as fresh as if they'd been painted in Eden, yellow flowers that were as bright as the sun, at the same time as

Frédéric was piloting his destructive planes under bridges and cities were being bombarded, in Munich *Eve's Flowers*, as if life were endlessly starting anew, for didn't Frédéric share with Daniel, in their naivety, a vast feeling of innocence that was spread over humankind, whether it was at times a holy and heroic humankind plunged into hell, losing nothing, as Max Ernst had done with the legitimate fury of his prophecies, in his terrifying collage-novel, there one saw the history of the last century file past, the Academy of Sciences with its death's-heads under an umbrella, the Ladies of Calvary, the Fairies of Destruction were invited to a ball, boats glided across blood-soaked floors along with severed heads, the painter was a provocateur, was sacrilegious, the sea, the forests were man-eating sites beneath the crows and snakes that made you bald, bodies were covered with cracks and burns as if they had lain in the ashes of the atomic bomb, the cities' outskirts were taken over by giant spiders, by grasshoppers that devoured the blue sky, those who were praying on a starless night, monks holding in their joined hand missals that were long rifles, and what did those images foretell, scourges, plague, first a painful cough, the scourge of chest diseases, and from the top of the mast could be seen castaways, everywhere castaways, choruses of castaways under a dreary sky, all of them, Charles, Daniel, Frédéric, Suzanne, were letting themselves be deluded by the diabolic power of the dream, a dream that would soon swallow them up as if under the wing of a nightmare, but what was most serious was what Daniel omitted, thought Adrien, in his happiness he had placed the sojourn of souls in the uniformity of actions, had forgotten to say that one day Suzanne and Adrien's daily walk to the tennis court, the gardens with their greenery shimmering in the sun, one day this stroll would not be repeated, pleasant though the habit had become over the course of a lifetime. Incessant music droned from the back of the garden, Venus's voice accompanying the grave and isolated sounds of the guitar, of the bass, so many festive nights that were still so long, said Samuel, who was descending the staircase from the high veranda to applause from Augustino, Samuel's a bird, cried Augustino in his high-pitched voice, Samuel appeared to Venus wearing a mask with green and blue feathers around the eyes, like a peacock's magnificent plumage, he strutted on the staircase, Samuel had made the head for the bird, which was also fitted with wings and breast, from various materials, from fragments of shattered glass, papier mâché, embroidered cloth, like a drawing glued together from collages and hardened gouache, for he had spent a long time working on it, like a cubist painter, and thus would Samuel be seen on board his boat, on Augustino's Noah's ark, all covered with feathers like the proudest of birds, long ago, his fore-limbs transformed into wings, and he was ready to take flight, to migrate with his family, his muscles were strong, he thought, veritable motors that would qualify him for flight and for landing, and singing, warbling swelled his throat, he would carry off in his claws the green iguana, the swamp fox, the tortoise, the deer run down by automobiles amid the evening flight of doves and turtledoves, or Samuel and Veronica would be dropped from a balloon into the hot air, like Guy and Pamela, the navigators with parachutes strapped to their backs who had been married in the air, in the Colorado sky, gliding hand in hand, they would make eleven thousand jumps, would skim over the clouds at two hundred miles an hour, Samuel descended the staircase of the high veranda, to the applause of Augustino, Samuel's a bird, cried Augustino in his high-pitched voice, and Jenny was surprised that he'd already wakened from his nap, but two nights, two more nights that are so long, said Samuel, never to sleep, never to obey his parents, and tutti son pien di spirti, thought Frédéric, wondering why he had fallen out of bed, and where was Edouardo, gardening in the yard, or was he in the garden waiting for Ari and his sculpture, and did that wave of voices, of murmurs, come from the garden, the TV set, or the streets, during these festive days and nights, was tonight the dinner with Adrien and Suzanne on the roof of the Grand Café that Isaac the architect had erected, weren't they all to meet on the highest points of the city, the Grand Hotel, the Grand Café, absorbed in constructing his dreams of genius, was Isaac not forgetting the poor people down below, those who left with no baggage, what noise from the passing airplanes, destroying, under the iron bridges, thought Frédéric, I'll tell Isaac tonight, he's used to my frankness, he won't be offended, Isaac, do you remember your childhood in Poland, why no, Isaac would tell him, you're thinking of my younger brother, Joseph, of my Uncle Samuel, I was smart enough to flee before all the others, Isaac, all those people in the smoking ruins, I saw them, you know, Frédéric would say, what was Frédéric doing, curled up in his blanket on his bedroom rug, where were they all — Ari, Edouardo — ah, the scrap of paper, I must reread what Edouardo wrote, to help me remember, thought Frédéric, but where are they all, why am I suddenly so alone, and Frédéric saw Edouardo's message on a chair by the bed, he reread the careful writing — Sunday, dinner at Suzanne and Adrien's — I just have to dress to go out then, Frédéric thought, because I have to convince Isaac this evening, the children of Munich, their mothers, I think about them every day, would I tell him how terrible it was for them all, the pin-striped suit, Edouardo got me this elegant suit, and the belt, otherwise the pants don't stay up, he said, where's the belt, tutti son pien di spirti, again that uncontrollable vertigo, that's it, they must be in the garden to watch the installation of Ari's sculpture by the fountain, an arc, a steel wire stretching towards the sky, a symbol of space, of liberty, what was it like to have a memory free to remember, a body free from all these worries, the belt, where is the belt, Edouardo often told me, don't lose it, and didn't Jean-Mathieu say he'd pick me up, I have time before Jean-Mathieu gets here to rehearse Grieg's "Lyric Pieces" for the concert, if I don't the teacher will rap my fingers, he'll run a match over my fingernails saying, if you don't play properly I'll burn your fingers, strange that I always thought he'd do it, Frédéric is at the piano already, Edouardo told Ari, by the fountain in the garden, the two of them on either side of the sculpture, looking for a place to set it down, no, not here, said Edouardo, it's too shady, the sun, always in the sun, said Edouardo, here, as it unwound the loose steel wire, the perpetual motion Ari had created, from an alloy of iron and resin to which his fingers had transmitted flexibility, magnitude, movement, would cast its spell on the light, would harness it, said Edouardo, and, very resonant, the notes Frédéric was playing on the piano faded away into the street sounds, and Edouardo said, his voice filled with longing, how much he thought about his mother at this time of year, about the Sierra Madre, Oaxaca, but his mother had told him it was his duty to be here with Frédéric, just as a few years ago he'd been with his sick father in Mexico, and you know, Ari, when I was born my mother thought I was so ugly, all wrinkled like a monkey, she didn't want me, it was the aroma of tortillas in our kitchen, said Edouardo, his nostrils still quivered when he thought about them, when I remember, Ari, that you're already a war veteran, before your fiftieth birthday, you don't look it in your untidy clothes, your hair like a horse's mane, a bad adventure, said Ari, a terrible adventure, said Ari, pushing back his memories with disgust, other veterans, real men of war, keep to themselves under pavilions, tents, on beaches reserved for them where they seem to be living in an exile that is bitter and hostile to everyone, what do they talk about among themselves, the dark crimes we committed over there, the bitterness in the face of the destruction of a race, a country, when I cycle past the campground I still shudder with fear, but what have I not done for the love of adventure, said Ari, what madness, art and sculpture can rehabilitate only a part of ourselves, the rest is in a muddy grave in Vietnam, there will always be generals to send adolescents to hell, so that they never really come back, and your adventure in South America, said Edouardo, and your adventure in Lebanon, though you were never allowed off your sailboat, what adventures, said Ari, four boys and four girls setting off on a sailboat in search of paradise, with their cargo of hashish under the deck, and we came back intact, with thousands of dollars in our pockets, intact but scared, an adventure still associated with the experience of war, with my wild reckless-ness in the face of danger, with a passion, a taste of death, these remnants of war, said Ari, suddenly embittered, his eyes lighting up only to look at his sculpture, lovingly, isn't it wonderful, he said, at the slightest breeze the steel will be set in motion, a sculpture is like a woman you love, move-ment, life, Fred will be happy, but we can't hear his piano now, why is he so silent, he must have gone back to bed, to sleep, said Edouardo, tell me everything, what was it like on the sailboat with the girls? Recklessness or innocence, said Ari, it was paradise, but as we drew closer to the shores and the piers where the sharp, shifty buyers were waiting for us, making only faint signs in the direction of our crew, dread crept over us, but out on the water, in the middle of the ocean, we were all inordinately happy barbarians, living naked

and caressed by the wind, so many embraces and kisses in
the sailboat's only shower, we were living with bodies and
minds totally relaxed on our magnificent sailboat which we
sold on our return, hashish dealers with dreams of buying up
whole islands, we were handsome, tanned by the sun and
wind, who wouldn't have envied the fate of these criminals?
And so goes our youth, said Ari, only in our dreams do we
see again the sailboat and the girls we drank rum with from
morning till night, making love with only the sky to shelter
us, rum and love-making drove away any fear, we knew that
another sailboat belonging to some friends had been
rammed by patrol ships, a careless young girl had been
killed, so goes our youth, said Ari, now the white sailboat
will return only in dreams, tutti son pien di spirti maladetti,
thought Frédéric as he walked uncertainly through the
crowd, he had forgotten to tell Edouardo he was going out
alone for a few hours, how did one get to that Grand Café
and its terraces that Isaac had built on the city's rooftops,
such rumblings of voices and drums, Atlantic Boulevard,
wasn't it here that you turned right, in the direction of a group
of blacks who were dancing and singing in the streets, a
defective truck was transporting Cornelius and his musicians
to those streets by the sea, they were sitting side by side on
straight-backed chairs, one of the men, was it thin Cornelius
who was coughing into his checkered handkerchief, seemed
to be shedding tears as he bowed his feeble body towards
the street, an old memory presented to his sight all those
who had been lynched, on a cliff, in a valley, necks held by
ropes used to hang from on the branches of all the trees on
Bahama Street, on Esmeralda Street, amid the abundance of
their blossoms, yes, it's here, on the right, that you have to
turn, tutti son pien di spirti maladetti, thought Frédéric, why
this vertigo, had his gait not been hesitant for a while now,

they were in the garden, positioning Ari's sculpture next to the fountain, Frédéric hadn't wanted to disturb them, the pin-striped suit would be perfect, the leather belt would hold the trousers snugly around his waist, but why did these dizzy spells, this odd kind of malaise, come over him, and suddenly Frédéric remembered the small bronze head, a bust of himself as a child, how skilful his fingers had still been when they were living in Athens, a musician, painter, sculptor, nimble fingers, an angel's fingers, he thought, it was the head of Frédéric, the child prodigy, the refined head of the young Mendelssohn, and suddenly here is the head of the old artist that replaced it, a sunken face, aged and crowned with white hair, another sign of God's cold indifference to mankind, and when we are on the highest points of the city, I shall say to Isaac, the Devil came here in the guise of a speculator to tempt you, he said, if you want, this island, this city will be at your feet, and you gave in to temptation, you drove the poor from their wooden houses, from their beaches, the style of your buildings, the way they were built, expressed your own desire for glamour, for magnificence, here a Moroccan garden, there a marvellous forest where birds imported from Asia sing in bamboo cages, sublime, you are sublime, Isaac, you even built a shell-shaped theatre where poets declaiming their verses can hear the waves of the sea, but all those dreams of genius drove the poor from their houses and you, Isaac, you will tell me, I saved this city that was in ruins, I was in the service of an idea, and I'll tell you, Isaac, when the speculators came to you on the highest points, where you could see the lamps of the Grand Café shining on the roofs at night, where fabulous stone animals sprang up, and the sculpture of a Greek boy dashing through the bushes, you didn't recognize the Devil in them, and just see how unhappy you are now, my friend, how lonely, with no descendants or friends, or just a few very close ones like your old Fred, for you fear the greed of men whose victim you've so often been, don't take offence, my friend, for I can still see them running in every direction, frantic, with no baggage, through the smoking ruins, tutti son pien di spirti maladetti, thought Frédéric, how could I forget to let Edouardo know I was going out alone, where am I now, what is my destination, there's Cornelius, taken to the cursèd tree in a horse-drawn cart, the slip-knot cutting through his neck, here he is crying into his hand-kerchief, I can hear their music, I'm dancing with them, easy, easy living, whether they were in the enemy's artillery, the infantry, their legs, their arms were torn to shreds as were our corpses, on a fencepost, on the walls of a pen, a Christmas of blood, of scarecrows burned at the stake, it was in Bastogne, a Christmas soaked in blood, December 1944, fingers chopped off, lacerated, December 1944, Bastogne, but where is Edouardo, I called to him from my room, Isaac will tell me I smoke too much, I'm ruining my health, no descendants, few friends apart from our gang — Charles, Adrien, Suzanne, his old friend Fred — and all those works of art around him, an Indonesian mask whose mouth twitches with cries, what will he find to reproach me for in my pin-striped suit, arms at my sides, a cigarette in my mouth, aren't you having a little trouble climbing the stairs, my dear Fred, we can hear your breath growling, you seem as youthful as ever because Edouardo takes such good care of you, but I don't want to hear a word about the innocence of this one or that, I shun the company of men, they're all guilty, I tell you, I can see that you don't get up till three in the afternoon, that you live only for music while I, I'm the servant of a machine, our mayor, Lamberto, would have understood the scope of my plans, the direction my work is taking, thanks to me the decency, the dignity of life, fill the souls of the poor, your bronchial tubes, my friend, you must look after your bronchial tubes, on Esmeralda Street they were in the back of a truck, sitting on hard chairs, their instruments propped against their knees, Edouardo knows the road to Isaac's house, its terraces, Edouardo, I know, will find me again, December 1944, amid the firestorms, and on the Path of Remembrance Charles was thinking of Frédéric, what would become of the dear boy when Charles shut himself away in a monastery to write, Fred who was so moving, but the TV set, the music by Grieg, the conflagration of an entire life and the silence that ensues; in that monastery, that retreat, thought Charles, one heard everything, Grieg's "Lyric Pieces," the celebration of Hanukkah to the joyous cries of North American children receiving presents, or the cries of Palestinian children in the city of Gaza, steeped in sulphur and smoke, everything, Charles would hear everything, from those fortresses of faith where each person prayed to God, beseeched Him, in mosques and temples, from the Ibrahimi mosque or the cave of Machpelan, so many vibrant sacred songs, psalms suddenly punctuated by moans of hatred or revenge, while the patriarchs are kneeling, their hands raised towards heaven, Charles would also hear the clandestine, the fleeting odyssey of cargoes of uranium travelling soundlessly from the Republic of Kazakhstan over the continents to Oak Ridge, but that odyssey would be fleeting, clandestine, and today, thought Charles, as he cycled under the palm trees, all you heard was the repeated tolling of a knell in a church, it was for Justin, tribute was being paid to him after all these years, his house, his family would be honoured, Justin, the pacifist, who like the mayor of Nagasaki had opposed a nation, opposed his emperor, a piece of steel in his lungs, in his heart, Hiroshima, a piece of steel, the guilt that had finally led to his death. And Christo Salvo, cried a voice, was it true then, what Mama said, and

Pastor Jeremy, or were those eyes seen through the hoods, under the white sheets, were they merely costumes for a masquerade night, thought Carlos, as he ran at top speed, we'll make a grand slaughter of them all, Carlos heard, was it true then, what Mama said, and Pastor Jeremy, about Negroes, homosexuals, for our brutality is not yet satiated, was that what could be heard through their hissing, their howling, under their fiery crosses, but where was frightened Polly in this crowd, Carlos thought, running at top speed towards the tables on the sidewalks, stopping only to gorge himself on spicy rice, on beans with honey, and barbecued meat, amid greasy, acrid smoke, and that was how he'd suddenly spotted Polly, Polly who, like him, was sniffing the aroma of perfumed food, Polly, who was hungry, who was thirsty, Polly alive and wagging her tail, and when Carlos said to her, follow me, she would obey his order, eager to follow, nipping at him to pull him towards the beach, the sun, the waves, was it true what Mama said, and Pastor Jeremy, that the White Horsemen had arrived, and they would be inseparable, thought Carlos, Polly would always be at his side, so well trained by her master that her head would be level with Carlos's left leg, that was how he would teach her the position, follow me, the position, sit, during their walks, when the leash was limp and elastic around Polly's neck, and Carlos would say, good dog, Polly, good dog, Carlos also knew that Polly was stubborn, but the way she lowered her head was so touching, and her eyes, moist with gratitude, had lit up when she saw Carlos again, those eyes of Polly's, always a little anxious under the curled tufts of her eyebrows, and Frédéric thought again about what old Isaac had told him, he had no descendants, but when he died his employees would discover that their children's education was paid for over the next twenty years, for, as old

Isaac had always said to Frédéric, though he too suddenly had little memory, recalling his childhood in Poland, Isaac was not the loathsome product of capitalism founded on the sweat of the poor, and wasn't that Edouardo whom Frédéric spotted suddenly, his Indian braid slapping his back, for Edouardo was walking quickly, he seemed very preoccupied, Frédéric called out to him, happily, Edouardo, Edouardo, isn't it tonight, cried Frédéric, that we're having dinner with Suzanne and Adrien, tonight, Sunday, or is it another day, tell me, Edouardo, do you remember, you whose memory is still clear, so clear that it no doubt recalls too many pointless things, and Frédéric thought that he had been saved from the crowd, which would have trampled him had Edouardo not been there, with his Indian braid slapping against his back, my friend, he repeated, while Edouardo's powerful arm held him up, my friend, is our date with Suzanne and Adrien tonight or tomorrow, Frédéric continued talking to Edouardo like that in the van that was taking him back to the house, looking at the holy images of male and female saints trembling before the rearview mirror, like the thin wood crucifix Edouardo wore around his neck, it sometimes happens that there are angels on earth, said Frédéric to Edouardo, everywhere, I know, said Frédéric, there are boys and girls like you, Edouardo, the universe is filled with a saintliness that is unknown to man, a saintliness that is secular and divine, as I was telling Isaac, everywhere boys like you, Edouardo, pitiful Mother Teresas who exhaust themselves with their work, in their homes, and who never experience the respect, the veneration they deserve, for life's like that, there is so much cruelty and injustice, and you, Edouardo, who in this world can appreciate your soul, your grandeur, do you know, and those poor people in Munich who disappeared into the smoking ruins, they too were saints, but did they not mock

Frédéric's ideas, and when they were nearly at the house, on the path lined with giant palm trees, Ari ran up to them saying, two boys came into Frédéric's bedroom while I was working outside, and what did those trouble-makers do but take off with the TV set and everything, everything, even Frédéric's precious records, they dumped it all in a bag and took off, and we know who they are, they're Pastor Jeremy's sons, the one who's called Le Toqué and his brother, Gregory, above all don't prosecute them, said Frédéric, I owe them a lot, no, don't prosecute them, but they're dishonest children, said Ari, they must be punished, and while he was speaking Ari saw the sailboat on its way to Lebanon, defiance and even dishonesty being merely a dream from now on, the girls on deck, a scent of water and salt, Frédéric thought of the empty spaces in his bedroom, tears sprang to his eyes as he suddenly noted that the bronze bust was gone from the table by his bed, they'll go to jail, said Ari, all that for a few chunks of crack, above all don't prosecute them, they're just children, said Frédéric, who was still looking for his music, for the bronze head, where was it anyway, and Frédéric, exhausted, lay down on his bed, saying he felt dizzy, wasn't it tonight, he asked Ari, our date with Suzanne and Adrien, no, no, said Edouardo, relax, it's not Sunday yet, well, I shouldn't have gone out alone, without you, said Frédéric, isn't that how we bring God's cold indifference upon us, but doesn't He go too far with his signs and manifestations? That's what I told Isaac on the roof of his house, God's cold indifference, His malice, when men are so innocent, so stupid in their innocence, but is it their fault? Look, the piano is still there, they didn't steal the piano, and all at once Frédéric announced that even if he was a man weakened by the wear and tear of age, he still played Grieg's "Lyric Pieces" as he'd done at his concerts in Los Angeles, when he was the little boy who had inspired the bronze sculpture, I'll take up sculpture again, he exclaimed, his face beaming with radiant joy, yes, my friends, believe me, Edouardo, we must order the materials, the hands, the fingers are still harmonious, balanced, it's a gift from heaven, I'll take it up again, and the sculpture will only be more perfect, for I always need to start everything again, until I die, was that the grace that awaited mystics, asked Frédéric, he had hopes of an imminent resurrection when he began again, modelling the small bronze head with its exquisite features would have swept him off his feet, he told Edouardo, for that's what it is, coming back to life, yes, but you need to rest, said Edouardo, those dizzy spells, those attacks of giddiness, you need to rest, of course, Frédéric seemed resigned to it, yet they are only signs of God's cold indifference towards me, nothing more, you must pay no attention to them, said Frédéric, I will triumph, you'll see, my friends, signs of His cold indifference towards me, for suddenly the bronze sculpture shone radiantly, it was reborn out of the world of shadows and the anguish of lost memory, the small bronze head was alive and, even more, it was coming back to life under Frédéric's skilful fingers, and while he was easing Frédéric's faintness, Edouardo applied a lavender-scented compress to his fore-head, I still think you should denounce those hooligans, said Ari severely, suddenly so many years separated him from the adventure of the sailboat heading for South America, for Lebanon, a young veteran of a war already forgotten, why did he feel so intolerant towards the pastor's sons, was he becoming like the rest of them, the younger son was lame, said Ari, ah, I'd have spanked them, the little devils, above all never prosecute them, said Frédéric, because thanks to them I've known relief from my pain, I've known deliverance, I used to have too many possessions and now I am at peace,

I passed through the door before it was time, deleth, that door mentioned by the sailor lost at sea, deleth, the door, you need a lengthy preparation to pass through it, said Frédéric, I have the sense of an imminent resurrection, and Edouardo said to Ari, let's go out now so Frédéric can sleep, what is the meaning of that word Frédéric keeps saying, deleth, he says, deleth, and Polly was running with Carlos through the waves, it was just to please her master for she wasn't sure she liked getting her muzzle and ears wet in the waves, sometimes she sneaked away towards the beach and its grass, her disobedient paws digging holes in the sand, but when Carlos said, follow me, she paid attention, her ears pricked up, her eyes, quick as a squirrel's, glued to the soles of Carlos's feet, feet that were pale pink under-neath, and how beautiful and new the world was suddenly for Polly, always they would be together, she and Carlos, she would defend him with her hoarse barking, too bad those big Labradors shoved her into the waves so disrespectfully, too bad she was still just a puppy hitched to the baggage carrier of a bicycle, but her master was a sturdy boy, a boxer, her master, Carlos, a future boxer, or so his father said, she would never want another master even if Carlos had neglected her for one whole day, leaving her in a nearly airless shed, that day Pastor Jeremy had moved the icebox, what's not done tomorrow will be done today, he'd said to Mama as he headed for the shed, it's a good eight years that icebox has been in the shed, and last year's yellowing Christmas tree, what are we going to do with it, Mama, let's wait till tomorrow, Mama had replied, standing on the lawn amid the roosters and hens, what are you all worked up about now, it's not Judgement Day, what's not done today, Papa, will be done tomorrow, and inside the rented house, shaded by the dense vegetation, Renata was thinking of the woman who had passed through here, who had written some wonderful poems, her existence had been erased, she had fled Berlin, going into exile with a mother, a father, both of them painters, on an island off Sweden, perhaps she'd left only a few legible words, help, help, before she was taken to a train, to this room where tension, disorder prevail behind the door, my illuminated spirit withdraws, help, for we are all of us fleeing Berlin, the train had taken them all to Treblinka, in what mental distress had she written, had she lived, the unknown woman's existence had been merely a ghost on whom a wind of madness had breathed, and Renata read those words in a letter from Claude, this was the end of her convalescence, the end as well of those objects of irretrievable satiation, O light smoke in the jasmine-scented air, objects on which she must no longer be dependent, that she must no longer clutch feverishly, her husband told her, cured, let her come home now and apply for the judge's position, he would support her, what was a woman on her own, a woman who was loved, doing in the dense vegetation of this rented house, when a clock told her that it would soon be evening, night, and that she would be no less alone, bereft of power, of sensual pleasure, those pernicious cigarettes, that gold cigarette case, she must renounce those objects, he would come here to collect her, she would walk to the beach with Claude, both of them permeated by the sultry air, the heat, intoxicated by their desires, he said he'd been thinking a lot since an accident involving a car some young delinquents had booby-trapped, he did not regret putting away those criminals who were still children, he was more apprehensive about the threats of revenge by their elders and their gangs, but how could he forget those faces behind the grilles in police cars, still young and innocent, the remorse stirred in them by fear, the tears on their plump cheeks, during the time of their separation Claude had often thought about the frequent subjects of their arguments, what was fair for Renata was not so for him, where ideas were concerned they were often irreconcilable, but he loved her, let her come home now, all his colleagues would support her, she could no longer deny that she needed the support of men, if he and she could not understand each other, were they not allies sensitive to each other's needs, he recalled the room that opened onto the Caribbean, that blue and tranquil sea, he recalled their love, during those days of their separation, he had known that Renata was first and foremost a mother, a woman, her story had always been inscribed in the story of humankind for its leniency, its tenderness that was unknown to man; man is incapable of feeling such tenderness, especially when he is in a position to judge the actions of dangerous criminals, he wrote, while Renata herself, even in the midst of a loving embrace, could feel as if it were her own the tragedy of a condemned man in a Texas jail, his death by lethal injection, the judge remembered his wife's profoundly disturbed expression when she had described the death, liquid, intravenous, of exemplary efficiency, the prisoner inflicting it on himself at the first light of dawn, it was during that time, when Renata was still in hospital in New York, that Claude had to uphold a guilty verdict for a gang of drug dealers, he was sorry they were all so young, like those young black prisoners, not even eighteen, continuing their schoolwork in the Jacksonville prisons, for every day the number of police and prisons increased for them, at the same rate as the inexorable resurgence in urban crimes committed by gangs of juveniles, attacking the elderly at night, for a long time, Claude wrote to Renata, that Texas prisoner had haunted him, for this time, as Renata had said in her anger, and he hadn't believed her, this time they had perhaps killed an innocent man, for more than half an hour, on a Sunday, the Texas prisoner had protested his innocence to the officers, and the innocence of those who, like him, had awaited their sentences for a long time in their cells, all his friends, he said; would he be murdered on a Sunday, he asked his parents, he who had never killed anyone, though his file was heavy with felonies, his beseeching request would only be interrupted when he died, in leather bonds that he had tried in vain to loosen with his arms, his shoulders; the vice would never be loosened even if he was innocent of the actions he was accused of, a crime in a Chicago bar, who would hear his complaint, his prayer, and his tears, Renata had always doubted the guilt of that man, he remembered her profoundly disturbed expression when the event was brought up, and yet that very evening had they not both forgotten everything to go to the casino, to go out, and he, Claude, had sent the judge a telegram, no, they had suddenly forgotten everything, and such was life, always demanding, distracting, numbing us with its pleasures, Claude had thought about it a great deal during those days when they were apart, he feared that while it was forbidden to consume alcohol before the legal age, in several cities in Canada and the United States, it would soon be legal to be taken to the electric chair, hanged, or killed by lethal injection, long before the legal age, and were we not heading for a massive extermination of youth, with more and more prisoners sentenced to death for minor offences, like the innocent man sentenced in Texas, they would be black, Hispanic, Chinese, few would be middle-class whites, none would be rich, in vain would the appalling cries of children in leather bonds be heard, this was a prophecy of Renata's about the repression they had discussed in the past, both of them, but to a man a woman's word was often too soft-hearted, too sentimental where the frailty of youth was concerned, and even at her husband's side, Renata was often in a state of solitary dismay, fearful of belonging to someone, and that was what he cherished in her, let her come home, but it is true, as she had always known, that a doubt, a mortal suspicion hung over the fate of the Texas prisoner, and the man, the accused, was perhaps innocent. And running from one end of the net to the other as if his feet had wings, with his racquet in hand, Tanjou could hear the Beethoven oratorio *Christus am Oelberge*, Christ on the Mount of Olives, to which Jacques had piously listened, he heard the angels' aria, the recitative by Jesus on the Mount of Olives, how would his Father, Who art in heaven, relieve them of all this dying, Raoul, Kevin, the animals' friend, tanned by the sun, smiling beside his dog, but the final photograph no longer celebrated his talent, his exchanges with Tanjou on the other side of the net, Kevin, already his photograph was no more than a memory, and Daisy, the actor, a marguerite, a small wildflower, Daisy, a plant that beautified the lives of others with its freshness, a white-petalled flower, its petals stripped away, disappeared into a grave, how would the Father Who art in heaven relieve them of all this dying, they were young, handsome, might the tragedy that was dogging them cease its foul deeds, Tanjou recognized Jacques's silhouette against the rosy whiteness of the sky, it was while Suzanne and Adrien were walking to the tennis court hand in hand, the gardens fragrant with flowers that had opened under drops of dew, dazzling red hibiscus, and Adrien was saying to Suzanne, she was still too serene and calm, thought Adrien, that manuscript of Daniel's has rubbed off on me so much that it's given me nightmares, I thought I could hear the wheels of the evil Carriage and the neighing of its horses, a few steps away a grieving shape appeared before me, was it a woman or a man, veiled in black, and said, follow me, follow me, I had a good pretext for refusing the sinister invitation, I had not yet finished my translation of the works of Racine, *Bérénice, Britannicus*, I told them, I managed to get away, but I can still hear the wheels creaking on the gravel road, so I shall tell my readers in my review, Adrien added, irritated by Suzanne's imperturbable serenity, I'll tell them, watch out for that young writer, reading this book will rub off on you like chlorine or the Bible's lessons of terror, wailing and gnashing of teeth, wailing and creaking of wheels along a gravel road at night, when the traveller is alone and without a guide, now, now, said Suzanne, don't get carried away, we too wrote books when we were thirty, when we were very young and very beautiful, like gods, we too have known success and glory, that's what we call the past, said Adrien, his sighs suddenly expressing all the dejection of his sorrow, that's what we call the past, very well, my friend, here now is eternity, whose gate will soon open onto other splendours, said Suzanne, the approaches to the River Eternity, and you know, Tanjou, Raoul shouted to his partner, gay and energetic, he seemed to have forgotten already that he'd been so sick a few moments earlier, you know, Tanjou, we'll be playing the Australians in the semifinals? They were beautiful, they were young, thought Tanjou, might the tragedy that was dogging them cease its foul deeds, Raoul, Kevin, with his brown complexion, his eyes sparkling under blond hair as silky as that of his dog, photographed with him, Raoul, Daisy, Marguerite, flower of the stage, transvestite dancer, clad in a tutu to dance the role of a prisoner who dreams of being transformed into a ballerina, flower whose white petals have been stripped away, Tanjou could hear the angels' aria, the recitative of Jesus on the Mount of Olives, how would his Father Who art in heaven relieve them of all that dying, the recitative from *Christus am Oelberge* to which Jacques had piously listened, and lunch with Jean-Mathieu was not till noon, with her camera's quick, sharp eye Caroline would record in minute detail the faces of those who were still in the garden so late, after the first festive night, two more days, two more nights, said the little girls, they had slept for a few hours and now had appeared again, framed in the doorways, in windows, Caroline took their photos while they were just carefree children, in a few years they would be like the young women in that area of the garden, who were talking about their lives *sotto voce*, one had been abandoned by her husband, the other was worried about the consequences for her children of a divorce, how long had she postponed her university studies, asked one of them, studies in marine biology and technology, or her return to classical ballet, how unnatural a thing is a woman's life, thought Caroline, once she entrusts it to a husband, a lover, when there is so much happiness in being alone, Caroline had been a lieutenant in the army, an airplane pilot, she had studied architecture, without will-power there was no success in life, women needed men too much, the young women in this section of the garden struck her as listless, what was a woman if she did not dream about establishing a relationship of power with a man, as men had done with women from time immemorial, a relationship of power with no dependency or servitude, Caroline rarely performed any lowly domestic tasks, in those days, she thought, southern families had servants, Jean-Mathieu had opined that Caroline's ideas were too shameful to be expressed, but how could one not be nostalgic for a time when, for families of a certain class, many chores had been lightened by black servants, a nurse, a gardener, they were like members of your family long since rooted in the same customs, between all of them, between masters and servants, there was freedom, equality, but Jean-Mathieu had told her she was deceiving herself, it was like when Caroline told Jean-Mathieu that she had only a modest fortune, could she afford to be extravagant as Joseph was towards Mélanie and Daniel, no, there's no such thing as a modest fortune, Jean-Mathieu had replied, from now on she would avoid those subjects when they met, and on the faces of these young women, Caroline observed, the first wrinkles were already being drawn of a life where one was born in order to become a woman, and with her camera she snapped Venus and Samuel, who were singing on the stage, Jermaine, who was looking at his parents with his melancholy slanting eyes, the beautiful child of a black activist man and a Japanese woman of aristocratic stock, thought Caroline, but didn't Daniel and Mélanie promote the flowering of such cultural mixtures around their children a little too enthusiastically, yes, perhaps, but you must remember that in the last century we too were immigrants, arriving in the port of New York destitute and persecuted, but now we have the most remarkable country, the most remarkable Constitution in the world, what a charming tableau Jermaine and his parents make, all three under the spell of the voices they're listening to, is it the cantata that Samuel sings in the school choir, I won't argue with Jean-Mathieu at lunch, but don't Daniel and Mélanie treat Julio, Jenny, and Marie-Sylvie as if they were the couple's superiors, encouraging them with their excessive liberalism to claim too much freedom, when they're merely employees, refugees with no roof other than their house, and Caroline photographed Jenny's noble face as she held Augustino in her arms, and the rather haggard face of Marie-Sylvie, were the stigmata she bore from the disastrous crossing on the raft or from her brother's madness, and now the little girls were coming back to perch in the doorways, the windows, saying, take my picture, Caroline, carefree children, who knows where the dawn of the new century would take them, under what conditions of life, unimaginable in the comfort of their homes, towards what kind of survival in gangs, in street gangs, by then Caroline, thank God, would no longer be in this strange world, unless she lived to be a hundred like her father, and as Caroline was recording these images with her camera's quick, sharp eye, the faces of the innocent children seemed to her suddenly to harden, like Samuel's face when he removed his bird's mask, beneath the mask he was dressed up as the singer Prince, thought Caroline, the girls who had grown up were no longer recognizable, they all resembled Samuel, crowned with feathers, with earrings and nose rings, eyes shadowed in mauve and black, cheeks streaked with colours somewhere between fire and ash, what would Caroline have done if they'd insisted, as they did with those journalists, those reporters, that she take photos of the children of Bogotá, sleeping in the streets at night on sheets of plastic or cardboard, smoking their pipes of basuco during the day, before bullets pierced their throats in the evening, then dying in the evening in the places where they had slept in dread of being killed in the morning, or that woman raising her fist in a California cemetery, Evergreen, in Oakland, which was the resting-place for the victims of the Jonestown massacre, a woman raising her fist and saying, remember, here lies a brother, a sister, a son, remember, and a camera like Caroline's would bear witness to the enormity of that disaster in the Oakland cemetery that was forever green, what would Caroline have done if she had been entrusted with those filthy tasks, to bear witness with her camera to the existence of so many disasters, fires, two firefighters kneeling by a poor burn victim who was living

his last moments in a swimming pool, having saved from
the flames a cat that would survive him like a soul, in that
limbo of an earth where its master had perished from his
burns, his hands still clutching the edge of the pool, clasped
by the hands of the kneeling firefighters, to what point
did you act out of empathy in the face of human tragedy,
if God had existed could he have acted with more sympathy,
more empathy, than those two men powerless in the face
of another's pain, on them, on those reporters, those journalists, was imposed the unbearable pilgrimage into these
tragedies; the procession of Moscow homeless to a shelter
where they were given soup, like the spectacle of blood-
streaked snowballs thrown by young boys in the streets of
Sarajevo, to what point could you feel empathy for human
tragedy when you were Caroline, a woman with a modest
fortune, they would avoid those topics during lunch on the
terrace, hadn't Jean-Mathieu also told her, you're charming,
Caroline, delicate like Jane Austen, whom you resemble, my
dear friend, but Jean-Mathieu could never resist flattering a
woman, Caroline's self-confidence was restored as she told
herself that when women were silent, and was it a lie to be
silent, no, simply one word placed in the silence, nothing
more, when women said nothing about themselves men
would be totally ignorant of their lives, what did they know
of the mysterious ties that unite women or the adulterous
loves of a woman and a man, what was kept silent was not
a lie, thought Caroline, on the terrace at noon Caroline
and Jean-Mathieu would avoid the topics that could damage
the ties between them, the future, for example, it was better
not to talk about it, were Caroline's premonitions legitimate,
she had no idea, but a woman's heart feels every nuance, she
thought, with the quick, sharp eye of her camera Caroline
thought she was already recording the images of the future,

the faces of those girls framed in doorways, in windows, were hardening in the same way as Samuel's face when he borrowed from the singer Prince his guttural voice and his cries, all of them, crowned with feathers, with earrings and nose rings, eyes shadowed in mauve and black, cheeks streaked with colours somewhere between fire and ash, they would advance in gangs, in hordes of barbarians and savages with their rap music, their African drums, they would take over this terrace by the sea, under the coconut palms, the Christmas palms where Jean-Mathieu and Caroline drowsily held forth about English literature for hours; their hair would be held down by the straw hats they wore, for age would have undone everything about them, the arteries would be too visible under the bluish transparency of their skin, their teeth, no, don't even think about what state their teeth would be in, age, then, would have undone everything, hair, teeth, in a weary tone they would exchange remarks about Jane Austen, thought Caroline, and at the approach to eternity, ready to return to the kingdom of heaven providing it was as attractive as a twilit salon where one goes for an evening cocktail with friends, they would see, looming up from beneath the vault of the palm trees, hordes of barbarians, of savages, girls and boys, rushing forward with their shouting and their drumming, crowned with feathers like Samuel, eyes ringed in black, cheeks streaked with colours somewhere between fire and ash, what would those young people do with the two old people, Caroline and Jean-Mathieu, dozing side by side on a terrace, their blue-veined hands on their knees, they would be as thin as dry wood, as firewood, no, at noon on the terrace Jean-Mathieu and Caroline would avoid those shadowy topics — old age, death — Caroline's vague premonitions would have bored her charming and cultivated friend, so here you are, absorbed in reading Jane Austen, Jean-Mathieu would say at lunch, the conversation would unfold amid the same enchanting calm, their faces bathed in light would be accommodating, amiable, and all at once Jean-Mathieu would say sadly, another one, my dear friend, we've lost another one, after Justin and Jacques I thought we'd had our share of sorrow, well, my dear friend, my dear Caroline, another of us has returned to the land of shadows, what can we do, my dear, what can we do, the number of our friends will keep diminishing, what can we do, the sweetness of the air, Caroline would say, think of the sweetness of the air, my friend, what a magnificent day, my friend, the blue sky, the sea on a windless day, think of the sweetness of the air, my friend, forget about the land of shadows, you must avoid those haunted topics, and those guilty, shameful thoughts when Caroline had been photographing Jenny's noble head, was society not evolving, Jenny would be a doctor when only yesterday black nurses weren't allowed in hospitals, but in Caroline's wealthy family there had always been a black nurse who came to the house to provide private care, the same was true in some of the great Boston families where such nurses were sometimes on duty, providing private care, Mary Eliza Mahoney was the name of the nursing pioneer who paved the way for liberation, for freedom, but they would avoid those topics, for all at once Jean-Mathieu would assume his accusatory manner, my dear, he would say, there is still so much racism in North America that the living conditions in our ghettos can only be compared with those of the Third World, you're deceiving yourself, my dear friend, our society is backsliding dismally, suddenly aware that a woman could never be right, Caroline would add in an anxious tone, my dear friend, how much empathy, sympathy are we capable of feeling for our fellow man? During their lunch, Jean-Mathieu would drum against his glass of lemon-ade or sparkling water, really, not to drink an icy margarita, a martini in a tropical country is absurd, but to your health, dear friend, you'll feel all the better for it, Caroline would say, you're mistaken, my dear, Jean-Mathieu would say, I used to be more tolerant, more compassionate, when I was a heavy drinker, the memory of an all-consuming thirst leaves you a little grumpy, quarrelsome, he would say, but most of all, thought Caroline, they would be conciliatory, amiable, bathed in a blue light like that of the ocean, under their straw hats, and isn't it time for reading in Spanish, asked Edouardo, placing a lavender-scented compress on Frédéric's brow, since we don't have a TV set now, they also stole our music, pick up your reading again, said Frédéric, didn't you say ha resucitado, you'll see, this time I'll be perfectly successful with the bronze bust, so Ari's already left, another woman, a mistress, sculpture or the flesh, or both at once, at his age I was like that too, the ability to love so much is one of life's treasures quickly squandered, ha resucitado, said Frédéric, do you remember the governor who censored my article, all about the families living on the railway tracks, the governor told me, no, this article must not be published, the story of those children so bereft of strength and defences that they're eaten by dogs, dogs as hungry as they are, both are killed by cars and trains, I remember the governor's indifference when my article was published, said Frédéric, who was growing agitated, isn't it time for a little rest, said Edouardo, going on with his reading, No estè aqui, pues ha resucitado, como dijo. Venid, ved el lugar donde fue puesto el Señor, said Edouardo, it's because of the railway tracks that I fought in the revolution, said Edouardo, Mas en angel respondiendo, a Spanish poem says you must give the song of your soul, said Edouardo, the song of the armed revolution, for those people piled up like scrap along the railway tracks, with their animals, the song of my soul, one day I walked across the frontier as I'd done so many times when I was a child, the rifles were now falling from my hands, I'd rather live in exile than be imprisoned, tortured, killed, said Edouardo, and always at this time of year I think about the Sierra Madre, No temais vosotras, says the Gospel according to St. Matthew, No temais vosotras; porque yo sé que buscáis a Jesús el que fue crucificado, Edouardo read to Frédéric, on whom sleep was descending, that was it, thought Frédéric, the sense of an imminent resurrection, with the modelling of the small bronze head, you would see in it the exquisite features of Mozart or Mendelssohn as a child, a youth, he who would compose the overture to *A Midsummer Night's Dream*, and the world would be overwhelmed by his precocity, ha resucitado, read Edouardo, ha resucitado, before the dizzy spells return, you must sleep, Bastogne, 1944, Frédéric repeated, our planes under the iron bridges, those wretched people in the smoking ruins, Bastogne, 1944, lacerated fingers, a Christmas soaked in blood, with the bronze bust I will triumph over those appalling signs of the cold indifference of God, said Frédéric in a voice nearly extinguished by sleep, and in the silence of the bedroom with its window open onto orange trees, lemon trees, could be heard once more the song of the cicadas, and Edouardo's words slowly dying out, ha resucitado, Frédéric, ha resucitado. And Claude would soon be with her, thought Renata, she would walk arm in arm with him to the beach, the two of them immersing themselves in the sultry air, the heat, irreconcilable, intoxicated by their desires, on her return she would apply for the judge's position, with her husband's support, would there be a return, was it already time to renounce those objects of irretrievable satiation, the pernicious

cigarettes, the gold cigarette case sparkling in the night of a
casino, a bar, in the presence of young men still unknown,
O light smoke in the jasmine-scented air, and what a feeling
of happiness to have found then again, Daniel, Mélanie, Samuel
who had grown so much over the winter, Mélanie, her
daughter in a sense, her child, they were the same height,
had secret similarities, what a feeling of happiness to be with
them all again, it was a few days after the terror of the ship
that had been wrecked on its way to Brest, to the church
where his oratorio would be played, that Franz left with his
sons for another woman, the sailboat, its figures from Goya
on the deck, Franz's sons whom she would never see again,
but what a feeling of happiness to be reunited with Daniel,
with Mélanie, Mélanie, her daughter in a sense, her child,
so many secret similarities, O light smoke in the jasmine-
scented air, on a pier, leaning out towards the ocean, she
would smoke for the last time, delighting in the immortality
of this moment above the water, she would take off her satin
jacket, no jewellery, no, she would wear no jewellery, she
thought, it would be a rainy evening, she would smoke by
the water, barefoot in her sandals, a raincoat tossed over her
shoulders, the smell of that flame in the wet air, for the last
time, how would she have judged Laura or any other woman
who killed her children, what did men know about the flow
of menstrual blood seething its fevers into their brains and
the cavities of their bellies where life was thrown into turmoil,
between love and fury, more and more women would suffer capital punishment, what did her husband know about
those eddies of blood, had he given birth to a child, we'll
leave that house, those servants who were my father's, wrote
the judge, they're ex-convicts who have long been in the
service of the family, they were condemned to serve their
sentences that way, under constant surveillance, but one day

I understood that they had us all under surveillance too, from a greenhouse, a garden, they spied on us and we didn't know how to elude their strict vigilance, the judge, like his father before him, had believed those prisoners could be rehabilitated, but a young woman he'd rescued from prostitution and taken into his house was already leading her daughter, still young, into that life, didn't parents and children suddenly end up back in the same physical and moral abandonment, trafficking narcotics, suddenly none of them had any homes except those places of degradation, shooting galleries, where they performed their rites, weren't we all of us victims of genetic anarchy, of hereditary flaws for which we were ourselves without surveillance, every day so many condemned men, repeat offenders, were the subjects of experiments in the prisons, their testicles exposed to radiation that caused tumours, cancers, but what could you do with those men, those women, who had no future, guinea pigs, subjects of experiments, like laboratory animals, a woman like Renata had denounced the practice of exposing prisoners in the jails of Oregon, of Washington, to radiation, but had anyone listened to her, all those former prisoners we kept in our service, wrote the judge, continued to keep us under surveillance, from a greenhouse, a garden, suddenly the judge discovered that they were among the men who had booby-trapped his car, the judge had thought about it a great deal, who knows whether Renata, a woman, had been right about the condemned man in Texas, the thought woke her in the night, but here, by the blue Caribbean, during her convalescence, they would go out in the evening, to the casino, shortly after a passionate argument, they forgot about the condemned man in Texas, said no more about him, far from everything, Renata and Claude were here to rest, to relax together, the judge had upheld the guilty verdict before his departure, and once Renata was alone on the beach she would hear again the orchestra musicians racing down the streets in their white suits, drawing joyous sounds from their instruments while a fine rain fell, she would see them all again, the West Indian against the whiteness of a wall, would he still be a man under his sooty rags, blocking the streets, the sidewalks, she would walk towards the stormy crowd that was scattering on the beaches, young people in black wearing felt hats, hobnailed boots, strapped in leather, their ferrets, their rats on their shoulders, suddenly this one, one of Franz's sons whom she had raised, a relative, a friend, they were all tangled in that blackish mass against the whiteness of a wall, wearing her raincoat, barefoot in her sandals, all her thoughts would be for that son, that lost friend or relative, and she would ask each one, what's your name, come with me, we'll be at the same table tonight, when would those light-hearted sounds the musicians drew from their instruments reverberate in her again, in the distance, no link of shame, suddenly, would they not be, all of them, men, women, children she had known well? And with the sharp eye of her camera, Caroline captured another face, that of Joseph, in a corner of the garden, one of the young orchestra musicians having forgotten his violin, Joseph was alone, playing the instrument, from which rose a slow lament, and Caroline was thinking of the eyes of a man, of the camera of a Russian soldier who had photographed the faces an army was releasing from the camps at Auschwitz, with an exhausted smile the youngest of them expressed the hope, the expectation that they would soon come back to life, that smile was fixed on Joseph's lips, a smile amid injury and grief, when life was being reborn from the ashes, but might God spare Caroline that procession of images of hell, might He let her be safe, to what point can one feel empathy, sympathy for the suffering of another, let Caroline be protected from those savage images, at noon she would lunch with Jean-Mathieu on the sunny terrace, the air would be mild, and Mère went into the bedroom under the oleanders, this would be the room where she rested near her daughter and her grandchildren, she lay down on her bed, let the young people enjoy themselves, thought Mère, two more days, two more nights, let the festivities continue, two more days, two more nights, this evening, from the pavilion on a pier, Mère would see the white heron striding regally into the waves while, stretching his neck, he set one foot ahead of the other with studied slowness, as the moonlight glinted on the darkened water, and Mère would hear as well the voices of Samuel and Venus tearing into the night, when they sang with their united voices, O let my joy endure, O let my joy endure.

ACKNOWLEDGEMENTS

My warmest thanks to the Canada Council for enabling me to write this book, and to my angelic friends, Claude and Erik Eriksen, Stell Adams, and Mary Meigs for their unwavering support; for their hospitality and generosity in Paris I thank the Saint-André des Arts hotel, Odile, Henri, and the late Philippe Le Goubin; and in Key West, Patricia Lamerdin and Dorothea Tanning, whose presentation of *A Little Girl Dreams of Taking the Veil* reintroduced me to Max Ernst. I also thank the late Gwendolyn MacEwen for her wonderful poetry, and Bonnie, who lets me spend hours writing at her Key West bar, Sloppy Joe's.

M.-C. B.